D1518753

Summer Shares

A Novel By

KEVIN PILKINGTON

ArcheBooks Publishing

Summer Shares

By

KEVIN PILKINGTON

Copyright © 2012 by Kevin Pilkington

ISBN-10: 1-59507-239-X
ISBN-13: 978-159507-239-9

ArcheBooks Publishing Incorporated

www.archebooks.com

First Edition: 2012

Dedication

For my brother, Thomas

She was gone when I woke up. The room was eloquent with her departure.

John Fante

Chapter One

Amagansett Dunes
Steps to the Beach
4BR, 2Bth beach house
10 min. walk from train
All amenities. Fun groups
Full share $1,000; 1/2 share $500.
Call Patty at (212) 263-5000.

This was the ad I found under the share column in very back of *The Village Voice*. It was sandwiched between the Gay Roommate Service and VD Clinics, a noble position to be in, I thought, for any house.

I figured a summer in the Hamptons would help me end my four-month mourning period. The loss I kept grieving over was called Laura. In November my two year relationship had come to an end. Actually, it had been disintegrating for over a year, but I kept holding on. That's what guys in my position do with girls like Laura—hold on. She had expensive tastes, and it finally got through to me that I was no more than fast food. I slowly realized that if I were going to spend the remainder of my life as a Big Mac, I'd have to find a girl who was going to accept the golden arch ambiance I could afford. And on my teacher's salary, in a city that builds monuments to the yuppie, it would prove a difficult search. In any event, I would no longer grieve the way I did on St. Patrick's Day.

I went to Tommy Makem's on Fifty-seventh Street by myself since I was too depressed to be with friends. Besides, a real Irishman like myself knows how to drink alone. Never quite understood the concept of drinking buddies.

Makem's, of course, was packed with leftover parade Irish in jeans and green sweaters and a few yuppies with crooked ties in gray suits. Those smug bastards, even today they aren't wearing green, and why should they when all the green they need is in their wallets. But what they all had in common were their complexions: no matter what they poured down their throats, it ended up red in their faces.

"Everyone! A Toast to Mother Ireland," some guy shouted from the back of the bar.

I didn't have a drink yet and couldn't toast the giant green woman I imagined squatting over a sea of Guinness, dropping red-faced babies in rapid succession. So I squeezed my way through the crowd under a roof of mugs they held high for the toast towards the bar. My eyes were already burning from the cigarette and cigar smoke. I found a spot near four fat guys who were wearing those bulky white sweaters that made them look like a flock of drunken sheep. I ordered a beer when a guy with a Saint Bernard head tapped me on the shoulder.

I turned to listen to him slur: "Where you from, me boy?" His brogue was obviously ninety-proof.

"The Upper East Side!" I had to scream to be heard over a song that had something to do with a rebel who killed twenty British soldiers. The rest of it sounded like he raped a herd of cattle after he knocked off the soldiers. I'm sure I heard it wrong but the cattle added drama.

"Not what part of the city," he yelled, "what part of the old country?"

"I'm not from the old country," I shot back imitating his accent.

I wanted to be left alone to work on my beer, but I caught the disappointment in his face. The fact of the matter was his brogue sounded like it was from the new country, county Bronx. But his drooping eyes seemed to say *play along, we are all brothers tonight.*

The city brings in guys like Saint Bernard and his buddies once a year, paints them green, puts their drinks in their hands and says today, you matter. You are all born in Ireland in places like Kerry, Dublin and Cork. If you haven't loved, love each other and if you can't do that, love a parade. Drink up gents, today you are the chosen. So, I, too, would be for a brief moment, one of the giant green lady's red-faced babies.

"But my dad is from Galway." My moment of compassion brought a grin to his big red face.

As he stared at me he yelled, "Boys we have a Galway man here!"

They hoisted their mugs in a salute. I nodded back my own.

Brothers.

I then turned, stared at my beer and began to cry. You see, when I have a few drinks I get maudlin, and, when I get drunk, I cry. Tears for beers, a drinker with heart. Anything and everything makes me open the floodgates. If it is no longer Friday, tears. What, the Yankees lost? More rain. Dyed your hair? You get the picture. But on that Saint Patrick's Day, I realized that there was no need to drink. I wiped my eyes, pushed myself through the crowd and out the door, drunk on Laura.

Going back to the ad again lifted my spirits. Three months near the beach would straighten my head out. This house would be all the shrink I'd need. Since I'd be teaching a summer session for six weeks, I would go out on weekends, then spend the rest of the summer out there from mid-July on. This called for a full share; I could come up with the thousand bucks. No sweat. I'd be able to relax, read what I wanted and try writing a bit more poetry.

The few things I'd written were not very good but did get published in some of those literary magazines that nobody reads with names like *Chicken Nuts, Egg Sucker* and *Rhino Horn*. But at least I could claim publication, and the school rewarded me with a small poetry writing class to teach during the summer session. I teach year-round because it's one of the things I do well, find rewarding, and with such few jobs available, I feel lucky.

There are a number of attractive girls in my classes, and since I had turned thirty in September, I'd added a mile to my morning run. I told myself I did it for me. Somewhat beefy at five-nine, I had to be careful; I'd become the master of my weight. Then, during a class this spring, age tapped me on the shoulder for the first time and whispered, "Chris, see the redhead in the last row? Look how her hair hangs seductive, limp over her left eye. All during class her right eye works hard for you, opens wide, takes all of you in. She listens to your voice, loves the way you move, but when she picks up her books to leave, she wishes you were a little younger."

Although I had to admit that the distance between my podium and their desks seemed slightly wider since hitting the big Three-0: the truth was I didn't want them. I wanted them to want me, not in the sack, but what I offered here: the seduction of Byron, Donne, Shelley; to share the passion they heard in my voice every time I read aloud; to forget Wall Street was just a few blocks away making and breaking millions; to crap on computers; that the forty-five minutes we shared together was the only real intimacy of their young lives, to crave what I craved: literature. I slowly realized that maybe I wasn't just running for me. I was also running for them.

So, Age, I decided, fuck you!

Sexual harassment was the other major reason I avoided getting involved with students, and it's also how I got my teaching position at Newman College. In nineteen seventy-six an attractive freshman accused Jerry Ludsberry, a popular English instructor, of trying to rape her. Newman College stood behind him, stated his credentials as impeccable and said that he had served the college honorably for over ten years.

However, according to a few very reliable sources on the staff, ol' Jerry, in his forties and the happily married father of three, conducted private tutorials under the sheets with numerous co-eds and had been sleeping with the jilted young lady as well. Eventually, she dropped the charges and the next semester, the department dropped Ludsberry.

With all the schools in and around the city, competition for students was stiff and our humble university didn't appreciate the negative publicity. The dip in enrollment during the semester I arrived to fill his spot was blamed on Ludsberry. Gonads as scapegoat.

During my first year, a student reporter for the school newspaper was doing an article on new teachers. He asked if there was a professor who had a major impact upon my life. I felt like saying Ludsberry. After all, he was instrumental in my obtaining a teaching position and showed me, through example, that risking a job you love isn't worth it, no matter how fine the student body.

Aside from relaxing, getting things together and doing what I pleased this summer, the house, according to the ad, was right near the beach. For me, a major pull. Hampton beaches are some of the most beautiful in the world, with all the amenities: sun, ocean, white sand, seagulls and women. Being in Amagansett also had appeal. I heard it was the least hip of all the Hampton villages, which were now overrun with the New York chic and wealthy. Being so far out on the Island, most opted for Quogue, South and West Hampton, which are forty minutes to an hour closer, and if you travel along the Long Island Expressway, that means a lot. So the town of Amagansett has remained a small strip on Montauk Highway and is still a bit sleepy.

I learned from Murray Bruin that there are still quite a few artists in the area. Murray is in his early sixties and a painter. Lean and a bit on the short side, no bigger than five-six, his lined and weathered skin makes him look more like a fisherman than artist. During a conversation he'll nervously run his right hand over his gray hair that has the texture and color of a Brillo pad after the last pot has been scrubbed. He rarely looks you in the eye, preferring to focus in on his shoes, the sidewalk or the street, but will sporadically glance up to see if you are still engrossed in what he has to say. And since he had taught for years, he tends to lecture, not discuss.

Murray was part of the Pollack, de Kooning crowd of the late forties and early fifties who lived on the Lower East Side where you could get by on fifty bucks or less a month, work all day in your studio—his was on Avenue A—then go over to the Cedar Tavern on University, drink and eat your fill with the little change you had in your pocket, and talk paint all night.

According to Murray, Pollack was a jerk, a nasty drunk. Legend as asshole. But everyone else argued theory and exchanged the necessary support they needed more than food. A friend of mine in the Art Department told me that in the late fifties, Murray had a major exhibit or two; de Kooning was already in the money, and Pollack was on the cover of Life, looking just tormented enough to earn his genius label. Murray's first exhibit had the type of success that got him a second in an even more prestigious gallery, the story went. However, the art critic, Clement Greenburg, who helped make Pollack, also helped destroy Murray Bruin. In his *New York Times* review he found little originality in Murray's abstracts and thought his best work to be nothing more than "pale Pollacks."

Over the years Murray had a few more minor shows, grew increasingly bitter about the entire art scene, and decided never to "play the game and suck up to those faggots" (his expression for gallery owners) again. He lives in a loft in SoHo he bought fifteen years ago when you could still afford one, has taught at the Art Students League, and when he needs the extra money, he teaches a painting class at Newman. The school takes him on, not because he is a good painter or teacher, but because he was the friend of innovators and didn't have the good sense to die young, to drive his car into a tree and the price of his pictures into the millions. I met him at a faculty party and then later in front of a magazine store on the corner of Eleventh Street and Sixth Avenue. It was there that I told him of my summer plans. He started lecturing me how he and his artist friends discovered the Hamptons and why they lost it the way the Village and SoHo were lost.

"During the summer we used to go up to the Cape. I don't know who, but one of us decided to go out to the Island. We all followed after hearing how beautiful it was, that here was tons of space and that it was only two and a half hours away."

"I read that you guys were into the hard light out there," I said, like a very interested student.

"Hard light." Murray repeated the phrase then grew quiet for a few seconds as if he were studying its validity, then smirked. "It was more like Hard-Ons. The beaches out there are still beautiful, but back then there were no people on them. You'll see, they are great humping beaches. Oh yeah, we worked plenty but screwed even more, man, under the sun, stars, girlfriends, wives. A great time, great time."

After running his hand over his hair, he raised his eyes for a brief second then shot them down again, Bruin style, focusing on an empty wine bottle near the curb. "Then the suits heard about us out there and figured it had to be hip." Suits was Bruin's name for wealthy businessmen, prehistoric yuppies.

"I guess that was bound to happen," I replied sympathetically but not bitterly, being part yuppie myself.

"Yeah, they don't know what hip is and always look to artists to lead the way," his eyes burning into that bottle now. "Like they followed us into SoHo and the Village. We can't meet their bucks. Fuckers. It happened out there. Only the big buck artists stayed on, de Kooning is still there in the house he bought in the Springs."

"Isn't Krasner, Pollack's wife, still in the Springs?" I asked, innocently.

"Who gives a fuck about that asshole's place."

I forgot. Greenburg's review strikes again.

"Anyway, man, enjoy it if you can afford it."

"It's only a share, Murray."

"Chow, man."

As he walked away, I yelled, "Aren't there quite a few writers out there still?"

"I don't know. Never read," he yelled back without turning around.

Chapter Two

I finally got the chance to sit down in my closet that passed for an office. My day was done, three classes over. For some reason I felt exceptionally tired, and during the second class my voice went hoarse. Maybe it was the first real warm day of spring, I thought as I picked up a pen to fondle. My first taste of sex in months. My entire body was clammy and my sport jacket felt a pound heavier, a reminder that summer was close and I should call about the share.

Don't procrastinate, I told myself, you found the ad on Monday and here it is a week later. Find *The Voice* and call! I had a tendency to put off major decisions, even minor ones, at times. This fell somewhere in the middle. But finding *The Voice* here would not be easy. There were books all over the room in stacks on the floor and in every available space of the bookcases that lined the walls. Except for a small clearing in the center, there were papers, newsletters, junk mail and papers I could no longer identify. I started lifting papers in my search, then found it in the back of the phone under some literary magazines.

I rustled open to the share page once again; the circle I made was still big and red around the ad. I skimmed down the house listings one last time to make sure there wasn't another house in Amagansett that had the same appeal. There weren't any others. Actually, there was one other, "a happy-go-lucky house ready for new adventures" that ended its ad with "all gay" and the guy's phone number. Nothing for me there. Sorry, Bruce, won't be calling any time soon. Done. I'd call Patty. Even her name was right. I always thought it sounded all-American and trustworthy. If it were to sound any more American, the ad would have said, "call Doris Day at 262-5000." I leaned over and dialed the number.

On the third ring, a receptionist in a high-pitched voice that sounded so distant she could have been speaking to me from Europe, answered the phone.

"Hello, Blax Advertising."

"Hi. I'd like to speak to Patty."

She seemed somewhat annoyed with my request. "Sir, we have three Pattys here: Franklin, Vickers and Smith."

She made it sound like a law firm.

"I'm calling in reference to the summer share ad in *The Voice* if that helps."

"You must want Franklin."

"Right," I said matter-of-factly.

"Just a minute please."

I leaned back in my chair, one of those metal institutional types that tilt and turn in all directions and sit on three legs with wheels. But because of the clutter around it, the only duty it could perform without too much difficulty was tilting. I stared at the dust in the strip of late afternoon sunlight that filtered in from the one tiny window over the bookcase until Patty answered.

"Hello, this is Patty Franklin," she said almost too pleasantly.

"Hi, Patty. My name is Chris McCauley and I'm calling about your summer share ad in *The Voice*.

"Oh, great, what information would you like to know?"

Her voice went from too pleasant to phony. I didn't trust her already. I'm suspicious of anyone who is totally happy or constantly "up," especially in New York. I decided to lower my voice a few octaves, hopefully creating a more serious and businesslike approach. Maybe it would settle her down as well, and besides I was considering investing what was for me a sizeable sum of money into a house filled with strangers. What if I got there the first weekend and disliked all of them? What if it got worse instead of better? It would be like throwing money away. Better ask about the people.

"Could you tell me about the people who are in it?"

"Sure, what would you like to know about them?" she asked.

"Oh, their ages, what they do—stuff like that."

"Most are between the ages of twenty-five and thirty-three. Some are in advertising like myself and my roommate who is also running the house, and others are in business. There is also a girl who's into acting but hasn't decided yet. Seems it's a money problem with her."

I really wanted to ask: How many girls were in the house? What were their vital statistics? Who had the biggest chest? What color was their hair? What kind of salary do you have to make before they make you a serious contender? Does salary matter? Do they like fast food? Will they eat at McDonald's?

"How many people do you have committed and how many will be there on any given weekend?"

"Right now we have seven committed, and we need one more and hopefully that will be a full share."

Here was my opening, the bit of daylight I needed. I slipped the next question in nonchalantly.

"How many girls?"

She giggled. I guess I wasn't as nonchalant as I thought.

"Right now, there are four girls and four guys. Do the numbers please you?"

I could hear the smile in her question and felt my ears go red.

"Sounds fine," I shot back quickly, angry at myself for the speed of my reply. Proof of embarrassment. I regrouped just as quickly and moved on.

"Well, Patty, I'm interested in a full share. I teach and do a bit of writing. I'll have a lot of free time from mid-July on, so I figured I might as well spend it near the beach."

"You teach? Where?"

"At Newman College."

"What do you teach?"

"English literature and a poetry writing class."

"That sounds exciting. So you like it?"

"Love it."

"You're lucky." She became quiet for a few minutes as if she were contemplating my luck, then asked, "Would you like to know something about the house?"

"Not really. If it has a roof, bathroom and a bed, I'm happy."

She giggled. This one sounded cuter than the last. "It has all that and more. You don't sound too fussy."

"I'm not."

"You sound like my kind of people."

I wondered what she meant by that. By this time, I found her voice quite pleasing and kept trying to envision what she looked like, but came up empty. I suppressed the impulse to ask her what her feelings were about fast food.

"Where do we take it from here?"

"Well, how about meeting Donna and myself for a drink? We have some photos of the house and it could help you decide if you'd like to commit."

"That sounds fine to me. Where and when?"

"Let's see. Is it possible that we could meet today?"

"Sure."

"Okay." It's four-thirty now. Our office is on Forty-fourth and Seventh. Could you possibly come up here?"

"No problem."

"How about if we meet at O'Neill's, it's around the block from our office on Forty-third. Is that okay?"

"Six o'clock at O'Neill's. Fine."

"We'll be in the front bar area. If we are a little late, please wait. We'll be there."

"No problem."

"Okay, Chris, see you then."

"'Bye."

"'Bye."

I hung up the phone. So far, so good. I had kept my hand on the receiver for a few seconds and noticed my fingernails were dirty. I couldn't believe I let them go. I've been fanatic about my nails since eighth grade. I grabbed the nail file I always carry and started cleaning.

When I think back to 1963, it is always filled with astronauts in their silver space suits that looked like aluminum foil, grinning up at me from the glossy pages of Life; John-John Kennedy saluting the American flag that was draped over his father's horse drawn casket, and Peggy Kelly's golden blonde beaver.

At five-foot-five, Kelly – no one ever called her by her first name – was the tallest girl in my eighth grade class at St. Peter's, a small Catholic elementary school in Westchester, New York. She was pretty, a bit on the chunky side, with curly blonde hair and was the only girl in class who was more comfortable talking and hanging out with the boys. Space travel for my buddies and Kelly became the main topic of our discussions. Those astronauts who smiled in the face of danger and the uncertainty of the unknown became instant heroes. Space, however, for myself and most of the guys was much closer to home. For us, girls were the unknown, the new frontier, and it was Kelly who played a major role in our exploration. She became the launching pad for our pubescent projectiles—Saint Peter's graduating class's state of the art hard-ons.

Kelly would carefully select what she considered the cutest boy in class during our daily recess break. She'd tap you on the shoulder and invite you over to her house to hang out. By the time she tapped me on the shoulder in October, I knew what it meant. Billy Mayer, the oldest looking boy in the class, was picked first. Billy started shaving in the sixth grade and looked about twenty when he was thirteen. It pissed me off that she considered that guy cute. He was also five-foot-ten and muscular. So I decided not to let him know of my displeasure. Anyway, Billy told me what she did. Kelly would meet you at the door of her basement, invite you in, hike up her skirt and let you see what she had, made you drop your pants, then play with your parts until blast off. I then made him tell me in detail at least five times.

I got the nod from her during recess. It was right after another attempt to pass a math test, so I was off in the corner of the school playground going over the problems in my head and still coming up with the wrong answers. Out of the corner of my eye, I noticed Kelly coming over to me.

"Hi, Chris. Why are you looking so sad?"

The tone in her voice reminded me of my mother's when she tried to be understanding.

"Hi, Kelly. I think I failed another math test."

"Yes, it sure was difficult," she said. "I don't think I did that well either."

That meant she only got about a ninety-four. Kelly was also one of the smartest kids in the class and loved math. Poor Kelly, I thought, no one hundred this time around.

"Anyway, I was wondering if you were doing anything today after school."

There it was, the green light. At that very moment, I became a specially handpicked member of the elite: a Saint Peter's astronaut ready to explore the unknown. Finally, space was within reach. I imagined myself in the newest photo in next week's Life, standing arm in arm and grinning with all the other astronauts: Cooper, Glenn, Chisum and McCauley. Heroes all. I tried not to show that I was excited, I didn't want her to know I had any idea of what would take place.

"I don't have anything planned. Why?"

"Well, I thought it might be fun to listen to some records at my house."

I tried to make it look good. "On second thought, I think I have to watch my brother this afternoon."

I searched, but couldn't find any disappointment in her face.

"That's okay, then," she said happily, "we can do it some other time."

Like hell. Time to regroup.

"Wait a minute. I have to watch my brother tomorrow. That's right, it's tomorrow. I keep thinking today is Thursday. So I can make it," I said quickly.

"Great. How about coming by at four? See you later, Chris." She then ran off to talk to some of her girlfriends.

After school, I changed into my most faded jeans and my Mickey Mantle tee-shirt, slicked back my hair, then took off my jeans and put on clean underwear. The only other time I ever changed my underwear during the day was when I went to the doctor for a dick and ball examination. Yup, Kelly was pretty special. Then I put on my desert boots and headed towards destiny.

The Kelly house was a large Victorian on a hill, ten minutes from my house. Its windows were huge; it was an expensive looking house except for its white paint that had begun to peel and turn gray. I headed around to the side, and before I knocked on the basement door, Kelly opened it.

"Hi, Chris. I'm glad you could make it," she said cheerfully. She always seemed cheerful. She ushered me in. The basement was large, dark and wood paneled, with family mementos on the walls along with some college football pennants. Over to the right against the wall was a leather couch, and to the left was a record player on a small table. Kelly was still dressed in her school uniform which consisted of a blue plaid skirt, blue knee socks, loafers and white blouse. She wasn't wearing her blazer. Her breasts looked enormous. She walked over to the record player and pretended a once-over examination.

"Darn," she said looking down at it, "this thing isn't working, Chris."

Nice touch, I thought, she wanted to get right to it.

"That's too bad. I guess I could come back another time." I was so fucking cool.

"Oh, no! Don't leave, we can still do other things," she said with a slight touch of alarm. Then she smiled again.

"Haven't Billy, Roger and Gus told you what we've done here?"

Gus! I didn't know Gus had come here, too! That really pissed me off. That dork was ugly and the shortest guy in the class. He couldn't have been more than five feet, and on top of that, his hair was curly. He was good in math, I'd give him that, but that's all I'd give him. That meant I was the fourth picked when I should have been first or at least second. Failing another math test and then Gus. It was becoming a day of insults.

"Well, they sort of told me a little," I said sheepishly.

"Let me show you something then."

She turned her back to me, grabbed both ends of her Saint Peter's school uniform plaid skirt, and slowly began pulling it up. My heart started to pound and I felt my ears redden. And then it appeared, her rosy, pink ass—the moon in all its glory, six years before any astronaut got that close.

Facing the wall, Kelly said she was going to show me something else. She began to turn toward me slowly. My temples started to throb, my mouth went dry. In a second or two, I got my first glimpse of beaver. This one was thick and blond. I stood mesmerized at the clump of hair. Kelly began to sway back and forth and speak in a kind of loud whisper. "Have you ever seen this before?"

"No," I said and forgot all about being cool. In fact, I spoke as if I were drugged, never taking my eyes off it, not looking her in the face but listening as if her voice were coming from a loud speaker.

"Why don't you unzip your pants, silly, and let me look at yours?"

I unzipped my pants, letting them fall around my ankles, then, like a robot, I pushed my underwear down around my knees. My rocket was already pointing to the heavens, or would have been if Kelly's breasts weren't in the way. Then all of a sudden, things started going wrong at mission control. I felt like my temples were going to burst; my heart pounded so hard I was sure it would break open my chest, my knees began to quiver and my balls ached. The rest happened quickly. There must have been some sort of malfunction in the missile head and there was nothing I could do to prevent the accident. I looked down at my hard-on, closed my eyes, and let out a loud moan, then shot all over the floor. When I opened my eyes, Kelly had already dropped her skirt to cover herself, looked at me with a confused expression and yelled, "Why did you do that for?"

I panicked. Had to get out of there.

I mumbled something about being sorry, yanked up my underwear and turned to run out. But in my embarrassment and haste, I forgot my pants were still around my ankles. I went crashing down face first into the cement floor. Kelly shrieked. The next few seconds are a blur. I remember grabbing my nose, feeling the blood flow into my hand, trying to wipe it away and snorting the rest back in, grabbing my pants with my free hand trying to pull them up, and Kelly yelling something about my being okay. As I let go of my nose to free both my hands for the difficult task of zipping up my pants, I looked down at my tee-shirt and saw blood stains all over Mickey Mantle's face. I felt myself get dizzy, but I had no time to pass out. I had to get out of there.

Pants secured, I ran toward the door. Too embarrassed to look Kelly in the face, I yelled "goodbye" over my shoulder with my hand back over my nose. She said "goodbye" and in a concerned tone, hoped my nose would feel better.

I was home within twenty minutes. My nose had stopped bleeding, but I felt miserable. I ran upstairs, got into the bathroom, took off my clothes and turned on the shower. For the first time in my life I felt unclean, with the kind of dirt you feel inside and can't get to with soap and water. But just in case I could, I'd try to. Maybe soap and water would somehow seep into my skin, clean away the last hour of my life. I didn't understand any of it, but I knew I'd have to get into the water. Then I thought if the water does get through my skin, it would be better if I were soaked. So I turned off the shower, got into the tub and slid back into the warm water that rushed from the faucet. When I went back for the bar of soap, I noticed how dirty my nails were and remembered what my mom had to say about them a few weeks earlier.

"Chris, if you don't clean those nails of yours, you'll never get a nice girl."

I jumped up, got out of the tub and started rummaging through the medicine cabinet to find a scissor. Instead, I came across my mother's nail file. I grabbed it and started on my left thumb. By the time I got to my middle finger, I felt more relaxed, calmer, even cleaner. In fact, with each finger I did, the better I felt. It just seemed to clean whatever dirt was inside. It did the job soap and water couldn't. I then got back into the tub and kept filing until they were immaculate, and then filed some more.

Chapter Three

I put my nail file away and decided I'd better head uptown to meet Patty and her roommate since it was almost five. I threw some papers in my briefcase, then gave the mess around me a quick once over to see if there was anything else I needed. Satisfied there wasn't, I made my way toward the door but first tripped over the Norton Anthology of English Literature.

Maybe it was the premature heat that pissed me off and made me do something I had never done before, I kicked the book. You see, I've always treated all books with the utmost respect, so it wasn't too much of a surprise that I instantly felt remorse. Plus, there was also guilt over the magnitude of the act. I had just kicked centuries of the great works of the English speaking world in the ribs. No sooner had I kicked it, I had it in my hands examining it for damage. Nothing. It looked fine. I placed it on the stack near my desk then turned and went out the door confident Shakespeare, Wordsworth and the rest of the boys would, in time, forgive me.

The air on Twelfth Street was much cooler than in the classroom or my office, but I decided I couldn't deal with the subway during rush hour and would treat myself to a cab. I walked over to hail one on the corner of Sixth. A woman was begging in front of Joe Jr.'s Coffee Shop. She looked to be somewhere in her late fifties to early sixties. On her head was a knit hat that covered most of her hair except for a few strands that looked like they tried to escape from under it but had given up and died in the attempt. An old stained raincoat that was a few sizes too big and might have been a man's London Fog in its more prosperous times hung over her. Her legs were bare and thin like two sticks ready to snap at any moment. On her feet were worn-out running shoes. The left was red and much larger than the blue one on her right.

She stood silently with one of those paper coffee cups in her right hand. There seems to be more people like that begging on the streets of New York every day, so you can be selective when it comes to putting change in their cups. If you are overcome with guilt because you didn't give any money to the old man on the corner, you can make amends with your conscience by placing some change in another woman's cup on the next block.

I have one weakness with all of them that makes me throw change in their cups: eye contact. And that's what happened this time, too. I happened to look in her eyes that stared at me from both sides of a very large, narrow nose complete with a purple growth on the left nostril. But it was those eyes that seemed to look through me as if they belonged to an old sage who knew everything about me, even my latest in my long list of sins, book-kicker.

I had thirty-five cents in my pocket that I threw into her empty cup, then walked to the curb. A cab stopped immediately; as I got in I heard her scream a high shrill voice, "What's the matter, Fucker, can't you spare a dollar?"

At first, I felt like laughing, then quickly felt embarrassed. I guess I could have given more, I mused, but then just shrugged it off to inflationary times, smiled into the eyes of the cabbie who was staring at me from his mirror, and said, "Forty-second and Sixth, please."

For some reason, the cabbie had a Mario Andretti complex. As soon as the light turned green, it was as if someone dropped a checkered flag. He floored the gas pedal. I fell back against the seat, then grabbed the hold-on strap near the window with my right hand and wedged my left onto the seat in an attempt to keep myself upright as we swerved in and out of traffic. A few times I closed my eyes, convinced we were going to crash into cars and trucks that we missed by inches. I was glad we were still in one piece when we stopped at the red light in front of Macy's. Miracle on Thirty-fourth Street, Part II. Only eight more blocks. The checkered flag dropped again and we beat three taxis next to us off the line by four seconds.

I made Mario drop me off at Forty-second when he stopped for another red light. Since I was still alive, why tempt fate? A lot could go wrong in just two blocks in a cab whose driver, I was convinced, was trying to break the sound barrier. I'd walk the extra two blocks.

I headed down Forty-second and got a kick, like I always did, from the skin flick titles showing in three porn theaters between Sixth and Seventh Avenues: "Night Nipples," "Dripping Lips," and, of course, "On Your Knees For Love." I always wondered who were the creative geniuses who came up with titles like those? There's probably a Title Committee, a handful of fat, balding guys in their sixties with cigars stuck in the corner of their mouths and money sticking out of their pockets, shouting out names at each other for the flicks they financed. And since none of them has had a stiff cock in years, the name that gives them the slightest tingle in their balls becomes the title of the next blockbuster.

I had seen a few skin flicks, but never had the desire again after my garter belt and high heel fantasies were taken care of by Sally Brown White.

During my last few months with Laura, when things started going bad, sex became increasingly infrequent. Every time I made advances, she made excuses. Then it was as if she hung a sign on her thighs, "No Trespassing." She eventually changed that to "This Property Condemned." It was rough, but I remained loyal. Just because my balls were turning a light shade of blue didn't mean I should go out and have sex with a stranger. That's what I kept telling myself over and over. I kept thinking she'd come around. It was about this time that I met Sally. She moved into the apartment below mine.

My apartment building is one of those renovated old tenements on 78th Street, between First and York. They are still common on the East Side even though more and more expensive high-risers are going up like so many hard-ons the city keeps jerking-off. I'm on the last floor of the five flight walk-up. There's a living room, kitchen and bedroom. Off the bedroom is what used to be a closet, which now has a toilet in it; the tub is in the kitchen next to my one and only sink. Not much of a penthouse, but even these set-ups are quite expensive. Luckily, one of my student's dad was a realtor and got me in at an affordable rent. Because the building is so old, there's always problems with the plumbing and it was bad plumbing that brought Sally to my door one morning.

It was a Sunday around eleven. I was by myself that weekend since Laura had gone home to visit her parents in New Jersey. My doorbell rang and when I opened it, there was Sally. She was dressed in a long pink robe with a wraparound belt that accentuated her small waist. Even in tacky, but sexy gold slippers with six inch spikes, she couldn't have been more than five-feet-four. Her long black hair had a schoolgirl sheen to it. She parted it on the side and let it hang rather coyly over her right eye. She looked to be between twenty-five and thirty, and obviously in good shape.

She smiled, extended her hand to shake mine and said, "Hi. I'm Sally Brown White."

I knew who she was and heard about her from Mr. Diaz, our super, whose broken English was as bad as his maintenance abilities. He stopped me in the hall the day she moved in.

"Hey, Mr. McCauley," he said with a rather hungry look in his face. "You should check out the fucks that moved in right below you in Twelve-B." He seemed excited and kept his voice low as if he were giving me a hot tip on a horse he didn't want anyone else to hear.

I was confused for a few seconds and concerned. Why would he be excited about some troublemakers moving in below me? "Did you say fucks, Juan?" I asked again, obviously troubled.

"Yeah, an incredible body. What a fucks!" he repeated excitedly, ringing his right hand up and down like a wet rag.

I then realized what he was telling me: A good looking woman, a *fox*, had moved in. I felt immediate relief. "Okay, Juan, I'll check her out."

I did see Sally a few times, but around the neighborhood and always from a distance. She was the kind of woman men noticed and she dressed to make sure they did. Every sweater or blouse she wore was always tight and even though long skirts were in style, Sally wore hers a few inches above the knee. The few times I did see her she was in heels. They were so high her feet would wobble a bit with each step as if she might fall over at any moment. She never did, of course, and each spiky step tended to give her tits that extra jiggle legends are made of.

"I hate to bother you, Mr. McCauley."

Before I could get a word out, she pushed past me and walked into the kitchen looking around as if she had been there before and lost something. Somewhat shocked, I didn't close the door but stood with it opened and watched her inspect my sink.

"Can I help you with something, Ms. Brown?" I asked with a rather incredulous tone in my voice.

She kept inspecting, didn't turn to make eye contact, then said, "Please call me Sally," as she began her inspection of my tub.

"Did you take a shower this morning, Mr. McCauley?" she asked as she inspected the tub from top to bottom.

I closed the door. "Why, don't I look clean?" I asked humorously. This made her stop the inspection and turn around to look me over. She ran her eyes up and down in a way that almost embarrassed me.

"You look clean, alright. In fact, you look squeaky clean."

Her eyes kept moving and when they stopped a little longer on my groin, I started to feel uneasy. I wanted her eyes to meet mine and get away from my balls.

"So, Ms. Broo...Sally, what are you looking for exactly?"

"A leak."

"A leak?"

"Yes. I was standing in my kitchen about twenty minutes ago cleaning my sink when I felt a drop of cold water splash on my back. I was nude. I always do housework in the nude and boy, did I jump!"

I envisioned her tits hanging in the dish water as she leaned over the sink to scrub her pots and pans.

"So, I looked up and since your apartment is right above me, I figured it was coming from your place. I immediately threw on my robe and here I am," she replied.

That means she was nude under the robe. The thought made me feel even more uneasy.

"Well, I did take a shower about forty minutes ago and the plumbing is so bad in this building, I must be the culprit." I started to walk over to the tub, acting concerned, and began inspection of it. "Let me take a look." Even if I did find something, I wouldn't know what to do about it, but I was nervous and wanted to move away from her.

"Never mind about the leak now," she said.

I stopped and turned to face her again even though I heard her and said, "Excuse me?"

"The hell with the leak. Got any coffee?"

"Yeah, but I'll have to make it."

"Great, while you make it, can I look around?"

"Why not?"

I felt like saying why? and don't look too closely at anything, you might discover the dirt I'm sure I missed when I cleaned yesterday. I looked for the coffee hidden deep in my refrigerator. Out of the corner of my eye, I watched her looking at the pictures I had up in the living room.

"Is this a photo of your mom and dad?" she asked.

"Yeah, it was taken about four years ago."

"You look more like your mother, you have her blue eyes, but yours are deeper, prettier."

"Thanks," I said, somewhat embarrassed but enjoying the compliment.

"Mind if I look at your bedroom?"

"Go right ahead if you like." I panicked for a moment as I put water in the coffee pot. Did I have any underwear or socks on the floor? No, I didn't. I remembered picking them up earlier and putting them in the hamper. I don't know why I did, since I usually let them stay on the floor for a day or two. I guess the gods intervened and made me do the unexpected.

After I plugged in the coffee pot and went to the cabinet over the sink for some cups, I heard Sally call from the bedroom.

"Chris, can you come here for a second?"

I put the cups on the kitchen table and headed into the bedroom. She was probably looking at the abstract painting I had on the wall, I figured, and wanted to ask some questions about it. When I entered, I don't remember if my mouth fell open, but I do remember stopping as if I hit a brick wall and feeling the blood rush to my face. Sally was sitting on the edge of my bed. Her robe was tossed over the chair against the wall. She was wearing a black bra and matching panties. Her tits looked enormous squeezed into those little cups, and heaved up and down with each breath she took as if they had a life of their own. Her left leg hung over the right, pumping up and down, causing her slipper to slap against her heel. She was stroking her knee, sliding her left hand around it seductively, in a slow circular motion. But it was her right hand that scared the shit out of me—it was attached to the bedpost in a handcuff.

"Hi, Chrisy," she said. Her voice oozed out of her mouth in a high sexy whisper.

"What is this?" I asked, trying to sound stern, but since I was mesmerized by the sight, I'm sure I didn't sound too convincing.

"I thought you might want to play a game."

I didn't want to play any game. I just wanted her out and then again, maybe I just wanted her. No, I didn't I told myself. Stop it. Get that out of your mind. You're in love with Laura. You don't screw around behind her back. Trust. If two people don't have that, they have nothing. Okay, so you haven't had sex with her in a while. It's just a phase, she'll get over it. You're not like most guys who fuck around behind their girlfriend's backs. You're Chris McCauley. Trust is your middle name. Trust...I stopped trying to convince myself that I didn't want Sally and I certainly couldn't stop the hard-on that was pushing against my jeans.

"So, do you want to play?" she asked.

"What game," I said, still trying to sound stern, "and what are you doing with that handcuff?"

"That's part of the game, silly. Come over here."

I tried to say something as my feet started moving, but couldn't when I realized how white her skin was. It was the color of milk and I found myself getting thirstier by the second. I was about to change my middle name.

"Chris, the first part of the game is finding the key to the handcuffs, and if you do, you can set me free and win the prize."

"What prize?"

"You'll see. Start searching," she giggled.

I was standing in front of her, then leaned over to unhook her bra. As soon as I unbuckled the strap, her tits just seemed to fall out like stuffed pillows. In the excitement, I didn't notice the key fall onto her leg. The pace started to pick up. I then saw the key, and leaned over to unlock the handcuff.

While I was fumbling with the key, her left hand was working on my belt and zipper. When I finally freed her hand from the cuff, and by the time I straightened up again, she had my pants unzipped and my hard-on out. She started to examine it, slowly moving her fingers along the shaft as if she were an art collector examining a piece of sculpture for her private collection. It was a safe bet to assume Sally had collected many such pieces over the years and had become a connoisseur, an expert, if you will, on cock art.

"How beautiful your prick is," she whispered, "what a powerful looking cock." It was her turn to be mesmerized.

I had never heard a woman refer to my hard-on as a cock or prick before. The few girlfriends I had didn't call it anything, and Laura always referred to it as "my thing." She'd say, "Your thing looks great," or "Is your thing hard yet?" I never realized it before, but every time we made love, it was as if it didn't belong to me, it wasn't part of my body. It was just a tool for her to get the job done. So when we went bed, it seemed like there was always the three of us; Laura, myself, and "the thing." Sally made me feel it was part of me, it was my body. At least this time there was just the two of us.

"It keeps getting harder, how do you do that?" Sally said, this time looking up at me. It wasn't, but I guessed it was part of the game. She also liked talking. That was also new for me, it turned up the heat.

"I have to suck you now, don't I?"

"You do, baby, you have to suck it." I was amazed at my reply. I felt free, uninhibited, caught up in a "game" in which Sally (excuse the pun) was the headmaster. She introduced me to a part of myself that I'd never met before and I liked him.

Moving both hands slowly up and down my cock, she started to make her tongue flutter around the head like a butterfly. Then, as if to brace herself, she grabbed my ass with both hands and took all of it, sucking and sliding her mouth back and forth, slowly at first, and then faster as if she were starving. She stopped suddenly, looked up at me again and said, "I want you inside of me," then fell back on the bed, ripped each string that went over her hips, pulled her panties from between her legs and flung them on the floor. With my pants still around my ankles, I fell on top of her and she helped guide my cock inside. It was wet and tight, but before I could tell her she told me.

"Feel how tight my pussy is," she groaned. More heat. I groaned in agreement. Her voice started getting louder until she was almost screaming.

"Fuck me! Fuck me! Oh, your cock is so hard! Oooo. Fuck mee!"

Sally's howling brought me back to reality for a few seconds. I know it sounds strange, but I thought of Mrs. O'Brien, the old lady who lives in the apartment next to me. I didn't want her to hear us. After all, the walls are quite thin. Every time I saw Mrs. O outside with a package, I'd offer to carry it up the stairs and she'd tell me what a nice young man I was. She knew I wasn't married, so I didn't want her to think I had sex. For some strange reason, I thought if she didn't think I screwed around, I'd remain "nice" in her eyes. I guess I just wanted to keep my title. But when Sally lowered her voice, I realized how ridiculous it was to care what the old gal thought. I began to concentrate again on the job at hand and went to Sally's nipples.

"Oooo, suck them," she purred, "I'm going to come!" She started banging her bent legs against my hips, my face was buried in her neck. "I'm going to come! Come with me baby!"

Music to my ears. I couldn't hold it any longer. Her voice started getting louder again as she dug her nails deeper into my ass. Her legs were banging against my hips now like flapping wings. If she didn't come soon, we'd probably start flying. I couldn't hold it any longer.

"I'm coming. I'm coming," Sally yelled.

"Me too, baby! Me too!" I yelled even louder, then collapsed exhausted on top of her.

We came together. Another first.

My pants were still crumpled around my ankles, my body was soaked in sweat, even my hair was wet. I must have looked like I had just taken a shower. I rolled over on my back, then looked over at Sally who was gazing at the ceiling. She basically looked the same. Her hair was dry and there was no sign of perspiration; the only hint that we had been through this together was that her lipstick was gone. I turned away and looked up at the ceiling too, then arched my back a bit to stretch. My body felt exhausted, but it was the kind of exhaustion I could learn to respect. I started to relax and began waiting—waiting for Sally to say something. Anything, as long as it was mildly complimentary like, "Chris, I've been with a lot of men, but you are by far the best," or something subtle like, "You fucking stud." I kept waiting. Come on, Sally, you stroked my cock, now stroke my ego.

Instead, she simply got out of bed, put her slippers on, then walked over to get her robe from the chair. After putting it on, she scanned the room, spotted the cuffs, unlocked them from the bedpost and put them in her pocket. She didn't look at me at all, and turned and walked into the kitchen. When she finally did say something, it wasn't exactly what I wanted to hear.

"Is this coffee done, sweetie?"

"Should be." I heard her pour a cup, drink it and then she finally gave me some recognition.

"You make a great cup of coffee."

"Thanks." It wasn't the compliment I was looking for, but it was better than nothing.

Her heels started clicking back toward the bedroom until she stood in the doorway. At last she made eye contact. "That was fun."

"Sure was."

"You can throw away those panties. They aren't any good to me now."

"I'll either throw them away or have them bronzed."

She laughed, then said, "Byee," as if she were singing it and walked out the door. Funny how sex made her sing. It just made me tired. I stared at the door for a few moments with my pants still anchored around my ankles, then turned on my side and went to sleep.

Later that afternoon, I went out to buy the Sunday *Times*. When I came back, there was Mrs. O'Brien struggling with a package near the front door.

"Hi, Mrs. O'Brien," I said cheerfully, "would you like me to carry that up for you?" I didn't wait for a reply and immediately went for the package.

"Thank you. What a nice young man you are," she answered with a big smile.

Great. She hadn't heard a thing.

Chapter Four

I turned onto Seventh Avenue. Times Square was already crowded with people moving in a hurry, staring straight ahead, their eyes fixed on nothing. Others looked down at their feet as if they were afraid of being recognized. But I recognized them. They were just working people making their escape, some to the nearest subways and train stations, and still others to the bus stops. Another work week was done. They wanted out and nothing was going to get in their way.

For a moment I imagined myself tripping, then screaming as they trampled me into the pavement. It was the kind of story *The New York Post* loved and would use for their headlines: COLLEGE PROF TRAMPLED TO DEATH BY RUSH HOUR CROWD... Story on page one.

I was, in fact, walking slowly, feeling a bit run-down, and I couldn't stop sweating. The crowd seemed to make the air even heavier and warmer than it was back in my office, and it were also making me feel somewhat claustrophobic. I was relieved to turn the corner onto Forty-fifth Street.

Most of Forty-fifth, between Sixth and Seventh, was dark, run-down, and shabby looking, but at least it was rather quiet. I spotted O'Neill's immediately.

It was easy to find. The large wooden doors and windows looked immaculate in comparison to the rest of the street. As I walked toward the doors, a derelict asked me if I could spare some change. I was going to make up for not giving more to the woman down on Sixth, but this guy was standing in between two parked cars taking a leak. I couldn't quite see myself waiting to give him money as he shook the last drop of piss from his honker, so I kept going, made sure not to make eye contact (didn't want to weaken) and went into O'Neill's.

Inside, I waited by the door for the hostess a sign claimed would seat me. While I stood there, I gave the place a quick survey. To the right was a long oak bar with a mirror of the same length behind it. In the bar area were a few tables that were empty. The girls obviously hadn't arrived yet. As usual, I was early. I shot a quick glance to the back of the room, which was the dining area. All the tables were empty too, except for one where an elderly couple were eating dinner. As far as I could tell, there was just one bartender, the old couple and a waitress. It sort of made me feel depressed, empty restaurants always did.

A hostess never arrived, so I grabbed a table, according to the plan near the window. When I sat down in a chair facing the door, the waitress came hurrying over, eager for something to do. I helped her out by ordering a draft. I then picked a napkin off the table and wiped my forehead. My stomach was feeling better, but I was still sweating rather heavily. There was, however, one of those wooden fans directly over me moving slowly but enough to cool me down.

When the waitress brought over the beer, the door opened. In walked two women, the one who was no more than five-foot-three looked like she tipped the scales at 200 pounds. Her hair looked dirty, and there seemed to be blemishes all over her face. Her friend, who was a bit taller, looked as if she hadn't eaten a meal in months. She made Olive Oil look ready for a stint in Weight Watchers.

They glanced over my direction, then headed toward the table. I felt my face drain. Gripping the arms of my chair, I began pushing myself up to greet them since most of the strength in my legs was suddenly gone. As they got closer, they began to smile but didn't stop. Instead they walked by and headed toward the back of the restaurant. I simply kept staring straight ahead and lowered myself back into the seat. I waited until I was sure it was safe and they wouldn't come back before I loosened my grip on the chair, then moved my fingers around to get the feeling back into them. Breathing easier, I understood what had just taken place, another warning from God. He was testing me again to prove his existence; He knows I used to question it from time to time. He was just toying with me like He did so many times in the past.

The Big Guy was saying: "See, Chris, those two could have been the girls you are going to meet at any moment. I know they are not your type, and I, in my infinite wisdom, decided not to let that happen. Don't ever doubt my existence and powers again. And, Chris, try to make the 10:15 at St. Monica's this Sunday."

I grabbed my beer and took a huge gulp—God's testing always had a tendency to make me thirsty. I put the glass down again and looked at it. It was the best tasting brew I had in a while.

"Chris McCauley?"

"I looked up. Patty and her roommate were standing next to my table and I hadn't seen them come in.

"You must be Patty," I said, getting up from the table to shake her hand.

"Hi," she replied with a smile. "Nice to meet you. Hope we aren't late."

"Oh, no. I tend to be early," I replied.

"And this is my friend, Donna Placido." Donna just smiled.

Patty was about my height with short, curly blonde hair. Her lips were full, but a bit too large for her slender face. Although she told me she was twenty-five over the phone, she looked a few years younger. Donna was on the short side with short black hair, was rather dark but looked about thirty. At a quick glance, they both seemed like they had pretty good bodies. They also looked rather tired, and since they hadn't put on fresh makeup, it reinforced the illusion they were fading. Their lips wore just a hint of the bright red lipstick they must have put on when the day began.

I was a bit surprised to find them wearing dresses, not suits. I assumed that since they were career women, they would be wearing conservative business suits complete with ties. It was the way Laura always dressed for Wall Street. I was convinced, however, that Laura's working uniforms were slowly suffocating the essence of her femininity. It was as if they helped her create the edge she thought was necessary to survive in "your world," meaning a man's world. Every time she used that phrase, she would glare at me and I'd have to remind her that it wasn't my world since none of the women at school wore suits. She'd just grunt and walk away. When she was dressed casually, she was a different person. "Would you please open the door, Chris?" or "Could you please answer the phone?" became "Open the door!" and "Get the phone!" when she was in pinstripes. So I found it refreshing to see two career women comfortable with their own identities.

As they sat down, I happened to glance in the mirror that was directly across from me. I couldn't believe it. I was wearing a white Budweiser mustache across my upper lip! I must have forgotten to wipe my mouth after my first gulp of beer. I gave myself a quick shave, wiping the back of my hand across my mouth. What a slob, they must have thought, he's sweating, looks ill and forgets to clean his mouth. I was embarrassed, but at least they didn't say, "Here's a napkin, slob, wipe the suds off your face." Instead they both got comfortable in their chairs; Donna kept smiling and Patty got down to business.

"Well," she began, "we should tell you right away that everyone has a full share in the house except for the two half-shares. The full shares have the option of going out every weekend and can spend time during the week if they wish. The two half shares will alternate their weekends and can only spend time during the week that coincides with their weekend. And since you are our last full share, if you decide to sign on, they'll be sharing your bedroom. Do you mind sharing your room with two different people? We will all be sharing bedrooms, but the rest of us, obviously, with the same person?"

"No, that's perfectly okay with me," I replied. Actually, the thought of sharing a bedroom with two different strangers wasn't very appealing. I already resigned myself to the fact I'd have to share a room with someone, but not two strangers.

"That's great. But I should also let you know that one is a guy and one is a girl. We thought you might have problems with that and we just like to be up front and honest about everything."

"I have no problems with that at all." Were they kidding! What luck! Forced to sleep in the same bedroom in a beautiful beach house every other week with a strange woman. What cruelty!

"Glad you don't mind having a female roommate then," Patty said.

I just smiled.

Donna, who was constantly smiling, finally stopped to speak to Patty. "Why don't you show him the photos."

Patty immediately began searching through her rather large pocketbook, found the photos, quickly shuffled through them, removed two and offered them to me.

"Here are a few photos of the house. It might help you make up your mind if you really want to commit."

"Thanks," I said, taking the pictures from her. As I shuffled through them, the waitress came by to ask if they would like a drink. Patty said no and that they were only staying for a few minutes. Donna was back in her smiling mode and was content to let Patty talk for both of them. It seemed Patty was the designated spokesman for the two in all matters.

The house didn't look like it was built, but more like it had landed. It was a gray contemporary that looked closer to a spaceship than a house. Apparently, most of the homes out there looked that way now, and the very old salt boxes dating back a few hundred years were in the minority. They certainly didn't blend in with the environment; there was nothing organic about it. I remember reading in an art class in college how Frank Lloyd Wright believed homes should become one with their surroundings. This thing would make him spin in his grave. Frank would never take a share in a house like this!

It was two stories, round on one side and square on the other with a deck circling it. There were also two slanted wings in the middle of the roof. I had no idea what they were for. I looked at Donna and said, "This sure is different looking."

She, of course, just smiled. The four bedrooms were empty except for beds and a bureau, the kitchen looked like it had all the modern equipment and the entire house was furnished with cheap, practical, beach type furniture.

"What do you think?" Patty asked.

"Looks great and a little like a spacecraft." She didn't acknowledge my comparison. I looked for a smile but didn't get one, so I looked at Donna. By this point, I knew I could count on her. Along with the smile, I even got a giggle. I actually liked the look of the place, or maybe it reminded me of my days as an astronaut. If *Life* were still being published, I'd be grinning from its cover in my silver spacesuit along with the title of its cover story, "Astronaut Returns to Space Program for the Summer Eighteen Years Later."

Patty jumped in with, "The beauty of it is the beach is right down the road."

As she said this, I happened to turn to the photos of the beach. We were in tune. I realized at that moment I was attracted to her and was already looking for things we had in common. We had timing. Okay, it wasn't much, but it was a beginning. On the other hand, can't timing be everything?

The beach was beautiful. It looked like it stretched north for miles until it became a thin white string. There were a few spaceship homes to the left, and the ocean was a deep blue with surf the color of the gulls that flew above it. I also saw what Murray Bruin pointed out. The beach would be great for "humping."

"This sure is a beautiful beach. How far is it from the house?" I asked.

"Just down the road, maybe three minutes," Patty said. Donna nodded in agreement, smiling.

"I guess you've been wondering about how we work the food arrangements," Patty said, with a concerned look.

It never even crossed my mind. "Yes, as a matter of fact, I was going to ask you about food."

"Well, Donna and I will get the staples, milk, sugar, etc., which we will all chip in for. As far as meals go, we'll have to leave it up to you people. If everyone wants to eat together, we will all pool our money, and if some have other plans, they should not feel any obligation to be part of the house dinners."

"That sounds democratic enough, even for a Republican," I replied with a smile. Not even Donna smiled at that comment.

"One other thing, Chris, we have a maid come in every Monday to clean up after us."

"That sounds like a good idea."

"We ran a house last summer without one and it proved to be a mistake. It tended to get trashed over the weekend and, of course, no one wanted to clean, including myself."

"Sounds like a good idea. How much will it cost?"

"No more than five dollars a person. Do you have any other questions about anything?"

"Not really."

"Well, if you'll excuse us then for a few moments. Is the ladies room in the back?"

"I think so."

They both got up and trotted off to the bathroom. I was never able to understand why women went to the bathroom together. When I was a kid, I figured they must have helped each other get on the toilet. At the time, it seemed like a logical conclusion. Later, in my teens, I asked my mom why women go off to the bathroom in pairs. I remember her gazing blankly at me saying, "Because that's what women do." I realized then it was another mystery in a man's life that's futile to question, and will always remain unsolved. But this time there was no mystery.

For Patty and Donna, the bathroom was to become a polling place where they would vote if they really wanted me in the house or not. I had made up my mind. I wanted in. I already had a crush on Patty. Donna didn't say anything but smiled pleasantly, the beach was beautiful, the house interesting, and I'd be sharing my bedroom every other week—as I convinced myself—with a beautiful woman. What more could a guy who was getting over a love affair possibly want?

I looked down at my beer. Take that, Laura.

The girls returned in a few minutes, their faces glowing with fresh makeup. Now they looked rested and refreshed with votes tallied. As they sat down again, we all smiled at each other and I have to admit, I was a bit worried. After convincing myself that this could be the greatest summer of my life, what if they didn't want me? Okay, girls, do you want me or not?

"Chris," Patty began, "both Donna and I would love to have you as part of our group, if you are happy with everything so far."

Victory! "I'm really impressed with the pictures you showed me of the house and the beach, and you girls seem quite pleasant. I'm sure the rest of the people in the house are pleasant as well."

"We tried to pick what we felt were the right kinds of people, but as you know, it's always a risk. Hopefully, everyone will get along nicely."

"I'm sure we will."

Actually, I had heard horror stories about how people in share houses ended up hating each other's guts by the end of the summer. Putting strangers together to live under the same roof for any amount of time is always a risk, but I quickly put that possibility out of my mind. This was going to be my summer.

"Do you have any other questions that we could answer for you now?" asked Patty.

"Nothing that comes to mind."

"You do know that our weekends begin Memorial Day and run through Labor Day. Also, you can use the house anytime you want during that time, but if you want to bring guests out on weekends, check with Donna and myself."

"Sure." I couldn't think of anyone I'd bring out anyway.

"We just don't want the weekend run over with strangers. It would be unfair to the shareholders."

"I understand."

Donna took time out from smiling a moment. "Tell Chris about the party," she said to Patty.

"Oh, yeah, we are going to have a party tomorrow night out at our place in Queens. It's open to anyone who wants to come, but we would like the people who are in the house to be there so they can get to know each other a bit before the summer starts."

"Sounds like a good idea."

"Do you think you can make it?"

Of course I could make it. I had nothing to do like all the empty Saturday nights I spent since breaking off with Laura. "I do have plans, but I'll get out of them and come by." Why let Patty think I wasn't in demand?

"Wonderful." She then rummaged through her pocketbook and took out a piece of photocopied paper.

"Here are the directions to our place in Queens. The party should begin around nine."

I took the directions, pretended to read them for a few seconds, then folded them up and placed them in my pocket.

"Thank you. There is just one other thing. When would you like me to pay you?"

"If you like, you can send me a check within the next two weeks. Is that okay?"

"Fine with me."

"If you have any more questions concerning the house, feel free to call."

"I'll do that. Thanks." A few moments of awkward silence followed where we all just sort of smiled at one another. For a pro like Donna it must have been second nature, but I always find those moments, no matter how brief, extremely uncomfortable. Patty put a stop to it. She was kind, too.

"Well, we should get going."

I wasn't in a rush to get anywhere. "I should really get going, also."

We all got up at the same time.

"I'd leave with you," I said to them, "but I've got to find the waitress to pay for my beer."

"It was nice meeting you and you, Donna." As you might have guessed, Donna smiled.

"We'll be seeing you tomorrow night then?"

"Sure will."

"Bye-bye."

"Bye." As I watched them walk toward the door, I was able to verify what I thought when they came in—they were in great shape. I then zeroed in on Patty's legs. Her shoes were high enough to make the muscles in her calves flare out ever so slightly with every step she took. Not bad. I could see already it was going to be a fun summer. I noticed too, that I had stopped sweating and felt much better than I had all day. Maybe I was more nervous about them than I realized. When the waitress came over with the check, I decided to sit down, relax, and have another brew.

Chapter Five

I slept late Saturday morning then went jogging along the East River. After I showered and had breakfast, I spent the rest of the day reading the papers and watching the Errol Flynn Film Festival on Channel Five. They showed *Captain Blood* and *Robin Hood*, my two favorites, back to back. I was anticipating watching those two movies during the day as much as I was going to the party that night.

Watching Flynn movies, however, was always hazardous to my health. I must have seen *Robin Hood* about twenty times over the years. Once, when I was around ten, I went outside after watching it and decided to climb an old oak in the back yard, the way Robin would have waited to jump down on one of the Sheriff of Nottingham's soldiers. I remember waiting for about an hour and the closest I came to seeing a Saxon was my younger brother, Tom, coming home from his guitar lesson. He'd have to pass under the tree to go in the back door. I figured I'd swoop down on him when he was right below me, which I did, but swooped three feet behind him and heard my right leg snap when I hit the ground. I spent the next six weeks on crutches with my leg in a cast.

On Saturday, the spirit of Flynn filled me once again. I had to take a piss while I was watching *Captain Blood*, but waited until a commercial. I knew I'd have to fight my way to the bathroom. So I jumped up from the couch, pulled my imaginary sword from its sheath, and began fighting the three pirates in my living room, quickly sliced them up and ran into the kitchen. Sure enough, two more were waiting for me there. I told them to step aside, but of course they wouldn't. They, too, would have to taste my cold steel. I smiled like Errol as I sliced their heads off one at a time, then ran into my bedroom. The coast was clear as I jumped onto my bed to get a better look. There were no more rogues in sight. With my sword still in hand, I leaped to the floor, but as I did my right foot got tangled in the sheets. As I fell, my hands shot out to break the fall. I wasn't hurt, but for a few seconds I looked at the floor. I felt rather foolish. I decided to put away my sword, enough blood had already been shed, and just walked into the bathroom.

I left my apartment that night for the party around eight-thirty. I grabbed a cab on Second and gave the cabby the direction sheet. I wasn't too familiar with Queens. The few times I had passed through it, I decided Queens and I would remain strangers. It always looked totally devoid of architectural character along with its frayed blue collar atmosphere. Patty and Donna's neighborhood was about twenty minutes from the Fifty-ninth Street Bridge and did little to change my opinion. All the houses looked identical: two story, brick homes with metal fences in front, only their numbers varied. It seemed Elmhurst would not bring Queens and me any closer.

The cabby said his brother used to live in the area "before he divorced the Missus," as we turned onto Seventy-eighth Street and dropped me off in front of 38-47.

I could hear music and other noises from the party on the sidewalk. It seemed to blend in with the traffic on the Long Island Expressway that was just a few blocks away. I opened the unlocked front door and climbed the narrow stairs to the second floor. I rang the doorbell, waited a few minutes, then as I went to ring again, the door swung open.

"Hello, I'm Aaron Goldstein, self-designated party greeter."

Aaron Goldstein was already shitfaced, about six-foot-one and quite thin. He was wearing designer jeans and a blue oxford shirt. His face was full and he had a booze induced glow.

"How ya doin', Aaron Goldstein."

"Come in, come in," he said, closing the door with one hand and holding a drink in the other. He then shook my hand, lost the grin on his face, looked from left to right as if to make sure no one was listening, bent over a bit and almost whispered in my ear, "What are you, an A or a B?"

What the hell did that mean? I hoped it wasn't a variation of the more common, are you A.C. or D.C.? I just got to the party and I had a live one on my hands!

"You got me there, Aaron. What do you mean?"

"Aren't you the half share guy? Just want to know if you are coming out on the A or B weekend?"

"No, I'm not the half share guy. I'm the full share guy. So I guess that means I'm A and B. I go both ways."

That made him laugh out loud which sounded somewhat like a nervous giggle. My remark made him put out his hand for me to slap him five. I slid mine across instinctively.

"You're okay. By the way I didn't catch your name."

"Didn't toss it." More giggles. "It's Chris McCauley."

"What line of work are you in, Chris?"

"Teaching. And you?"

"I'm in advertising – and women whenever I get the chance," he added with a smile.

"That must keep you busy."

"Just the women do." He giggled, drained his glass, then said, "And speaking of women, what about the two babes who are running the house?"

"They seem quite nice."

"Shit. That's not what I mean, what do you think about their bods?"

"Those are nice, too."

"That's an understatement."

I just looked at him.

"But there's one problem," he said, staring into his empty glass, "I haven't decided which one I want yet."

It was time to shake this asshole. "Well, take your time, Aaron, the summer hasn't even started yet." That seemed to put him at ease.

"Yeah, you're right, I got time. Anyway, let me give you a quick tour of the place without moving. To your right, as you can see and hear, is the living room where people are dancing."

We were standing in the hallway where most of the living room was blocked from view. But I could make out various parts of bodies as they danced into the hallway and into view for a second or two. The girls had a Marvin Gaye tape on. Another positive sign. After meeting Goldstein, I needed one in a hurry.

"Now, over there," Aaron turned on and pointed with his glass across the hall and to my left, "is the kitchen and next to that is the dinette where you'll find drinks, a keg and assorted dip shits. And over here to my right is the most important room of all. Aside from being their bedroom, it has a kind of powder you might want to try." He looked at me, giggled, and snorted twice just in case I didn't get what he meant. "You're on your own now."

"Thanks." I quickly left him and headed toward the kitchen. There were two guys who looked like they were in an intense conversation as I walked through to the dinette. I stopped there to check out the action in the living room. It was a rather large room that was furnished, like the rest of the apartment, in leftover college posters and furniture from real life—the kind you find in your mom's or aunt's house. There were anywhere from fifteen to twenty people dancing. I spotted Patty in the middle of the crowd but I couldn't tell with whom she was dancing. For the first time, it dawned on me she might have a boyfriend.

The table in the dinette was filled with little sandwiches, chips and dips. None of it looked appealing or even touched. So I went for the keg, it was time to drink down some fun and catch up. As I was filling a plastic cup I found on the table, I heard: "Chris! Glad you could make it!"

I turned around to face Donna. She was sweating and her eyes were slightly glazed.

"I wouldn't have missed it."

"Did you get the chance to meet any of the summer people yet?" I was surprised to hear her initiate a conversation since all she did yesterday was sit meekly and smile. "Just Aaron Goldstein."

"A wonderful guy."

Glad she thought so. "He sure is." Some guy from the living room crowd screamed out her name.

"Just a second," she yelled back without turning around.

"Boyfriend?" I asked.

"No, just a fuck buddy."

I didn't think I heard her correctly. "Excuse me?"

"He's just a fuck buddy. Ever since my divorce six months ago, I've been into sport fucking." Her divorce explained the real life furniture. But I couldn't get over the change from yesterday. So much for first impressions.

A big guy with a beard who looked like a lumberjack dressed in a plaid shirt and jeans came over and put his arm around Donna.

Donna introduced us. "This is Dan. Dan, meet Chris."

We both said "hi" and shook hands. He seemed anxious and immediately said to Donna, "Come on, baby."

43

She said to me, "Dan is going to go with me to my room and help me powder my nose. See you later."

"See you later," I said, as they walked unsteadily towards the kitchen, then into the hall.

I drained my glass and looked out into the living room to see if Patty was still dancing. She was still going at it and was even dancing with Goldstein.

It was time to refill my glass, but before I could, a girl came over to me with her arm stretched out holding a full glass.

"I can see your glass is empty, so this is for you," she said, cheerfully.

I wondered how she saw anything, with eyes that seemed no wider than slits. I took the glass. "And I thought you had to pray to get your prayers answered."

She laughed at my remark but it was a bit forced, party etiquette. As she did, the short brown curls that framed her round face shook like tiny, silent bells.

"You're Chris McCauley, right?"

"Yes, I am."

"When you walked in, I asked Patty who you were."

Her comment made me wonder why Patty didn't come over to say hello if she had spotted me first.

"Well, I have no one nearby to tell me your name, so you are going to have to help me out."

"Debbie Gelfand." She then took hold of a wine glass she found on the table as if she needed a prop more than a drink, and took a sip. Her nose curled over her upper lip, and when she drank from the glass it seemed to curl down even further to take a sip of wine, too.

"You teach," she said, sounding more like she was telling me, not asking.

"Yup." I decided not to ask her how she knew. "What do you do?"

"I'm an actress," she said, then quickly shot her eyes out to the people dancing.

"An actress. Have I seen you in anything?"

This brought her eyes back. "You couldn't have seen me in anything."

"Why not?"

"Because I haven't acted in anything."

I sensed she was uncomfortable with the statement and thought I shouldn't pursue the matter, but she did. "I've been taking acting classes for the past few years."

"That's great."

"What's great about it? If you don't get up and perform in front of people, it's pointless." She was staring into the living room, expressionless and not really looking at anyone. I didn't know what to say next except, "Well."

She didn't hear it. "But I'm about to go on auditions soon." I tried to sound enthused, "When?"

"As soon as my analyst thinks I can. In about a month or two."

"That's good news." She didn't hear that either.

"You know what I really hate?"

"No, what do you really hate, Debbie?"

She looked at her wine. "As soon as people hear that you are an actress, they want to know what you acted in or whatever it is you are going to do next, gives you validity. If you haven't acted in anything, they seem to think you can't really be an actress. It's not fair. When my mom tells people she's a housewife, it seems to be enough. They accept it and never ask her where was the last room she vacuumed, or what table will she clean next." She then looked up at me. "See what I mean?"

I did and was pissed with myself for asking if I had seen her in anything. "Yeah, I do." I figured I should change the subject, but she beat me to it.

"So, you're one of the share people?"

"Yes, I am."

"So am I," she said cheerfully. "As a matter of fact, I'm your A girl."

"Excuse me?" I said, somewhat puzzled.

"I'm one of the half shares and you and I will be roommates on the A weekend."

Since I hadn't eaten much of anything that day, the beers were quickly creating the desired effect. I was already buzzed so it took a few seconds for me to decipher what she said, and when I did, I needed another beer in a hurry. She began examining my face closely for my reaction. Instead, I looked at my glass and said, "I need a refill," then walked to the keg and filled my glass.

I needed time to collect myself and get over the shock. My fantasy of having a beauty in my bedroom was over. I felt like she had died within the past twenty-four hours and the girls elected Debbie to break the awful news. Another fantasy gone. Nicole Something, may she rest in peace. I wondered if hospitals had fantasy morgues where fantasies that die suddenly would stay until they were claimed again. I even saw the coroner filling out the forms: Cause of Death: Reality. I was drunker than I thought, but if I had a few more brews in me it could have been worse—I might have started crying.

When I walked back to where Debbie was standing, she was still waiting for my reaction.

"Sooo, we are going to be roommates," I said, trying to conjure up some enthusiasm, but with little success. Debbie was no Nicole, but I guess, not many women were.

"I just know our weekends will be a lot of fun, but we might have a problem though," she said with a smile.

I felt like saying there'll probably be a few problems. "Oh, really? What's that?"

"Do you sleep in the nude?"

"No, I don't," I said matter-of-factly.

"Well, I do," she said teasingly.

It was time to get serious. "I promise I won't look."

She made her voice squeaky. "Not even a peek?"

"No!" I snapped, a bit surprised I sounded irritated. I didn't want to give my real feelings away, and I certainly didn't want to hurt hers. It was time to change the subject.

"Did you try any of this food," I said, as I turned to look over the table.

"No, I can't eat any of this stuff. Nothing greasy. I'm on a special diet."

Good. A topic I should be comfortable with. "Are you trying to lose a few pounds?"

"No. I have a touch of colitis."

How charming. "That's too bad."

"Yeah, most things go right through me. As a matter of fact, do you know where the bathroom is?"

"I think it's that way." I pointed down the hall. I wasn't sure but I wanted Debbie to get going and I wasn't in the mood to get into the colitis issue.

"Okay. Well, I'll see you later, roomy," she said, as she turned and headed toward the kitchen.

"See you later." Much later I hoped. I really needed another beer, but before I could go back to the keg Goldstein was on his way over.

"Great party, ha man?" He put his palm out for me to slap him five. I skinned him. After Debbie, it was a relief to see a familiar face, even if it belonged to Goldstein.

"Saw you talking to the Gelfand babe."

"Yeah, she's nice."

"I tell you what, buddy, I'll let you have her. She's not my type."

"Thanks. That's real big of you."

He started laughing then opened his hand again for skin. I slapped it with my own and laughed with him. I was beginning to like him.

"Did you try any party powder yet?"

I had never tried it. For some reason, it tended to scare me.

"No, I haven't."

"Try it before it's gone. It's good shit!"

"I will."

"By the way, one of the clients I work for is Planters Peanuts. See the mixed nuts," he pointed to a bowl on the table, "don't eat them."

"Why not?"

"I did a taste test," he tended to use advertising slogans and clichés, "They're not Planters and if they're not Planters, they're not nuts," he said seriously.

"I got to get the babes straight on what nuts to eat, Planters or mine." He started laughing as he put his hand out for more skin. Slapping him five was becoming automatic. When something in the living room caught his eye, he said, "I gotta mix, Chris, catch you later."

"See you later." I watched to see if he was going after Patty. I was relieved to see he stopped to talk to a couple, then felt someone gently touch my arm.

"Hi, Chris."

"Hi."

It was Patty. "While I was dancing, I saw you come in and when I got a chance to come over, it looked like you were in a heavy conversation with Debbie. I didn't want to intrude."

Great. She noticed me, maybe she was interested after all. Unlike Donna who wasn't what she seemed yesterday, Patty was the same—sweet and polite. "We weren't discussing anything heavy. Actually, it was just small talk." By this time, my head was spinning, but as far as I could tell I wasn't slurring any of my words. In order to make a good impression on Patty, I decided to stop drinking for a while.

"I hope you're having a good time." She sounded sincere.

"Yeah, I'm having a really good time," I said enthusiastically.

"Did you get to meet any other share people?"

"Besides Debbie, just Aaron Goldstein."

"He's something else, isn't he?"

We both smiled in agreement. "He sure is," I added.

"You have to meet Russ and Jody. They are the couple who'll be in the house. And can you believe they have been going together for five years!"

No, I couldn't. Five years sounded like a lifetime. But I was glad to stay on the topic. It would be the easiest way for me to segue into her life and find out if she was going with anyone.

"Five years sure sounds like it's serious."

47

"Most of my friends can't make a go of it for five months." There was an ample supply of regret in her voice.

"Well, relationships are difficult." I offered these pearls of wisdom in a very sympathetic tone.

I couldn't get over her sensitivity and sweetness. She'd give a kind old lady a run for her money, but I found it very appealing. I realized that most of the women I had associated with socially over the last two years were usually Laura's friends—aggressive Wall Street types who buried sincerity and sweetness along with their grandmothers. Patty was truly a breath of fresh air that I was ready to inhale. This was also the time for me to innocently clarify her availability.

"I can't believe you are not seeing anyone."

"No. No, I haven't been dating anyone seriously for over a year."

The road was clear. Time for a compliment. "I'm sure you have to beat the guys away from your door."

She smiled. "Not exactly, but thanks for thinking so. And how about you? Are you seeing anyone?"

"I actually had to break off with someone a few months ago."

"That's too bad and sometimes it's worse when you have to end it."

This was no time for honesty, and integrity was out of the question. "It was difficult for me to tell her it was over. I just hated to hurt her, she was so in love with me, but it had to be done."

Patty listened intently.

I didn't like lying, so I decided to end it quickly but before I did, I had to assure her of my sensitivity. "But I made it clear that I'd always be there if she ever needed me. Even so, I stayed awake nights for a while hoping she wasn't too hurt and that she'd get over me in a hurry."

"Were you in love with her?"

"There were things I loved about her, but I wasn't *in* love with her."

"Then it was for the best," she said, trying to sound comforting.

I shook my head slowly in agreement.

"Hey, you guys," Patty said looking over my shoulder, "come here, I want you to meet someone."

I turned to face a tall guy about thirty and a woman about the same age, but much shorter.

"I'd like you to meet Chris McCauley. Chris, this is Russ Palmer and Jody Gottlieb. We are all going to be sharing the house together this summer."

The three of us exchanged hellos and shook hands. Both of them said how they were looking forward to the summer and what a beautiful spot it was. Patty listened and beamed, feeling proud that it was she who discovered the spot.

I liked Russ immediately. He had an easygoing manner, a comfortable smile and a slight Midwestern accent. Jody seemed a bit distant, or maybe it was because Russ was so relaxed. She also wasn't as short as I first thought. Standing next to her boyfriend, who was at least six-feet-two, tended to take a few inches away from her. And, although she had an accent too, it was definitely New York. It dawned on me after a few minutes that Jody was a pretty version of Barbara Streisand.

I said, "You know, Jody, I've been trying to decide who you look like and I finally have it."

"I hope, hope, hope it's not Barbara Streisand. Everyone tells me I resemble that ugly thing."

"Come on, babe," Russ said, "she's not that ugly."

"Yeah, and she's got a great bod," Goldstein said as he hurried past us toward the kitchen.

"No, I wasn't thinking of Streisand, but a cousin of mine."

"You have a Jewish cousin?"

"No, that's why I didn't think of her right away."

"Is she pretty?"

"Sure is."

"Good. I like this party already. I'm with my sweetie," she put her arm around Russ, squeezing a smile out of him, "and I've been told I don't look like Barbara Streisand."

I was glad I didn't end up hurting her feelings, especially since we'd be spending every weekend together and the summer hadn't even started. I was also pleased with myself for dumping Streisand on a moment's notice and coming up with an unbelievable substitute that everyone seemed to accept. Grace under pressure. Hemingway would have been proud.

Looking at Russ and Jody, I wondered if they could be considered "the perfect couple." Over the past few years, I had been hearing the expression quite a bit from my mother, who was receiving a lot of peer pressure. All her friends' kids were getting married, and neither myself nor my two brothers or sister, all hovering around thirty, were even remotely close. Every few weeks Mom would call to say, so and so's son got engaged, how adorable his fiancée was and that they made "the perfect couple." My mom was passing out perfect couple awards to everyone. I never bothered asking what the criteria was. If it had to do with physical appearance, Russ and Jody didn't make it. They were almost stereotypes of the sections of the country they were from. The laid-back Midwesterner and the neurotic New Yorker. But if it meant simply being at ease with one another, sharing affectionate embraces and glances, then Russ and Jody were a perfect couple. Or, at the very least, the tall and short of it.

"We were on our way to the keg," Russ said. "We better get to it before it runs dry."

"A smart move," I replied.

Jody rubbed his stomach. "I've got to make sure he doesn't drink it dry."

"Keep an eye on him," Patty said smiling.

"I never drink too much, don't believe her," Russ said teasingly. "Looking forward to the summer, Chris." He took Jody by the hand and headed toward the keg. "Catch you later."

"Nice meeting you, Chris." Jody said as he tugged her along.

"Nice meeting you guys."

"Aren't they a perfect couple?" said Patty.

"They sure are."

We both stood silently for a few moments watching the people dance in the living room. Goldstein was passing through again with a drink in each hand. He stopped to scold us.

"You two aren't drinking?" He almost sang it. "How do you expect to have a good time if you don't drink? You have an obligation to this party to get sloshed, make fools of yourselves and vomit before dawn. And don't forget to introduce your nostrils to the party powder before it's all gone." He then walked back into the living room.

We both laughed, then grew quiet again for a few moments and went back to watching everyone dance. I started to feel slightly uneasy. Patty was swaying to the Rolling Stones song that was playing. It was my cue to ask her to dance, which I didn't want to do. It's not that I dislike dancing, it's just that I have no sense of rhythm. It got so bad over the years that I stopped snapping my fingers to songs since I always snapped in the wrong places. The few times I did dance I was convinced everyone on the dance floor was watching me in disbelief from the corner of their eyes. And if they were smiling or laughing, it was at me and my latest moves. The few times I didn't have a problem with it was when I was drunk, but I needed a few more beers in me to reach for my dancing shoes. "Start Me Up" by the Stones came on, forcing Patty to pop the question.

"This is the great song. Would you like to dance?"

Fucking Stones. "Sure, I'd love to."

As we went into the living room, someone from the kitchen called from the hallway. A guy and a girl were waving Patty over.

"That's William and Mary, friends from work."

"I thought they were a college in Virginia."

Patty looked at me confused.

"Sorry, a bad education joke."

She smiled. "I'll be right back."

I was grateful for the momentary reprieve. Patty came back over in a few minutes looking a little concerned.

"It's Donna."

"What happened?"

"She's had too much to drink and she never really did coke before. I didn't want that stuff in the house, but she insisted. I certainly would never use it."

I tried to make a few more points. "I've never used it either." But I don't think she heard me, she seemed upset.

"On top of that, she still isn't over the breakup of her marriage. She's in the bedroom now crying uncontrollably with vomit all over herself. I better go look after her."

She didn't wait for me to say anything. She just turned and hurried down the hall and into the bedroom. Shit, and I wanted to dance. Relieved that I didn't have to try out my latest steps. I headed for the keg.

On my way to the spot near the table, Goldstein came over grinning, then stared like he was witnessing a murder.

"What's the matter, Aaron?"

"I'm going to blow chunks."

"What?"

"I'm going to puke." He put his hand over his mouth, then broke into a wobbly run towards the bathroom past Debbie who was walking towards me holding her stomach.

"He doesn't look too good," she said.

"And how are you feeling?" I asked.

"Not too good. I just spent the past half-hour in the bathroom."

"You got out just in time. That's where Aaron was headed when he passed you. The bathroom is in more demand than the keg."

"I'm going to split, my stomach is giving me too much trouble. So, I guess I'll see ya in a few weeks."

I told her to feel better and that I'd see her on Memorial Day weekend. She was the first to leave; it was around midnight, but people started to trickle out soon after her.

I got a chance to talk to Russ again and found out he was in advertising, too.

Although he was already a Senior Vice President, he, unlike Goldstein, found his work boring. He later told me he couldn't remember the name of the other guy in the house who was going to be my roommate on the B weekend. Apparently, Patty mentioned it to him, but that was a few beers earlier. What he did remember was that the guy couldn't make it to the party.

I had my last beer around one, then decided to take off. I said goodbye to Pat and Jody and a few people I hadn't even met. I didn't however, get a chance to say goodbye to Patty. She basically stayed in her room nursing Donna. I did catch a glimpse of her briefly, as she hurried into the bathroom with a washcloth, but then it was back into her room just as quickly, clicking the door behind her. I would have said so long to Goldstein, but I couldn't. He was passed out on the couch.

Chapter Six

I loved my Volvo. It's true my feelings for her intensified every time I had to travel any distance. And since it was Friday of Memorial Day weekend and I was loading up my car for the ride to Amagansett, which was at least two and a half hours away, my love ran deep. Not being the least bit mechanical, I was afraid my car would break down and I'd be stuck on some dark country road for hours. It had actually happened to me twelve years earlier, although it was in my first car, an old 1960 used Pontiac. But I've never been able to shake the fear of it happening again.

During my junior year in college, I decided it was time for a new car, and with my mechanical expertise, it had to be a dependable one. After much research, a loan from my dad, and the go-ahead from Motor Trend Magazine, I bought my Volvo. It was a 1971 142E, the model to introduce fuel injection, so it had some extras: black leather upholstery, AM/FM radio, A/C, and it was not just gray, but metallic gray. She was beautiful and because of my brother Tom's car-headlight-gender theory, my Volvo has always been a woman.

As soon as I drove out of the showroom, I headed for home to show it off to my folks. I pulled into the driveway, got out, looked it over once again, then went in to see if my mom or dad were home. They weren't. So I headed to the refrig and grabbed a can of soda. A few minutes later my brother Tom came in from playing basketball. He was three years younger than me, five inches taller and a bit too good-looking for my taste. He had the kind of facial features that look like they were chiseled from stone. I could only assume that one of our Irish ancestors got loaded one night and made love to a rock. Tom and I always got along, however, and I actually liked him more than many of my friends.

"Great car, Chris," was the first thing he said as he came into the kitchen.

"Thanks."

"The color is cool."

"I dig it too."

He then headed over to the refrig, opened it, inspected its contents for a few seconds, then grabbed a quart of milk and started gulping it down. It was a style of drinking we perfected over the years. A glass, we found, slowed the process. After slugging down half the quart, he mumbled something about being hungry, went back to the refrig and opened it. As he was bent over the refrigerator surveying its contents, he asked what turned out to be a very important question. "What is it, a guy or a girl?"

I was confused for a minute. "What do ya mean?"

He emerged from the refrig with a hunk of cake in his hand, took a bite and answered with his mouth full of chocolate layer. "Is your buggy a guy or a girl?"

"How the heck am I supposed to know?"

"It's easy. Check the headlights."

"What's this gonna prove?"

"If the headlights are big, it's a woman's tits. That means it's female. And if they're small, you got yourself a guy."

I gave this explanation a little laugh, as if I couldn't take it seriously.

He took another gulp of milk. "Give me a few minutes. I'll go up and change, then take me for a ride."

"Okay."

As he walked upstairs with the milk and cake still in his hand, I started thinking about what he said. I couldn't exactly remember how big the headlights were. All of a sudden it mattered—I didn't want to drive around in a guy. I yelled up to my brother, "I'll meet ya outside!" Hurrying out the door, I walked to the driveway and bent down in front of the car to get a good look. I was relieved. It was all woman.

While I was putting my beach chair in the trunk, it dawned on me that my relationship with my Volvo was the best and, after ten years, the longest I had with any woman. Every time I wanted to turn her on, she responded, gave me a smooth ride and never broke down. For our tenth anniversary, to show my appreciation, I bought her a new coat—in this case, one made of paint. To my way of thinking we were right up there with any of the perfect couples my mother could point to. We proved that even with very different backgrounds, we could make it work.

Patty had sent everyone in the house directions. They looked pretty easy. All I had to do was take the Midtown Tunnel to the L.I.E. and stay on it until Exit 70. From there, I crossed over the Montauk Highway and followed that all the way out to Amagansett. I had given Aaron Goldstein a call during the week to see if he wanted a ride out. Since he lived down on Thirty-Eighth and Second, I wouldn't have to go out of my way. I also would have enjoyed the company.

He appreciated the offer, but said he had to make a pitch for a new toilet paper account. I can't remember the brand name, but he began referring to it as the Butt Wipe Account. So he preferred to take the train this time where he wouldn't be tempted to talk and would have more room to spread his work out. He hoped I'd offer rides again over the course of the summer. I assured him I would. He thanked me, but before he hung up he wanted to know if he could ask me some questions over the weekend about the kind of butt wipe I used. It would help him with his pitch. I laughed an told him, "no problem." He said he knew it was a shitty thing to ask, laughed at his pun, then said he'd see me out there. He reminded me that I should be ready to party "heavy duty." I waited for him to laugh but he didn't; duty wasn't a pun. So my maiden voyage out to the summer house was going to be a solo run.

I listened to the weather reports; all predicted a beautiful weekend. I guess the clouds that snuck in like enemy aircraft, Friday evening, weren't picked up by radar. Around 9:30, there was a heavy downpour that lasted for almost twenty minutes. When it stopped, I took off on schedule.

I drove to York, turned onto Seventy-Seventh, then over to Second Avenue. The downpour broke what little humidity there was and seemed to make the wet streets sparkle. Or maybe Mother Nature got fed up with how dirty the city was getting, came in with a bucket and scrubbed things until they shined. Perhaps everyone was washed away in the process, or had simply deserted the city like they did on every holiday weekend. It was a good sign. With half the city going to the Hamptons, that meant they were already there and I'd have a smooth ride out.

Turning off Second Avenue. I headed down into the Midtown Tunnel at Thirty-Eight Street. Driving through it, and all tunnels for that matter, made me uneasy. It struck me as the perfect place as any for a disaster. I imagined the water smashing through the way the Red Sea crashed on the Pharaoh's army in "The Ten Commandments." I was positive that myself and the two cars ahead of me had enough sin among us to merit the punishment. I even pictured Moses, as Charlton Heston, standing near the toll booths raising his staff and commanding the East River to crash in on us. I convinced myself to get out before it happened. I stepped on the gas, passed the car in front of me, which goes against tunnel safety and etiquette, and got out in a hurry. I pulled up to the toll booth relieved that I was on land, even if it was Queens, and that Moses was nowhere in sight. I handed my two bucks to the toll taker, noticed his name tag said J. Moses, then continued on my way.

Patty predicted there would be little traffic at this time, and she was right. Things got a bit congested around LaGuardia Airport, but once I passed it, traffic thinned out again. By the time I reached Huntington, I was already feeling relaxed. I rolled down my window a bit to let a slice of air rush in. For a brief moment, I detected a strange fragrance. It wasn't the familiar scent of garbage, soot or urine--some of the more common ingredients I grew accustomed to in the hot city air. It eventually dawned on me that I was inhaling fresh air.

I decided not to turn on the radio, but instead I listened to my Volvo. Her engine hummed a tune even I could snap my fingers to. I began to gently tap my hands on the steering wheel. Since I created my own rhythm, I didn't miss a beat.

With the city at least an hour behind me and no tall buildings in sight, I noticed how much closer the sky was. Without Manhattan skyscrapers holding it up, the sky just seemed to lower itself and settle right above the highway. I found it comforting. I guess it always is, whenever the stars are in reach.

Chapter Seven

I reached the town of Amagansett around 12:30, found the turn right before the Mobil station, which lead to Bluff Road. Bluff ran parallel to the ocean; the sky was crowded with stars, but there was enough room for a big round and happy moon. It grinned down as if to welcome me and cast a blue glow that kept the night so clear, I could have read the name of the tiny road signs without my headlights. A few yards past Atlantic Avenue beach was a large, white square sign. Written across it in ornate lettering was Treasure Island Drive.

I turned onto it and to the right, at the end of the road, looking even more like a spaceship than in pictures, was the house. I pulled in to the driveway next to two other cars. As soon as I got out of the car I took a minute to stretch and noticed there was only one light on downstairs. The astronauts seemed to be sleeping. I got my suitcase out of the trunk, quietly closed it, then tiptoed up the walk to the front door.

The door was unlocked and opened into the living room. The light was coming from the kitchen which was straight ahead. Pasted on the refrigerator was a sign titled "A-Weekend," with our names, and arrows pointed to everyone's bedroom. My name and Debbie's had an arrow with "east wing" printed on the arrow.

Again, I tiptoed down the short hall to a closed door. I opened the door quietly and peeked in before entering, just to make sure it was the right one. The room had a warm blue glow from the moonlight that shown through the large, glass sliding doors to the right. Debbie was sleeping on her back, breathing heavily, but not quite snoring. Her eyes were closed, but her nipples were staring up at the ceiling since her sheet was tucked under her rather large breasts. She wasn't kidding—she did sleep naked. A woman of her word.

Gently, I closed the door behind me and as I walked on my toes to my bed across the room, I stole one more quick glance at her chest. I didn't want to wake her, be caught in the act, and create any misunderstandings. It was the tits I wanted, not the rest. She was what Vinny Byrnie, a college buddy, used to call a "parts girl."

Byrnie explained to me once that a "parts girl" is basically an unattractive chick who may have great legs, ass, or as in Debbie's case, great tits. These were the only kinds of girls Byrnie dated. His reasoning was that unattractive "parts" chicks were grateful to have boyfriends and so they treat you like a king and in the process, great body parts are there for you to do with as you please. I never bought into his theory and wasn't about to now.

As I put my bag down gently at the food of the bed, I wished those tits of hers were removable. I envisioned myself detaching each one as Debbie slept and taking them to bed with me. But since I couldn't, I pulled down the sheet, took off my shirt, kept on my shorts and climbed in. Facing the wall, I curled up into a very large fetus and within a few minutes was asleep.

•

The next morning, I woke with the sun warming my face—I appreciated the warmth, but not the light. I was used to my dark bedroom at home. In fact, since it was in the back of the building, it was extra dark and always insured me a few extra hours of sleep. I looked over at the glass doors to see if there were curtains waiting to be drawn. No such luck. I looked over at Debbie who had her sheets pulled over her head. I gave it a shot. Still too bright.

Disgusted, I pulled the sheet off my head and looked at the clock on the night table between the beds. 8:00 A.M. It was early but time to concede defeat. The sun was the winner. I flipped the sheet over the side, swung my legs over the bed, sat with my feet on the cold, tiled floor, then got up, took a tee-shirt from my suitcase, and tiptoed past Debbie, the mummy, and out of the room.

The kitchen was all white, with streams of sunlight coming through the high windows like long golden ropes tied to the floor. Although there was no one around, coffee was perking on the counter next to a tray of cups and doughnuts. The smell of the coffee drew me to it immediately. I poured a cup, grabbed a doughnut and walked into the living room expecting to find the angel who set up breakfast. There was no one around, the entire house was still sleeping.

I decided to have breakfast on the deck in back just off the dining room. As soon as I slid the doors open, I felt the intensity of the sun. Only 8:15 and already it was heating things up. In a few hours the day would really be cooking. I took the sunglasses from my pocket, put them on and surveyed the deck for the most comfortable looking chair. There was a long lounge in the corner designed especially for me. I immediately parked myself, began sipping my coffee and checking out the surroundings. There was no lawn in the backyard, but there was plenty of sand. Bits and pieces of houses peeked over dunes whose bumps and mounds looked like hundreds of Debbie Gelfands sleeping with sheets of sand pulled over their heads.

In a few minutes, the doors opened and Russ walked out. He was wearing one of those bright red Hawaiian shirts with green monkeys all over it, even brighter blue shorts, wraparound sunglasses and was barefoot. His hair hadn't been combed and looked curlier than what I remembered at the party.

"Mornin', Chris," he said while yawning.

"How ya doin'."

"Okay, but I couldn't sleep that late with that," he pointed to the sun as if he were aggravated, "blarin' in the windows."

"That was my problem too, and now with that outfit of yours in front of me, things are even brighter," I said with a smile.

He started to laugh. "This is the latest in Hampton attire. If you like, I'll tell ya where you can pick up some of these duds. That is, if you want to be hip."

"No thanks," I smiled back. "I've never really been too hip and certainly not hip enough for those things."

"Suit yourself, then."

He had a good sense of humor. I began to like him more. A few minutes of silence followed. We both looked around some. Russ turned, walked over to the door, slid it open, stuck his head in to see if anyone was there, then closed it softly. He walked over to the edge of the deck and leaned over the rail as if to make sure no one was there. Then he walked over to where I was sitting.

"Coast is clear," he said with a smile as he pulled the waist of his shorts open with his left hand, and stuck his right in toward his balls.

I tensed for a second and maybe it was noticeable.

With his hands still searching his groin, Russ smiled and said, "Don't worry, Chris, I don't want a blow job."

"Good news," I said, grinning back and slightly embarrassed he noticed me flinch.

"But I do want a cigarette," he whispered as he pulled out a pack of Winstons.

"Now we're both happy," I wisecracked.

"To tell ya the truth, I gave these up months ago," he smiled, but continued whispering as he put one in his mouth and lit up.

"It sure looks like you quit."

After a long drag he stopped, whispering, "At least that's what Jody thinks. I told her six months ago I'd stop. Couldn't handle her crabbing about lung cancer anymore. Yup. That's what she thinks. Honesty in a successful relationship is utmost, Chris."

"Nothing like honesty, Russ." I started to get the impression that things between these two weren't quite so rosy. But it was a bit early to think about revoking their Perfect Couple Certificate.

"So, are you seein' anyone?" Russ asked.

"Nah. Takin' a break."

"In between beaver, so ta speak."

"So ta speak."

"But there is so much tuna out there just waiting for your hook," he said, grabbing his crotch for emphasis. "You lucky bastard."

I just smiled. "C'mon. You got Judy."

"You mean I had and had and had," he said disgustedly. "I've had that pain in the butt for five long years."

That did it. No Perfect Couple Certificate for these two.

"I wish I were out here alone this summer. You don't know how lucky you are."

I thought it strange, since I didn't consider myself lucky at all. What I really wanted was a relationship and to collect my own Perfect Couple sheepskin. Someone I really understood who really understood what I was all about; a girl who didn't care about how much money I made, what kind of clothes I wore, or if I craved an occasional Big Mac. After Laura, a girl like this would truly be a breath of fresh air. Perhaps that was it. All I really wanted from a woman was fresh air. Maybe a successful relationship was no more than a question of breathing. With that thought, I inhaled the clean Hampton sea air, took another sip of coffee and focused back onto what Russ was saying.

"For that matter, the sex with Jody has been bad for a while."

"Oh?" I said, sounding more surprised because I was actually lost in my own thoughts, but I also didn't want to hear about a couple's sex life no matter how well I knew or didn't know them. "Maybe we shouldn't get into that, Russ."

"Why not? I hardly know ya."

"That's what I mean."

"But that's why it's easy to talk about. If I really knew ya, I wouldn't tell ya anything."

"I see," I said, as if I didn't understand his logic at all. But since he wanted to get into it, I figured, what the hell. "How long has it been bad?" I asked, sounding a bit like a shrink.

"Like I said, awhile."

"Three weeks, four weeks?"

"Longer," he said, uncomfortably.

"Three months?"

"Fuck. Try three years."

"That is awhile," I said not holding back my surprise.

"Chris, I gotta get out of this thing," he flicked his cigarette over the railing, "but I can't do it alone. I need help."

Luckily, I didn't have to respond because the doors slid open. It was Goldstein, looking very thin and very white. He was only wearing blue running shorts and since his hair was very tightly curled, it always looked the same.

"Chris, Russ, morning," he said, smiling and walking over with his palms out to slap him five. "Lay down some skin, men, the summer has officially begun," he said as he gave his left palm to me, smack, and his right to Russ, smack. He then began to sniff the air. "What the fuck..." he trailed off, then sniffed again. "You guys smell that?"

"Nope."

"No."

Confused, he said, "Sure you do...shit, it's fresh air! Damn!"

"It takes a few minutes to adjust, but you'll get used to it," said Russ.

"Yeah, but will my lungs?" Goldstein put out his palms. Smack, smack. "So now for today's agenda. After turning a golden bronze on the beach, what do ya say we go to the Laundry in East Hampton and get some steamers? You guys interested?"

"The Laundry was a bar, but I was never crazy about clams. "To tell ya the truth, I've never been crazy about clams, raw or steamed."

He looked at me for a second then started laughing. "What we have here is a failure to communicate. I love that line. Did you see the movie?" He didn't give me time to reply. "I'm not talking about clams, I'm talking about women."

"Oh. I guess I should have known." I put my palm out this time. Smack.

"Let me explain. A steamer is a woman anywhere from twenty-five to forty-five who was married at least once and needs a man in a hurry because she's used to getting it during her years of carnal bliss."

"So she's hot to trot," said Russ, smiling and going for his balls and another cigarette.

Goldstein watched him put his hands in his pants but didn't flinch. Guess it looked fine to him. "Right," Goldstein said more excitedly. "Out here the Laundry is where they all go, it's a fucking steamer pot. So what do ya say— interested?"

It didn't really appeal to me and now that I knew what a "steamer" really was, it appealed to me less. But it was the first weekend and just in case everyone would be out, I didn't want to be stuck in the house alone. Besides a little male bonding wouldn't hurt.

Goldstein kept looking back and forth for our reactions.

"Sounds okay to me," I said.

"Great. How about you," he said looking over at Russ.

"Count me in. That's if I can dump Jody for the night."

"That's the spirit. I knew it. You're just involved, not dead." He then put out his palm for Russ, who smacked it with conviction.

The doors slid open again. Patty and Donna walked out, both with coffee in their hands. Patty was wearing a one-piece, red bathing suit with a t-shirt over it. Donna, on the other hand, was just about covered in a black string bikini. Before they could say hi, Goldstein commented on Donna's suit.

"Impressive beach attire, young lady," he said with hungry enthusiasm. Donna laughed out loud, enjoying the instant recognition.

"Glad you like it, Aaron."

"What's not to like," he said, going over to put his arms around her shoulders. "As a matter of fact, it's the "not" I like most." He then gave her a low wolf giggle. After we all greeted each other, Patty and I made eye contact.

She walked over to where I was sitting. "So, you made it."

"Sure did," I said with a smile.

"When you didn't arrive by midnight, I thought you might have gotten lost."

"No, the directions were great. I took your advice and left late."

"Great," she said, raising her voice a bit for emphasis. She then looked away and up at the sky as if noticing it for the first time. While she was looking, I noticed a freckle under her chin and for some reason, I had an impulse to get up and kiss it.

"Isn't it just beautiful," Patty said dreamily. A woman in love with the sky.

"The best."

"What a good way to begin the summer."

Before I could answer, Donna let out a loud, flirtatious laugh.

"Hey, quiet over there," Patty said as if she were scolding, "Jody and Debbie are still sleeping."

"I love it when you are angry," I said with a smile.

She looked down at me with a quick smile, then back over to Donna who was laughing even louder.

"These two are terrible. I can't help it. You should hear what they're saying."

"Don't believe her," said Russ, lighting up another cigarette.

"And did you see where he keeps his cigarettes?" laughed Donna, pointing to Russ's crotch.

Russ looked over at Patty, took a long drag and said, "It's a long story."

"I'll bet," Patty said, as she turned to me and let them go back to whatever it was that was making them laugh.

"Donna is in her element," she said as if she were her older sister.

"What d'ya mean?" I asked, but had a pretty good idea.

"She craves male attention. Can't live without it."

"The bathing suit sort of demands it. And you know what they say about a bathing suit. If it fits, wear it."

"I know," she said, lifting her eyes up in the process and frowning disapprovingly.

She was letting me know that she and Donna had their differences. This one was a difference I went for. I was a fan of subtlety and understatement. Besides, I thought, if you and I are going to have a relationship, Patty, no skimpy string bikinis for the eyes of horny, drooling men! Hopefully, I will give you all the male attention you'll need. On the other hand, I knew that at my best, I was the jealous type and at my worst, I was the insanely jealous type. But, of course, as I often do, I was getting ahead of myself. By tomorrow we might not even like each other. But I quickly disregarded that option.

"She really deserves the attention, though." She was coming to Donna's defense in a hurry just in case I was getting the wrong idea. Another fine quality. She was a true friend.

"How do ya mean?"

"She was married to a real bas...*creep* for five years."

She didn't curse either. "That's too bed."

"He certainly didn't give her any attention, but maybe I shouldn't be telling any tales out of school."

"That's a cute expression."

She perked up when I said this leaving the serious Donna marriage saga behind.

"It's Pittsburgh."

"Is that where you are from?"

"Yep. Can't you hear it in my accent?"

I could, but I told her that I couldn't. I wanted to play. "No, I can't. Really?"

She began to give me a quick accent lesson.

"Say town."

"Town."

"We say ton."

"You guys say fire. We say far."

"That's cute."

"Sure," she said, as if I weren't telling the truth.

"No, I mean it," I said, trying to convince her but laughing in the process.

"See, you're laughing."

As we were talking, I was trying to decide why she looked slightly different than she did at the party. I figured it must have been her hair. Although it was straighter, it had a childlike luster and sheen. At times, it actually caught the reflection of the sun, and at others, it seemed to caress it. Perhaps this was the last vestige of childhood holding onto her and not willing to let go—even if it meant stretching all the way from Pittsburgh.

This is what I enjoyed most about getting to know a woman who possessed subtlety—it was the discovery. As I shot a quick glance over to Donna who hadn't stopped laughing, I could see there was nothing to discover and there would never be with women like her. They're an easy read. However, women like Patty are an explorer's delight, it takes time to find out what makes them act and react, and to unlock the fine nuances of their mystery of whatever it is that makes them beautiful. It started to appear strange that she and Donna could be such close friends. At that moment, they seemed very different, or it could have been just the difference between a one-piece and a string bikini.

We were interrupted by the door sliding open. Jody stuck her head out, greeted us all, then looked over at Russ. He quickly flicked his cigarette over the railing. If the sun hadn't made her squint, she might have caught him, but instead said, "Mornin', sweetie."

"Morning, babe. Come on out," Russ called back cheerily.

"It's too bright. I'm going to have breakfast inside. Have breakfast with me?"

"I had it."

"Pleeze," she said, like a three year old kid.

"Alright. Be right in."

"Oh, goody," she said, then slid the doors closed.

As he walked towards the door, Russ looked at me grinning. "Almost caught me.

I smiled back.

After he went in, Patty said, "Aren't they adorable," more of a statement than a question.

"Yup." She'd find out soon enough.

Chapter Eight

Aaron was a 4, Russ was a 6 and I was an 8. But after twenty minutes under the intensely hot sun, we were all smearing ourselves with a 15 sun block. The three of us sat in our sand chairs like three oily kings holding court before the crashing surf. The beach was beautiful, the sky was a deep blue, and if there were any clouds in the sky, they must have been stuck over South Hampton since there was none above us for miles. There were a few seagulls that flew so gracefully it was as if they were choreographing a ballet specifically for our entertainment as we baked. And then there were the occasional small planes flying very low a few yards off shore towards Montauk. Some were so old it looked like glue and luck held them together, as they just about pulled large banners advertising the local "in" club or a "favorite" beer of the Hamptons.

I thought the beach would have been more crowded, but the familiar smell of suntan oil, distant radios and the laughter from the few swimmers who braved the still frigid waters were comforting to me and started to lull me to sleep. Russ was already dozing to my left and Aaron was staring from behind his glasses at the crashing waves. The girls said they might go shopping, except for Debbie who was still sleeping with the sheets over her head when I went to get my bathing suit. As I started to nod out, Goldstein started to talk.

"Chris, so you're not seeing anyone?"

The sound of his voice jolted me a bit and I snapped my head back too quickly, hitting the back of my beach chair.

"Sorry, man, didn't realize you were sleeping."

I tried to politely deny it. "Naw, naw. I wasn't really sleeping."

"Go back. Sorry."

"It's okay, really."

"I insist. Catch a few more Z's."

I gave in. "If you insist," I said smiling as I tilted my head back against the chair and closed my eyes. In a few seconds, I was beginning to doze off again.

"I plan on getting married next year," Goldstein said matter-of-factly.

I called it quits. He wanted to talk and there was no way I was going to sleep. I sat up, cleared my head and looked at him. "Did you say you are getting married?"

"Yeah."

"Who's the lucky girl?"

"I don't know."

This confused me. "What do you mean?"

He turned away from the ocean and looked at me. "I mean, I haven't met her yet."

I thought he was just joking and that I should play along. "Well, I'm sure you'll both be very happy."

"I'm serious, man," he said, slightly aggravated.

"Well, great," I said, shifting to a more serious tone, not wanting to upset him.

"I mean..." he stared back out at the ocean, "I'm convinced this is the year and there is someone out there for me."

"I'm sure there is," I said trying to sound supportive.

He looked at me. "Where are you from?"

"Westchester."

"You see, I'm from the Midwest."

"Where exactly?"

"Right outside of Chicago—Lincolnwood actually, and I came here right out of grad school because the best jobs in the ad game were here."

"Do you like living in New York?"

"Yeah, but my values are Midwestern and I'm almost thirty."

"You're ready for the wheelchair," I said jokingly.

He smiled. "Most of my friends and almost everybody I know back home has a wife and 2.7 kids by now."

"Yeah. But you are not back home. This is New York and most New Yorkers don't get married before sixty," I said, surprised at myself for saying it very matter-of-factly.

"I guess. But I can't shake the twenty odd years of mid-American values because I'm a visitor to another city."

He stared back out at the ocean, then added, "Which feels like another planet most of the time."

I stared out at the ocean too. Russ began to snore.

Goldstein looked over at him. "Look at Sleeping Beauty over there. He's from my section of the map and he's in a relationship for a few years. They seem right for each other. Probably marry soon."

"Yeah." Guess he hadn't heard. We sat silent for a few minutes before he continued.

"The thing is, without someone special, everything else is pretty empty. It's really a shame. I have a great job, make great money, got a nice apartment, but with no one to share it with, it doesn't mean shit."

"How long have you been in New York?" I asked.

"Four years."

"You haven't met anyone in four years?"

"No one worthwhile. And I keep being reminded of it by my parents. Every time they call to check up on how I'm doing, I'll tell them about a pitch I'm on, the heavy hitters that I deal with or about a bonus I got. They just listen, say nothing, then ask if I'm dating anyone special. All the other shit they just toss out the window, then they tell me I had better find someone to make it all worthwhile. Of course, before he hangs up every time, my dad has to tell me that a truly successful man is the one who has a wife and family who loves him."

This was the last conversation I thought I'd be having with Goldstein. I remember Yeats saying we all wear masks, man's way of hiding from the rest of the world. Maybe getting stoned, the partying till you drop attitude and chasing any available woman was the mask Goldstein chose to wear. For whatever reason he had, he also chose to take the mask off with me. At that moment, I preferred it off. But since I didn't know him that well, maybe he was just trying to get more sun on his face.

"Well, your folks sound like good people."

"They are. They're great. But they don't understand how difficult it is to find someone who is right for you in New York City."

"Yeah, it's tough," I said, sounding like a man who knew.

"Shit. That's why I'm out here. That's why we're probably all out here."

I had to agree. "Guess so."

"How about you?"

"How about me?"

"Aren't you out here looking for someone?"

For some reason the question made me uncomfortable, even though it was basically true. It was time for me to loosen the straps on my own mask. "More like I'm getting over someone."

He adjusted himself in his chair and leaned a little closer. "Was it serious?"

"Three years of serious."

"Wow! That's a long time."

"Sure is."

"What happened?"

"Basically, it was a question of money. Whatever I made wasn't enough."

"I'll tell ya. If she was dissatisfied with the money you made, then she wasn't worth it."

I was beginning to like the unmasked Goldstein even more. "Besides, I'm out here to get some writing done."

"Short stories. Right?"

"No. Poems."

"I don't read much poetry," he said apologetically.

"That's okay. No one does."

"I gave up on it when I found out it stopped rhyming." He then put out his palm. Smack.

I was glad he didn't pursue the Laura issue since I didn't feel like getting into it. Besides, he wanted to continue talking about his own problem.

He turned and just looked out at the ocean for a few minutes. "Yeah...so...anyway, I figured coming out here might help me make my year's deadline."

Before I could answer, he looked past me and down the beach. "What the fuck is this coming our way?"

I turned and looked. A few yards away was a woman in a white jumpsuit. She had pink gloves on that reached up to her elbows, sunglasses that came to a point on each side like the kind they stopped wearing in the 50's, and on top of her head was a large, black, round straw hat in the shape of a serving tray. In her right hand she held an opened pink umbrella with ruffles around the edges.

"Maybe we are getting too much sun, Aaron."

"Maybe. But she is coming over to us."

"Hi, guys." It was Debbie Gelfand.

"Keep going," said Goldstein, pointing to his right, "your spaceship is three miles that way."

"Very funny," she said smiling.

"Be careful, you might get some sun," I said.

"Why do you think I'm covered? Don't you boys know about the damaging effects of the sun? I don't want to wrinkle up like a prune, especially since I'm an actress." Then she added with a smile, "I must keep my skin pure and smooth."

Russ began to stir but didn't wake.

"Wait a minute," Goldstein said, as if he had just gotten an idea, "if you let the sun at your skin and start to wrinkle, I can get you a job pitching prune juice."

"No thanks, Aaron."

"C'mon. The agency is looking for a new Prune Lady."

"Let them look elsewhere. I have no intentions of ruining my skin. Anyway, I'm a serious actress."

"Suit yourself."

"Where are the girls?" I asked.

"When I woke around noon, they were on their way into East Hampton to shop for bathing suits or something."

"You obviously don't need one," said Goldstein sarcastically.

"No, I don't. Thank you very much." Then she looked over to me. "So what time did you get in last night, Chris? I didn't hear you."

"Late. I tiptoed into the room. Didn't want to disturb you."

"Well, I hope I was properly covered. You know I sleep naked," she said smiling.

"You were covered. Didn't see a thing."

"Are you sure?"

"Positive. The room was dark," I added with a bit of irritation which I hoped she hadn't heard.

But she did and added defensively, "Just don't want to make you uncomfortable, that's all."

"You didn't. Don't worry."

"Well, I guess I'll just stroll down the beach a little. See you guys later."

"Later," I said.

"Don't forget what I said about the prune job," said Goldstein smiling.

She acted as if she didn't hear and as she was walking away, she turned and said, "Don't stay out in the sun too long. It's not good," then strolled on. A couple, a few yards away smearing suntan oil on each other, stopped to watch her walk by, said something to each other, laughed, then started smearing again.

Goldstein was shaking his head as he watched her go. "She's a trip." He turned back to me, "So what did ya see last night?"

"Her tits."

"Nice?"

"Not bad."

"Yeah, but the rest of the package is bad news."

I didn't feel like pursuing it and neither did he.

"Maybe I should try to join Sleeping Beauty over there," he said after a few moments, then put his head back against the chair and tilted his face towards the sun.

I stared out at the ocean and began to wonder why Laura and I never came out here. We usually rented a beach house for a week in Connecticut on the Long Island Sound. The beaches were pretty enough, but there was no comparing the relatively calm waters of the Sound to the majestic waves crashing before me. I also remembered how she loved to go to the theater, and for some reason, we went during the summer more than any other season. I wanted her sitting next to me at that very moment and show her how the Sound beaches were like off-Broadway in comparison to this. I wanted her to share with me this big production number taking the place just a few feet away, and seeing for herself that this was truly the great White Way.

Russ started to yawn, "Christ, this sun is hot. It's even giving me strange dreams."

"Strange dreams?" I asked

"Yeah. I thought there was a woman standing in front of us in a weird outfit, holding an umbrella."

"That doesn't sound good," said Goldstein.

"We better get back," I added.

We all got up, folded our chairs and headed back to the house.

Chapter Nine

Donna was the Kitchen Commander, a title she gave herself since she took charge of the first large dinner. At times, she sounded more like Kitchen Dictator the way she served up orders for us to carry out, but she did it pleasantly and no one seemed to care. I think we were all grateful since no one wanted the job or responsibility of cooking for seven people.

The main course would be a French dish consisting of scallops in a cream sauce with mashed potatoes on top. There'd also be vegetables and a strawberry rhubarb pie for dessert. They got all the ingredients after they went clothes shopping, at the Farmers Market on Montauk Highway. It was the local fruit, fish, vegetable and rip-off stand according to the girls. The wealthy considered it chic to shop there, so there was always a few hundred thousand dollars' worth of foreign cars parked in front. Patty joked that sunglasses were required shopping attire inside. They would have shopped at the local I.G.A. up the road, but by the time they got there, it was already closed. They made sure to point this out because it would mean that everyone would have to kick in a few extra dollars at the end of the weekend. They hoped no one minded. No one did.

The job Donna gave me along with Russ was to peel potatoes. I was hoping for a salad assignment since Patty was working on it, but Jody got that slot. The setting of the table and peeling the corn was Goldstein's job. Debbie assisted Donna in the sauce for the scallops. There were no complaints; everyone seemed to enjoy their assigned task. All in all, we were a well-oiled machine.

Russ and I took our spuds out on the porch to peel. Russ leaned over and whispered, "The good news is Jody is going out with Donna and Patty tonight."

"Really? Where?"

"Some place in South Hampton. It seems an aunt or uncle of Patty's is out for the weekend and they're going to visit for a while."

"Why is that good news?"

"That means I can go with you and Goldstein to the Laundry."

"Oh, yeah."

"I told Jody we're just going to walk around Sag Harbor. So play along if she asks. If she knew I was going with you guys to the Laundry, she'd cut my balls off."

"But if she cut your balls off, you'll have more room for your cigarettes," I said grinning, then dropped my potato in the bag.

He watched the potato drop in the bag, then said, "Funny."

"Don't worry," I added seriously.

"Great."

"Make sure you cover your tail and tell Goldstein."

"Already did," he said, then grabbed another potato and started peeling.

Donna was a good cook. The scallops with mashed potatoes on top was very tasty and very heavy. Russ and I ate half of what Donna served in individual cooking bowls. The girls each ate about a quarter of what was in front of them, and then there was Goldstein. I never saw anyone with that kind of appetite. He cleaned his bowl, finished mine, then downed Russ's and polished all that off with second helpings of vegetables. He started eyeing Donna's bowl but decided not to eat it.

"I shouldn't," he said rubbing his stomach, "I don't want to make a pig of myself."

We all applauded. He did, however, have enough room for two pieces of pie for desert. And after he finished his three cups of coffee, feeding time was over. I always admired guys like him who could really shovel it down and never put on a pound. When it came to eating, they were truly the eighth wonders of the world.

While we were drinking coffee, Patty mentioned that her aunt and uncle were staying in South Hampton for the weekend. She was going to visit them tonight and she invited the girls along. As soon as she mentioned it, Jody looked across the table at Russ and sweetly asked, "What are you going to do tonight, sweetie, while I'm gone?"

"Chris and Aaron were talking about walking around Sag Harbor."

"What's there?"

"It's the oldest whaling town in the U.S. Thought we'd look at old buildings."

"It's really a quaint old town," Goldstein added.

"Oh, fun," Jody said excitedly.

"And you know how I love anything that's got to do with history, babe."

"But, sweetie, will you have a fun time without me?" she said in her little girl voice.

"I'll try, babe."

The girls smiled warmly. These were the signs and sounds of a loving relationship.

We all helped clean off the table and put things away.

Later, Jody leaned over and crouched where Russ was reading the paper to kiss him goodbye, then followed the girls out the door. As soon as the door closed shut, Russ threw the paper on the floor, jumped up and yelled, "Men, it's Laundry time!"

"Yes!" Goldstein yelled from the hallway as he quickly walked in with his palm out for Russ. He looked at me and yelled, "Steamer Time!" as he walked over with his palm out. Smack. Looking back and forth at us, he added, "But first, pre-Laundry preparations," as he turned and walked back into his room. In a few minutes he came back into the living room. "Sorry, men, I wasn't able to get any coke, but I have this." He lifted his right hand holding up two joints.

"Better than nothing," said Russ, taking one from his hand.

"Don't be too depressed," said Goldstein, "this is strong shit. The best. One knocked me on my ass the other night and you're looking at a man who can smoke."

I wasn't too thrilled at the prospects of lighting up. I wasn't much of a dope smoker. A few years before, I tried what was considered weak grass at a party and it totally knocked me on my ass.

When Russ took a hit and handed it to me, I said, "I don't think I'd better."

"What da ya mean, 'I don't think I'd better'?"

"I had a bad experience with that stuff once." I shrugged, "I'm Irish. Can't you guys roll up any beer in those instead?"

They laughed, but were persistent.

"C'mon, Chris, it's steamer time!" Aaron yelled taking a hit on his.

Peer pressure. I took it from Russ and sucked down some, held it, coughed as I exhaled, regrouped, then sucked down some more. The seals of approval followed.

"Alright!" said Russ.

Goldstein followed with "That's my man!"

In a few minutes, the room started to sway. When it began to spin, I was already lying on the couch. The rest is unclear, but I remember the guys looking down at me and I said in a voice that sounded like someone else's, "I better stay here, I don't feel so good." I figured if I closed my eyes the room would stop. When I opened them again, it didn't even slow down. I also couldn't tell who was talking, it was as if their voices came together as one.

"Boy, does he look fucked up! Let's get him up."

I remember being lifted and guided into a car. I was lying in the back seat, the car was moving and it was the cool air blowing in from the window that cleared my head a bit. I sat up. The first thing I recognized as I got up was the Snowflake Ice Cream stand which meant we were on Montauk Highway. Goldstein was driving; we were in my Volvo.

Russ turned around and said, "How ya doin' champ?"

My head was clearing, but things were still off center and Russ's voice sounded to me like it was in water.

"Better, I guess."

"When was the last time you smoked?"

"It's been awhile."

Goldstein looked in his rear view mirror. "You just aren't used to it. Told ya it was strong shit."

I just smiled and laid my head back, letting the cool air blow against my face in full force. It was refreshing and seemed to be bringing things more into focus for me. When we reached East Hampton we turned right onto Newtown Lane. The town looked crowded with tourists, or maybe it just looked that way because of all the weed in my brain.

The Laundry was just to the left of the East Hampton Train Station. "Here we are, boys," said Goldstein, "the biggest steamer pot for miles." He put his palm out to Russ. Smack.

We drove into the parking lot; it was packed. We backed out and found a space two blocks away. When I got out of the car my legs felt a little rubbery, but I was in a lot better shape. The breeze that came in the windows helped more than I thought. In fact, I was starting to feel pleasantly high.

"How ya doin'?" asked Russ. His voice didn't sound like it was in water anymore. It was dry and belonged to him.

"Feelin' good."

Goldstein came over after locking up the car and slapped me on the back. My body, however, was overly sensitive and it felt like his hands shattered some bones. He said, "Men, we have work to do. Let's get to it."

He put his arms over our shoulders, and as we headed towards the doors, I yelled, "Crabs! Here we come!"

They both laughed.

"That's steamers, Chris," said Goldstein, "steamers."

The doors opened into the bar area which was packed. To the left behind a partition was the dining area which was equally crowded. But all the action was taking place along the bar. The air was heavy with smoke and the Stones were singing rather loudly over the sound system.

Let's spend the night together,
Now I need you more than ever.
Let's spend the night together, now...

At a first glance, the average age looked to be forty and over. After a second, closer look the emphasis was on "over." Everyone seemed deeply tanned, as if they had spent the entire year on the beach and not just the past day or two. Almost all were dressed in white which accentuated their dark, leathery skin. The few who seemed to be in decent shape wore tightly fitted outfits. The rest, who were overweight and out of shape, wore tightly fitted outfits. They were the living, bulging testament for the one-size-fits-all style of dress.

As we made our way slowly through the crowd, I noticed most of the women had plunging necklines, sagging chests and wore lots of gold jewelry. Then I saw that most of the guys had plunging necklines, sagging chests and wore lots of gold jewelry. The women who were not being hit upon by aging studs smiled as we passed or turned to check us out with their hungry eyes. If they were steamers, then we were the fresh, young bait.

At the end of the bar a small group was leaving. We headed for their spot, filled in the hole and ordered beers. When the brews came, I quickly took mine and sucked it down. I wanted to keep my high and not let this place get to me. I ordered another. As soon as I started working on it, the buzz came back a little stronger. Now all I had to do was avoid making eye contact and inadvertently send the wrong message to a waiting steamer. We were being closely watched and the predators were ready to pounce.

Goldstein had to go to the john and said he'd be right back. Russ just kept sipping his beer, smoking cigarettes and looking around. I focused on my glass where my eyes would be safe. A big guy, who was tan, of course, and built like the Pillsbury Dough Boy, made his way over to Russ. They shook hands and exchanged hellos. Russ introduced him to me, but I really couldn't hear over the noise even though I smiled, shook hands and pretended I did. The only thing I could make out was that they once worked together. Russ bought Pillsbury a drink, and then he headed back with his drink through the crowd to where he came from.

In about fifteen minutes, Goldstein returned with a woman in tow.

"Men," he announced, lifting his voice above the noise, "this is Brenda."

"Hi, guys," Brenda said in her high-pitched Queens accent which cut through the noise.

He then put his arm across her shoulder. "This is Chris."

"Pleased to meet cha."

"And over here is Russ."

She leaned over to shake. "Pleased to meet cha."

Brenda looked to be in her early forties and was on the short side, though her teased hair gave her an extra few inches. Extra time in the sun gave her a few extra wrinkles that extra makeup could cover up. She was squeezed into the white jumpsuit with its zipper pulled down in front to show a few miles of cleavage. Her eyes were glassy and she seemed a bit unsteady in her heels. Even though I was still mildly high, I could see Brenda was juiced.

"You know what Brenda claims?" asked Goldstein.

It was time to play. Goldstein threw out the ball and Russ was the first to swing.

"No, what?"

"She claims older women can give better head than younger ones."

Brenda started laughing and playfully hit Goldstein on the arm. "I'm not that old, Alan."

"The name is Aaron, babe, Aaron, and who mentioned your name?"

She tried to look serious but couldn't and started laughing again. "I meant mature women are better at it because they have more experience."

"Makes sense," said Russ, faking a look of interest. He glanced over at me, "Make sense to you?"

"Guess so." I wasn't interested and sounded it.

"Then she tells me," Goldstein put his arms around her shoulders again and hugged her a bit, "that she likes giving head to more than one guy at a time."

This made Brenda giggle. "No, not every 'toim... but I've been known to do more than one guy at once."

"Really?" said Russ, now faking surprise.

"If they're cute, dat is," she added quickly.

Goldstein jumped in. "Cute is the word here. I told Brenda that I had two good-looking buddies here. So what da ya think?"

"Yeah. They're cute," Brenda said sheepishly.

"So, I said to Brenda, you think my buddies are cute, why not show us what we've been missing."

She giggled some more. "I wasn't really serious."

To get her more in the spirit of giving, Russ asked, "What are ya drinking, Brenda?"

"Rum and something."

"Rum and something, it is."

She giggled again. Russ turned and ordered her the rum and whatever.

"Ya know," said Brenda, you goys look kinda young." She looked serious and was obviously thinking over her proposal.

"It's just the surroundings, babe," said Goldstein laughing. "So whaddya say? You got three cute guys here."

Russ handed her the drink.

"I don't know," she said, then took a hit from her glass.

Goldstein looked at us and winked.

"Forget it," said Russ, "there isn't any place to do it anyway."

Goldstein shot him a lethal glance.

"Whaddaya mean? There's a place outsoid we can go," said Brenda, almost irritated.

The child psychology was quick and effective. Russ looked over at Goldstein and smiled. Goldstein smiled back almost apologetically as if to say sorry I doubted you.

"So, let's go," Goldstein said to her enthusiastically.

"Not so fast," Brenda said, looking a bit drunker. "I have to tell my goilfriend I'm going out for a few minutes."

"Okay, babe," said Goldstein.

"Hold this," she said, thrusting her half empty glass in his hand. "Be right back."

When she walked toward the back of the room, Goldstein turned and said, "Are you men ready for a steamer B.J.?" He thrust out his palm toward Russ. Smack. Then to me, but I guess I was a little slow with the skin. "C'mon, man," he said. Smack.

My high had taken a turn for the worse. I was becoming very depressed. Another drink would have just made things worse and I'd probably start crying. What was I doing here? This was a garage, a repair shop specializing in aging, broken machines: broken marriages, broken hearts and broken down bodies where nothing could be fixed permanently. Just mended with a quick poke here or a suck there to get things going for a weekend, for a night, or for a few minutes out back. Then the machines would break down again and be back here waiting and hoping for the right mechanic to try and patch things up.

I started wondering about what Laura was doing. Did she have a boyfriend yet? Stupid question; of course she did. She was beautiful, successful and under thirty—The American Dream. And the new guy probably had the big bucks she required. The three of them, Laura, Big Bucks and his thing were probably in bed at that very moment going at it. And here I was, high, surrounded by steamers and not feeling the least bit mechanically inclined.

"I'm back," said Brenda, smiling and grabbing Goldstein's arm.

"Ready?" asked Goldstein.

"Yeah, but I told my girlfriend I'd be right back."

"Of course. No problem." Goldstein said assuredly. He put his arm around her shoulder and said, "Lead the way, babe." Then he turned to look at us and winked. Russ put his drink down, grinned and followed their lead. I gulped down my brew, put the empty glass on the bar and reluctantly made my way through the crowd.

Once outside, I lagged a few feet behind feeling depressed and mad as hell at Laura for already having a boyfriend. I was simply staring at the ground and following the sounds of their footsteps. We ended up at the side of a white clapboard house on the other side of the parking lot. Large hedges acted as a divider, so the Laundry couldn't be seen. However, you could hear people walking on the gravel, the slamming of doors and the coming and going of cars. The house had its windows boarded up; it was obviously empty.

"Okay, Alan," said Brenda, as she squatted down and started pulling down his zipper.

"Shit, she's really doing it," said Russ to me in a rather loud, surprised whisper.

Goldstein was leaning against the house, his pants around his ankles and his hands resting on her moving head as she worked on him. You could hear her moaning as she was sucking.

In a few minutes, Goldstein began slapping the side of the house with both hands and as soon as he started saying "Shit... Damn... Shit" Brenda's left hand waved Russ closer. She was out to prove her point. Goldstein just leaned against the wall with his eyes closed. As soon as Russ moved closer, she turned slightly to her left and helped him pull down his pants to get at the goods. His back was towards me, but the sucking and moaning sounds had a familiar ring.

Once into it, the work sounds stopped and Brenda said, "C'mon baby, relax," then started things up again. It didn't take long before Russ started to hunch over, and with his legs buckling, he let out a groan. Job completed.

Goldstein was zipping up his pants. Brenda got up wiping her chin with her right hand, and tried helping Russ pull up his pants.

"So what da ya think, guys," she asked rather proudly.

Russ turned as he was buckling up and quietly said, "You forgot Chris."

"I told you guys more than one. I didn't say three." She looked over at me as she got her lipstick out from her shoulder bag. "Sorry, honey, but two is the limit." I think she smiled, then put the lipstick on her bottom lip and rubbed her two lips together. As she was putting the lipstick back in her purse, she said, "I'm not some bimbo, ya know." She didn't seem high anymore. Sucking cock had a sobering effect on her.

"That's okay. No sweat." It didn't really make any difference. I was still depressed, still a bit high and was wondering if Laura had stopped fucking Mega Bucks by now.

Brenda looked at Goldstein. "So, what da ya think?" she asked again.

"Not bad."

Then she looked at Russ for a reply.

"Yeah. Not bad."

"Not bad?" she said incredulously.

"Yeah, you know, pretty good," said Goldstein, "but you weren't any better than any younger chick."

This pissed Brenda off. "Yeah, well you came too fast, and I thought your buddy here," she nodded toward Russ, "wasn't going to get it up!"

"Brenda," said Russ mockingly, "I'm insulted. Why don't you leave, but before you do, give me my come back."

"Fuck you, guys," she said, then turned and quickly headed down the walk and back towards the Laundry.

They both laughed and gave each other skin. Smack. Then they apologized for my not getting a tune up. I assured them it was okay.

"Let's get going," said Russ, as he grabbed a cigarette from his shirt pocket. "I don't want Jody to get suspicious."

We headed toward my car. I told Goldstein that I didn't like driving even when I'm a little high, so he could drive home. When he unlocked the door on the driver's side, I climbed in the back seat. He started the engine up, made a U-turn and headed for Newtown Lane. He looked over at Russ as we passed the train station. "Were you really a no show for a second or two?"

Russ looked at him like he didn't understand.

"Trouble getting a woody? A hard on?"

"For a second. It was the first time I ever cheated on Jody. Guilt came in on a breeze and settled on my dick."

"Funny how guilt affects the wrong head sometimes."

"But I rallied in a hurry," laughed Russ.

"You just had to break the ice. Next time it'll be easier," Goldstein said. He then looked quickly over his shoulder at me. "When we come back we'll make sure you get yours first."

"I'm not coming back," I said, more coldly than even I expected.

Goldstein and Russ shot a quick look at each other. I expected them to ask why, but I was glad they didn't since I didn't think I owed them an explanation anyway.

As we headed down Montauk Highway, we said nothing to each other. After a few minutes, I laid my head back against the seat, closed my eyes and wondered how many years my Volvo had left.

Chapter Ten

I was sitting on the couch staring at nothing and thinking about even less. The entire living room was pitch black except for a bright light shining on me. For some reason I started counting to ten. Before I reached six, a big gust of wind blew the front door open. I turned towards the door that became illuminated with a blue light, then jumped to my feet. Laura was standing there naked with just an overnight bag hanging from her left shoulder. I wondered how she could stand the cold with no clothes, since the wind gusting around her was frigid.

"Laura," I yelled in shock, "how did you know I was here?"

"Never mind that," she said, rushing towards me then throwing her arms around my neck so forcefully it hurt.

I tried to put my arms around her, but for some reason I couldn't move them.

"Chris," she said almost frantically, "I love you and want you back."

"You do?"

"It was wrong the way I treated you. Please say you'll forgive me. Please. Please!"

I couldn't believe what I was hearing. "Of course I forgive you."

She then kissed me. I tried to put my arms around her but they wouldn't budge. When she pulled her mouth away, I asked, "But what about Mega Bucks?"

"He's gone. Dust. Vapor. History. It's you I want."

"But I don't have the kind of money that would make you happy, remember?"

"I was a fool. I found out money is nothing without love. But let's stop talking and make love." She then took my hand and led me to the couch.

I was becoming nervous. This was much too overwhelming for me, but I desperately wanted to make love to her. If only I could get my arms going! How could I make love to her without the use of my arms, hands?

As we sat down, she said, "One thing, darling, it was a long trip and I'm a bit hungry. After we make love, I'll be famished. Is there a McDonald's nearby?"

I knew then she was a changed person. I was convinced. "Of course there is, sweetheart. There is a McDonald's in South Hampton and across the street from it there is a Burger King." I became excited with the prospect of making love and fast food. "As a matter of fact, there is a Snow Flake just ten minutes down the road on Montauk Highway."

"Wonderful," she said smiling, then went to open her shoulder bag that was sitting near her feet. "One more thing."

"What's that, honey?"

She pulled out a long knife. "First, I'll have to cut off your thing."

I was perplexed. "My thing?"

"Yes, darling, your thing," she said smiling.

I jumped to my feet. "Why do you want to do that?"

"Because it always got in the way. By cutting it off, I'll be less inhibited and won't have to worry about getting pregnant. Don't you see? It will make me feel totally free and I'll be able to enjoy the parts of your body that are safe."

I got up and started to back away from the couch, but my legs were becoming increasingly difficult to move. I tried reasoning with her. "How could we possibly make love without it?"

"You'll see. Trust me."

"How about going for something else?" I frantically looked myself over. "Here, take an arm, take both! They don't work anyway. See!" I started to move my shoulders back and forth, causing my arms to hit against my sides.

"No, darling. Sorry. The thing must go." She reached into her bag again and took out a long knife sharpener. It was then my legs stopped. I couldn't move them either! I couldn't step back any further. I started to panic and broke out into a sweat. Laura got up, gave the knife two quick strokes against the sharpener, then started walking towards me smiling.

"Please, Laura, don't." Sweat picked up the pace and started pouring out of me. I started to yell, "Laura, please, this is insane!" But she kept walking towards me, smiling. When she was standing right in front of me, I broke down—pleading with her not to do it.

"Stop your whimpering, idiot," she said aggravated, her smile gone. "I told you we'll go for a Big Mac or Quarter Pounder!" As she lifted her left hand with the knife to de-thing me, I shut my eyes.

When I opened them, I was staring into a blaring light. I was drenched in sweat and out of breath. After a second or two, I realized the light was the sun shining through the bedroom window and that I had been dreaming. Even so, I checked to make sure my thing was where it should be. It was shriveled, but in one piece. I obviously woke up just in time. I looked over and was even happy to see Debbie, or the lump I knew was Debbie, sleeping with the sheets pulled over her head. The clock read 11:00. Even if it were 5:00 A.M., I would have gotten out of bed. Couldn't risk another dream.

I took off my soaked tee-shirt, climbed out of bed, searched for a pair of shorts in my dresser, put them on, then tiptoed out of the room. Coffee was brewing. I stopped off in the bathroom to take a leak then headed for the caffeine. Surprisingly, I felt no effects from the dope and beer, but I was still feeling the effects of the dream.

The house was quiet. Seemed like everyone was still sleeping. When we got home from the Laundry around 1:30, the girls still weren't home. Russ was relieved since we beat Jody. He told us he was going to tell her we were home by 11:30. He figured she would quiz Goldstein and me to make sure he wasn't lying

I remember laughing and saying, "Yeah, you're right, Russ, trust is everything in a relationship."

I was heading towards the porch to drink my coffee when I looked in the living room and saw someone sleeping on the couch. As I walked over to see who it was, Patty lifted her head from under the blanket.

"Good morning," she said, still sounding half asleep.

"Sorry. I didn't mean to wake you."

"No, that's okay. I never sleep soundly on a couch."

"If you don't like couches, why don't you stay in your bed?" I said, as I maneuvered to the chair across from her.

"It's a long story."

I wanted to stay and talk to her. "If you make it a short story, I'll listen."

She smiled and sat up.

When she moved the blanket away, I shot a quick glance to her chest to get a better idea of its size. She was wearing a large football jersey. There was no way of telling.

"As we were coming home last night from my aunt's, Donna wanted us to stop for a drink, but I was too tired and Jody said she wouldn't go near a bar without Russ. So Donna said we should drop her off at Tomatoes."

"Where's that?"

"It's right down the road from us on Montauk Highway."

"Towards Montauk?"

"No. Amagansett."

"Is it a bar?"

"A restaurant, but after ten it becomes a disco."

"She'd go in for a drink by herself?"

"Yeah, she does that."

"How did she plan on getting home?"

"Being escorted."

"So she stopped off for a man, so ta speak."

"I guess," she said, frowning disapprovingly.

"So around three o'clock, Donna wakes me and asks if I mind sleeping on the couch because she has a buddy with her."

"Fuck buddy," I said knowingly.

"She always leaves that part off with me. And that's the end of the short story," she said, lifting her eyebrows in a forced smile.

From where I was sitting, I could look down the hallway to where their bedroom was. The door opened quietly and out walked Fuck Buddy. He was tucking his shirt in his pants and yawning. He looked around six-three, was very thin, pale and needed a shave. He was the kind of guy who had a five o'clock shadow by noon and although he was bald, the hair that grew on the sides was pulled back into a pony tail. Three earrings hung from his left ear and his black shirt that was tucked into his black pants was open to the waist. A gold cross hung from a chain that gleamed against a black brush of chest hair. For a second, I thought Donna should get her eyes examined or perhaps it was very dark in Tomatoes.

He stopped, looked down at Patty, and then at me. "I'm Felix Catapano," he said, in a very raspy, Brooklyn accent.

Patty said nothing and seemed a bit stunned.

I said, "Hi."

"My friends call me Felix da Cat for short." He looked at Patty and then over at me for a reaction.

"Interesting," was all I could come up with.

"Yeah. But some just call me 'Da Cat,' but I don't go for dat. It reminds me of Cat Stevens and I can't stand da fucka's music."

"Under the circumstances, I don't blame you."

"Yeah. But I love cartoons, and Felix da Cat, let's face it, is a classic. We both wear black."

"I see the connection now that you point it out."

He began sniffing the air. "Is dat java I smell? You don't mind if I pour a cup," he said, as he headed to the kitchen.

"Go right ahead," I answered, even though he wasn't waiting for my okay.

When he was out of sight, Patty looked at me in disbelief. I just shook my head.

When he emerged from the kitchen sipping his coffee, he said, "Tell Diane..."

"That's Donna, Felix."

"Ha?"

"Her name is Donna."

"Oh... yeah... Tell her I'll call."

As he walked towards the door, I said, "Make it soon. You don't want to break her heart."

This made him stop, turn around, and then look at me somewhat confused. "Oh, yeah. Yeah. I get cha." He took another sip, headed out the door and said "chow" without turning around.

Patty, still in a state of shock and staring at the door, said, "What am I going to do with her. What a sleaze that guy is! I had no idea! Last night I was so tired and it was so dark, I don't even remember seeing him."

"It's amazing what a little sunlight can do."

She looked at me. "I hope he never comes back."

"Yeah. We'll run out of coffee cups."

Chapter Eleven

Dr. Doze. Mr. Sandman. These were just two of the nicknames I heard students use when referring to Bill Lujack. Bill was our classical scholar who had been with Newman College for twenty-five years. The university was proud of Dr. Lujack. After all, he had published five well received books on the Greeks and Elizabethans that were even reviewed in the Sunday *New York Times Book Review*. He was addressing this meeting concerning the objectives of the summer session English courses. I had planned to stay out at the house for the week, but was notified there would be departmental meetings, such as this, that I had to attend.

Dr. Lujack was about sixty-two, had thick red hair which was invaded by gray strands, wore horn-rimmed glasses and was in his blue suit. He always wore the same blue suit, no matter what time of year. He was even more famous for his blue suit among the faculty and student body than for his scholarship. Bill Lujack, Ph.D., and his suit for all seasons. If he had no intentions of ever buying a new suit, it was becoming obvious he had even fewer intentions of buying new teeth.

During the first week of my first semester, he came over to me in the faculty lounge to "welcome me aboard." It was very brave of him to do since he seemed painfully shy and when he flashed a smile, a quick one as if to get it over with in a hurry, I noticed his front tooth was missing. Then, just before Christmas break, we met in the faculty lounge again. He asked me how a student of his was doing and as he spoke, I noticed that another tooth was gone. Strangely, the one he had already lost was still missing in action.

At the end of the spring semester, when he said I could teach a poetry workshop, I noticed another gone and no replacements had been brought in. I also found it necessary to slowly back up every time he spoke to me, since his breath was rather foul. However, when I was safe and out of breath range, he made it a point to move closer. If there was a wall behind me, I was in trouble.

We were in a large classroom in the building on 12th Street for the Lujack address. I grabbed a seat in the back, a leftover habit from my undergraduate days. As he spoke about our overall objectives, I decided I could forgive him for wearing the same blue suit every day, his bad breath, and even his not bringing new recruits to fill the gaps in his mouth. After all, he was a brilliant scholar. If the university didn't give a damn about what he wore or if his molars were doing their job, why should I? But this was the first time I had heard him address a group that I was part of. It became clear, immediately, that besides being a brilliant scholar, he was brilliant bore. Dr. Doze and The Sandman were names that fit him better than his suit. He mumbled, kept coughing, and never made eye contact with his audience. If greeting a new faculty member was painful, then this was obviously torture for our noted scholar.

I began to zone out, thought a bit about my first weekend in the Hamptons and of the trip back into the city. It was raining Monday morning. Everyone decided to take off early since the weather was bad and by leaving by noon, the odds of getting stuck in traffic were minimal. Russ and Jody were the first to leave. Debbie hitched a ride with Donna and Patty; Goldstein asked if he could ride shotgun with me. I was glad to have the company.

However, I wished that I didn't have a car and could have ridden back with Patty. It would have given me a chance to talk to her some more. It was difficult to get in a one-on-one with her with so many people around. Of course, Donna and Jody would be in the car as well. I pictured us driving home, asking Patty to pull over, and telling the other two they'd have to get out and hitch the rest of the way home. Before I could go on with this fantasy, Lujack began coughing into the mike and brought me back to where I didn't want to be.

A few uneasy moments followed as his coughing turned more into hacking as if he had been smoking for fifty years, even though he deplored tobacco of any kind. As he continued hacking and trying to clear his throat, I thought maybe another tooth was making its escape and had gotten lodged in his tonsils. A few of the faculty began to shift uncomfortably in their seats, sneaking quick glances at one another. Some seemed somewhat amused, while others looked more annoyed with our choking scholar. After a few moments, which seemed more like hours, he recovered, apologized, and went on with his talk. I drifted off again and began thinking about potatoes.

Driving home from Amagansett we passed quite a few potato fields that filled the damp air with a musty aroma. I had never smelled potatoes before even though my mother made them for my father who insisted on having them for supper every night. Boiled or baked, they were always piled in a bowl and placed at the center of the table. My dad said they were his native food and just as we all needed air to live, an Irishman needed something else: potatoes.

His favorite were Idahos and he said he could tell if they weren't by simply cutting them with his knife. It was how easily the knife moved through them and how the potatoes fell open that proved they were from either out west or impostors. Once my mom couldn't get her hands on Idahos and slipped some Maine's into the bowl. They never made it to the spud expert's mouth since they didn't cut open like the real thing. However, after thirty odd years, the relationship between Dad and the Idaho seemed to be on shaky ground. He complained they weren't tasting as full of flavor as they once did. Supper just hadn't been the same over the past year or so.

Passing the last field before South Hampton, I thought I'd play matchmaker and introduce him to some of these Long Island spuds. It might just turn out to be an affair, nothing more than a dinner or two. Or it may turn out to be something more meaningful and with a little butter and salt, supper might become what it once was., I decided I'd pick him up a bag next weekend, when the hacking began again.

The meeting was over. Everyone quickly got to their feet and hurried for the door. Becky Samuels, who taught Romantic Literature, must have taken the one seat that was left behind me while I was daydreaming since I didn't remember seeing her come in. Becky was in her late thirties or early forties, very bright and a great figure. She also had beautiful, vibrant eyes, rarely smiled, was rather aloof, and wasn't very popular with the rest of the faculty. This seemed to suit her just fine since she was a militant feminist and 90% of the English Department was male.

Becky had the office next to mine, so we tended to see a lot of each other. We actually got along quite well and I enjoyed her dry, sarcastic sense of humor.

Many of our colleagues just found it sarcastic—at least the 90% that was male.

Every time she went to the faculty room for coffee, she would knock on my door, if it were closed, and ask if I needed a cup. I usually did. When she returned, I'd ask her to sit if she wasn't busy and we'd shoot the breeze. We covered most topics, but shied away from anything personal. She did allude to the fact that she was once married, years ago "in another life." It was a mixed marriage and didn't have a chance. She was Jewish and he was a chauvinist. That was all I knew about her life away from school. I also learned she didn't care for terms of endearment.

During finals, I brought her a cup of coffee to her office. We started chatting when her phone rang. She basically answered to whoever was on the other end with a few "yes's" and "no's." Then her face grew red and she slammed the phone down. For a second she forgot I was standing there as she stared at the phone. After a second or two, she looked and said with her teeth clamped together, "He called me *dear*."

"Bastard," I said jokingly, just in case she wasn't entirely serous. She was. Her face remained flushed.

Becky walked a few steps towards me as the rest of the faculty was heading out of the door from the Lujack talk. Keeping her voice low enough for only me to hear, she said, "another invigorating talk by our esteemed colleague."

"Are they always this invigorating?"

"Always. At least they have been for the eight years I've been here."

"That's encouraging."

"Know what I've decided?"

"No, tell me."

"The next time I have to listen to a Dr. Doze speech, I'm going to get up and push what's left of his teeth down his throat and really give him something to cough about!"

I stared at her for a second and said matter-of-factly, "I bet you would."

When she saw I was convinced she really might do it, I saw Becky Samuels smile for first time ever.

Chapter Twelve

My second trip out to Amagansett on Friday night went even smoother than the first. Goldstein had called me during the week to ask for a lift. I was glad to have the company and told him I'd pick him up at 10:00. As soon as he got in the car, he began telling me what an exhausting week he had pitching a new account. After I paid the toll at the Lincoln Tunnel, he put his head back against the seat and fell asleep. So much for company.

There was even less traffic than the previous Friday and we reached the beach house in a little over two hours. When I pulled into the driveway and turned off the engine, the quiet woke Goldstein. He lifted his head, began rubbing his eyes and asked, "Where are we?"

"At the house."

"Already?"

"What da ya mean, already?" I said good-naturedly. "It's been over two hours since you checked out."

"Sorry, man. Must have been more tired than I thought. Some company I turned out to be."

"No problem. It went fast. There was little traffic. I made good time."

"Great. Now it's time to get to the bathroom, take out the huge Goldstein python and empty my bladder."

I laughed as we both reached in the back seat to get our bags. Patty's car was in the driveway and a new T-Bird was parked next to it. I realized that this was the B weekend and that it must belong to the other half share and my new roommate.

The living room light was on, but the house was sleeping. Goldstein whispered he was going to take a leak and go right to bed. We bid each other good night and headed for our rooms. I quietly opened the door and saw the B guy was sleeping. I tiptoed past his bed, put down my bags, stripped down to my boxers and got under the sheets. The moon was grinning into the large glass doors. I stared into its face for a few moments, tried to make out the Little Dipper then turned on my side, facing the wall, and in a minute or two, I was out.

•

The next morning the sun was bright by 6:00. I was able to block it out by putting the pillow over my face and slept until 8:30. Then I smelled the coffee, gave up on trying to sleep in that light, got dressed and walked quietly past my roommate. I stopped off to take a leak and then headed for the coffee. Donna was putting donuts on a large tray.

"So you're the angel who gets the coffee going."

A large smile spread across her face. "I'm not exactly an angel, but I did put out the coffee and donuts last weekend."

Donna was barely covered in her string bikini and I have to admit, for a second, I wanted more than just a donut. "I forgot to say good morning," I said, as I poured a cup.

"Morning," she said as she poured herself one. "So how do you like the house?"

"Great. It's a beautiful spot."

"Everyone thinks the same."

"How could they not?"

She took another sip. "We really didn't get a chance to talk last week."

"Guess it's tough with so many people."

"Did you have a good time last weekend?"

"Yep."

"How was Sag Harbor?" She didn't give me a chance to answer. "That's if you really went."

"Yeah. We did."

She started laughing coyly. "C'mon, Chris, this is Donna you're talking to!"

I laughed. "Okay—you got me. Guilty."

"I thought so."

"Never got close to Sag Harbor."

"Where'd ya go?"

"The Laundry."

"Oh. That's a hot place. How was it?"

"Okay."

"Just okay?"

"Yeah," I said with a high pitch to my voice for emphasis.

"I bet it was better than that," she said, smiling as if she knew something.

She almost made me feel like I needed my nail file. It was time to change the subject. "So, what kind of a week did you have?"

"Hectic. And you?"

"Boring. Had to go to a series of meetings for the summer session."

"When's it begin?"

"Monday."

"More coffee?" she asked.

"Sure."

As she poured she asked, "Where's that cute orange bathing suit?"

"Still in my bag."

"It's beautiful out. Are you going to the beach later?"

"Sure am."

"Make sure to wear your orange bathing suit."

"If you insist."

"I do. I love it and it looks great on you."

"Thanks."

She took a sip of coffee. "You know, I've had my eye on you," she said while staring into her cup.

I guess this meant I might be fuck buddy material, but since neither eye belonged to Patty, I really didn't care. "You have?"

"In fact, when I first met you I thought you were very sexy."

Under normal circumstances, this compliment could have meant something, however, it came from the same woman who picked up Felix da Cat. "I'm sure you must have changed your opinion by now."

"O *contraire*. I think you're sexier."

I felt like asking her what Patty thought. How did I rate on her sexy scale? In any event, I wanted to change the subject again but didn't have to; Russ and Jody walked in.

After exchanging good mornings, we all grabbed more coffee and donuts then went out onto the deck to have breakfast.

By ten, Goldstein joined us and so did Patty, but my roommate hadn't appeared. Patty told us his name was Walter Kornbath. All she knew about him was that he was originally from Philly, came from old money and wanted to spend time out here to get over a recent breakup. Another broken heart, I thought, welcome to the club.

I decided to head out to the beach and made the announcement to the group. My ulterior motive was to see if Patty would go with me, but she didn't bite. They all said they'd meet me there later.

I headed for my bedroom to put on my bathing suit. I opened the door quietly, hoping I wouldn't wake Walter. However, he wasn't asleep. He was on his stomach reading a magazine and was buck-ass naked. This took me by surprise. I've never been very comfortable with male nudity. Over the years when I found myself in a locker room, I always showered and dressed as quickly as possible while other guys walked around naked and as comfortable as if they were in three-piece suits. I've shared rooms in the past with my closest buddies and even they couldn't tell you the length of the McCauley hose. I'd like to think they were as uncomfortable about it as I, since they never paraded in front of me either. And then there were guys like blue-blooded, white-butted Walter.

He looked up at me, put down his magazine, then sat up on the edge of the bed. Extending his hand to shake, he said, "Hi. I'm Walter Kornbath. You must be Chris."

I made sure to keep my eyes on his face. He looked about my age, had a receding hairline, and a thin mustache rode his upper lip. I shook his hand. "Nice to meet you."

"Excuse my apparel, but it's quite warm in here."

It didn't seem that warm to me. "Yeah, it is warm."

"It sounds like everyone is up."

"Yeah. They're on the deck having breakfast."

"I'll have to get out there and meet them."

"They're nice people," I said, then headed over to my side of the room to unpack some clothes from my overnight bag.

"What time did you get in last night? I didn't hear you come in."

I looked over at him to talk to while I unpacked. He was on his side with his dick facing me. C'mon, whip on those shorts, Walt, make me feel better. "I got out about 12:30, quarter to one."

"I was exhausted when I got here and went right to bed."

"What do you do for a living?"

"I'm a stock broker."

My dad once referred to them as used car salesmen. "Sounds interesting."

"Not very," he said, making it sound as if it wasn't. "Patty tells me you're a poet."

"I've written some and gotten a few published."

"Now that's exciting," he said, making it sound as if it were.

"In fact, I'm teaching a poetry workshop starting Monday."

"Wonderful! You know, Chris, I've been writing poetry for years."

He couldn't be all bad. "Good for you."

"Yeah, but I don't know if it is any good. There really isn't anyone I could show it to. If anybody at work found out, I'd probably lose my job," he added with a laugh.

I knew what was coming and I really didn't want to read the poetry of a naked stock broker.

"Do you think I could show you some of my stuff?"

"Be glad to look at your work." I felt like saying, that is, if you cover your balls immediately.

"Great. I'll bring some next time I'm out.

I went to the dresser and found my two bathing suits. I remembered what Donna said about my orange suit, so I grabbed it. Maybe she was right. Maybe I did look sexy in it. After all, there was Patty to consider. Before I went into the bathroom to change, I said to Walter, "I'm heading out to the beach. Why don't you come out later?"

"Thank you, I will. I'm going to grab some coffee first and meet everyone."

"See ya later," I said as I walked out of the room. Closing the door behind me, I felt relieved that I didn't have to look anymore at Walter or his dick.

Chapter Thirteen

Everyone trickled out to the beach by noon, applied all the necessary oils and baked for a few hours. We walked back to the house a little redder or darker than the previous week, took our respective showers, then sat down to a cold dinner. Patty and Donna recommended we hop into the cars later and go over to Bay Street, a disco in Sag Harbor. I wasn't thrilled with the idea but I knew sooner or later I'd have to dust off my dancin' shoes.

Bay Street was on a wharf that was once used for fishing and whaling ships to unload their catches. The major catch now was tourists who parked their cars on it when there weren't any parking spaces along Main Street. The town of Sag Harbor still looked the way it must have 300 years ago with its saltbox homes, churches sitting like giant seagulls on the hills overlooking the harbor, and its quaint, narrow side streets.

Inside, Bay Street looked like a giant box with a large dance floor in the center. It was crowded and the music was turned up so loud the walls seemed to throb. The minute we were ushered in by two muscular, tanned, blonde guys, Patty started jumping up and down as if the music had gotten got into her feet and she couldn't help herself. She stopped jumping, took Donna's hand, and they both hurried out to the dance floor. Russ and Jody got lost in the crowd; Goldstein, Walt and I made our way to the edge of the dance floor and inspected the crowd. Everyone looked around our age and was having a good time. There were a lot of attractive girls and not a steamer in sight. Walt said he had to find the "lavatory." As he headed off into the crowd, I wondered why he didn't say the men's room, john, or head.

"Look at all this tuna," Goldstein shouted into my ear.

I smiled at him but was inspecting the so-called tuna.

After a few minutes he shouted into my ear, "Some great lookin' fish here, man, just waiting' for my hook."

I smiled.

"Catch ya later," he said, then headed off to dance or fish.

I looked out over the bobbing heads and the vibrating and sweating bodies to see if I could spot Patty. In the process, my heart jumped three times whenever I spotted a blonde head and thought it might be Laura. The first two really weren't her size but it didn't really make any difference since their hair was blonde. The third was just about her height and when she spun around, I almost felt like running up to her and yelling in her face for not being Laura. But finding only three possibilities was an improvement. During the first few weeks of our breakup, I used to spot at least ten girls a day who turned out to be impostors. So only three meant I was probably getting over her.

I finally spotted Patty in the middle of the floor still dancing with Donna and shaking everything she owned. It was obvious that if I wanted to get closer to her tonight, I'd have to join her on the dance floor. There was no getting around it. The only way I could get out there soon was to chug down a few brews. So I looked to see where the bar was and slowly made my way through the crowd.

The bar was far enough out from the dance floor so that the bartender could hear your order. As I was about to ask for a Bud, Walt appeared.

"This is on me," he said as if I had no choice but to accept.

So I did. "Thanks."

He smiled. He tended to smile a lot, the way Donna did when I met her at O'Neals. But where her smile was natural and came from her heart, Walt's seemed a bit forced and didn't quiet go with the rest of his face. It was as if he took smiling lessons and hadn't gotten the hang of it yet.

"So, Chris," he said as he handed over my brew, "what is your situation?"

I wasn't sure what he meant. "Pertaining to what?"

"Are you involved, ever been to the altar? You know."

Most guys would say have you ever been married, hitched, getting any, getting laid? But Walt wanted to know my "situation."

"No, Walt, I'm not involved."

"Actually, Chris, if you don't mind, I prefer Walter," he said smiling.

For some reason this irritated me. "Sure," I said, then started working on my beer and realized I didn't like Walt, I mean Walter.

"Has there been anyone special as of late?"

I didn't want to get into a conversation about my love life with him or be forced to think about Laura since I thought about her most of the time already. I just wanted to sip on my Bud without the conversation he was beginning, or better yet, without him around.

"Yeah, we broke up a few months ago."

"That's too bad."

Even though he was looking at me, I kept looking out at the dance floor checking the various women whose asses I wanted to bite. I finally spotted the most succulent. It belonged to a brunette who had hers wrapped in a skirt so short and tight it looked like an ace bandage.

"Yep." I answered, then drained my bottle. I needed another one. That bandage was making me thirsty. "Time for another one of these," I said, looking at my empty bottle.

"The next round is still on me."

Who was I to argue? "You're on." As he went over to the bar, I began looking for Patty again. She was still out there. I figured two more brews and the spirit of John Travolta would slowly begin entering my body and I'd be able to cut in on Donna.

"Here you are," Walter said handing over number two.

"Thanks." We clicked bottles. I took a hit then found the bandage again and adjusted my eyes.

"I broke off with someone recently, too," Walter said, obviously wanting to pursue the topic.

"Too bad."

"That is the reason I wanted to come out here this summer."

"I've got a feeling that's why most of us do," I said with a knowing smile and still glued on the bandage.

"I guess you are right," he said. He took another sip then added, "It's been difficult for me to get over her."

He was talking to the right guy. "How long did you go out with her?"

"For about two years."

"Long time."

"Yes, it was. But what made it really difficult was that she left me for someone else."

"That happens," I said concentrating on how the bandage was beginning to shimmy.

"True, but it was for another woman."

That got my attention. I peeled my eyes off the bandage and looked at Walter. "Another woman?"

"Yes. Someone she dated for a while before we met but never could get out of her system."

Walter wasn't smiling anymore; he was staring over my shoulder at nothing. It was one of those stares that I was very familiar with. They are used quite a bit by guys like Walter and myself during the first few months after a breakup. They usually come in two parts. During the first long stare, the eyes seem to say my ex busted a few ribs to get at my heart. She ripped it out of my chest and just happened to step on my balls in the process before she left. Then the blink finally comes and during the second part, the eyes say: she didn't mean to bust my ribs, she'll return my heart as soon as she finds the time, and my balls just got in the way and it was my fault they got stuck on one of her heels as she walked out the door. Making excuses for the beloved was an intricate aspect of the second part of the stare.

Although I wasn't crazy about Walter, this changed things. This was common ground we were standing on and we were both hurting. I wondered how many women he saw tonight who were his girlfriend until they turned around with someone else's face. Poor bastard.

I had to do something to immediately help and I did. "How about another brew? This one's on me."

"Thanks," he said with an appreciative smile that was real this time and fit just fine on his face.

When I went over to the bar, caught the bartender's eye and put my fingers up in a V for two more Buds, I wondered about losing your girlfriend to another girl. I had never thought about it before. I tried placing myself in that position. Even though Laura hadn't left me for another guy, I was sure Mega Bucks was in her life now. But what if there was a Mary Mega Bucks? Was that worse? I thought about it for a few moments and began thinking it wasn't so bad.

Ever since I was a child, I had always seen my mother, aunts and their friends hug and kiss one another. In general, women were more affectionate with one another, so taking it a bit further didn't seem so out of the ordinary. But then when I envisioned Mary Mega Bucks with Laura, beaver to beaver, I started to burn. By the time the bartender handed over the Buds, I was even more pissed at Laura for humping Mary. And why wouldn't she be going at it with Ms. Bucks? A powerful woman with a lot of bread.

I stood there with the bottles in my hands, staring at the floor and realized I had to stop it. It was bad enough being convinced Laura was seeing a guy; I couldn't deal with the possibility of another woman. I'd leave that angle for Walter to deal with. I rationalized it was loss we were dealing with and that was where the pain was for both of us. It didn't matter if you broke up for reasons too numerous to mention, or that it was because of another man, or, for that matter, another woman. The point was the two of us were wounded and had begun the healing process, in part, by coming out here. I also realized that part of the prescribed medication was the dark bottles I was holding in my hands. I walked back to Walter and handed him his brew.

"Thanks," he said.

"My pleasure."

We clicked bottles. I took a hit but Walter wanted to continue where he left off and I wanted to hear more as well.

"It's really difficult on the old ego losing your girlfriend to another guy, but even stranger when the other guy turns out to be another woman."

I just nodded my head. I was too intrigued and didn't want to interrupt his story.

"Of course, there is another side to this."

Before he could go on with the other side, Goldstein came over to us. He was somewhat out of breath and glistening with sweat from dancing. "I can see you dudes are sucking down brewskis, which is important, but get out there already, and do some dancing!"

"We will, soon enough." I said.

"As a matter of fact," he said, looking back towards the dance floor, "One of you should get out there and cut in on Donna and Patty. They've been dancing by themselves ever since we got here like a couple of dykes."

Walter turned away from him and took another hit on his Bud. I pretended I didn't hear and started searching again for that bandage.

Chapter Fourteen

I awoke at around eleven on Sunday morning and began feeling for the clamp I was sure my head was wedged in. When I realized it was throbbing on its own and that the large piece of sandpaper in my mouth was just my tongue, I decided to head for the beach and sweat the beer out of me.

I downed too many brews at Bay Street and never did get to dance with Patty. When it was time to ask, I was too drunk and she was too tired from dancing nonstop for the three hours we were there. I never got a chance to hear the other side of Walter's story either, or if I did, I was too shit-faced to remember.

It took another hour to get up, put on my bathing suit, grab a towel, then tip-toe past Walter who was sleeping under his sheet Debbie Gelfand style.

The rest of the house was sleeping and I assume hung over as well, since there was no coffee brewing or donuts that looked like they were dipped in mud and placed neatly on the big tray shaped like an apple. So I walked out the door.

I had been lying in the sun for almost an hour when a voice greeted me.

"Hi, Chris."

I briefly opened my eyes, but that's all I could move. It was Jody, looking wide awake, happy and very flat-chested in her one-piece, shocking pink bathing suit.

"You look like you're hurting," she said as if I had gotten run over by a beach buggy.

"It's also the way I feel."

"You were pretty crocked when we left last night," she chuckled.

"If you say so. I don't remember."

"Don't feel so bad. Everyone was." More chuckles.

Her voice was high pitched, but even more so in my present condition. It became a mild form of unusual punishment. All I wanted was to be left alone and to sleep.

"Even Russ got sloshed, since I let him have a few extras."

I closed my eyes, titled my head towards the sun again and listened as she opened the beach chair she was carrying and sat down.

"The sun will be good for you. You'll be able to sweat what's left of the poison out of your system. Ya know?"

"That's my plan."

A few moments of silence followed. A few moments of heaven. But she wanted to talk, even to a man who was obviously suffering.

"Everyone is still sleeping," she said as if she were disappointed.

I didn't answer. Maybe she'd catch on and realize that my lack of enthusiasm to converse was a sleep wish. No such luck.

"I didn't think that there were any attractive girls there last night. Ya know?"

I felt like saying: Maybe you were in the wrong place. Didn't you see the at least twenty knockouts? What about that bandage? Or those three blondes that looked like Laura.

Shit... *Laura.*

A quick funk passed over me like a cloud. I let it pass. I also had the feeling that if I said there were some hot numbers there, Jody would want me to identify them. For now it was easier to agree with her. "I didn't either."

"Either did Russ." But she wasn't very good at hiding the doubt in her voice, so she decided to thoroughly erase it. "Did he tell you that he thought there were any attractive girls?"

I was too drunk to remember what her bullshitting boyfriend said. But I had a feeling that he did and if I told her he did, he'd have one hell of a Sunday. I didn't want his blood on my hands. "He told me what he told you." Although I still had my eyes closed, I could feel her smile and the tension in any doubts she had about him break, for the moment anyway.

After a few moments of silence she launched into what I found out was a favorite topic: her relationship with Russ.

"I'm really fortunate to have found a guy like Russ. Don't you think so?"

She didn't give me a chance to answer.

"I think so. He's successful. Caring. Loving. Honest. And he's totally happy being with me. Of course, he knows he fulfills all of my needs. And it's obvious I fulfill his. So why shouldn't we be content? I mean, we are happy all the time. Well, not all the time. At least 98% of the time anyway. I can be a pain sometimes, I guess. But, ya know, I don't even notice other guys anymore. I'm lucky I noticed him. Of course I was looking then. Did he tell you we met in graduate school? He used to sit right next to me and wouldn't have even said hello if I didn't say it first. He says he noticed me right away but I don't think he really did. Ya know? After two months of 'hellos' I got fed up. I'd try starting a conversation after class but all he ever did was smile and say, 'yes' or 'no.' So Midwestern. Don't ya think? I think so. I don't know why I went after him. It's not like I went after guys. I always let them come after me. Wait a minute. I know why I went after him: he was sexy in a quiet way, tall and good-looking. My type. Although, at first, he was a man of just a few words—sort of like Clint Eastwood. Goddd! I love Clint Eastwood! I've seen all of his movies, but my favorite, favorite, favorite is Play Misty for Me. Did you see it? Ya gotta see it. Anyway, he reminded me of Clint Eastwood. Of course, Russ was much more sensitive. Soughtta like Alan Alda. Come ta think of it, he's a combination of both. Ya know, a Clint Alda kinda guy..."

All I had to do as she went on about her life with Clint Alda was to shake my head in agreement in the appropriate places. And since she asked questions but didn't wait for answers, I was basically able to zone her out. The sound of her voice, originally annoying to my throbbing head, simply became a kind of white noise that blended in with the crashing surf.

It actually started to lull me to sleep, when I heard my name come at me in a much louder and shriller pitch.

"Chris! So what do ya think?"

I had to raise my head and look at her. "About what?" I couldn't and didn't try to hide the fact that I had stopped listening. But it didn't seem to bother her.

"About me and Russ."

"What about you and Russ?" I said still confused.

"Doesn't it sound like we have a wonderful relationship?" she said, as if they wouldn't make it if I didn't think so.

I had to come up with something to make her happy and maybe even shut her up and let me sweat in peace. And I had to come up with something in a hurry, which was difficult in my present state, but I did. I wasn't sure if it would work, but it was worth the gamble.

"Ya know Jody," I said as sincerely as I could, "I don't know you guys that well, but it's easy to see one thing."

"What's that?" she said, tilting her body slight close to me with a very concerned look and almost seemed to be holding her breath in anticipation to what I was going to say.

"You two are obviously a perfect couple."

The tension and concern in her face immediately lifted, she sat back in her sand chair, broke out into a smile and said, "Reallyyy." She stretched the word out as if she were singing it. The only thing that could have made her happier would have been if I were a priest and had just pronounced them man and wife.

She then stared out at the water for a few seconds as if to savor her moment of triumph: The Perfect Couple Award. She looked at me, smiled and placed her head back against her chair, tilted her face up to the sun and closed her eyes.

I peeped at her for a few more moments. She looked content and now wanted to enjoy the sun and think about her relationship quietly. It had worked. I laid my head back against the blanket again and shut my eyes.

I started dozing off when I heard someone approaching.

"Hi, guys."

I opened my eyes to see Patty standing between Jody and myself in a flowered bikini. She was holding onto a large beach bag. I tried sitting up, but felt a bit dizzy, so I propped myself up on my elbows.

"Hi. Is anyone else up yet?" Jody asked.

There are some very wiped out looking people strolling around," Patty said with a smile.

"Did you happen to see Russ?" Jody asked, sounding almost worried.

"No, I didn't."

"Well, I better go back and see how hung over he is; get him some aspirin or something." She then got up, dusted off her butt as if there were sand on it and headed for the house. "See you guys later," she said on her way.

"Okay," said Patty, then she looked down at me. "And how are we feeling this morning?" she said as if she were parodying a concerned mom.

"I've felt better."

"Yeah. You were pretty ripped last night," she said back in her normal tone of voice.

As we were talking she took a large towel out of her bag and spread it out next to me. As she worked, I checked out her body since it was the first time I saw that much of it. She was in better shape than I thought. Her hips were very round. My throbbing head started to clear.

Sitting down on her towel, she looked into her bag and said, "By the time I asked you to dance, you were gonzo."

"You asked me to dance?"

She looked over at me smiling. "Yep."

"I don't even remember you asking," I said incredulously.

She took out a bottle of suntan lotion, poured some in her hands and started smearing it over her legs.

"Yeah," she said with a giggle, "but all you kept saying was something about a girl that was bandaged and that you wanted your nail file." She stopped smearing the lotion on her stomach then looked over at me smiling and waiting to see what I had to say.

"Shit. I don't remember any of that. I must have really been rocked." I was a bit embarrassed but more interested in helping her apply that lotion.

"By that time everyone was bombed except for Donna and myself because we were dancing all night."

"Jody looks pretty good," I added.

"Yeah. She was keeping an eye on Russ who was going at it too."

"Just a house of lushes," I said with a playful tone in my voice.

"Just a house having fun," she tacked on with her own playful tone. She then leaned over, took her sunglasses out of the bag and laid back on her towel.

I stayed propped up on my elbows looking at her and fantasized making love to her, right there. Of course there was no one on the beach and we were sliding around on each other, putting that Hawaiian Tropic to good use.

"So," she asked, "do you start classes tomorrow?"

"Not until Tuesday, but I have to go in tomorrow to do a little preparation."

"Looking forward to it?"

"Not right now feeling the way I do." The truth was, as soon as she had arrived I started feeling a lot better.

"You'll feel better soon," she said like a concerned mom again. "Where is your school located?" she asked seriously.

"On 12th between Fifth and Sixth."

"I have to do some work down near you tomorrow. I think it's on 18th and Sixth."

"Really?"

"We have to give a presentation to a possible client."

I saw an opening, I had to ask her out. This was the perfect opportunity; I couldn't think about it too much. It always took me a few days to build up the courage to ask any girl out. I took three weeks and endless hours of rehearsal before I got the nerve to call up Laura after we met at a mutual friend's dinner party. I remember practicing a little speech and even wrote it out.

The night I called her, I got so nervous that when she said "hello," nothing came out of my mouth. I slammed the phone down and then had to wait until the next day before I could try it again. I was afraid that if I called her back that night, she'd somehow know that I was the person who'd hung up on her. So I had to practice my speech for another twelve hours.

When I finally called the next night, I was so nervous I forgot what I memorized and simply said who I was and would she like to meet me for a drink. She did. It taught me that spontaneity can be everything it's cracked up to be.

To ensure an atmosphere of spontaneity, I said, "Say, if you are going to be near Newman College, why don't we get together for dinner?"

She turned her head towards me, pulled down her glasses and peered over the top at me. "You want to get together for dinner?"

"Yeah. I mean, since you are going to be right nearby."

"Well," she said rather slowly as if she were thinking it over.

That made me uneasy. She didn't jump at my offer. Insecurities started taking over. Shit. I shouldn't have asked, but it was too late. The few seconds she spent mulling it over felt like the twelve hours in between phone calls to Laura. I started to become defensive and decided to retreat. "I just thought since you were in the neighborhood..."

"It would be nice but I'm not sure it would be a good idea."

"Really?" I asked not knowing what to say and probably sounding a bit defeated as well.

She must have sensed my dejection as she hurriedly added, "It's not that I don't want to go, or that it's not a nice offer. You certainly are a pleasant guy."

Pleasant guy. Great. What an insult. I would have preferred sexy (I did have on my orange bathing suit), attractive, too hot to handle. Anything but *pleasant*. My head started throbbing again, but I didn't know how to retract my offer. All I could come up with was, "It's okay if you don't want to go."

"But I do," she added quickly.

I didn't get it. "I don't get it."

"It's just that it's not a very good idea, perhaps, to get involved with someone in the house this early in the season.

"Involved?" I said obviously sounding confused.

"I don't mean involved really. But what if we liked each other and then things didn't work out and by August we couldn't stand the sight of each other?"

I started to feel better. She wasn't rejecting me. It was being in the house together that was the problem. Then I actually started feeling pretty good. "What if we did get involved," she had said. My hangover lifted.

I then laughed a bit and felt my confidence come back. "Who's talking about getting involved? I just thought it would be nice to have dinner."

She giggled too. "It would be nice. But it's just that there are so many horror stories about shareholder romances. They always turn sour and then one or both of them stop coming out. So you see why I'm hesitating."

"Well, if we get involved and it becomes another horror story, I'll stop coming out to the house."

She giggled again, "You'll have to."

"Why?" I asked smiling.

"Because I help run the house." She then pushed her glasses up over her eyes for emphasis, turned her head and faced the sun.

I laid back, squinted at the sun, then closed my eyes and thought about what she said for a moment or two, then said, "Patty?"

"Yeah?"

"How about meeting me in the lobby of Newman College at 5:30?"

After a second she said, "I can be there by 6:00."

Chapter Fifteen

I was in my office by noon to prepare my syllabus for my class Tuesday. This meant I had to type it, which was no easy task. I'm a two-finger seek and peck typist and although I never enjoyed sitting in front of a typewriter, I always enjoyed one in the hands of a real typist. It was a sound that I grew up with. My mom used to type and basically did all the secretarial work for my dad's business.

Most week nights he would dictate letters that she would type in the little office that he had built right below my bedroom. The steady sound of her fingers hitting the keys tended to keep my brother Tom, who was my roommate, awake. For me it became an odd sort of lullaby that actually helped me fall asleep. Even now at night on 78th Street, when I hear rain hitting the skylight above my bedroom, it sounds like someone is working at my mom's old Corona. If anyone happens to say the next day that it rained like cats and dogs last night, I know it was really the alphabet.

I would have been more excited about teaching my first poetry writing class, if it wasn't that I was meeting Patty at 6:00. I kept checking my watch, hoping the afternoon would rapidly come to a close but, of course, it dragged.

Around 3:00 I was halfway through typing my syllabus page, when Becky Samuels stopped by with a cup of coffee.

"What the hell are you typing?" she said as she handed over the cup. "You've been going at it for two hours. It must be a novel."

"Try a syllabus."

"You mean as in a page in length?"

"Yeah. I never told you I was the world's worst typist."

"You must be up to two words a minute."

"More like three and a half."

She walked over and looked at it and then at the page I was copying from. "Give it to me. I'll do it," she said.

"No. It's okay. I have only a half a page to go and it should only take me another twenty-four hours."

"C'mon," she said snapping her fingers in the process, "hand it over."

"Really?"

"It'll only take me a few minutes."

"If you insist," I said as I ripped the page out of the typewriter and also handed over the page I was copying from.

"My hero," I said jokingly, but really meant it.

"Sure, sure," she said smiling then walked out the door. As soon as she was gone, she was back. "I almost forgot to give you this," she said, holding onto a large computer printout.

"What's this?"

"Class list. Your enrollment for your writing class tomorrow. Lujack asked me to give it to you."

"Hey," I said as I scanned the sheet, "there are only eight students." I was very surprised at the low enrollment.

"Stop complaining. It means less work for you."

"I guess you're right," I said, seeing the logic in her statement.

"It's summer. Coast a little. Besides, during the summer season you get quite a mix of characters. There'll be one or two undergraduates and the rest always seem to be out-of-towners, usually from Mars, who take courses to fill up their time."

"In that case eight might feel like eighty."

"You got it. Be back in a few minutes with your syllabus," she said, turned then was gone again.

I completed all my preparations for class. To keep busy, I even straightened up my office. I was doing a bad job of killing time. It was more like I was just wounding it.

At a quarter to six my office was straightened. I looked around for something to do for the next ten minutes and in the process noticed my nails. I decided to work on a few, got out my file and went to work. At five 'til, I got out of my seat, put the file in my pocket and headed for the lobby.

I spotted Patty first. She was sitting on one of the benches near the front door, flipping through a bulletin the school keeps with other pamphlets on tables across from the elevators. She was wearing a white blouse, flowered skirt and high heels. As I walked closer she must have felt me staring at her—she looked in my direction, smiled, then got up. Her skirt fell just about her knees and her heels were high enough to cause a slight flair in her calves, as if they too were greeting me.

"Hi," she said with a warm smile, her full lips shining with gloss.

"How are you?"

"Just fine. I was skimming through the bulletin and deciding if I should take a poetry writing class," she said teasingly.

"Oh, really?"

"Really. Have any suggestions?"

"McCauley. But it might not be a good idea since you'll probably end up getting a crush on him."

She didn't answer but just laughed.

"So are you hungry?" I asked.

"You bet. Where are we going?"

"To Gene's. It's right around the block on Eleventh. It's not very hip, but the food is good, it's quiet, and they don't rush you."

"Sounds good to me. Let's do it."

Gene's was everything I said: unhip, our shrimp dishes were good, it was practically empty and we talked for over two hours.

Patty got me to talk about myself, but by the time our coffee and cheesecake arrived, I had learned quite a bit about her.

Her parents were basically unhappy together. Mom was a bit of a gold digger; she had married Patty's father because blue blood ran in his veins and he was supposed to take over his father's lumber business. His father and his logs were worth a few mill. But as soon as her parents picked up their Perfect Couple Certificate, he had a falling out with Papa Franklin over some mysterious issue, was disinherited and went to work in an insurance company. There weren't enough bucks in insurance to keep her mom happy. All through grammar and high school, Patty tried hiding from her parents' shouting matches. When it came time to enter college, she chose Syracuse for two reasons: it offered her a scholarship and it was a few thousand miles away from the battling Franklins.

She then decided she wanted a career in advertising and the only place to go, as far as she was concerned, was Manhattan.

A week after graduation, she came to the city with three hundred bucks in her pocket and nowhere to stay. Manhattan was "overwhelming" and it scared the "heck" out of her.

"You mean shit don't you?" I said, trying to look serious.

"That too," she said with a quick smile.

She took a room at the Westside Y and in a month had a job at Blax and met Donna who was working there and needed a roommate. "The rest, as they say, is history," she concluded as her fork slid through the last piece of cheesecake.

I kept thinking she had balls. I admired her since I couldn't imagine coming right out of college, and with a small town background, to live in a city known for swallowing people up, or at least spitting out what was left. What was even more surprising was that she had been in the city for almost three years and didn't seem tainted by it. She was pleasant, sweet, optimistic and still had a milk-fed, small town aura about her. Somewhere between her coming to the city from college and my last bite of cake, I realized I was hooked on her.

What she did omit from her bio, however, were romantic involvements. I wanted to know what kind of guy she went for so I could make the necessary adjustments. The only way to approach the subject was to come out and ask, good naturedly, of course, "So what about your love life? You seem to have omitted any reference to boyfriends," I said with a smile.

She looked down into her coffee. "There really isn't much to tell, except for the usual high school crushes and one or two brief relationships in college."

I liked what I was hearing. Hardly touched by the hands of men. I was always aware of my shallow side; like all helplessly heterosexual males, I lusted after women and tried to slide home with a few over my spotty romantic career. But, of course, any girl I got involved with had to practically be a virgin, which meant she should have had no more than one or two boyfriends. I too was guilty of keeping the double standard alive.

When we were first dating, Laura told me she wasn't very experienced sexually. She claimed there hadn't been many men in her life. The first night we went at it, I felt like my balls were in the hands of a skilled mechanic. Later as she rested in my arms, it dawned on me that maybe she had been around more than she let on. When I asked her where she learned a few of her maneuvers, she lifted her head from my chest and said in a little girl's surprised voice, "Why? Doesn't every girl do it like that?"

I was already in love and she was crafty. So at the time it made perfect sense. I found out later she really had quite a few notches on her bedpost before she added mine.

"There was one stupid thing I did though," Patty said frowning.

"Oh?" I felt my stomach drop a bit. "What's that?"

"Well, it's not like I'm proud of it or anything," she said staring into her coffee again. "I don't even know why I'm mentioning it."

"Because I asked you."

"Well..."

"Yeah?" I said coaxingly.

She looked up from her coffee. "When I moved into Donna's, there was a couple who lived downstairs. I got to know them—you know, can I borrow this, do you have that? Soon they invited me down for dinner, drinks. Stuff like that."

"Uh-huh."

"Well, Joan and I would have real girl talks and she confided in me that she really loved Logan, her husband, and that they had a wonderful marriage except for one thing."

"Which was?"

"She didn't enjoy sex and she felt terribly guilty because Logan was starting to complain and she was afraid that he would take up with some bimbo." She took another sip of coffee. "I can't believe I'm telling you this. I haven't told anyone about it. Not even Donna."

I knew what was coming and the knot in my stomach was beginning to tighten. But I couldn't show that I was bothered. If I did she might not tell me what happened. "Go ahead. It's good that we can be open with one another."

"Okay. Anyway, she asked me since I was young, pretty and she knew that I was a good person, would I consider going away with Logan for a weekend?"

I couldn't believe the offer. "She asked you what?" I asked, even though I heard her.

"Yeah. She asked me to go away with her husband for a weekend."

"Now there's a considerate wife," I said jokingly, trying to hide my jealousy. "Of course, it was to go to bed with him," I added sounding a little pissed.

"Yeah."

"So what did you do?" I asked even though I knew what she did.

"We went away to this little inn called The Griswold Inn in Essex, Connecticut, on some river there. At first I wasn't going to do it, but I hadn't done anything risqué in my entire life. Besides, I was only twenty-one and I liked both of them. Logan was around thirty-eight or nine and rather cute. I wasn't seeing anyone. So, you know."

I acted very calm and listened intently, but I couldn't deny the fact that I was doing a slow burn. Fucking Logan. Prick. What a scum bag. Horny Logan and his undersexed wife! Sounded like a carnival act. I was burning alright but I acted as if I didn't care. "Did you have a decent time?"

"Pretty good since I hadn't been with any guy for a long time."

I could almost understand her going, but she wasn't supposed to like it. I was getting a crash course in what brutally honest meant.

"I see," I said not concealing my disappointment as well as I should have. Patty heard it in my voice and tried to rectify things.

"Even though I was young and rather naïve, I started feeling quite guilty," she said as she mashed bits of cheesecake with her fork.

She looked guilty as she said this, causing my jealousy to quickly take off. I switched gears and wanted to help erase the guilt she had felt.

"Hey. Forget it. You were young, and hadn't been in the city very long. Everyone is supposed to do something silly around twenty-one or twenty-two. Besides you only did it once, so let it go."

She looked up at me, still looking guilt ridden. "No, I didn't."

Shit. "You mean you went away with him twice?"

"No. It was more like four times."

Fuck. Jealousy was still in the air and I inhaled it, but it was also easy to see she wasn't feeling very good about what happened with shithead Logan. She was trying to clear her conscience. I was also flattered that I was the first person she had told this to. Could I have told her about Sally Brown White? Nope. And I wasn't even going to try. She was being honest which was a totally new approach for me and was something else to admire her for. It was also an opportune time for me to turn in my Double Standard Badge and get on with the maturing process, which was no easy task. Most guys don't mature, they just get older.

"So what do you think of me now?" she asked with a concerned look.

I decided to take her lead and be honest with her. "Well, you did what you had to do. You were young and probably learned a great deal. I'm also flattered that you confided in me."

"I certainly learned a lot—never go near a married man again. And I'm confiding in you because I like you and trust you," she paused for a moment, looked me in the eye and added, "and I sense there might be something special between us."

She warmed me with that comment. All I added was, "Thanks. I think so too." We both gave up eye contact, feeling slightly embarrassed by what we just exchanged.

After a few moments of silence, I asked, "Do they still live in the apartment below yours?"

"Oh no, no. They moved to Atlanta over a year ago. Joan wanted to be closer to her family. And I had been avoiding them for at least six months before that."

"Uh-huh."

"There really hasn't been anybody serious in my life since college."

I liked the sound of that. We had refills of coffee, talked a little more and then I asked for the check.

When we walked out of the restaurant, the night was on the warm side but there was a strong refreshing breeze. It made the trees rustle as if they were applauding our return to the street. We stood for a moment until I asked her if she wanted to walk a bit.

"Sure," she said, "we should walk off our dinner or at least the cheesecake. I was also thinking about something. If it's okay with you, I'd rather not tell the other guys in the house that we had a date."

"Okay, but why?"

"It's just that I was in a house last year and two people started dating and everybody in the house tended to watch every move they made. It became a game for everyone. The couple was labeled the "love birds" and, you know, were teased and stuff like that."

"I understand."

"I'm a very private person, I guess."

"So am I."

She smiled at me, then took my hand which surprised me. I squeezed it gently then we began to stroll, hand-in-hand, towards Fifth. We tried picking out our favorite brownstones that have been standing gracefully shoulder-to-shoulder for over two hundred years in this section of the West Village. We peered into their large windows that add a touch of nobility to their facades.

In one that was brightly lit, I saw myself reading a book with a pipe in my mouth. Laura sat in the chair across the way from me, under the large portrait of an 18th Century woman. She put the book down. She stopped reading to tell me that it was time for bed. We headed upstairs to our bedroom that I could see from the street had oak beams across the ceiling. A fireplace flickered the room warm and romantic.

Back on the sidewalk Patty asked, "What are you thinking about?"

"I was just wondering how old this house is."

"Very. Like everything in this part of tawn."

"You mean town. There's that Pittsburgh accent flaring up again."

She just smiled.

We began walking again then stopped next to The First Presbyterian Church on the corner of Fifth. There were no street lights next to it and it tended to block any light coming from the avenue. It made the last section of the sidewalk rather dark. We stopped and turned to face one another.

"I should really get a cab," Patty said, "and head home. I have a busy day tomorrow."

"Okay," I said disappointed that we couldn't walk some more.

"I had a really nice time."

"So did I."

She then leaned over and kissed me gently on the lips, then pulled back. I took the bait, put my arms around her and went for her mouth that quickly opened. Her lips felt like moist cushions.

As we kissed her hand slid down my chest to my already hard cock and began gently squeezing it. We kept going until we heard someone approaching, then stopped. As we turned to walk to the corner, I put my arm around her shoulders and she rested her head against my chest.

At the corner, we stood quietly and waited for the first available cab. I let a few pass in an effort to steal a few more seconds with her, then hailed one over. As I opened the door for her, Patty turned to give me a quick kiss.

"Thanks again," she said, "I had fun."

"So did I."

"See you this weekend."

"See ya."

I watched the cab pull away, my cock still at attention. I then turned and faced the First Presbyterian Church that was sitting like a big dark monster of faith. If it had been open, I might have gone in to thank God for giving me the good sense, that night, to wear light weight khakis.

Chapter Sixteen

O nly five students arrived for my first workshop. The other three never showed; it just meant even less work for the next six weeks.

I decided to have each one of them say a little about themselves and something about their writing backgrounds before I took over. I felt it was important to immediately create some sense of community, so they wouldn't feel like a group of strangers coming together to write poetry.

They were a mixed lot. The person I asked to start was in her mid-fifties, had been writing for years, and now with her children on their own, had more time to pursue her own interests. Next to her was a man about the same age who was stiff and impeccably dressed in a three-piece suit. He was an investment banker with a very stiff lower jaw. I wondered how he got his words out at all since that jaw seemed to be constructed of steel. In back of him was an undergraduate whose hands constantly vibrated as if they ran on batteries. He also had a pronounced stutter, but he was here for the right reason: he loved poetry. Two seats to his left an Asian girl was taking the class because it fit into her schedule

There was one more student who sat all the way in the back against the wall. I asked her to say something last because she looked rather disturbed. I was a little nervous that she might be one of those out-of-town Martians that Becky Samuels warned me about. She looked to be in her late twenties, was very thin, had what at best could be called a crew cut, wore a plain, black dress with black stockings and rocked back and forth every few minutes.

When I said, "You're next miss," she stopped rocking, looked at the other students who were facing me, then broke into a quick burst of high-pitched giggles, bordering on hysteria. It made me flinch, and the other students turned and looked at her. Martian discovered.

She abruptly stopped giggling when she noticed the others facing her. "My name is Marguerite Mulhullon." She paused, thought for a moment and quietly giggled to herself. "I started writing poetry when I was ten after my little brother almost died. She started rocking back and forth again. "I tried to kill him," she said, then started to quietly giggle again.

This bit of information made the older woman turn away from her and look at me with her eyebrows raised. She had an expression on her face that seemed to say, "We have a live one here."

I thought: Great, I'm beginning my very first workshop with a homicidal maniac. I hoped she was finished, but she wasn't.

"It was just that he teased me all the time. A real pain," she said with a very blank expression. "Then I started writing again in college but dropped out to live in a commune in Utah. I did a lot of drugs out there." More giggles. "Let's see. Then I lived with Eldridge Cleaver all the time he wrote *Soul On Ice*. Every time he had writer's block I gave him head." She began laughing hysterically again and speeded up her rocking in the process. "He said it got him over his block and made him write better. I was really angry that he didn't give me a dedication in the beginning of the book. After all, I had to suck him off quite a bit."

This last bit of information made the investment banker turn and face me. He looked shell shocked.

She paused for a few minutes.

I thought she was done and simply said, "I see." It was all I could think to say. But she wasn't finished just yet.

"When Eldridge left me, I came here and got an apartment in the East Village with a very sexy chick who was a performance artist." She laughed hysterically again. "She used to put an avocado in her ass when she was on stage, and ask if anyone in the audience wanted to come up and eat some. That's how we met. I was in the audience one night and hadn't eaten a thing in about three days. I was coked out." More hysterical laughter. "Anyway, I started mixing too many drugs and ended up in Bellevue. I've been out for about three months and recently decided to get back to my poetry." She stopped smiling and seemed to concentrate on her rocking.

I heard someone say in a shocked whisper, that wasn't meant to be heard, "Avocado?"

All I could say to her was "Thanks." I was just relieved that she stopped.

I quickly handed out my syllabus and took some time to go over it. During the rest of the class, we discussed the various forms their poetry might take and why free verse wasn't really "free" at all. I concluded by telling them to bring me their poems before class so I could Xerox enough copies for everyone.

After they left the room, I was rather satisfied the rest of the class went smoothly and grateful that Marguerite hadn't uttered another word or had any other outbursts of hysterical laughter. She did, however, keep rocking, and since it was a silent endeavor, it was fine with me. She must have rocked a few miles during the entire class.

I gathered up my papers, put them in my briefcase, then sat on the desk and looked out the window at the Village rooftops. I just wanted to make sure the three wooden water towers were sitting in launch position. They always looked like fat rocket ships to me. The one on top of a Tenth Street apartment building was narrower than its fellow water holders. So I made it my spacecraft.

I first noticed them back in the fall when things were coming apart with Laura. I had called her from my office, which ended up in one of our end-of-the-relationship phone marathons. I was trying to convince her that we owed it to each other to iron out our problems. Those discussions always left me drained and feeling like I had run ten miles. I wasn't very smart to get into it with her before a class, but during those last few months, I was everything but smart.

I found out my Wordsworth class was being changed that day to the Eleventh Street building. Walking into the room, I can remember feeling that I had to get away from my own life and realized my already frayed emotions were continuously being clawed and the relative stability I had known was being shredded. I felt exhausted, defeated, trapped.

I was giving an exam to that class, so I couldn't get lost in Wordsworth poetry or stroll with him and his sister Dorothy along the paths of the Lake District.

After passing out the exam booklets, I gazed out the window for the first time and found my escape: a fleet of wooden spaceships. While my students wrote, I chose the slender one on Tenth as my command vessel. The vague letters on its side I could just about make out brightened into U.S.A., the water it held became its fuel.

I got into my spacesuit, climbed up the ladder attached to its side and before climbing into the cockpit, turned and waved to the crowds and reporters on Sixth Avenue. I got behind the control panel, checked my instruments, and blasted off. A perfect launch.

I orbited the earth twice. When I returned, I made a perfect landing back on top of the apartment building and got back to class just as my students were completing their exams. I can remember feeling invigorated and refreshed. I had found my escape.

I acquired many frequent flier miles over those next few months. Laura might have had my balls, but I still had my imagination.

I realized I hadn't taken a trip in about two months and wondered that if things were to take off with Patty, I should really learn to keep my feet on the ground. But when I got off the desk and headed for the door, it was comforting to know those water towers were still in launch position, just in case.

Chapter Seventeen

I didn't get a chance to see Patty the way I wanted to over the next three weeks. Blax was making a major pitch for a new client, so she was working late hours. That meant no week night dates. And when I did see her on the weekends out at the house, I went along with her request not to let the others know we were interested in one another. I was finding that more and more difficult with each passing weekend. If by chance we found ourselves alone, we would kiss quickly, and she would grab my cock and squeeze it. That was about the extent of our intimacy. I was beginning to find these brief encounters, at best, difficult.

On the Saturday before the Fourth, we were all on the deck having breakfast when she got up to go inside. I waited a few moments and felt it necessary to make the announcement that I needed more coffee before getting up and going inside.

When I walked into the kitchen, Patty was facing me as if she had been waiting. I quickly walked over to her; we threw our arms around each other in a tight embrace, slammed our mouths together and practically swallowed each other's tongues.

Stopping to catch our breaths, she whispered, half-jokingly, "I thought you'd never get here."

"This is crazy," I said half out of breath.

"What is?"

"This."

She knew what I meant and drew back out of my arms. "Maybe," she said almost sounding guilty, "but for now it's easier."

"For you maybe. When are we ever going to get closer?"

She seemed to enjoy my frustration and acted coy. "What do you mean?"

"You know."

She reached down and squeezed my inflated cock. "There'll be plenty of time for that. What's the rush? Be patient."

What's the rush, I thought. How can I be patient? I felt like saying my right nut is blue and it's rapidly spreading to my left.

"Look," she announced in a comforting tone, "I just want to be sure before we do it."

"Sure about what?" I asked in an exasperated, loud whisper.

"About us."

She didn't give me time to answer and then cut me off at the pass.

"What if we meet for dinner one night this week?"

I was willing, however, to take what I could get. "When?"

"How about Wednesday?"

"Okay."

"Let's make it early, around six, right after your class. It'll have to be quick, though. About an hour and a half."

That ruled out getting her back to my bedroom for dessert. "How come?"

"I'll have to get back to the office since we make our pitch on Friday."

I was quiet for a second or two, depressed over the lack of dessert. I was on another forced diet.

"Okay?" she said, sounding more like a mother or some adult trying to get a child to smile.

I couldn't help but feel she was slightly enjoying the position she was in. She had the goods that I was desperately trying to buy. I began to calm down. "How about Knickerbocker's?"

"Sure. Where is it?"

"On University and Ninth."

"Great."

On Wednesday we met at exactly six at Knickerbocker's. Over a dinner of chicken and fish and white wine, she told me about Blax's marketing pitch and how after that week things would slow down and we could see more of each other during the week.

I told her that my class was going well and how the one student I had thought was going to give me trouble, had so far turned out to be no trouble at all.

We also discussed the people in the house. Patty basically liked all of them, found Debbie a little weird, Walter a little stiff and distant, and that Russ and Jody weren't exactly the perfect couple after all. Apparently, Jody complained a lot to her in private.

We finished dinner in about an hour; I told Patty she still owed me about a half hour more. Since I had known there would be no dessert at my place, I had come dressed for the occasion in my light weight khakis. I suggested we stroll a bit before she hopped a cab back to her office.

The last few days and nights had been rather warm and humid for June and tonight was no exception. As soon as we walked out of the air-conditioned Knickerbockers, made even cooler by the jazz pianist who played while we ate, the street air felt oppressive. It struck me like a heavy film, causing my hair to stick to my forehead and the back of my neck. Although she complained about the heat, Patty looked as cool and refreshed outside as she did in the restaurant. In fact, she was so dry looking, I was almost embarrassed to put my damp arm around her. If some men don't mature, then most women don't sweat.

I thought I'd nonchalantly lead us over to the corner of Fifth and Eleventh, stop next to The First Presbyterian and work in a proper send-off. However, since Patty was in a hurry to get back to the office, she walked a little faster than usual and it was she who guided us until we were standing on the dark side of God once again.

She began things by nibbling on my lips and mumbling something about wanting me. Hearing this flipped my switch: my cock sprang into the attack position and my damp arms tightened around her. In between kissing, I kept saying, "When, when?"

This made her slow up and pull her face back out of kissing range. She looked at me and whispered, "soon," followed with a quick kiss on my chin, "soon."

My hair was plastered to my forehead, my shirt was glued to me with sweat. Patty looked even cooler and dryer than before. I wanted to say, "How soon? How about setting up a date? I'll supply the bed. Don't bother bringing any clothes. You won't need them." Instead, I said nothing.

"I've really got to get back to the office," she said and kissed me on the chin which meant she didn't owe me any more time.

Just before she got into the cab I hailed over, she gave me another quick kiss on the lips, whispered "soon," kissed me again and said, "See you Friday. Thanks for dinner."

As I watched her cab pull away, I was feeling frustrated and irritable in my sweat drenched clothes. Even the street lights were dulled, covered in a heavy veil of humidity. For a second I wished that someone would have invented tiny filters, for nights like this, so I could place one in each nostril to clean the air of all the soot I was inhaling. I pictured the walls of my lungs stained black like the grime blackened buildings all over the city. Who needed cigarettes with air like this?

It was even hotter in the cab I got into. "Seventy-Eight and First," I told the cabbie.

Instead of taking off, he turned and smiled.

I figured he didn't hear me. "Seventy-Eight and First, please."

He kept smiling at me. I glanced at his license on the dashboard. Hussan Harari. In his attached photo, he was wearing a thick black beard that made his dark features even darker. He looked sinister, perhaps even like a terrorist and nothing like the cabbie grinning rather childlike at me.

Great. He heard me alright—he just didn't understand English. This irritated me even more. What happened to the good old days when cabbies were certifiable but at least they were American? This bird kept smiling.

"Okay, chief. I WANT TO GO TO," I said loudly and very slowly, "SEVENTY-EIGHT AND." I held up my index finger, "ONE." I then pointed uptown.

He shook his head yes as if he finally understood and sprang into action. I felt a small surge of accomplishment or maybe I was bilingual and didn't know it. He stepped on the gas and flew across the street cutting off two cars that slammed on their brakes, then headed across town on Tenth. Between Second and First a car pulled out from a parking space and cut in front of us, causing Hussan to bang on his horn and yell, "Fucka, fucka, fucka." At least he was picking up some English.

When we got on First, as soon as we reached the light, it turned green, which meant we were good for about ten blocks without hitting a red one. As soon as we reached a light Hussan would start bouncing up and down, laughing loudly like a monkey, like Cheeta, in all those Tarzan movies, then pointed to the light while looking back at me and saying a slew of words in some Far Eastern language that sounded like he had a mouthful of pebbles. It was obviously a game he discovered: An American game that he could even win at for a few blocks. Welcome to New York.

Entering my apartment building was always a momentary relief from the humidity and heat. But as soon as I started to climb the stairs, things began to warm up. I quickly opened my door and headed for the A.C., turning it up full blast. Being on the top floor made my apartment oppressive in the summer heat. But my air conditioner was big, mean and hated heat. In a few minutes, it was kicking the heat out of the place, really cooling things off.

I got out of my damp clothes and hopped in the shower. It felt good to wash the sweat and grime off. After toweling off I grabbed my nail file to clean the frustration out as well. I headed for the couch to work on a few fingers when the phone rang.

"Hello?"

"Chris?"

"Yeah."

"Hi. It's Donna."

There was a lot of noise in the background, mostly music and laughing. "This is a surprise. What's up?"

"I'm with a few friends at McMullen's and since you are only a few blocks away, I thought you might join me for a nightcap."

I certainly wasn't in the mood, didn't especially want to spend time with her and there was no way I was going to go back out into that heat. "Nice of you to offer but I've had a long day and just got comfortable."

"C'mon, Chris, don't be a party pooper." She said, rather blitzed.

"No, really. Some other night."

"Boooo," was followed by a laugh.

I felt guilty. "*Any* other night."

"Sure, sure. Suit yourself."

"Thanks again."

"See you on the weekend." Click.

I felt sincerely relieved that I had stood my ground and hadn't given in to her offer.

I headed over to the couch with my nail file still in hand, plopped down and started working on my index finger. Whatever irritability and frustration I had been feeling earlier was being filed away. By the time I worked my way over to my other index finger, I felt like I was on Valium. Just as I started to work on my pinky, I was startled by a knock on my door. The front door to the building is locked and visitors have to be buzzed in first before they start the climb to my penthouse.

I walked over to the door and opened it slowly with the inside chain still latched.

"Hi, sexy." It was Donna.

I took the latch off the door and opened it for her to walk in. "How'd you get in the front door without buzzing?" I asked as she walked in the kitchen, inspecting it with the eyes of a first time visitor.

Without looking at me she said, "Some cute guy who lives on the third floor was letting himself in and let me in too." She was buzzed and filled the air with a mix of perfume and booze. I actually found the aroma so pleasing, I figured if someone bottled it, they'd make a fortune. Chanel No. 80 Proof at Bloomingdale's and fine stores everywhere.

She slowly walked into the living room and sat on the couch. I jokingly said, "Have a seat."

Her black and white print skirt rode up when she sat, showing some extra leg. She immediately kicked off her shoes and said, "You certainly are dressed for the occasion."

I was just wearing gym shorts. "It is hot and I wasn't expecting company."

She laughed. Her eyes looked glazed. "I'm not company. We're old friends. We even live together."

"We do?"

"On weekends, silly."

"I guess you're right."

She looked like she didn't need anything and had already had too much of something. But I played host. "Can I get you something?"

She laughed. "We'll soon find out."

I wasn't quite sure what she meant, though I had an idea. "Well then you'll let me know," I said, sitting down in the chair across from the couch.

She patted the cushion next to her and said, "Come sit next to Donna."

She liked what I had said and started laughing or maybe she wasn't laughing at all. The booze was. I was tempted however; she looked attractive and being slightly drunk made her sexier. But I hadn't even gotten things with Patty going and I wasn't about to let a quickie with Donna get in the way.

She kept smiling. "If you don't sit here, I'm coming over to sit on your lap."

I laughed. "Okay. I'm coming."

She said, "You were supposed to stay there," as I came over and sat next to her. "I guess I could sit on you here, too."

"You only want to do that because you obviously had a few too many."

"I had a few tokes, too. But that's not true. If I were straight, I'd still want to sit on you."

"You make me feel wanted," I said with a grin.

She tried out a seductive stare, put her hand on my leg and said, "Don't you want me?"

Since she asked. "Not tonight."

She quickly took her hand off my leg and in an irritated tone said, "Why, aren't I good enough? I guess I'm not Patty, right?"

I played dumb. "What do ya mean?"

"C'mon. Patty's my roommate. I'm her closest friend. She told me you guys have gone out a few times."

"Okay, you got me," I said, trying to sound humorous since I sensed her irritability.

"And if I know her, she's going to take at least a year before she lets you get her pants off." She started smiling again. "So while you wait, here I am."

I didn't like her putting Patty down that way. Besides, she was betraying Patty's friendship by moving in on her territory. It was my turn to feel irritated. Even though Patty wasn't there, Donna made me feel closer to her. I had to make it clear to Donna which side I was on.

"Does she know you?" I asked rather accusingly.

"What's that supposed to mean?"

"Well, if my closest friend was interested in a girl, I'd make sure, even if I were interested, to stay away from her."

"Aren't you a good boy," she said sarcastically and sounding less buzzed.

"It's just that there are boundaries in friendship that you shouldn't cross over."

"Yeah? And what do you call these boundaries?"

"If you want a label, stitch on loyalty."

"Really, Mr. Morality?"

"Really."

"Come off it," she said stone sober. "First of all, you haven't done anything with Patty yet. We all began at the same starting gate. What do you guys know about boundaries anyway? You all go after any girl you want, everyone's fair game. The great white hunters cock their cocks and hunt the white-breasted, helpless female." She was on a roll and becoming angrier as she went on. I didn't even try to interrupt.

"Just like the prick I used to be married to. I'm home making like Donna

Reed, cooking, cleaning, keeping his dinner warm, while he was out humping everything that moved. A year after our divorce, my baby sister told me he even put the make on her." She stopped for a moment, looked up at the ceiling and almost yelled, "She was only *fifteen years old*!"

I winced.

She put her head back against the couch, closed her eyes and continued: "He always talked about having a son. I figured if I got pregnant, it would make our marriage stronger. We tried for months. When nothing happened, I got the blame. He started calling me 'Dear Desert,' 'Sister Sahara.' When I finally talked him into seeing a doctor with me we took some tests and found out it was he who was shooting the blanks. Then things really went to shit. He started drinking even heavier than he had been, sometimes didn't even come home for days, and when he did, it was to slug me."

I wanted to say I was sorry you married a bastard, that he hit you, and for all the pain he caused. But I didn't even try, because I knew she wouldn't let me.

She lifted her head off the couch and turned to look at me, her eyes were glistening with tears. "Five years in that torture chamber was enough. As soon as I got out, I decided this time, I'd do things differently. If it's a man's world, live it like a man. If I wanted to go out and get laid, I'd do it. And you know what I found out?"

"What?"

"A lot of you guys can't handle it. It's not herpes or the clap you are afraid of, it's role reversal." Her discovery made her smile. She stared at me, then offered me a challenge. "So, Chris, are you woman enough?"

"I don't think I'll ever be woman enough for you, Donna."

"Too bad." She then got up from the couch, braced herself on its arm and got back into her shoes. "I better get going," she said with a forced smile and headed for the door.

I got up and followed her.

"Cute place you got here."

"Thanks."

She opened the door and turned, "I won't tell Patty I was here, if you won't."

"When were you here?"

She smiled. "See you on the weekend. I can't believe it's the Fourth already."

"See you then," I said, closed the door and put the latch back on. I stood there for a moment, listening to her heels click down the stairs, as if to make sure that she was really leaving.

I went over and sat back down on the couch. The apartment was quite cool by now, and as I listened to the hum of the air conditioner, I thought about what Donna said. I hated to admit it myself, but she was right—I didn't like being hunted.

Chapter Eighteen

The entire house was on its back. It was Saturday morning, the Fourth, and all of us were on the beach by eleven, oiled and facing the sun. Since it was the big weekend, Debbie and Walter were both invited out. I had even offered to give up my bed to Walter and sleep on the couch, but it turned out he had to go home for a Philly family reunion.

We were all working on our tans for "the" party that night. A wealthy client of Russ was throwing a big bash at his oceanfront mansion in South Hampton. Russ's account group who worked on a successful campaign for him was invited to the bash. They were told to bring anyone and everyone they wanted; so Russ invited all of us. He heard this guy threw a Fourth party every year and that they were pretty incredible: tons of food, assorted stimulants, babes (he added when Jody wasn't around) and a few well-known faces.

"A *real* party," he said, emphasizing real.

The sun was hot but there was a cool breeze that came every few seconds to lick the sweat off your skin and make it feel almost icy in the process. The sky was so clear, it was as if Mother Nature woke up early, dusted the clouds away and polished until the piece of sky right above us shined.

The beach was a bit more crowded than on previous weekends and when I looked down at Atlantic Avenue Beach, which was always a smudge of people in the distance, I could tell that it was even a larger smudge than usual.

I decided to take a break, sat up and saw that everyone seemed to be sleeping, except for Goldstein who was sitting up reading *The Times*.

"Did you read about the fag disease, Chris?" he said in a low tone, in an attempt not to wake anyone.

"No. What disease?"

"It seems homos are contracting this disease that is killing them after they butt-bang each other."

"I remember hearing something about it on the news recently."

"At least hopelessly heterosexual guys like myself are safe," he said skimming over the page, then playfully added, "if you are thinking of going homo, I don't think this would be an appropriate time."

"Thanks for the warning, pal."

He looked at the water, folded the paper, and getting to his feet he said, "Think I'll cool off," then headed towards the surf which was relatively rough.

Patty, who was lying next to me sat up and smiled. "Beautiful, isn't it?"

"Sure is."

She looked over at the others who were still dozing. "We certainly are an ambitious lot."

"Sure are."

"Where's Aaron?"

"Out there," I said pointing towards the water with my chin. He was standing with his back to us, ankle deep in the surf with his hands on his hips.

"I might have to join him in a few minutes," she said as she reached over and rubbed my hand. Our sex for the day.

When Russ sat up, she quickly took her hand away. God forbid if she got caught in the act.

Russ looked at Goldstein. "Check out Mark Spitz," he said with a laugh.

We looked at Goldstein who was trying to avoid being knocked over by a wave. It crashed into him and seemed to swallow him up for a few minutes. We started laughing and waited for his next move. His arms came out of the surf first and seemed to be thrashing.

"Anything for a laugh," Russ said shaking his head.

"What a goof," I added.

Patty just laughed.

Goldstein started to yell something which was muffled by the crashing waves.

"Now I guess he's supposed to be drowning," Patty said with a laugh.

His arms were flailing wildly and I caught a quick glimpse of his face before another wave washed over him. It was a look of panic and fear of a man in trouble. Russ and Patty must have noticed it when I did, since the three of us jumped to our feet without saying a word and raced to the water.

As we ran, I heard Patty behind me yell, "God, he's drowning!"

Russ and I crashed into the surf, and since we were running at full speed, immediately fell. I felt like I was in a dream, where the faster you want to run, the slower you go. It was as if there were a thousand little hands in each wave grabbing my ankles and making me fall. Luckily, he wasn't that far out and I reached him before Russ.

Goldstein was coughing and choking on the waves that kept washing over us. I grabbed him by the wrist and tried telling him to stay calm but the waves kept filling my mouth. Russ got to us a few seconds later and rather than help, he seemed to make matters worse. The three of us kept hanging onto each other. We were getting nowhere fast. Patty had the good sense to stay on shore. If she had come out to help, we all would have drowned.

What helped us was that we weren't over our heads and were eventually able to get our footing and head towards the shore. As Russ and I guided Goldstein, we were all coughing and choking. It was hard to tell who was saving whom.

By this time Jody, Debbie and Donna were with Patty at the water's edge. The three of us crashed at their feet as they circled around us with a few other strangers who had noticed the action. Goldstein was on all fours coughing up water. We all started to smack him on the back, except for Jody who was concerned about Russ, who was annoyed that she wasn't more concerned about Goldstein.

"Shit. I'm fine," he said to her as he sat with his arms wrapped around his knees. "He's the one who was drowning." That shut Jody up, as she realized there just might be some truth to what he had said.

"Yeah," Goldstein said, as he turned to sit on his butt.

"At first we thought you were kidding," said Patty.

"It's a good thing they were awake," said Donna. "The rest of us were sleeping."

"You were really drowning?" asked Debbie rather firmly as if to make sure he wasn't kidding.

Goldstein slowly lifted his head in her direction with a disgusted frown on his face, as if to say are you out of your mind?

"You're lucky," she replied to the look on his face.

He then leaned back on his elbows, looked out at the water for a few seconds and said, "Especially since I can't swim."

"What?" I asked in disbelief.

"What the fuck?" Russ added.

"Are you nuts?" Donna almost yelled.

Patty, in a concerned mother's voice said, "Aaron, even good swimmers don't go in on a day like this with the surf this rough."

The few strangers that had come over walked away.

"I wasn't going swimming," Goldstein said, still a little winded, "I was just going to stand there to cool off when some big ass wave knocked me over."

"The next time you want to stand in the surf, don't," I said, "or make sure one of us is with you."

"Besides," said Russ, "if you drowned, it would have ruined our weekend."

Donna smiled. "Yeah," she said, "but we probably would have still gone to the party tonight."

"I would have wanted it that way," said Goldstein.

"Since everyone is okay, let's go back to our towels to get away from these waves and relax," suggested Patty.

As Russ got to his feet, Jody said, "You're a hero, sweetie." She was serious and this seemed to annoy Russ more.

"Yeah, right," he said, then looked down at me and raised his eyes toward the sky. As they walked away, I heard him say to Jody, "I wish I hadn't given up smoking. I could use a cig now."

For a second I wondered if the cigarettes he kept down by his balls fell out as he ran into the water.

"Are you okay?" Patty asked Goldstein as if to make sure.

"Well, I could still use a little mouth to mouth."

"He's okay," said Donna sarcastically, then turned and headed back.

As I stood up, Patty said, "Nice going." It was a quiet trophy that I gladly accepted.

I offered my hand to Goldstein who grabbed it and got to his feet. We walked back toward the others.

Debbie was still with us, walking next to Goldstein. "If you still need a little mouth to mouth, Aaron," she said, trying to sound seductive, "just let me know."

Goldstein looked at me, smirked, then turned to her and said, "If it turns out that I suffered any noticeable brain damage from this experience, I just might."

Chapter Nineteen

The homes along the ocean on Dune Road in South Hampton were enormous. None had lights on, making the older Tudors look like dark, ominous castles. Further down the road, the homes became more contemporary, but they too were dark, silhouetted against a sky lit up with a full moon and millions of stars that glittered like diamonds. I became convinced that they were actually diamonds, or some other exotic jewels. How else could anyone possibly afford these palaces beneath them? Mere stars were for the skies over Quogue and Amagansett where the size of a home was in reason and within reach.

The bigger the homes grew in size, the more bizarre looking they became. They seemed to be constructed out of large circles, triangles and domes.

Pat, Jody and Goldstein were riding with me in my Volvo; and since Russ had directions, we led the way. Patty and Debbie rode right behind us with Donna in her Toyota.

I drove slowly so we could examine every home we passed. As soon as we were in front of one, Jody would say in disbelief, "Holy Gosh," and Goldstein would add, "Fuckin' A." They were both right. These homes were "Holy Gosh, Fuckin' A monstrosities."

After we passed the last house, there were no more for at least a mile. Then in the distance, we spotted our destination. It was the only house with lights. From where we were, it looked like thousands of diamonds had fallen from the sky and landed in a large pile.

"There it is," said Russ.

Goldstein, sounding hungry, said, "Party time!"

I pulled up in back of a Rolls that was last in a long rope of parked cars. Donna pulled in right behind me; as we got out, we all expressed our amazement at the size of the homes we had passed. Then we became silent and somewhat awestruck as we cast our eyes in the direction of what Donna called the "Party Palace." We walked past what must have been a few million dollars' worth of cars. A few limos were parked among Porches, Mercedes and Jags.

When we passed a Dodge, Russ said, "How'd that get in here?"

I was glad that I had bought my Volvo that new coat of paint. I had nothing to be ashamed of.

When we reached the driveway, Patty and I stopped for a few minutes to examine the "Palace" in detail. The others headed inside.

It was larger than all of the homes we had inspected and certainly the strangest looking. At each end of the house was an enormous round ball constructed mostly of glass and what looked like chrome. They were connected by a long glass tunnel. The entire house looked like an oversized barbell the Jolly Green Giant might use to pump up his green biceps. Under the tunnel, the driveway continued towards an oceanside aglow with neon lights. I could make out a piece of tennis court and a section of a pool. Since there was so much glass, it was easy to see that the barbell was packed with a few hundred people.

After a few minutes more of inspection, Patty simply said, "Wow."

We headed for the door.

Inside, I couldn't help but notice the abundance of beautiful girls. These were the kind who lived on magazine covers and probably wouldn't bleed if you tore the page. The guys looked like they could afford them. Many were dressed in Calvin Klein whites or pastels—the appropriate showcase for tans. Almost everyone had that "new money" look. But scattered about in their own little clusters were couples, dressed in blue double-breasted blazers and tastefully cut white dresses. They looked like they had just stepped out of a Ralph Lauren ad, or in reality, spent some afternoons posing on the lawns of their South Hampton mansions for the pages of *Town and Country*. They stood with drinks in their hands talking among themselves, almost oblivious to what was going on around them. They were at this party because it was an important one, but that didn't mean they had to be a part of it.

We were standing in a large sunken living room. Across the room, in front of a window that covered the entire wall so you could look out at the pool, tennis courts and ocean, was a long bar. Five bare-chested, muscle-bound bartenders were serving drinks. They only had on black bikini bathing suits and white collars with black bow ties. Formal beach attire. Waitresses walked around with trays of hors d'oeuvres. They too were dressed formally in black bikinis, white collars and bow ties.

A large group was dancing in the middle of the room to a Michael Jackson tune from Thriller. A black DJ was spinning the songs from a stage set up next to the bar. To my left, people were coming in and out of the tunnel. I noticed a blonde walk out, who I could have sworn I'd seen in the movies or on TV, but I couldn't place her.

Patty took hold of my hand and said, "Let's get something to drink." It sounded like the right thing to do, since I was already building up a thirst.

She led me through the crowded dance floor, and for a few, brief shining moments, I got caught among three beautiful girls. I stood still as they laughed, after noticing my predicament, and danced around me. They too were tall and curvaceous in their tans, bikinis and tank tops. I simply began smiling at the cleavage sisters and started admiring the view. I then saw Patty turn around to see where I was. She smiled and beckoned me with her index finger. I told the girls I'd see them later, but they couldn't hear me over the music.

"Having fun?" Patty asked sounding slightly jealous.

"Couldn't help it. Got caught in the middle of some new steps."

"I better keep my eye on you," she said with a smile.

"What do you want to drink?" I asked.

"White wine would be nice, but first I have to find a bathroom. Be right back."

I leaned over the bar and asked a bartender what kind of beer he had. He proceeded to rattle off about ten names, with a few imports I had never heard of before, then smiled. He had perfect teeth.

I stuck to the basics. "Make it a Bud and a glass of white wine."

As I waited, I looked out the window. There was a large deck with tables and chairs. The entire deck was filled with the rest of the "old money" crowd. More couples in finely tailored Polo, Armani and Donna Karan outfits. At closer range many of the older men could have given Douglas Fairbanks, Jr. or Cary Grant a run for their money in the distinguished department. They all obviously felt more comfortable on the deck away from the spectacle taking place indoors. It was even more obvious that they were the oil and everyone else inside was water. And, as everyone knows, water and oil simply don't mix. The tennis court was empty, but there were some swimmers in the pool.

The bartender brought over my brew, which I immediately took a hit from, flashed a perfect smile and placed the glass of white wine in front of me.

"Is that wine for me?" a voice on my right asked.

I turned to see where the voice came from. It belonged to a brunette in her late 20's or early 30's. She was about my height and dressed in pink running shorts and a tank top, with a matching pink sweatband around her head. She was in great shape, had a cute, turned up nose, and her deep tan added an extra sparkle to her white teeth.

"Well, it wasn't, but feel free," I said, with a smile before taking another hit on my Bud.

"Thanks," she said, then took a tiny sip. "Isn't this an outrageous party?"

"Sure is."

"My name's Belinda," she said smiling and thrusting out her hand to shake.

"Chris," I said, switching the Bud to my left hand to take hers. It was incredibly soft.

"Do you know Benjamin?"

"Who?"

"Benjamin Chard-Allman, the dude who's throwing this bash."

"No. A friend does."

"He was a client of mine."

"What do you do?"

"Now I own a gym in Huntington called Body Sweat."

"You look like you're dressed for it, without the sweat, of course."

She smiled.

"A great name for a gym."

"I think so," she said, then was quiet for a few seconds as if she were contemplating how great the name was. "You should meet Ben, he's a great guy."

Great guys always are until you meet them. "I bet he is."

"Yeah. He gave me the funds I needed to open the gym. No strings attached."

"He sounds like a great guy."

She shot a glance over my shoulder. "There he is."

I turned to catch a glimpse of the great guy himself.

"He's the bald one."

He was talking and laughing with the cleavage sisters and one of the waitresses. His head was completely bald and looked as if it had been waxed. On his chin was a gray Van Dyke and he was all in white; his shirt was open to his navel, looked like it wouldn't cover his round belly if it were buttoned. He looked pregnant—a good guess would be his sixth month.

Looking at him, I said to Belinda, "He's not a very good advertisement for Body Sweat." With Michael Jackson still singing his ass off, and since I said it as though I were thinking out loud, she asked me what I'd said. I turned to her and repeated it.

"Oh, he doesn't go to the gym."

"I thought you said he was a client."

"He was, but that was my last job."

"What job was that?" I said, then lifted my bottle and began to drain it.

"I was a call girl."

That gagged me a little. She said it so nonchalantly, it was as if she said she was a lawyer. So I decided to double check. "You were what?"

"A call girl."

I turned to the guy with the perfect teeth and asked for another Bud. Then I said to Belinda, "That sounds like an interesting job."

"It was very good to me."

I was intrigued. "So how does one get into the profession?"

"I can tell you how I got into it."

"Okay."

"In my early twenties I got a job as a cashier at a topless place in Times Square. I didn't dance topless, just worked the register.

When she said this, I shot a quick glance at her tits. They were rather small, but my glance wasn't quick enough. She caught me looking and knew what I was thinking.

"Shit. I'm not that big anyway. So one night this Italian sailor comes in for a few drinks then tries comin' on to me. He was kinda cute and I hadn't been laid in a while, so when he invited me back to the ship he was on, I figured, what-the-hell." She then made a what-the-hell face.

I responded with a quick what-the-hell shrug of my shoulders and took another gulp of beer.

"The next morning he goes over to his wallet and puts five hundred dollars on the bed for me. I looked at him and said, "No," meaning I'm not a hooker, but since he spoke so little English, he thought I meant it wasn't enough. So he put down another three-hundred bucks. After I left I thought, 'Hmmmm.'" She looked at me with her eyes wide open, moved her head slowly up and down as if the sailor had just given her the money and the idea to start hooking had popped into her head for the very first time.

"Hmmmm," I replied.

"Then one thing led to another, I hooked up with a high class madam and went to work.

"Did you make a good living?"

"Sure did. I was high class merchandise," she said seriously then stepped back and put her hands on her hips for me to inspect the goods. "I charged five hundred bucks an hour."

I checked out the merchandise. It looked fine, but two hundred and fifty would have been more than generous. But what did I know—besides, these were inflationary times. I was beginning to find the conversation quite interesting. I had never spoken to a call girl before, or even a former call girl.

Questions began creeping into my brain and since my beer was starting to loosen me up, I began to ask. "Was there anything you wouldn't do?"

"Yep. No anal for me. I'm not that kind of a girl."

At first I thought she was kidding, but she wasn't. "Of course not."

"But I did get into spanking. There was this spoiled young rich dude who ended up paying two thousand for two hours of getting his butt spanked."

I remembered my mother and father spanking me as a kid. There's no way I'd pay for that pleasure again. The idea of someone spending two thousand dollars to get his ass smacked seemed ludicrous and rather funny. I started to smile, which seemed to upset Belinda.

"It's not funny. The poor guy needed it the way you might need to get laid."

Her comment made me think of Patty. "You're right."

"After all, it started in his childhood. As a young boy, he'd go to his maid's bedroom and look at her things. I think it was his first crush. Then he ended up finding her underpants and would, you know, rub them against his face and smell them, you know. I guess she caught him and started spanking him. You know how it goes—a deep psychological thing took over. So if it weren't for people like me, he'd never get off." She took a sip of wine and looked at me for a reaction or if I had another question.

I decided not to pursue the spanking stuff, but I did have another question. "You musta made a bundle."

"A mega-bundle."

"Hope you stocked it away."

"Nope. I started putting it up my nose. I think most of South America went up it."

"Too bad."

"Yeah, but that's sort of how I changed professions. During a session with Benjamin, he told me that I had not been looking like myself and figured I was doing drugs. He said he'd get me into a rehab center and then set me up in a business, no strings attached."

"What a guy."

"Yeah. I didn't even have to fuck him anymore. But I did, and still do, of course. So now I've been running Body Sweat for about a year and doing great."

"A happy ending."

"Ya know, I didn't get your name."

"Chris."

"Are you a one-name kinda person, like Cher?"

I smiled. "Chris McCauley."

"So, Chris McCauley, are you here by yourself?"

Before I could answer, I heard Patty say, "Did you get me that glass of wine?"

I turned around to face her, Goldstein and Debbie. "I had it but..."

"You gave it to that fox you were talking to," Goldstein said already sounding shit-faced.

I turned to introduce Belinda, but she was gone.

"Who was she?" asked Patty trying not to sound even remotely jealous since she couldn't let onto the others that we were becoming an item.

"She runs a gym called Body Sweat."

"Sounds like my kinda place," said Goldstein.

"Sounds more like a whore house," Debbie added with a giggle.

I didn't even try to explain. "Let me get you that wine," I said to Patty, turned and ordered another.

"Is this an awesome party?" said Debbie looking around. "There is a famous director here who I just have to meet."

"Who is he?" asked Patty.

"I don't know, but I just got to talk to him."

"If you don't know who he is or his name, how do you know he's here?" Goldstein asked sounding drunk and annoyed.

"I overheard two girls talking in the bathroom."

"Speaking of the bathroom," Goldstein said to me as I got a glass of wine from another bartender with perfect teeth and handed it to Patty, "did you check out the rest of this pad?"

"Not really," I said, taking a hit from another Bud.

"It's really incredible," added Patty.

"Yeah," said Debbie, "if you walk through the glass tunnel, on the other side is a game room, poolroom, bedrooms..."

Goldstein cut in. "Huge bedrooms, just waiting for me and one or more of these beautiful babes."

"Go easy young man," Patty said, then winked at me.

"Oh yeah," Goldstein said, "in the poolroom that soup guy was talking to a small attentive audience. What the fuck is his name again?"

"Soup guy?" I said not knowing who he could be referring to.

He looked at the three of us for help. "You guys know. The fag who drew the soup cans."

"You mean Andy Warhol?" said Patty.

"Yeah. That's the guy."

"Andy Warhol!" said Debbie lifting her voice in disbelief. "He's a great artist. He's not a fag."

"Yeah, right," Goldstein said smirking.

"In the poolroom?" she asked again making sure she got the location right.

"Yep."

"I gotta see him," she said, then headed in the direction of the tunnel.

I looked at Patty. "It's my turn to go to the head."

I handed my beer to Patty, and said I'd be right back. I headed in the direction of the tunnel, but had to make my way through the dancing crowd. The Beatles were singing "Birthday," as I kept banging into body parts: an arm here, a tit there. Since I was already a bit buzzed, I didn't care, and the dancers I was making contact with didn't care either.

Walking through the tunnel, I stopped in the middle of it to survey the tennis court and pool. No one was playing tennis, but there were a few swimmers in the pool. It looked like they were skinny-dipping, so I squinted with my blurry eyes to get a clearer look. Sure enough, a girl climbed out of the pool, looking long, sleek and very naked. Her wet body glowed under the lights. I noticed that no one on the deck seemed to notice; it made me feel like a Peeping Tom. Was I the only pervert staring? Feeling slightly embarrassed, I headed on to the bathroom, but shot one last look back at her before reaching the poolroom.

The room was enormous and had two long leather couches on each side of it. The walls were in hunter green covered with old hunting prints and portraits of famous racing horses. Someone, I thought, should go out and tell the blue bloods they can come in now if they'd like, there's a room decorated especially for them. A small group was standing in front of the large window that looked out over the ocean.

One of the guys recognized my quest for the grail and called out, "It's that way," and pointed to the door.

I smiled, walked over, and as I went to open the door, it was pushed from the other side. For a brief moment, I stood eye to eye with Andy Warhol, "the soup guy." He was exactly my height, was so pale he was almost transparent, wore an out-of-season black turtleneck and very dark sunglasses. But what caught my attention was his hair. It was a white wig that stuck out on all sides, as if it were in a permanent state of shock. It reminded me of the feathers on a dead sea gull I had seen on the beach that day.

I said, "Excuse me."

He just smiled.

As I stood over the toilet and unzipped my pants, I found it rather humorous that I was taking a leak right after, and in the very spot that the famous "soup guy" with the dead sea gull on his head had taken a leak. I was a little more drunk than I thought. It felt good to lose the beer.

Chapter Twenty

I made my way back to the bar, but Patty and Goldstein were no longer there. I looked around for a few minutes then ordered another brew. I kicked that back then decided to walk outside and have a look around. I spotted Donna on the deck flirting with two blue-blooded guys; she threw a quick glance in my direction, but that was it. She was obviously on the hunt and couldn't waste valuable time on me.

"Hey, Chris," someone to my right called. It was Russ. He was standing a few feet away with Benjamin Allman.

At close range, Allman's bald dome was even shinier and he looked to be around sixty. Around his neck was a heavy looking gold chain. If he fell into a pool with that around his neck, he'd never come up. I walked over.

"Chris," said Russ, "this is Benjamin Chard-Allman. The man who's throwing this party and who I talked about so much."

The only thing Russ said about him was that he was a big-shot in advertising and that he threw this huge party every Fourth. I was buzzed but knew enough to go along.

Russ was simply doing his duty. I think it's called ass kissing.

142

"Oh. So this is Mr. Allman," I said trying to sound like I knew all about him. I put out my hand to shake his. He took it but looked over my head as if he were looking for someone else.

"Nice to meet you," he said, giving me a quick smile along with some quick eye contact before he began searching the crowd again.

"Chris teaches at Newman College and writes poetry," Russ said straining to be pleasant.

"Poetry!" said Big Ben in disbelief. "A dead art form. Who reads that shit anyway?"

I didn't think it necessary to be polite after that comment. I let the beer take over. "If it's shit, I guess shitheads." I glanced over at Russ who was still smiling but now had a few beads of sweat over his lip. However, since Allman wasn't interested in me, or in Russ for that matter, and kept looking for someone, he didn't hear me anyway.

"Fuck the poetry. Jingles are where it's at."

"Yeah, you're right. I'm going to teach Jingles 101 in the fall, then Advanced Jingles in the spring."

"Great. Great," he said in a hurry as he continued to search the crowd.

"I thought you'd be impressed."

He seemed to spot whoever it was he had been looking for. "Gentlemen, there is someone I have to talk to. Catch you later," he said not looking at either of us.

I watched him walk over to two beautiful women, who each took an arm and walked with him inside.

"Fucking asshole," I said to Russ as I watched Allman disappear. Then took a hit of my beer that was warming in my hand.

"Major fucking asshole," was Russ's reply. "Can you believe the women here?" he said in the same breath.

"Pretty outrageous."

"And I can't approach one," he said disgustedly.

"Yeah. Where's Jody?"

"Patty came by and told us she saw Bianca Jagger, so Jody went to see if she could spot her. She wanted me to come of course, but then I saw Allman. She figured I was safe, so she went without me."

"Where did Patty go?"

"I don't know, but my few minutes of freedom are over."

Jody was back. "Chris, isn't this just a fantastic party?"

"Yep, sure is."

"I just saw Bianca Jagger."

"Really?"

"She was at the bar talking to some dreamy guy, but she's nothing to look at."

"That means," said Russ, "that she's good-looking."

"What's that supposed to mean?" Jody said, obviously annoyed.

"It means what I said. Whenever someone is even mildly attractive, you say that they're not."

"I do not."

"Yes, you do." Russ looked over at me. "It just means that she is jealous of anyone, girl that is, who is better looking than she is."

Jody raised her voice, "Bullshit!"

"Okay," said Russ, "Chris, take a look over there at the blonde with the tray in her hand."

I turned to look. She was one of the waitresses in a formal black bikini. Like all of the waitresses working at the party, she was a knockout. It just so happened that she was equipped with a few extras that set her apart from the others: the longest legs, the biggest boobs and naturally blonde hair. In short, if there was a heaven, she could very well be it.

"So Jody, what do you think of her?" asked Russ.

She looked over at the waitress and quickly back at Russ. "What do you mean, 'what do I think'?"

"What do you think? Is she good looking or not?"

Jody turned to look at her again, then began to examine. Her face seemed to tighten. "Her legs are too long, her chest is too big, and she's not that good looking."

"See," Russ said raising his voice in exasperation, while glancing over at me, "that woman is one of God's best tries and Jody thinks she's unattractive."

"Shut up Russ," Jody said pissed off.

"You shut up. You're so fucked it isn't funny."

"Why, just because every bimbo you see, you think is beautiful and I don't."

They had never fought in front of me before and I wasn't going to hang around and watch. I would never argue with a woman I was involved with in public. I was always aware of the strangers around me and immediately became embarrassed. Towards the end of our relationship, whenever Laura laid into me in public, which was often during the last few months, I always clammed up and waited to fire back behind closed doors. When I saw other couples fighting with one another in public, I'd still become embarrassed but this time for them. These two were heating up, so it was time to move on.

"Look, I'll see you guys later," I said, but they didn't answer me. Russ was in the middle of calling her a neurotic, jealous bitch and she was calling him a mean bully or something close to it and looking as if she were trying not to cry.

I put my empty bottles on one of the nearby tables and walked down towards the pool area. There was a couple in a white terry cloth robes sipping drinks at a table, their hair still wet from swimming. In the pool, a girl was doing laps; she looked like she was wearing a very tiny bikini or she was simply nude. I tried not to stare.

As I walked over to the fence to look at the beach, from the corner of my eye, I saw that she had finished the laps and was climbing up the ladder at the far end of the pool. I turned to see what she was wearing. Just pool water and nothing else. She had short blonde hair, round hips and a great looking ass. She hurried over to a chair, picked up a towel and began drying herself off. She must have felt me looking at her because she suddenly shot a quick glance in my direction.

Embarrassed, I turned my eyes toward the beach, walked over to lean on the fence and gazed out at the ocean and thought about her ass. I started to think about a small birthmark on the side of her right cheek that was quite visible in the strong lights that lit the pool area. For some reason it was familiar. Since I hadn't been with that many women, I started to go over the asses I had the pleasure of being close and personal with during my rather lackluster career as a stud. I couldn't place it. I eventually blamed my minor fascination with it on the abundance of beer in which most of my internal organs were marinating.

"Excuse me."

I turned to face the swimmer who was now covered in a pink terry cloth robe. Her blonde hair was slicked back from her swim, beads of water were glistening like tiny jewels all over her face, and her lips were slightly vibrating, a sure sign she was chilled. My immediate impression was she was more sexy than pretty.

"Aren't you Chris McCauley?"

"Yes, I am."

"I thought it was you. Except for the mustache you haven't changed a bit."

I was surprised that someone at this party knew me and I immediately tried to place her face. I felt like asking her to take off her robe so I could get a better look at her naked limbs. Perhaps it would jog my memory. And if not, at least I'd have another look at that perfect ass.

I said, "I'm sorry, I can't place you."

She started to laugh. "Maybe this will ring a bell." She moved a few feet away turned around and with her back facing me slowly began sliding her robe up her legs. As she did this, she looked at me over her shoulder and began smiling in anticipation of my recognition. When the robe slid past her birthmark, it clicked. I yelled out her name as if I were a contestant on a game show.

"Peggy!"

She let her robe drop down and turned around to face me again. "I knew that would jog your memory," she said with a big grin.

Not only did it jog my memory, the day in her basement eighteen years before came rushing back along with all the embarrassment that went with it. For a few seconds, I was thirteen again, wearing a bloodstained Mickey Mantle tee-shirt.

She came over and wrapped her arms around me. I put mine around her, resting my chin on her head. When she released me to stand back and chat, her robe opened and she did nothing to close it up. It was strange meeting again for the first time in almost twenty years and even stranger with her beaver looking up at me.

"So what's been going on with you for the past eighteen or twenty years?" I said jokingly.

I had literally not seen her since the eighth grade. Her family had moved right after we graduated that year. I can remember avoiding her after that basement incident. I was too embarrassed. When she tried to talk to me, I came up with some excuse and hurried off. If she caught my eye in class, I quickly looked the other way, or buried myself in a book, even if it was a math book.

"Should I start at the beginning?"

"If you mean after eighth grade, sure."

She laughed. "We moved to Stamford, Connecticut, where my folks immediately got divorced. That was just fine with me since all they did was fight. After high school I went to the University of Colorado, but since I always had a hard time finding a parking space, I figured it wasn't worth it and dropped out after three weeks."

I laughed. As I listened to how she spent time out West, did a lot of drugs, then straightened herself out and began doing secretarial jobs, I hoped she wouldn't bring up that afternoon in her basement.

"I was always free-spirited. Hell, I even started young. Remember?"

Shit, here it comes I thought. "Yeah. I guess you were." I flashed a quick smile and glanced down at her beaver. Still blonde. It hadn't changed a bit.

"I was too much." She laughed some more and obviously wanted to reminisce about basement afternoons. "Back then there weren't too many thirteen year olds as brazen as I was."

"There sure weren't." I was thinking of some way to change the topic before we got around to me in the basement.

"I think I ended up with most of the guys down there by the time we graduated." She ended her comment giggling.

I laughed too, rather uneasily.

"As you can see," she paused and opened her robe to show me her tits and blonde bush, then closed it. "I'm still free and I guess a bit of an exhibitionist."

"Whatever floats your boat."

"I guess," she said staring at the ground. Then she started to smile. "I can still remember the funniest thing."

I braced myself. My past was coming back to get me in the balls one more time. Whoever said, "Child is the father to man," knew what he was talking about. You can't ditch your childhood. I braced myself. Okay, let Peggy watch me fall on my face one more time.

"You remember Billy Mayer?"

"Sure."

"Remember he looked fifty at thirteen?"

"The first guy to shave in the class. In fact, I think he actually started shaving in third grade." We both laughed.

"Well, he came over and I go into my little routine," she started laughing. "I turned around to flash my pubic hair and his little hard-on starts exploding. Then he turned to run out. He was so fucking embarrassed he forgot to pull his pants up and went crashing face first into the floor." More laughter.

A reprieve. The fates had stepped in, decided to keep the action intact, but confused the characters for her. Or maybe there have been too many faces in her past, and too many drugs in the mid-seventies. In any case, it wasn't me who made a fool of himself in her basement, it was Billy.

"But I remember when you came by."

Fuck. Maybe she was just setting me up and was going to tell me it wasn't Bill after all.

"Really?"

"Yeah. You were all over me, grabbing my chest and you had a stiff little hard-on that just wouldn't go down." She was smiling from ear to ear.

So was I. More luck. "Well, things haven't changed much when it comes to that kind of stuff." This time I was smiling from ear to ear.

"Still hot and ready, huh Chris?"

"Afraid so."

She kept smiling but I didn't get the sense that she was coming on. She was simply talking about her childhood. For her, strangely enough, it was a warm memory and nothing more.

"So Chris, tell me what you've been up to."

It took me all of ten minutes. I was surprised how easy it was for me to condense twenty years of my life in a few minutes. But I actually enjoyed editing life down to the bare essentials. Nothing like the basics to give one's life greater significance.

Peggy wanted to know if I was married and when I returned the question, she said, "Yep. I'm Mrs. Benjamin Chard-Allman." She said it sarcastically as if it were a title she didn't need.

"You're married to Big Ben?" I said not hiding my surprise.

"Yeah. The big bald guy who's old enough to be my father."

I know what he looks like. We met."

"What you met is what you get."

"Interesting," was all I could come up with.

"Not very. But he—excuse me—*we* are very wealthy."

"Where'd you two meet?"

"When I came back from Colorado, I got a job as a temp in his office. He spotted me, called me, wined me and dined me and asked me to marry him."

"Looks like you said yes!"

"Shit. Why not? I figured some gals get married for love, others for bucks."

I might have looked as if I didn't like her reason for marital bliss since big bucks and Laura were still a sore spot, or maybe Peggy was feeling a little guilty. She tried explaining.

"The romantic in me wanted to fall in love, but I've never been in love, so why not go for the green now and I figured my love would turn up some time down the road. Since we stopped sleeping together after the first few months of our marriage, you can bet I'm looking."

"You guys don't sleep together?"

"Nah. He prefers hookers."

I felt like saying I know. "Why?"

"Because he's used to paying for everything. Hell, he's paying my way." She added a what-the-fuck laugh. "But don't worry about my love life. You're not talking to any frustrated wife."

I smiled. "Somehow I didn't think I was."

"I've gone through quite a few guys and Ben usually sets me up. Wants to keep me happy."

"Sounds a little bizarre."

"My life has been bizarre for so long, it seems perfectly natural to me."

All I could do was nod my head in agreement.

"My present boy toy of the moment is the blonde bartender."

"There are five blonde bartenders."

"The cute one with the perfect teeth."

They all had perfect teeth but I pretended I knew who she was talking about.

"Speaking of drinks, how did you end up at this party?"

Before I could answer, the couple who was sitting at the table and had been swimming with her called and waved her over. She looked back and yelled, "Be right there." She then said, "I've been holding them up. Gotta get going!"

"Okay."

"But if you are going to be here for a while, we should have a drink later."

"Great."

"Boy, it has been really wonderful seeing you after all this time."

"It's been fun."

She reached to stroke my mustache. "This is a nice addition."

"Thanks."

"See you later."

I stuck out my hand to shake but she leaned up and gave me a peck on my cheek and hurried over to her friends.

I turned to look out at the ocean. There was a pleasant warm breeze which, for some reason, felt exotic. Perhaps it traveled in from some far off locale like India or France. Or maybe Chard-Allman purchased it, since he buys everything, and had it imported for the party. A full moon lit up the beach with blue light. I noticed a woman sitting, looking at the ocean. There was also someone lying next to her. I wondered where Patty was and decided to look for her, but first I wanted to stroll down to the water.

Walking down another series of steps onto the sand, I stopped to take off my shoes and made my way to the water's edge. Since I didn't want to invade the couple's privacy, who were the only people besides myself on the beach, I purposely stayed a few feet away. As I passed them, I heard Patty call my name.

The guy lying next to her was Goldstein, who was snoring rather loudly. "Where have you guys been? When I came back to the bar, you were gone."

"Apparently, Aaron found the coke room just before he reached us. After you went to the bathroom, it all kicked in and he was a goner. He insisted on going for a swim."

I interrupted her. "Asshole."

"I finally convinced him he didn't know how to swim and tried to make him remember he almost drowned today. But he insisted on coming down to look at the ocean. I figured I'd better come with him just to play it safe."

I looked at him again. "He looks safe now."

"Yeah. As soon as we got here, he sat down, fell back and zonked out."

"Smart move."

She looked down at him sleeping, then up at me. "It was just so beautiful I thought I'd stay for a few minutes then get someone to help me drag him a little further away from the ocean. Besides, it was nice to get away from all that noise."

"It is kind of noisy," I said just to agree, even though it didn't seem very loud to me.

"Where have you been?"

"Bumped into an old friend."

We both grew silent and looked out at the ocean.

"Sure is beautiful."

"Sure is," she said with a sigh. "Want to go for a walk?"

"Great." I looked down at Goldstein. "Sleeping Beauty isn't going anywhere, but let me drag him a few feet away from the water."

"Good idea. We don't want him washed out to sea."

"Sure don't." I bent down, grabbed him by both wrists and dragged him a few feet. He didn't stir.

Patty took off her shoes, then took my hand. The tide was low and the sand was firm and cool under our feet. We walked up the beach until the sounds from the party were washed over by the surf.

Patty was rather quiet except to comment on the next dark mansion we approached. Then she stopped, put her arms around my neck and gently kissed my lips. We embraced, tightly locked our mouths together, then fell onto the sand. She began kissing me all over my face and kept whispering, "It's time." I was finding out that it's always time when a woman says it is.

I couldn't believe what was finally happening and started fumbling with my belt buckle. Patty helped me with this difficult, but important maneuver, then helped me push my pants down to my knees. She immediately started stroking my cock as I slid my hand up her skirt to remove her panties, but they were already gone. There must have been a look of surprise on my face; she smiled at my discovery then leaned back to make things even easier.

I began to unbutton her blouse and luckily she helped me with that too, otherwise I would have never gotten it open. Then I lifted her bra up and went for her breast with my mouth and worked the other nipple with my fingers. She began arching her back, and the sound of her moaning made the warm air hot. I moved my hand down between her legs to make sure she was ready. As I got on top of her, she held onto my cock to make sure I was on target. I was. It was custom-made, the perfect pussy, or maybe for the first time, it was simply the right woman. She squeezed her legs against my sides then slid her hands onto my ass to assist me in each thrust or to press me against her and to push deeper.

Overhead the moon was grinning and the stars burned on my back.

Chapter
Twenty-One

"I'm in love."

At first I thought Becky Samuels was kidding when she walked into my office to make this surprising announcement. Since she made it a point not to share anything personal with me, it was only natural to think some kind of joke would soon follow. But there was a strange, almost confused look on her face, and she made it a point not to look me in the eye. Then she shot a quick glance at me to see what my reaction was and just as quickly looked away again. The tone of her voice and the look on her face made it seem as if she were telling me she contracted a fatal disease. "I have three months to live," would have been just as appropriate.

"That's great," I said, sounding cautiously upbeat.

"I guess," she answered, as if she were giving in to the situation and not totally agreeing with me.

I was intrigued by her reply. "Well, isn't it?"

152

"Not if you fall in love the way I do."

"What do you mean?"

"I never walk into it or even crawl. I always fall." She looked at me with a concerned expression. "And when anyone falls, your chances of getting hurt are greater."

I tried to ease her fears. "Falling in love doesn't always mean getting hurt."

She frowned disgustedly. "C'mon."

"It's true," I said, now sounding like I was trying to convince myself.

"Yeah, well how about you and Nora?"

"Laura."

"Yeah, Laura."

"What about us?"

"Didn't you fall in love with her?"

I bristled, "What's that got to do with it?"

"Well did you?"

"Yeah, I did."

"You see!"

I did, but pretended I didn't. "See what?"

"You fell for her and look what she did to you. During most of the spring semester you looked like you got your head kicked in."

"So what," was all I could get out.

"I just don't want to walk in here in a few months like I got my head kicked in."

I was still on her side. "It doesn't mean you will. Maybe it will work out. Did you ever consider that?"

She stared at the wall again, then began, "It's just that when I got divorced..." She stopped herself, not wanting to resurrect the pain.

"Look, go with it. Take the risk."

She looked at me again. "Do you still love Nora?"

"Yeah," I said, sounding more disgusted than I intended.

"The fucking thing is that after all this time, I still am a little in love with my ex-husband. And after what he did to me."

I wanted to know what he did, but didn't think I should ask. There were boundaries with Becky I didn't feel comfortable crossing. However, I decided to give it a try, but before I could get the question out, she asked me one.

"Do you love what's her name?"

"Patty?"

"Do you?"

"No. We've only been dating a few weeks."

"Are you using her for methadone?"

I didn't get it. "What do you mean?"

"You know. The way junkies use it to get off the drugs they're really hooked on."

Maybe I was, but never thought about it like that. Was I using Patty to get over Laura, or was I dating Patty because I was trying to get on with my life? Maybe the truth was somewhere in the middle.

"No, I don't think so," I said, sounding a little perplexed.

"I got into a methadone type relationship a few months after my ex and I broke up. It just created more problems. So I got out of it and said the hell with this relationship stuff."

"Until now," I said with a smile.

"Yeah. At least this isn't a methadone relationship."

"Hey, and even if you are falling, it's still worth the risk."

She smiled then sighed. "I guess there isn't even the hint of rationale in these matters."

"There never seems to be."

"But at least I'm questioning and examining this time."

"So you really aren't falling, after all."

"Yeah. Maybe not. By the way, we are going to spend a week together out in the Hamptons.

"Oh, really? Where?"

"A motel in East Hampton."

"That's right near the house I'm in. I'll give you the phone number. Maybe you and..." It dawned on me I didn't know her boyfriend's name. "What's his name anyway?"

Rather than tell me immediately, she seemed to hesitate, then said, "Steve."

"Maybe you and Steve can get together with me and Patty for a drink out there."

"Maybe." She didn't seem too thrilled with the idea. "Well, I have a class in a few minutes. Can you believe how fast the summer session went?"

"Just two more weeks," I said sounding relieved.

She then turned to walk out.

"Hey Becky." She looked back over her shoulder "It really is good news."

"What is?"

"Your fa...your walking into love."

"I hope so."

"I'm rooting for you."

She smiled warmly. "Thanks," then walked out the door.

I was pleased Becky wanted to share a bit of her love life with me. It was the first time she shared anything personal; usually it was all school related. During my break up with Laura I had to share with Becky what I was going through. It was obvious that I was getting my balls kicked in. One day I walked past her in the hall on my way to the office. She came by a few minutes later to see if I was okay. I guess I looked pretty bad. I gave her a quick run down of what was going on. She didn't offer any advice. She must have sensed I wasn't looking for any, just an ear to moan into. But she did listen and simply told me it would get better and to "hang in there." Although that's all she said, it seemed to help at the moment.

Over the next few days she'd pop in with extra coffee and simply ask how I was doing. It was during one of her check-ins that I learned she was once married. But that's all she revealed about her personal life. So I was glad to return the favor and was pleased that she felt comfortable enough to share what seemed like an unexpected turn in her life. It sounded like there had been no love involvement for quite some time. It was long overdue.

I leaned back in my chair and thought about her methadone comment for a moment, shrugged it off and thought how quickly the summer was going. It was mid-July and there were only two more weeks of school left, then I could spend the rest of the summer out at the house.

Everyone was still pretty much getting along, but some cracks in the seam were starting to appear. By now everyone knew Russ and Jody were far from the perfect couple since they began bickering in front of everyone, and didn't try to hide it. Every time Russ got me alone, all he wanted to talk about was dumping his "bitch" and getting new pussy. Donna became more sour and if something wasn't going smoothly in her life, and it seemed by mid-July nothing ever was, she let the entire house know about it. She dragged in two more "fuck buddies," but she always seemed worse after they left.

Walter missed both of his weekends after the Fourth and since he was alternating with Debbie, he hadn't been out since his first weekend. He became known as the Phantom. Debbie actually became sweeter and more sure of herself when her shrink gave her the green light to go on auditions. But she became more depressed when she never received callbacks. And although July was half over, Goldstein still hadn't gotten laid.

I looked up at the books on my shelf and spotted the word Science on the spine of one of the titles. I wondered what title it was but was too lazy to get up;

it reminded me that aside from math I was never much good when it came to science either. No matter how hard I worked at it in high school and college, I could never pull anything higher than a C. Patty admitted she always had a difficult time in science as well. How ironic that we were both pulling an A in chemistry—the indefinable science that takes place between two people in heat.

Even though no one in the house knew we were dating except Donna, I couldn't give a shit now that I was getting laid on a regular basis. If Patty didn't want anyone to know, it was just fine with me. And now that I was getting laid, it even made sense.

I always thought I was having good sex with Laura—and I was—it was just that now I was having great sex with Patty. It sort of came as a surprise. When we made it on the beach for the first time in South Hampton, it was very good, but I thought it was because I had waited a while to get her. But after that night, I couldn't seem to get enough of her. It wasn't just any one thing about her that got me going, it was everything. Her voice over the phone, for instance, was enough to set off the buzzer in my balls that sent tiny electrodes into my cock and maneuvered it into the attack position. Her cute flowered skirts had the same effect on me that short tight skirts always had. And when she walked in her heels, her calves flared with silent seductive moans, enticing me, making me want to get down on all fours and lick them.

At first I didn't understand why I lusted after her the way I did. She was simply a cute girl from a small town and certainly not my idea of what a "hot" woman should look like. I never saw her in tight skirts, a tight blouse or any of the Sally Brown White outfits that usually turned me on. I just didn't get it. But then I discovered heat is where you find it, so sit back, blame it on chemistry and have a great time.

Patty wasn't just *into* sex, she was *passionate* about it. As soon as I'd get my clothes off, she'd wrap her fingers around my cock, close her eyes and hiss loudly through her partially closed lips. It was as if she was charging her battery for the work ahead, with those electrodes that came up from my balls. And the fact that she always acted as if I were the last man on the planet to have sex with did wonders for my ego and my dick.

Since we were excelling in chemistry, we tried an experiment or two. After dinner at Gene's one night, we took a cab up Sixth Avenue to my apartment. The cab was sectioned off from the driver's seat by a partition that seemed like a small wall. On top of it was one of those plastic enclosures that is supposed to be a protective shield against possible muggers.

As we headed uptown, Patty reached over and began massaging my crotch. I was looking out the window, was pleasantly surprised and closed my eyes, shutting out the shops along Sixth to enjoy the hand job. Nearing Forty-Second Street, I heard Patty move towards me to begin working my zipper down. I quickly opened my eyes to see if she was doing what I hoped she was and shot a quick glance to make sure the cabbie wasn't on to us. He wasn't, and Patty had my cock out in the process, stroking it with her hands and flicking her tongue around the head, teasingly. She was playful, having a good time and making me squirm. I was hoping she'd take it all in her mouth by Fifty-Sixth Street. I had never had a cab ride like that before and the old adage that the cabbie might catch us or that someone might see us, just intensified matters.

By the time he crossed over to Fifty-Ninth Street to head up Third, Patty was working pretty hard and tightening her grip. The go ahead sign. It was just as well, since I couldn't hold back any longer. Unfortunately I timed it perfectly with a pothole. As soon as I began to come, the cabbie hit a crater, the entire cab shook and I jabbed my rod so deep into Patty's mouth, I felt it touch the back of her throat. She immediately took it out of her mouth as she loudly gagged and coughed. I looked quickly into the cabbie's rear view mirror to see if he caught on. But he kept his eyes on the road and said in a loud Spanish accent, "Sorry."

Patty stopped coughing, kept down so the driver wouldn't see her lift her head up from my lap, and slid back over to the other side of the seat.

I put my cock back and zipped up, then looked over at her and said, "Sorry, you okay?"

She nodded that she was. We both sat quietly for a few moments looking out at the Upper East Side until we looked at each other and began giggling. It was the first time sex ever made me laugh.

I had an experiment I wanted to try myself. Laura never let me, what she called, "perform cunnilingus." The first and only time I tried, she clamped her legs shut and told me never to try it again. She said it was "gross and disgusting" and how could I enjoy doing something like that? There are some things you just can't explain, so I didn't even try.

Patty was different.

If it had to do with sex, how could it be disgusting? The first time I got down to work, I knew it was where my tongue belonged by the way she moaned. And it wasn't so much that I liked the taste, there wasn't any, it was more the feel of those pussy lips against my tongue. They reminded me of the petals on the roses that grew in the back yard when I was a kid. I remember finding the roses so soft that I had to touch them with the tip of my tongue and thinking nothing on earth could be so soft, so delicate. But now I was touching something even softer with my tongue, in a totally new garden. I was licking Eden.

It was the night of the cab job. I felt terrible that we hit that pothole and I made Patty gag, even though she kept giggling about it. I wanted to make it up to her. When we got into bed, I immediately kissed my way down between her legs and decided to try something different. I thought I'd simply spell my name on her pussy, using my tongue as a pen.

I slowly licked a C then an H. Her body went limp; I wasn't sure if she liked it or not, but decided to go ahead with the R. As I started the S, she began moaning quietly. That was the all clear signal. She was in luck, I thought, that my name was a long one. When I put a little extra pressure on the L, she started moaning louder and in between moans began saying, "Oh God!" I felt her body begin to quake, and her legs stiffened—I pressed harder making her come all over the Y.

I was stuck between her legs, clamped tightly against my ears and feeling the aftershocks vibrate through her body. When she finally relaxed, I crawled up next to her and put my arm across her breasts.

She turned to kiss me and said, "God that was great. Where did you learn to do that, or whatever it was?"

I thought for second. "In the first grade."

Chapter
Twenty-Two

The next morning I was facing Patty when I opened my eyes. It must have been before 7:00, otherwise she would have been up getting ready to leave. She usually got into work by 8:30. But she was staring up at the ceiling with her arms folded behind her head. It was a position that was uncharacteristic of her and, it always seemed to me, a position that was uncharacteristic of most women.

"You're up early," I forced out of my mouth before a yawn managed to fill it.

She turned to me smiling and said, "Morning."

I closed my eyes and asked her what time it was.

"Around seven."

"Why aren't you jumping into the shower and getting ready for work?" I asked, focusing my eyes on her as she turned and looked at the ceiling again.

"Because I was thinking."

"About what?"

"Things."

"Like what?"

"You know, goals. The future."

"Isn't it kinda early in the morning for that," I managed to get out before another yawn.

She smiled, "It's never too early."

"Want to share some of them?"

"Sure. If you're sure you want to hear them so early in the morning."

"Yep, I do."

"Well, I was thinking about going to work today and how I hate filling another man's pocket with the money I make for him."

"I can understand that."

"I've always had this dream of starting my own advertising company. Do the kind of work I want to do, fill it with only the best people and let them put some of that money in my pocket for a change."

"Sounds good to me."

"It wouldn't have to be too big an operation, but I'd demand quality work and that's what Franklin Advertising would be known for."

"Catchy name," I said with a smile and more awake. "Where would you have it located? Here in New York?"

"Not necessarily. Chicago, Boston, California."

It bothered me that she didn't say New York, but I wasn't quite sure why.

"Of course, being a woman will make it more difficult."

"But if there is a woman who can do it, it's you."

She turned to look at me, smiled and said, "You bet." Then she faced the ceiling again.

I thought about what she said. The part that Franklin Advertising didn't have to be too big but would be a quality firm said a lot about her. If Laura had had similar dreams, it would have to be the biggest firm in the U.S., Glitz Advertising. And of course, rake in the biggest bucks. But Patty emphasized quality because I was finding out more and more that she was a quality person.

"Then I was thinking about other things," she said.

"Like what?"

"How I would really like to get married some day and have kids."

The defense alarm went off in my head. A red light started flashing behind my eyes. Here it comes. She's going to tell me she's falling in love with me already and did I feel the same about her? I'd just have to be honest, tell her she's a quality person, that there is a lot I admire about her, the sex is great, but I've only known her for a few weeks. And if push came to shove, I'd have to admit that I still wasn't over Laura. I was feeling bad for Patty already. I'd have to proceed cautiously with my questions.

"When would you like to get married?" I asked.

"Not for a few more years."

A good answer. I relaxed.

"I'd like to get my own business going first." She turned to look at me. "That's going to take up a lot of my time. Long hours. Little free time."

"I guess. So you really can't have kids right away."

"No, not right away." She turned to face the ceiling again. "Raising kids is a full-time job. It'll be tough running the company and raising a family. I figure my husband and I will have to be financially comfortable enough so I can at least take some time off to spend with the children. I don't want them to think a nanny is mom."

"A nanny too!" I said sounding as if I were impressed.

"Since I'll have the business to run, I'll definitely need a nanny. I don't know if I can have it all, but with a few compromises along the way, I might get close. Let's face it. Being a parent is probably the most important job in the world, as far as I'm concerned. I want more than anything to be a successful mom. I spent eighteen years with mine, so I know what it's like not to be." She was quiet for a minute or two, shifting her gaze down to her feet. Inspecting them she said, "But I guess there are no perfect parents and certainly no perfect kids. Mom tried her best. So did Dad."

"I'm sure you'll be a great mom."

"That's my plan."

I turned on my back. "How many kids would you like to have?"

"Ten."

The figure startled me. "What? Are you a Mormon or something?"

She laughed. "Okay, so it's an unrealistic number, but I can't have just one because it would make life too lonely and deprive it of bossing its younger brother or sister around. And I couldn't have just two because if they didn't get along they wouldn't have anyone else to choose from. I think I'd rather be an only child than to have one other sibling I spent all my time fighting with. So I guess a more realistic number is four. I'm sure though they'll all get along beautifully and love each other anyway no matter how many I end up having."

"At least four is a workable number."

"Just what do you mean?"

"Just that having a kid now is an expensive proposition."

"Expensive proposition?" she said as if she didn't understand.

"Yeah. Having a child costs big bucks. I would think having four is a large family by today's standards and would be economically draining for the parents."

"Perhaps you weren't listening," she was obviously annoyed, "I'm going to have a career that will enable me to afford a large family and I'm assuming my husband will have a career as well."

"Good point. What about your hubby?"

"Hubby?" she asked, sounding like she didn't understand this word either.

"Yeah. Your husband. You better hope he's making a really good salary."

"The only thing I hope, concerning my husband, is that he'll love me. I don't give a shit about his salary."

She was pissed. "Shit," was the first curse word I ever heard come out of her mouth.

"If he makes ten dollars to ten million doesn't mean anything to me. It's the size of his heart not his wallet that matters to me. Will he be loving, understanding, compassionate, passionate, there for me when I need him and there for our kids when they need him? That's what matters. I won't need him for his money, because I plan on making my own—this means I'll have to marry him because I love him. Strange concept, isn't it? At least strange for many women in New York. And if he only brings in ten dollars a week, we'll pool it with my salary so we can afford four kids and maybe even five."

She looked at me anticipating a reply but I couldn't give her one. I felt a little foolish the way I had when I was a kid, every time my mother gave me one of those lectures that always bothered me mostly because I knew she was right.

We both remained quiet for a few moments and stared at the ceiling. I focused on a brown water stain that I thought resembled a dog's head, along the lines of a Scottish Terrier. It's the closest I'd ever get to having a pet in the apartment.

I thought about what Patty had said. It basically reinforced what I had thought about her—that she was a "real" human being with her values and heart in the right place. She also gave me hope that there were more women like her out there on the streets of New York. It didn't make any difference that they may not be from the city, as long as they ended up here. If and when things didn't work out with Patty, there would be more gals from Pittsburgh, or Seattle or Des Moines who shared her goals and were ready to take her place.

I began to feel depressed. Why couldn't I have heard something similar come out of Laura's mouth? I could never imagine Laura coming even remotely close to what Patty had just said. At least not to me, the guy bringing home ten bucks a week.

Since money wasn't an issue for husbands as far as Patty was concerned, it certainly made me a contender. That was probably what she was leading to anyway. Why else would she bring up the subject of future goals? I got myself ready and still felt an honest response would be the best way to handle things. I thought I'd force the issue since it was getting late and she'd have to get up any minute and get ready for work.

"So do you have any contenders?"

"Contenders?" The tension left her voice. She seemed relaxed again and really didn't understand what I meant.

"Just guys who you'd consider marrying."

She thought for a second. "Not really."

Very cute I thought. She's yanking my chain. I'd play along with her until she got around to me. "No one, huh?"

She thought for a second or two. "I have this feeling that the same thing will happen to me that happened to my Aunt Sara."

"What's that?"

"When she was about nineteen—she's sixty-five now, and still a striking looking woman—she was riding a bus in Pittsburgh. When it came to a red light, she looked out the window and saw a guy about her age standing on the corner. She said this funny feeling came over her and she knew that one day she'd marry him. About an hour later, she stopped in a drugstore to have a cup of coffee. Someone sat down next to her and when he asked to borrow the menu, she turned and looked at the guy who was standing on the corner. They started talking. He asked her out and forty years later they're still married."

"That's wild."

"Yep. But that's how I know it will work with me. As soon as I see my future husband, I'll know immediately."

Where did that leave me? I was all set to tell her that we would need a lot more time since I couldn't even consider getting married after knowing her for such a short time. Not to mention I was still hooked on someone else. Now all I wanted to hear from her was that she might have heard a bell or two when she saw me the first time at O'Neals, nothing more. Why shouldn't I be a contender, even if I didn't want to be one, yet?

When I turned to look at Patty to pursue the matter of my contention, something stopped me. I realized it was ego time again and like any full-blooded American male, I was responding to the call. The truth was I really didn't want to be a contender. I just wanted the satisfaction of saying I wasn't ready and to sound mature, even though maturity had nothing to do with it. In some strange way, I just wanted to take a swipe at Laura, at Patty's expense. Patty certainly deserved better. I started to feel foolish again. Not the kind of foolishness I felt as a kid, but the kind a thirty year old man feels.

"It's getting late," Patty said, "I better get ready for work." She leaned over, gave me a quick peck on the cheek then hopped out of bed. She was naked so I propped myself up to watch her walk into the kitchen towards the shower. I loved watching her naked ass as she walked, it was almost perfect and her hips just accentuated its roundness. It always shook just enough to give me a hard-on.

Chapter
Twenty-Three

It was the last week of July and the first week I'd spend alone in the Hamptons. Summer school was over and now I had nothing to do but spend the rest of the summer reading, trying to write some poems and going to the beach. I planned to go into the city sporadically to check my mail, have dinner with Patty, and spend the night with her for dessert. It was a schedule I could live with. It turned out that I didn't spend the first week alone, however.

Walter called Sunday night after everyone left. He had taken the week off and was going to spend Monday night through Thursday out at the house, but was going up to the Cape for the weekend to visit friends.

"I hope that is okay with you, Chris," he said to me over the phone, making it sound as if it were my house.

"Of course," I said, even though I did mind, "it's your place, too."

He laughed. "That's right, it is. See you tomorrow."

"See you then."

Before hanging up he said, "Chris?"

"Yeah?"

"I have some poems I'd like to show you if that's okay."

"Sure bring 'em."

"See you tomorrow."

•

I woke around nine o'clock on Monday morning. I slept a little later because the sky was overcast. The lack of sun gave me the extra hour. I was still rather tired because the house kept me awake. It was full of sounds I never heard on weekends when it was full. After I got into bed and turned off the lights, I thought I heard someone trying to open the front door. I got up to make sure it was locked. To play it safe, I spent the next ten minutes making sure all the doors and windows were securely locked.

When I got back into bed and turned off the light again, everything was so black I couldn't see the bed next to mine. There was no moon or stars out to help things. I put my hand in front of my nose- couldn't see that either. Then the house started to creak and snap but these sounds didn't come from the front door. It was as if the house had a life of its own, and since it was nighttime, it was simply breathing as it slept. It spooked the hell out of me. No longer a spaceship, it was now a sleeping giant and I was simply a vacationing college professor it had swallowed. A piece of meat in its stomach it was trying to digest.

Rather than make breakfast, I took a quick shower, threw on shorts, tee-shirt and sneakers, got in my Volvo and headed to Estea's, the coffee shop in Amagansett. I took Bluff Road so I could look out at the ocean. Atlantic Avenue Beach looked empty, as it should have considering the weather. Everything was gray: sky, ocean and even the tiny snack stand, with its fresh coat of gray paint, almost disappearing in its gray surroundings.

Heading towards Indian Wells, the only sounds I heard were the crashing waves along the shore and the occasional gusts of wind or a distant squawk of a gull. For the first time I was experiencing the sounds of purity, the Hamptons cleansed of the thousands of weekend Manhattanites who glut the northern tip of the Island every weekend. Until Labor Day, Monday would take on a new and very different appearance. It would look like Errol Flynn, in green tights as Robin Hood, casting out the invaders, sending them scurrying back down the L.I.E. and into the city. I turned left on Indian Wells and into Amagansett.

Even the town was empty. The constant string of cars that headed towards East Hampton and Montauk on weekends was nonexistent. I had the uncommon luxury of parking any place I wanted. I took a spot near the gas station. Crossing the street, I stopped in the middle to look towards Montauk, then towards East Hampton, and couldn't spot a car for miles. Not a car in sight. It was such a pleasure that I had the urge to order breakfast and have it in the street.

Instead, I crossed over in front of Stephens Talkhouse and headed for the General Store to get a paper to read while I had breakfast.

The General Store was run by an Italian family who owned the pizza shop and the new Italian restaurant, Felicia's, at the end of the block. The oldest of the clan was the father, who was also the slimmest; he spent his time running the pizza shop, while his son, daughter, daughter-in-law, and various family members worked at different times in all three. They were rather heavy and seemed much too large for the otherwise small town.

Since the main part of Amagansett was really one block, and all three of their stores were on it, it appeared as if they ran the town. There was the Square directly across the street that consisted of small boutiques but it wasn't making a go of it. No matter what store opened there, it became another in a few weeks. If you bought shoes in Cole Hahn in June and went back in July to buy another pair, you'd probably have to settle for ice cream instead in the Haagen Daaz that took its place.

It seemed strange that the stores that couldn't make it there, when just two miles away, in East Hampton, cash registers kept ringing. The only stores that stayed were the three run by the Italian family and, of course, the famously overpriced Farmer's Market. It was situated closer to the train station and really not part of the town. It snagged most of the East Hamptonites who figured if fruits and vegetables were too expensive, they must be chic enough to eat.

The Italian son in his early thirties had a striking resemblance to John Belushi. I mentioned this to the people in the house one weekend, and from then on we referred to the entire family as the Belushis.

The Belushis liked to fight on occasion with a customer but they mostly fought among themselves. And always in Italian: very loud Italian. When I walked into the General Store, true to form, they were going at it, but this time in English. John was arguing with his younger sister about going to college. Seemed she wanted to go and he wanted her to stay where she belonged—working with the family. After a few minutes when they realized I was in the store, they switched over to Italian so I wouldn't understand what they were fighting about. I was able to understand three words, however. "Fuck" which came from John and "Albany State" that screeched out of his sister's mouth.

Along with *The Post* I picked up two local free papers. One was *The Hamp-*

tons, which always featured a beautiful girl in a skimpy bikini on the cover. It was put out only during the summer and inside there were a lot of advertisements for the local hot spots like Marrakesh, Tomatoes and Bay Street. There was the usual article on some famous artist out here for the summer or some has-been TV or movie star appearing in a summer stock production at East Hampton's Guild Hall. It was filled with photos of chic parties at the homes of some of the more famous residents. The well-known literary artists and movie people seemed to alternate weekends. One weekend there were shots of Calvin Klein's party at his place in Sagaponic, George Plimpton's home in Sag Harbor and even Allman's Fourth of July bash. Of course, none of us made the photos from the party, but Lauren Bacall, Warhol and Bianca Jagger did.

The section I liked best was called "Hot Shots." There were random photos of couples looking like they were having a great time at one of the "hot" clubs. Since all the shots were staged, the couples always looked like they were "supposed" to be having a good time and never just having a good time. They would be sitting at tables drenched in sweat from dancing which created ideal conditions for the photographer to snap women with the biggest chests. And it just so happened they were usually braless with their blouses plastered against their tits and hard nipples. I guess the paper was trying to prove only well-endowed women went to this club and were excited to be there.

The other paper was *Dan's* named after its founder, Dan. It was only a few pages long, wasn't hip and wasn't meant to be. It was filled with advertisements from local stores that were open year-round. The poorly written articles by Dan himself were noble in their intent. They dealt with the plight of local fishermen, upstanding citizens who had died during the previous week, environmental issues, or mundane local school board problems. The reality of living in the Hamptons during the summer months could be found in both papers.

I walked over to the counter to pay for *The Post*. John had stormed into the back room cursing in Italian.

His sister turned to me and smiled, "That's thirty-five cents, please." She was actually quite sweet when not dealing with the rest of the Belushis.

After breakfast I was going to go into East Hampton and check out the books in Book Hampton, but it started to rain so I headed back to the house. When I pulled into the driveway and got out of the car, I heard the phone ringing. I ran in, picked up the receiver and said, "Hello."

"Chris McCauley, please."

I didn't recognize the voice, "This is Chris."

"Chris. Hi. It's Becky Samuels."

Becky's voice sounded a little deeper over the phone. I was surprised to hear her since she wasn't supposed to be out until August and she gave me the impression that she wasn't anxious to get together in the first place.

"I didn't think you were supposed to come out until August."

"Change of plans. Anyway, I'm out but the sun isn't."

"Yeah, it's pretty dismal, but the rest of the week is supposed to be beautiful."

"That's good news."

"Where are you staying?"

"At the Dutch Motel."

"Where's that?"

"On Montauk Highway, between Amagansett and East Hampton. It's actually closer to the town of East Hampton."

"Are you with your friend?"

"Yeah. Steve is with me and I was thinking, since the weather is so lousy, why don't you come by and have a drink and then maybe we can do something later?"

"Sounds great."

"Bring your new girlfriend, too if she's out."

"This will be a solo trip. The poor woman, like everyone else who doesn't teach, has to work."

She laughed. "Why don't you stop by around five?"

"Okay, see ya later."

I was pleased she called and was interested in meeting her boyfriend. I couldn't imagine her with a boyfriend or how she looked outside of school for that matter.

I spent the rest of the day reading, watching television and then went for jog when the rain let up. I was taking a shower after my run when Walter arrived. Since I wasn't expecting him until later that night, I didn't hear him come in. Stepping out of the shower, I remembered I forgot my towel in the bedroom; I left the bathroom to get it and as I was walking down the hall, Walter who was in the room walked into the doorway. I practically jumped out of my skin.

"Hi, Chris" he said with that smile that still looked uncomfortable on his face.

"Shit, Walter!" I said the way you sound when you get the shit scared out of you.

His smile left. "Sorry, didn't mean to startle you."

My first impulse was to cover my cock with my hands, but instead I hurried past him to get my towel on the bed. For some reason, the last guy I wanted to be naked in front of was Walter. I quickly wrapped the towel around me, and as I gathered up my clothes said, "I thought you were coming out later tonight?"

"I did too," he said as I hurried past him and back to the bathroom, "but I got done with my errands sooner than expected."

Before I got out of the bedroom, I dropped my tee-shirt and as I bent down to pick it up, my towel came undone. Walter said, "oops" and although I didn't look at him, I could feel that unnatural smile spread across his face.

I just wrapped the towel around me again, and held it together with my right hand, got up and headed to the bathroom. I was pissed. Picking up the shaving cream can, I angrily pressed enough foam in my hand for three shaves. Looking at all the cream in my hand made me calm down and reason with myself. Smearing some on my face, I wondered why I was so mad at Walter?

I just wasn't sure about him. There was something strange about him that I couldn't quite get a handle on. Maybe it was his uncomfortable smile or his being very comfortable buck-ass naked the first time we met. And I still didn't like it that I couldn't call him Walt. None of my reasons were very substantial and by the time I finished my shave, I decided to give him the benefit of the doubt. However, even though he might be an okay guy, it didn't mean I had to sleep in the same room with him with three other empty bedrooms available.

Walking back into the bedroom, Walter was lying on the bed, fully clothed, reading *The Wall Street Journal*.

"Walter," I said as I went to get my wallet and keys on the dresser. I turned around as he put down the paper and looked over at me with his unnatural smile, "I was thinking. Since we have three other bedrooms, I thought I'd take one so we can each have some privacy."

He stopped smiling. Looking rather concerned, he said, "A fine idea, but let me take another room. I don't mean to force you out."

He sounded genuinely upset. I felt a little guilty about being mad at him. "You're not forcing me out. Hell, I'm going to be here most of August, so I'll take another room."

He started smiling again. "If you insist, then."

"I do."

He watched me put my keys in my pocket. "Are you going out for the evening?"

"Yeah. A colleague of mine is out here with her boyfriend for a few days. She's staying at the Dutch Motel and invited me over for a drink."

"That sounds pleasant. I have nothing to do and since I really don't know anyone out here, would you mind if I came along?"

Shit. I hesitated. "Well..."

He saw that I wasn't thrilled with his offer. "If it isn't an imposition."

How could I say no, even though he was the last person I wanted to bring along? "Sure, why not?"

"Wonderful," he said smiling broadly and sounding relieved. "Would you like me to drive?"

"No, c'mon, I'll drive," I said as I walked past his bed.

•

The Dutch Motel was no more than a few minutes away. It was next to a tiny group of stores. Since the building ran inland, I had never noticed it before. We pulled in and parked next to the office. I had forgotten to ask Becky which room she was in, so I went in to ask the clerk. A tough, unfriendly-looking woman around fifty and not very friendly said it was in the back next to the pool. I thanked her as she walked, without saying a word, into the room behind the desk. A real sweetheart.

Outside, I told Walter it was around the back. There was another building back there that wasn't visible from the street. In the middle of the two buildings was a large swimming pool. Even though it was still overcast, there were six to eight women sitting around it on lounge chairs. A few had bathing suits on. There wasn't a man in sight. I turned to Walter who was checking things out.

"Not bad," I said. "All babes."

He smiled in agreement.

I knocked on 12A, which was the last door. I heard Becky call out, "Just a minute." Hoping I wasn't early, I checked my watch to see the time. Maybe she was going at it with Steve and I was interrupting the proceedings. But it was ten after. I was okay.

In a few seconds, I heard footsteps approaching the door. Becky opened it. She had obviously just taken a shower. Her hair was combed back away from her face. She had on a tight fitting t-shirt, a short jean skirt and was barefoot. This was a different Becky Samuels than the one I knew at school. She was relaxed and comfortable. There was a warm pleasing smile on her face as she greeted me.

"Chris. Hi." She then gave me a kiss on the cheek. Another surprise.

"Hi, you look great," I said as we waked in and as she peered at Walter.

"You're just not used to seeing me this way," she said, closing the door behind us.

"Becky, this is Walter Kornbath, one of the people from the house."

"Hi, Walter."

"Nice to meet you," Walter said as he put out his hand to shake hers.

The room was L-shaped and rather large. It was your typical motel room, with a large double bed in the middle against the wall and cheap paintings on the walls. Naturally, the paintings had something to do with the ocean.

I could hear Steve in the bathroom that wasn't visible from where we stood. I was hoping he'd hurry out. I was anxious to meet him.

"I hope you don't mind my coming along," Walter said to her.

"Not at all. Glad you came."

"So, where's your better half?" I said. "I'm anxious to meet him."

She smiled. "In the bathroom."

We heard the bathroom door open and out came Steve: a slender, very attractive woman about twenty-six. She was in a pink terry cloth robe and her hair was wrapped in a towel. I almost fell over but tried not to show the slightest bit of shock, since I could feel Becky watching for my reaction. As soon as I said, "Nice to meet you," the smile on her face disappeared as she stared past me at Walter."

"Hi, Stevie," Walter said sounding like he was being forced to say it at gun point.

She greeted him coldly with, "Walter."

I forgot my own shock as I looked back at Walter, then turned to face Stevie again, then Becky. I turned to face Walter once more, and said, "You two know each other?"

Walter looking ill said, "Yes, Stevie and I were going together and recently broke up."

"Oh," I said and looked at Becky, who was looking as uncomfortable as I was feeling.

"We were going together until she met someone else."

"That must be me," Becky said sounding as if she were owning up to a theft and annoyed that she was referred to as "someone."

I didn't know who to look at. All I knew is that I wanted out of there. Stevie wasn't saying anything, just looking at Walter.

"Of course," Walter continued, "it took a month or two for Stevie to tell me as she was kept busy sleeping with both of us."

This angered Stevie. "Walter! You have no damn right to say that!"

"Perhaps," he replied then looked at Becky. "It was nice meeting you, Becky."

A tiny smile appeared on her face in acknowledgement.

"Chris, if you do not mind, I will wait in the car." Zombie like, he then turned, opened the door and walked out, closing the door quietly behind him.

Now we were three. I had never felt both so awkward and so shocked at the same time. I was bombarded with a series of emotions. I wanted to beat the shit out of Walter for asking to come here with me. At the same time, my heart went out to him for having his heart broken by this woman who I was expecting to be a man, who turned out to be the lover of my friend. I was also annoyed with Becky for not trusting me enough—Stevie could have been a woman, it wouldn't have mattered. Stevie was a woman! My head was spinning. The few minutes the three of us were sharing felt more like a few hours.

"Well," I said looking at both of them.

"Well," answered Becky.

"Hey, I'm sorry about all of this," I said awkwardly.

"It's not your fault," Stevie said, "you'll have to excuse me. It was nice meeting you, Chris." She quickly turned around and walked back into the bathroom.

As she walked away, I said, "Nice meeting you."

Becky looked uncomfortable and pained. "I'm so sorry, Chris. Rather than tell you, I thought it would be better to show you."

I reached up and gently touched her cheek. "Forget it. There's nothing to be sorry about. How could you have known I was going to bring him? Walter. *The* Walter."

She sighed.

"It's a small world and I'm finding out it's even smaller in the Hamptons," I said.

"You better go see if he's okay."

I nodded my head in agreement. "I'll check on him. We'll get together in the city, but I'll make sure to bring Patty."

"Good idea," she said as she walked me to the door then kissed me goodbye.

"Enjoy the rest of the week. It's got to go up from here. Talk to ya later."

"Take care."

I walked past the pool and knew now why there were no men around. The women looked the same but I was looking at them differently. Near the ladder at the head of the pool, a girl was sitting on a lounge chair. Another was sitting on the edge of the chair with her hand on the other's leg. They were talking quietly. I began imagining them in bed, nude, and licking each other's pussies. As they were going at each other, their faces slowly turned into that of Becky and Stevie.

Chapter
Twenty-Four

Walter was sitting in the car with his head back, resting against the seat. He didn't look good. He wasn't supposed to. I wasn't mad at him anymore. How could I be? He'd just had his guts ripped out. I'd look the same way if the characters had been changed. The thought of my going to the motel and ending up meeting Laura and her new lover would have been devastating. And what if the lover was a woman? Fuck! Poor Walter and I were comrades again.

In the car, I looked at him. "I'm really sorry this had to happen."

"It wasn't your fault, Chris."

I wanted to help him get over the catastrophe as soon as possible. What do ya say we get some brews and knock 'em back on the beach?"

"Sounds like a good idea."

As we pulled out of the parking lot and passed the Dutch Motel sign, he looked at it and said, "They should change the name of this place to the Dyke

Motel."

I stopped at Belushi's, picked up two six-packs of Rolling Rock since that was the only brand they carried, and headed to the house. Walter was silent the rest of the way.

We didn't bother going into the house; we each took a six-pack and walked out to the beach.

The day ended with a beautiful evening. The sky cleared and the sun had turned into a brilliant orange ball. It started melting and slipping down the sky until it touched the ocean. Walter opened a brew and chugged it down in one continuous gulp. He then heaved the bottle. It made a long high arch before landing past the surf. I was impressed with the heave. He began working on another as I gulped mine down and then threw the bottle with all of my might. It didn't even reach the water. I was embarrassed with my effort and said to him, "The wind," as an explanation for my poor showing, even though there was hardly a wind blowing. Walter stood mute and probably didn't notice my throw since he didn't acknowledge my weak excuse. I grabbed another then looked at the sun again. Half of it was submerged and the water around it was dyed orange as well.

Walter hadn't said much since we left the motel, but when he did it was direct and to the point. "Bitch."

We were both on our third brews. Walter was setting the pace. My second bottle, I just dropped near my feet—wanted to save myself any further embarrassment of another feeble throw. Walter, on the other hand, was impressive with his second throw, too. It went a little further than the first.

By our fourth brews, except for Walter's one word summation of Stevie's character, we still hadn't discussed what took place at the motel. I was approaching a buzz since I had eaten nothing that day except for breakfast. Bending over to get another beer, I thought I heard crying but figured it was the beer kicking in. When I straightened up, I looked over at Walter who had moved a few feet away. His back was facing me and his shoulders were shaking. He was crying. My heart sank. The poor bastard began crying loudly; he wasn't trying to hide it. I didn't know what to do. At first I thought I'd ignore it and let him cry himself out. But his shoulders were really shaking by now, so I thought I'd try to console him.

"Walter?"

His shoulders kept shaking. Gently, I placed my hand on his left shoulder. He turned, almost spun in the process, threw his arms around me and buried his face in my right shoulder. It was my day for being stunned. I stared out at the ocean, not knowing what to do with my hands, so I kept them at my sides. I also looked around to see if there was anyone on the beach watching us. I was relieved to see we were alone.

Walter kept crying. I wanted him to stop and to take his arms off me. If I consoled him, perhaps it would speed up the release of his arms. I gently began patting him on the back with my right hand and said, "Look, man, it's going to be alright. Take it easy."

It worked. He slowly stopped crying. I was relieved to feel him lift his head, but he kept it above my shoulder for a second or two, then turned and kissed my neck. I immediately pushed him backwards with both my hands, then grabbed the side of my neck and began rubbing where he kissed me. I yelled, "What the fuck was that, man?"

He looked at me as if he were confused. "What was what?"

"You fucking kissed me on the neck," I yelled, holding my hand on the spot as if I were bleeding.

"Look... Look I'm sorry," he said wiping his nose, "I thought you knew or at least understood."

"Knew what?" I yelled even louder.

"That I'm bi."

"No, I didn't. I just figured you were fucking weird. And since I'm hopelessly heterosexual, I don't like being kissed by another guy." I was getting angrier and felt like I was a victim in one of those horror movies who is tricked and bitten on the neck by a vampire. I'd probably find two holes where Walter, the vampire, stuck his bisexual fangs.

"I thought you knew," he said sounding as if he were trying to reason with me and calm me down. "Both Stevie and I are bi, we traveled in the same circles. That's how we met."

"I don't give a shit about your circles or your sex life as long as you don't cross over towards me." I had it. "I'm going back to the house." I turned, started walking quickly and continued rubbing my neck. I couldn't get the feel of his lips off it.

Walter raised his voice so it could be heard over the surf. "I wanted to tell you at Bay Street but I didn't get the chance."

"Fuck you," I mumbled.

By the time I got to the house, I felt nauseous. Too much beer on an empty stomach wasn't mixing very well with the kiss from Walter.

I ran up to the bathroom on the second floor, hopped in the shower and let hot water stream down on my neck. After about twenty minutes of water therapy, I knew I could use my nail file, but it was in my bedroom. With the kissing bandit probably down there, I wasn't about to get it. I decided to stay in Patty's room and try to sleep the evening events away.

I crawled into bed wondering how I would handle Walter tomorrow. If he were staying until Thursday, I thought I'd go back into the city. I didn't want to be in the house alone with him if I could help it. As I began dozing off, I heard the door slam.

I got out of the bed and looked down at the driveway. Walter was getting into his car with his overnight bag. He threw it in the back seat of his T-bird, started up the engine and drove off. I wasn't going to have to face him tomorrow after all.

"Thanks, Walt," I said out loud, then got back into bed.

Knowing he was gone settled my stomach. I thought back over the evening. It was one of the strangest, no *the* strangest I'd ever experienced. For some reason a Woody Allen joke about being bisexual popped into my head. He said that if you were bi, you had more chances of getting a date on Friday nights. I'd always thought it was funny. Tonight I didn't. I turned on my side, closed my eyes, and in a few seconds fell asleep.

The next morning a loud banging and rattling downstairs woke me from a deep sleep. I looked at the clock on the table near the bed, it was 6:30. More banging. I got out of bed, put on my shorts and looked out the window. In the driveway was a very large white '59 Cadillac. It looked like Ahab finally killed Moby Dick and left him in the driveway. I went downstairs.

By the front door, a black woman was fumbling with a bag, brooms, and a vacuum cleaner. She was short, very round, and in a sack dress that covered it all. On her head was a Met's baseball cap and her feet looked stuffed into sneakers that had no laces.

"Hi," I said.

I startled her. She checked me out first before a big grin pushed aside her heavy cheeks, exposing a gold cappped tooth and a black hole where a tooth was missing. "Hi, I'm Bessie Tennessee from Alabama. Who you?" She spoke loudly as if I might be hard of hearing.

"I'm Chris."

"Nice ta meet ya, Mr. Chris."

"Nice to meet you."

"Did you come in from Alabama?" I asked jokingly.

"Naw. Was born dere but because of my last name don't want nobody thinkin' "I's from Tennessee. Proud I's from 'Bama. Ha! Where you from?"

"Upstairs."

She looked puzzled. "You must be a share people."

"Yep."

"Done never met no share people in dis house except Miss Patty and Miss Donna. Dey hired me to clean da house. Day two nice young ladies. Ha."

I knew someone cleaned the house. Patty or Donna collected five bucks from everyone each Sunday to pay her. It never crossed my mind that I'd meet her.

"So you're the cleaning lady."

"Yup. Come every Tuesday. Ha."

For some reasons she added "Ha," to almost everything she said. It was her way, I guess, of giving emphasis to what she was saying.

"Well, I'll be seeing you a few more times, since I'll be out here most of the summer."

"Dat be nice. You seem like a real nice man."

"You seem real nice too." My returned compliment broadened her smile.

"Yup. I clean houses five mornings a week, den go to work in da potata house."

For a second I didn't know what the potata house was. Then I remembered I saw a factory that packed potatoes in South Hampton.

"Tha's some heavy schedule."

"Bin doin' it for twenty year. Got ta put tree kids through school. Got no man to help me. Ha."

Incredible. Here's a woman with little or no education working her fingers to the bone so her three kids can get one. "What time do you get up in the morning?"

"Bout five. Clean a house den get to the potata house by 8:30. Den work dere till six."

"Wow."

"Yup. Clean houses only in da summer. All yous share people need ya houses cleaned. I do it for da extra dollars. What do you do?"

"Teach."

"Edgecation. Dats very fine a you. A teacha." She placed her hands on her hips and kept smiling, proud of my being a teacher.

I looked out the window. She was making me feel a little embarrassed.

"You da kinda person who be guiding my babies tru school. Edgecation is the most important gift America can give its young people. Ha." After she gave me her "Ha," she looked at me seriously for a response.

"Yep. Education is very important. How old are your kids?"

"Sevon, leven and eighteen. Oldest is going to college in da fall." She smiled proudly.

"That's great. Where is she going?"

She looked down at the floor, trying to think of the name. "Damn. I never can remember dat itty bitty name." She looked up. "You must know it. It's up dere on da water."

It wasn't much of a clue. I shook my head.

"Ya know, it's dere on da water in Connecticut."

"You don't mean Yale, do you?"

She grinned. "Dat's it. Yale. It's a good one, ain't it?"

"One of the best."

"My baby been working three jobs dis summa to help me pay for her school-in' year. Da rest da school gives her."

"She got a partial scholarship?"

"Dat's right. A skull-or-ship."

"That's very impressive."

She smiled proudly. "Yup. Ain't no man to help. My man weren't no good for any kind of seaport. He'd stay home for a spell, den take off for a couple of years. Den when he'd get tired, he'd come home to rest a spell. Over da last twen-ty years, he done come home and gone so many times I lost count." She laughed. "Da last time he come home it was ta die. He had poison in da blood."

"I'm sorry."

She looked at the floor then up at me. "Gave him a real nice send off. Bought him the best box I could and suit too. Didn't want him arrivin' at da Pearly Gates lookin' da way he always did. Raggedy as all get out. He looked good laid out too. Dat man always did look good on his back if ya know whats I mean." She burst out laughing. "Well, I betta get to cleanin' dis house, soes I can get to da potata house on time. Ha."

"It was nice meeting you."

"Fine meetin' you too professa. I guess we be meetin' next Tuesday again."

"Guess so."

She leaned over to get her cleaning materials out of the bag. I went back up to Patty's room and sat on the edge of the bed. Finally, I thought, I met someone out here, besides Patty, who is real, who would never be invited to posh parties except to clean up after them; someone who never had any formal education but broke her back to make sure her kids did; a woman who kept taking back a hus-band who only came home when the world tired him out, and then showed him the respect he didn't deserve when it killed him.

I laid my hand against the pillow and closed my eyes. It was still early and I was still tired. My last thought before falling back to sleep was that Bessie Tennessee from Alabama was some woman.

Chapter Twenty-Five

"Conrad toilet paper
Is the only one to buy
Smooth, soft and sturdy
See for yourself
It's double ply.

Never settle for another brand
If your grocer doesn't have it
Take a stand.

Don't let him tell you
The tissue paper he carries is the same.
It's just a ploy
Don't settle
Conrad is the real McCoy..."

Conrad was the new toilet paper Goldstein's account group was working on. His loyalty to his client went beyond the call of duty. Not only did he bring up the subject of toilet paper on numerous occasions, one weekend he saw new rolls of Charmin in the shopping bags Patty and Donna brought back from the I.G.A. He took them out of the bags saying, "Nobody takes a dump until I get back." He ran out of the house, returned the Charmin and came back with Conrad. He put them on the kitchen table and smiling, said, "Now we can all dump again."

About 9:30 on Saturday morning, he yelled that everyone had to get up and come into the living room. I was already awake. The sun was shining by 7:00—which meant I was up for good. Even Debbie complained about the sun shining in the room as I left to sit on the porch. As usual, however, she just pulled the sheet over her head and went back to sleep.

"C'mon everybody. Wake up," he yelled. "Get in here. I want you to listen to something extremely important."

I was the first to walk in, took a seat and said: "Hope this is important, otherwise the others will lynch you."

He was holding a tape in his hand, standing next to a tape deck. "Of course it's important, or I wouldn't wake everyone."

Patty and Donna walked in wearing the large tee-shirts they had slept in. Both were yawning and looked very tired. Donna was annoyed. "This better be good, Aaron. Patty and I worked late last night and needed to sleep late this morning."

"It's important. Believe me," Goldstein said reassuringly.

Both Patty and Donna were showing a lot of leg. Their tee-shirts rode up when they sat down. Their calves pressed against the couch, flared out nicely. I thought I'd do a comparison test. Donna, I had to admit, had a good little body; her legs were formidable competition, but Patty's were a little longer and her thighs firmer. Patty won on points.

Russ came down, walked into the kitchen, and then came out with a cup of coffee and a cigarette. By coincidence, everyone had gotten out late Friday night. I had a tough time tanning on the beach that day. The sun tired me out, as it usually does, forcing me into bed by 10:00. Seeing the cigarette in Russ' hand meant one thing: Jody wasn't here. He was wearing a bright purple Hawaiian shirt, yellow shorts and his wraparound sunglasses.

"You're smoking," Donna said, making it sound more like a question.

"Jody's going to string you up by the nuts," I added.

"No she's not." He took a drag. "She couldn't come out this weekend. She had to help her mom take care of some stuff."

"Then I guess there will be less fighting this weekend," Donna noted dryly.

Russ just looked at her. Before he said anything in response, I distracted him. "Take a seat for this very important event."

"It better be. I never get up this early." He took a seat next to me.

Out of the corner of my eye, I saw Patty give Donna a little slap on the leg for the comment she'd made to Russ.

Debbie came out wearing Dr. Denton pajamas. The last time I had seen them was on my sister when she was three or four years old. These PJ's were the real thing, complete with a buttoned bottom flap over her butt. I found it strange. Not because she was wearing them, but because she only slept naked under the sheets. She was wide awake, taking a seat on the couch next to Patty. "Sorry I'm late."

"I thought this was Walter's weekend?" Goldstein asked.

Patty had been yawning. When she stopped she said to Goldstein before Debbie could answer, "It is, but he called me at work yesterday morning and said he wouldn't be out this weekend or the few others he had remaining. So I called Debbie and told her she might as well come out and use up Walter's share."

I said nothing and decided to keep my mouth shut—not even tell Patty what happened. At least not for a while.

No one seemed to care; and didn't even ask Patty any questions about why he'd given up the rest of his weekends.

Goldstein began. "Then that's everyone. As you all know, I've been working very hard on the Conrad account."

"Yeah, every time I wipe my ass I think of you," Russ said trying not to smile.

"Russ!" Patty yelled.

"Gross." Donna added disgustedly.

Debbie laughed.

Goldstein was all business, not acknowledging Russ's comment. "I knew three of you are in the same field, so you know how important jingles are."

Goldstein continued. "So would you listen to it with both your professional ears and consumer ears?"

Donna was annoyed. "Shit."

"How exciting," Debbie said. She looked excited, too.

Patty said nothing.

"I feel a little inadequate, I just have consumer ears," I added.

"Great," Goldstein said, "it's the inadequate people who buy." He turned, put the tape in and pushed play. A woman started singing:

"Conrad tissue paper
Is the only one to buy..."

Goldstein started nodding his head in time with the music. When the jingle was over, he asked anxiously, "What do ya think?"

Donna was disgusted. "I don't know. We've been listening to this kind of shit all week at Blax. I come out here to get away from it. I'm going back to bed." She got up and stomped back to her bedroom.

Goldstein watched her leave and when she was out of ear range said, "As the summer goes on she just gets sweeter." He looked at Patty. "Patty, what do you think of it?"

"I honestly think it's fine, but Donna was right about working a lot this week. I'm kind of wiped out too. Let me listen to it later and then we can talk about it. But right now I've got to get some sleep." She got up and headed for her bedroom.

"Thanks, Patty." He watched her walk out and said, "Great legs on that girl."

"I've heard worse," Russ offered before getting up and going into the kitchen.

Goldstein looked at me. I really didn't know if it was any good, but it did sound like hundreds of other jingles I'd heard over the years. "It sounds as good as any other I've ever heard."

"Not exactly a rave." He sounded depressed.

Debbie cut in enthusiastically, "I think it sounds great."

Goldstein looked at her like he had forgotten she was there and was surprised she had an opinion. "Really?"

"Yeah. It was a catchy, peppy tune, that tells you it's a real good product and never settle for anything less."

"Exactly!" Goldstein was excited. "Tell me more." He sat down next to her. It was the first time he had ever been interested in anything Debbie had to say.

I left them discussing the jingle, went into the kitchen, poured myself a cup of coffee and walked out on the deck. Russ was sitting on the railing with a cup of coffee and another smoke.

"Can you imagine that chump getting us up for that?"

"I was up." I took a seat.

He flipped the cigarette into the sand and took a deep breath. "Smell that, Chris?"

"Nope, what?"

"Freedom. Of course you wouldn't smell it. You're free."

"You must be referring to the little woman."

"Yep. Believe me, it's great being out here alone and not having her check my every move."

Any second he was going to tell me how he had to break it off with Jody.

"I gotta get out of it man. Get my hands on some new pussy."

"It's out there." I took a sip of coffee.

"What the fuck am I still doing in this thing?" He looked down at the deck floor.

"Good question."

He looked up. "What do you mean?"

"I don't know, except we know all the things that are wrong with Jody. Now what's wrong with you?" I was surprised at my question and expected him to laugh it off or tell me to stuff it. Instead he sat quietly thinking the question over.

He lowered his voice to make sure no one else would hear. It was a between-you-and-me tone. "I'm still with her because I hate being alone. In fact, I'm scared of being alone. I don't like myself enough to spend too much time with me. That's my fucking problem."

"That's not so strange."

"When I think about it, it started when I got the job in New York. I was coming from the Midwest to big and frightening New York City. Jody was after me, and she was from New York. I figured rather than do it alone, what the fuck, I'd do it with her."

"Makes sense."

"Having her around is now like a drug. It's not good for me but the thought of letting go scares the livin' shit out of me. I'd have to face the city by myself."

"Yeah, but you've been here long enough now to know what to expect."

He took out another cigarette and lit up. "I guess so. There are other emotional issues I have to address." He then took another drag and inhaled so deeply, as he was thinking, that smoke must have reached his toes. "I know too that I'd probably want a babe waiting in the wings to take over when I dump Jody."

"Wow. You really don't like being alone."

"Fucked, huh?"

"Give yourself some time to be alone first. Test the waters. See what it's like to live with you. Maybe you'll end up liking yourself after all."

"Yeah. I know. You're right. But right now I could really go for some new beaver. Real sex. I'm out here in the summer, New York's playground, and I can't get anything because I'm under surveillance. Shit. I still dream of that blow job I got from that steamer at the Laundry."

I forgot the Laundry and he was still dreaming about it. "That seems like a long time ago. Shit. It's already August 12th."

"Yeah, the summer is almost over and I haven't gotten laid yet."

"It could still happen."

He grinned. "I should talk. Look at you. You haven't gotten any either."

I was trying to be encouraging and the fucker was busting my nuts. Or maybe it was a simple case of misery loves company. But having my nuts broken made me say, "That's what you think."

Russ became all ears. "You're nailin' someone in the house, aren't ya?"

I could have named someone else who was out there but not in the house. However, I figured it was already the 12th and we only had a few weeks to go. I went along with Patty's secret all the way—so far. If I let the cat out of the bag now and she was teased, she'd only have to endure it for three weeks. I didn't see any point in hiding it any more. I answered, "Yep."

He took out another cigarette. "It's Patty." He struck a match and lit up.

I smiled. "You'd make a great contestant on Jeopardy. Chris is fucking someone in the house. Your answer please. Who is Patty?"

He smiled, took another drag and said, "I actually saw you guys through the window," he pointed with his chin to the kitchen "grab a quick kiss two weeks ago."

"And I thought we were doing a good job of hiding things."

"Good point. Why were you?"

"Patty's idea. You know. Summer romance, same house. If it didn't work out. Getting teased. Stuff like that."

"Makes sense."

"I guess."

"So how's it going?"

"Pretty good."

"How is she?"

This is the famous question guys are supposed to ask other guys when they want to know how a woman is in the sack. Of course, I was expecting it. "Great. Almost as good as me," I said and made sure not to smile.

Russ looked at me to see if I would smile. When I did he said, "She's got a great bod."

I was feeling cocky and answered as if having a great body to make love to was a common experience for me. "You think so? It's not bad, I guess."

He knew what I was doing and sort of grunted to acknowledge my comment, then added, "Do you think it will last past Labor Day?"

"Hope so."

"She seems like a real decent girl."

"She really is," I said sounding more sincere than I intended.

"What's with the other one?"

"Who, Donna?"

"Yeah. The first few weekends she was sweet as hell. Then she became bitchier and bitchier. A real sourpuss."

"Probably has something to do with the male species."

"She's fucked enough guys out here. She doesn't seem to be having any problem. Shit. I even thought about doing her. It would be a good place for me to start."

"So why don't you?"

"Not now. I've spent the past few years with a bitch, why trade her in to fuck another one? She does have a hot body, though. But I really don't like her now and it's obvious she's not enthralled with me."

"Yeah, it's too bad she's always pissed."

"It's strange she and Patty are such tight friends. Patty is always so sweet. She is sweet, isn't she?"

"Sure is."

"And then there's Donna, the perennial P.M.S. queen."

"I don't get it either."

"They say opposites attract. It must apply to friends, too."

"Maybe."

"Now that I have some breathing room this weekend, I'm going to try and talk everybody into hitting some clubs tonight."

"Shouldn't be too difficult."

It didn't take much convincing on Russ's part. Everyone wanted to party. The girls wanted to try the Laundry first since they had never been there. Except for Donna, they didn't think we guys had been there either. Donna, after sleeping the rest of the morning, woke in a better mood. And when she heard we were all going out she really cheered up. She even teased Russ, Goldstein and me in front of the girls. "I'm surprised the guys haven't been to the Laundry yet. I hear they got some hot women there."

"Hot steamers," Goldstein said under his breath.

"What did you say, Aaron?" Donna asked still smiling.

"Just that I could really go for some steamers. I love shellfish."

We spent what was left of the afternoon on the beach. And since Donna was in such a good mood, she made a lasagna dinner. She said we needed the extra carbohydrates since we'd be dancing the pounds off tonight. Of course that didn't apply to me.

I got ready early that evening so Debbie could use the bedroom to take the extra time women always need. I sat in the living room.

Russ came down with a package in his hand. "Since I knew I was going to be free this weekend, I brought a little blow to celebrate and since I'm such a sport, I brought enough for everyone." He sat at the dining room table and started cutting lines with a razor.

Goldstein came in, spotting Russ at work. "Yes! Yes! Yes!" he yelled. "We're going to have a great time. Yes indeed!"

Patty and Donna walked down both dressed in minis and heels. Goldstein looked at them and whistled. "Check out these two hot numbers. Sandwich me ladies."

Donna didn't hear him. She was too interested in Russ working on the lines. "A man after my own heart." She was excited. "Look at all the lines."

"Go easy, Donna," Patty warned.

Donna looked at her frowning. "Yes, Aunt Patty."

Debbie came in wearing a tight pink jumpsuit with purple polka dots. She had green evening gloves that reached up to her elbows and was holding a long cigarette holder. On her feet were strapless heels. She looked at Russ. "Do you have a cigarette I can borrow?"

Russ looked up from his lines. "You don't smoke."

"I need it for the holder."

"Then get rid of the holder."

"I can't. It goes with my gloves."

I pointed to her toes. "How are you going to dance in those shoes?"

"I'm not. I'll take them off as soon as Aaron asks me to dance."

Goldstein smiled. "I want the first dance to be mine."

She smiled back. "As you wish, sir."

I was waiting for Goldstein to make some wise-ass remark to her the way he always did, but he didn't. He went back to watch Russ work, then looked back at Debbie, running his eyes up and down to check her out. I guess a way to a man's heart is through a jingle. It looked like there was more than toilet paper between them.

"Okay, ready," Russ announced.

Goldstein said to Donna, "Ladies first."

"What a gentleman," she said, walked over, took the bill Russ rolled and two lines disappeared.

Goldstein and Debbie went next. Even Patty, in the spirit of things, did a line. I backed off. The guys didn't push me, they knew if I did I'd never make it out of the house. I told them I'd catch up on beers later.

Russ, Goldstein and Debbie got into Donna's car. Patty got in with me. The first stop was the Laundry. In the car, Patty said, "Hi, babe." The blow was kicking in. It was the first time I had ever seen her high and it was the first time we were alone together in the Hamptons. She was smiling and looking at me as I drove with my eyes on the road. "Did I ever tell you, I love the way you make love to me?"

"No, never."

She leaned over, stuck her tongue in my ear and began rubbing my cock. I liked her high.

Chapter Twenty-Six

The Laundry was packed. The parking lot was full and there were cars lined up on both sides of the street. We ended up parking at the East Hampton train station.

We walked in as a group or tried to walk in after some difficulty. It was so crowded we could hardly get the door open. The outside bar was also hopping. Not much had changed since the Memorial Day Weekend. Steamers were out in greater numbers, which was only natural with the summer quickly heading towards the finish line. And there were just as many gray-haired Romeos on the hunt. They all still had their brown leather skin draped in chains and stuffed in tight white outfits. Not to mention the maze of sagging tits and gray curly chest hair.

Marriage counselors should be aware of this place, I thought. All couples who are thinking about divorce should come here as part of their therapy on a Friday or Saturday night. After gazing around the room, they'd hurry home scared and immediately try patching up their differences, realizing even a bad marriage is a fate better than the Laundry.

The girls looked like our dates, so the steamers kept their distance but eyed us from behind their dark tans and thick make-up.

Patty said she felt like jumping out of her skin. She wasn't used to getting high and had never snorted anything. She needed to dance and was disappointed there was no dance floor. Even Donna didn't like the men who were staring at her. I heard her yell, over the music that was blaring, into Patty's ear, "What a bunch of losers."

Russ took orders and got us all drinks. He handed me two brews since I had to catch up to them. I chugged the first one down fast. As I tried to reach past a couple and place the empty bottle on the bar a woman in the back of me said, "Hoi," in my ear. I turned to face last Memorial Day Weekend. It was Brenda. I got nervous and looked over at Patty. She had her back to me talking to Donna. "Hi," I said, "how are you doing?"

"Foine. You're the guy who didn't get his turn. Aren't ya?" A smile spread across her face, teeth sparkling against the backdrop of her tan.

I looked to make sure Patty still had her back to me. I didn't want to have to explain Brenda. "Yeah. That's right."

Her smile disappeared. "I see ya still hangin' round with these loosahs." She pointed with her chin in the general direction of Russ and Aaron.

I guess she was still offended. "Yep."

She smiled again. "Well if ya dump them layta come see me. I'm just with my girlfriend."

I shot another quick glance at Patty. "Will do."

"Boye," she said then made her way through the crowd. Russ and Aaron didn't notice her.

I eased my way over to Patty. She turned to face me. "We gotta get out of here. My heart's pounding. I gotta dance and work out some of that crap I took."

Donna added, "Let's rock. This place sucks."

"Fine by me." I caught Russ's eye and tilted my head towards the door, to signal we were going. As I lifted my brew to finish it off, I noticed at the end of the bar a blonde ponytail on a tallish woman. I had to check it out. I put the bottle on the bar. Patty, Debbie and Donna headed for the door and I headed for the ponytail. I reached the guys but kept trying to see who owned that tail.

"Where ya goin'?" asked Russ.

I didn't look at him. "Be right with ya. Meet ya by the cars with the girls in a second. We're going to hit someplace else."

I continued my way through the crowd towards my destination. I almost knocked a drink out of someone's hand, and heard, "Hey, watch it!"

"Asshole" came next after I stepped on the foot of someone else. I said "sorry" to no one in particular. I felt like I had snorted a few lines too, the way my heart was pounding.

I finally made it. She was standing with her back to me, talking to someone I couldn't see. It was Laura. I stood there for a few moments, took a deep breath and tapped her on the shoulder. She turned. I exhaled. It wasn't her.

She didn't say anything as she searched my face to see if she knew me before offering a cautious "Hi."

"Sorry," was all I managed to get out. Turning quickly around, I made my way back through the crowd, my heart still pounding. I spotted a drink on the bar. It looked lonely. I picked it up and gulped it down and continued to the door.

Everyone was standing by the cars when I got there.

"Where were you?" Russ asked.

"Had to go to the john."

"Bullshit," Goldstein said, "you were heading towards some blonde."

"Really," Patty said. The coke was making her sound slightly more jealous than she intended.

"I had to take a leak." I tried to sound convincing but knew I didn't. "So, where are we going?"

"The Jag," Patty said. "It's only a few minutes away on the Three Mile Harbor Road."

"Great. Let's go."

"Same seats," Debbie said sounding like an excited kid.

Patty told Donna to follow us since she knew the way. In the car she seemed a little cool. I figured it was the coke. "Go down Newtown Lane," she said, "then take a left and stay to the left of the windmill. It's only about five minutes from there."

"Yes, captain," I said jokingly.

"So was it her?"

Shit. "Who?"

"What do you mean, who? Don't insult my intelligence. The woman you've been pining over. Laura."

"No, it wasn't Laura. I was just going to the bathroom and I'm not pining over her."

How the hell did she know I was pining over Laura? I thought I was hiding it from her. She knew I was lying and remained quiet the rest of the way.

The Jag looked like a square made of cinder blocks with a good size parking lot. Two big guys took the five dollar cover and stamped your hand in case you wanted to leave and come back. Your stamped hand proved you paid. Except for the restaurant in front, it looked similar to Bay Street on a smaller scale. Near the entrance was a bar, at the far end of the dance floor was a stage with a DJ spinning tunes. To the left of the dance floor were sliding glass doors that opened outside onto a patio and another bar.

Patty started jumping up and down to a Wilson Pickett song as soon as we walked in. It was just like she did at Bay Street, but with a little coke in her there was a little more bounce in her jumping. She and Donna immediately headed onto the dance floor. The place was crowded, without a steamer in sight. Walter would have loved it. There were a lot of good-looking girls and guys.

Russ brought me a beer.

I smiled and taking it said, "Good man."

"A lot of pussy here. I'm going to scope 'em out," he said.

"See ya later."

He walked to my right and got swallowed up by the crowd. I looked over toward the bar and saw Goldstein and Debbie talking into each other's ear, so they could be heard over the Temptations. Whatever they were discussing, they were enjoying themselves. It was a sight I wasn't used to. All summer he'd have nothing to do with her and when he did, it was just to bust her chops. What a difference a jingle makes.

> *"Ain't too proud to beg*
> *Sweet Darlin..."*

I looked out over the bobbing dancers and found Patty. She was dancing her cute little ass off. I took another hit from my brew, on my way to becoming pleasantly shit-faced.

Goldstein walked over holding Debbie's hand. She was holding her shoes and a cigarette holder in the other. "Will you watch these while we dance?" she asked.

"Sure, just placed them near my feet." I was beginning to slur some words and feeling so good, she could have asked me anything I would have said, "sure." I watched them walk onto the dance floor as Patty and Donna came off. Patty was smiling. Although she had been dancing non-stop, as usual there wasn't a drop of perspiration on her.

"This is my night to fly," she said before kissing me on the lips. She must have forgotten about Laura. "I'm going to the bathroom, then getting another drink. When I get back you and I are finally going to dance."

I was feeling so good, I'd even dance. "Sure."

She left me Donna who was looking a little damp around the edges from dancing. "Looks like you caught up with us, Chris."

I must have looked pretty smashed like the rest of them. "Sure," I was into one word answers now and "sure" was easy for me to get my tongue around.

Russ showed up with a cigarette and a fresh drink. "Say, Donna, want to dance?"

"No thanks," she said. As soon as she turned Russ down, a guy with short black hair and a thick beard tapped her on the shoulder. He was wearing a tee-shirt that said, "Take this. It's yours," with an arrow pointing down toward his dick. He asked her if she wanted to dance. She smiled, shook her head yes and followed him out onto the dance floor.

Russ took a drag on his cigarette as he watched them begin to dance. "Fuckin' bitch," he said before dropping his cigarette on the floor and crushing it with his foot.

Patty came back with a drink and brew for me. "As soon as we finish these, we dance." She took a sip. "Boy, am I smashed."

Russ and I answered in unison, "Me too." It made her laugh.

"What are ya drinking?" I asked her.

"Bourbon and soda."

"Sounds like it has balls," said Russ.

"It's what they call a Tennessee Tranquilizer."

"Tennessee?" I asked.

Her eyes closed as she slowly nodded her head yes.

I lifted my bottle. "Here's to Bessie Tennessee."

"Who's that," Russ asked as he lifted his glass.

"A woman I should fix you up with after you dump Jody."

Patty started giggling, "I don't think she's Russ's type."

"At least she's real," I countered.

The DJ interrupted us with an announcement he made over a song that was already playing. "Let's reverse gears and travel back through the years. It's time for the real deal. The Godfather of Soul, Mr. James Brown, singing 'I Feel Good.'"

The DJ forced the inevitable. It was time to dance, but I was drunk enough not to care. Patty took my hand and pulling me onto the dance floor, she didn't give me a chance to put my beer down. Most of what happened next was a blur. I do remember Patty bobbing up and down, spinning and waving her arms. I quickly found a move for me that worked. I simply lifted my feet as if I were walking up tiny steps. Hell, I figured that since I walked up the stairs to my apartment millions of times over years, this was a natural. I eventually got so caught up in my stair climbing that I closed my eyes. I became convinced that the other dancers were so envious of my dancing, that they were watching me trying to learn my complicated maneuvers. The "78th Street Boogie," I was sure, would spread from the Jag across the country. It would become more famous than the Hustle. All because of me. And to think I used to hate to dance.

I eventually opened my eyes. There was actually a little space around me; couples would shoot a glance at me smiling. They were obviously jealous of my dancing dexterity and the intricacies of the "Boogie." I closed my eyes again but shouldn't have. I missed one of the tiny steps I was climbing and almost fell over—crashing into a couple who caught me. Patty came dancing over and, giggling, took me by the arm and guided me off the floor. I was pretty sure I heard someone clap as we left.

Laughing, Patty said, "You're more smashed than I am. Let's get you some coffee." We walked outside and took a seat at a table. "Stay here," she said, "I'll get coffee."

I was drenched with sweat. There was a cool breeze that would pass through on occasion. It felt great. Every time it rubbed against me, it made my skin feel like I was sitting in front of an open freezer. Patty brought over black coffee for me. She didn't have one because she said the caffeine would speed her up even more.

Goldstein and Debbie, who was bare foot, came over. The first thing Debbie said was, "I can't find my shoes," sounding as if she didn't care. "I went back where I left them with you, Chris, but they were gone."

Goldstein reached up and touched her chin with a brush of a finger. "Don't worry about it. I'll buy you a new pair."

Debbie smiled sweetly, "You don't have to do that."

"Fuck. I'll buy you an entire shoe store."

Everyone was feeling no pain. Goldstein looked down at me. "That was some dance you were doing out there."

I smiled, "Thanks."

He started laughing. "Looked like you were climbing steps. Where the hell were you going?"

I just smiled.

Patty said, "Don't make fun of my little dancer." She leaned over and kissed me on the cheek. The coffee and the fresh air were clearing my head, which made me even more surprised at Patty's open display of affection in front of the others. Maybe she wasn't giving us away, the coke and booze were.

Goldstein looked at us squinting his eyes as if he were seeing us as a possible couple for the first time. "Wait a minute. How long has this guy been your little dancer?"

"Since early July." She turned and looked at me. "Who cares if anyone knows, summer's almost over anyway." It was Patty giving us away. And the coke had nothing to do with it.

Goldstein looked at me. "Nice going you sneaky bastard." He put out his palm.

I grinned and smacked it.

"You mean you guys have been going out? And you didn't tell anyone?" Debbie said surprised and excited by our secretive romance.

Patty and I nodded our heads yes.

She answered with, "Cool."

Russ came over with a drink and a cigarette going. He looked shit-faced too. Before he could say anything, Goldstein said, "Did you know these two were getting it on?"

Russ looked at us then at Goldstein. "Yeah, I did."

Goldstein was surprised. "You did?"

"Yeah. I saw them suck face in the kitchen. They thought no one saw them. Today Chris told me they were."

I looked at Patty to say I was sorry about telling Russ, but she was looking in at the dance floor, probably looking for Donna.

"Has anybody seen Donna?" she asked. Bingo.

Russ was taking out another cigarette." Yeah. She's been dancing all night with some weird looking guy."

"What time is it?" asked Debbie.

Russ looked at his watch. "2:30."

"What do you say we get goin'," she said looking around at us.

Everyone agreed it was time to leave.

Patty got out of her chair. "Let me get Donna."

We all watched her walk in and remained quietly watching the crowded dance floor. Patty returned in about five minutes. "Let's go. Donna is gonna stay and get a ride from the guy she's with."

"We all know what kinda ride," Russ said and followed it with a sarcastic

196

drunken laugh.

Patty asked Goldstein to drive Donna's car and said she would drive me and Russ since she was in better shape than either of us. I got up and wrapped my arm around Patty for more support than affection.

Chapter Twenty-Seven

All the way home Russ, who was pretty ripped, cursed out Donna from the back seat. He'd say something derogatory, then say he was sorry to Patty because she was Donna's good friend. "Could you imagine that bitch, sorry Patty, wouldn't dance with me, then dances with Charles Manson's twin brother?"

We had the windows open and the air was helping both Patty and me but was doing nothing for Russ. "She has been pissed all summer. What the hell is wrong with her? Huh, Patty?"

"She has her problems, like everyone else," Patty said.

"You are such a good friend to her. You'd never say anything against her."

"I don't like saying anything against anybody."

Russ sat up and leaned his head between us.

"Chris, you are one fucking lucky guy to have found Patty here."

I didn't answer him. There wasn't any point. I just looked over at Patty and smiled. It was strange to see her drive my Volvo.

"And speaking of fucking," Russ rambled on, "if Donna and I were the only two people stranded on a desert island, I still wouldn't fuck her. I'd rather jerk off. And after I did, I'd nail my come to the sand so she couldn't use it. Sorry I said that Patty, but I'm just telling the truth."

"I know Russ. It's okay."

When we pulled into the driveway Donna's car was parked. As soon as we entered the front door, Russ flopped on the couch. "I don't think I can make it to my room."

I turned to Patty, "I'll stay with you in your room. Donna won't be home tonight."

Patty frowned, "I'm disgusted with her. Too many guys. I'll lock the bedroom door so she can't get in." She walked into the kitchen first then came out smiling, "I'm still high. That's not the bedroom."

"See you in a few," I said, "I want to take a quick shower first." I felt like I had a salted film over my entire body from sweating so much. I was still buzzed, but pleasantly so. There was a towel I had left on my bed that I wanted to take into the bathroom with me.

I opened the door quietly, in case Debbie was already in bed. She was, but she didn't have a sheet on top of her, she had Goldstein.

Shocked, I immediately said, "Excuse me," and started to close the door, but in the process didn't hear them stop or acknowledge me. I was still drunk enough to think if they were oblivious to me, I might as well go over and get my towel.

I walked quietly around their bed. They were both grunting. I grabbed the towel and as I turned to leave, I had to take a quick look at the action. The room was bright as usual, making it easy to see. Goldstein was really drilling. Debbie had her legs bent at the knees and her arms wrapped around him so tightly it seemed she was making sure he wouldn't roll off. In between grunts, she kept saying, "That's it. That's right. That's it..."

I never heard anyone screw before. I found it a turn-on and, surprisingly, somewhat humorous. Humorous because, I reasoned, I wasn't laying any pipe. I walked out, took one last look then quietly closed the door.

The shower felt great. I still had a nice buzz and the sight of those two screwing had inspired me. I was ready for Patty.

She was naked, lying on her side and facing the wall when I entered the bedroom. I climbed in next to her, kissed her back then slowly ran my hand along her hip before reaching over to rub her nipple. She moaned and whispered, "I don't have my diaphragm."

I interpreted this to mean she didn't want any sex tonight. Before I could feel disappointed, she reached back and slowly stroked my cock.

She whispered again. "There's baby oil on the night table."

Something was going to go on after all. My spirits lifted. I turned on my back and reached for the bottle. The bed shook as she got on her knees. She then took the bottle from my hand, squeezed some oil in the palm of her hand, rubbed both hands together and then slowly applied the oil. Her right hand slipped up and down my cock, around the head, which sent tiny shocks through my entire body. I had been watching but let my head fall back against the pillow during the shock treatment. I closed my eyes as her left hand circled and gently squeezed my balls. I thought this would continue until her hand slid and squeezed me into a frenzy and made me come.

After a few seconds she stopped and whispered, "Get on your side," as she got on hers with her back facing me again.

I wasn't sure what she was up to and the oil felt so good, I hated for her to stop. I reluctantly got on my side and put my arm around her waist. I thought the fun was over and she wanted to sleep. When she nestled her ass against my cock, I closed my eyes thinking she was just getting comfortable. In a few seconds she moved her ass away from me, reached back and began feeling my hard-on as if she were feeling it for the first time. She even tilted it down, placing it between her cheeks, resting the head against her anus. Things clarified in a hurry. She wasn't feeling my dick like she had never felt it before. She was measuring it. Would it fit? She wanted me to go somewhere I had never gone before, with her or anyone.

The idea of having anal sex had never crossed my mind, because it never crossed my mind with Patty or anyone else. I assumed it would be too painful. The few women I discussed it with I wasn't sexually involved with. They all said it never appealed to them because of the pain factor. Even a few of my guy friends wanted no part of it. My brother once said, "Stay out of there! Why do you think God, in His infinite wisdom, created pussy?" However, I always found the idea titillating, never thinking I'd ever get the opportunity.

I started pressing the head of my cock against her anus; it felt like an impossibility but the possibility of getting inside kept me going. To help matters, I leaned over for the oil, squirting it on my cock. Patty reached back smearing it, basting it for me then guided it until the rest was up to me. Slowly, I started to push, stopped then started again with a little more pressure. I was going to stop, afraid that I might hurt her, just when her ass began to open. I stopped once more, closed my eyes to concentrate, to feel her ass encircle the head of my cock.

She began taking short rapid breaths as I pushed a bit more and when she moaned I slid in all the way up to my balls.

Patty immediately reached back to grab onto my thigh so I wouldn't move. My face was buried in her hair against her neck; I found myself taking short rapid breaths, fighting for air with her. Gasping, I tried to kiss the side of her face but ended up kissing her ear. A few seconds later I began to move; she tensed, tightening her grip on my thigh. I waited a few more seconds then slowly started again. Her body began to relax, her grip loosening on my thigh. Feeling her body give in forced me to relax too. I began breathing normally as I stroked my way into a smooth rhythm.

It felt better than any pussy: tight, virgin. Patty started using it like it was a pussy. Moaning, she began pushing it up against me so I could go deeper.

When I stopped she took over, moving her ass back and forth as she continually moaned. The tightness of her ass had taken its toll on my balls. At this rate I was going to come any second. I breathlessly told Patty it was getting near that time. She began panting loudly moving her ass faster to help matters along and coaxing me on, "C'mon, c'mon, c'mon." That last "C'mon" did it. My body stiffened. Tightening my grip on her shoulder, I exploded, groaning so loudly I was sure the others in the house heard me.

We both laid there exhausted before I eased out of Patty and turned over on my back. I felt like my entire body had just been shattered. The only thing I could say was, "I think I'm still alive."

Patty turned on her side to face me, placed her hand on my chest, sliding it slowly over the sweat I was drenched in again. "I'm glad," she whispered. "That means we can do it again soon." She kissed me on the cheek before closing her eyes. Within minutes I was asleep.

I began dreaming that I was swimming for my life way off shore during a storm. Behind me in the distance was the beach. The only house was ours, silhouetted in black against a purple sky. Ahead of me was a large ocean liner also silhouetted in black with a spotlight on its name. Between the ocean liner and myself was a life boat. In the front of it Laura was sitting with both her hands clutching only its sides. She looked panic stricken and was trying to keep from capsizing. In the back, Patty was leaning over the side with her arm stretched out, hoping that I'd be able to swim close enough for her to help me on board. Laura started yelling, "Let him go! Let him go! He'll make us capsize!"

The more I swam, through the turbulent waves, the further away they seemed. I kept swimming and after what seemed like years, Patty's hand was within reach. One more wave washed over me before I lifted my tired hand out of the water and grabbed Patty's. Laura was screaming while Patty helped me into the boat. Once I got myself onto a seat, I looked at Patty to thank her but she was gone. In her place was Bessie Tennessee. I was confused. Where had Patty gone? But I was grateful to be on board.

"Youse lucky I was able to reach ya. Ha!" Bessie said over the noise of the storm.

"Thanks so much, Bessie."

She started laughing and Laura kept screaming. I went to turn and tell her to stop, that we'd be fine just, as a large wave crashed over us. When I opened my eyes my heart was racing.

I looked around the room and at Patty sleeping next to me. It was just a dream. I was relieved, but why could I still hear Laura screaming? I listened more intently. It wasn't Laura but someone was screaming. It sounded like it was coming from the next room. I got out of bed to investigate. As I was putting on my pants, Patty woke.

"Who's yelling like that?" she asked without opening her eyes.

I walked towards the door. "That's what I'm going to find out."

The yelling was coming from Russ's room. The voice belonged to Jody. "You damn pig! You have to fuck every guy you meet don't you!"

"Fuck you!" another woman screamed. It sounded like Donna. "Who the fuck are you? His mother? No wonder he's sick of fucking you!" The thumping of footsteps followed. Donna came out of the room, naked holding her clothes in front of her. She stomped past me looking very pissed and not looking at me. She stormed into Patty's room and slammed the door.

It looked like Russ finally got some new pussy and was caught by his old one. Though I didn't get it. Donna didn't care for Russ, but under the right weather conditions it seemed like she was capable of bumping just about anyone. It was Russ I didn't understand. He made it quite clear that he couldn't stand her.

It sounded like Jody was having a one-way screaming match—I couldn't hear Russ's voice. Since I couldn't go back into Patty's room and couldn't just stand in the hall, I decided to go down and make some coffee. Their bedroom was on the way. I told myself: don't look in – but I couldn't help myself. The yelling had stopped because Jody was sitting at the edge of the bed crying. Russ was sitting up in bed, bare-chested with the sheet pulled up to his waist. We looked at each other for the brief moment it took for me to pass-by. At the bottom of the stairs, I heard their door close.

Goldstein was standing in the kitchen wearing a pair of running shorts that looked familiar, drinking a cup of coffee. He greeted me, "Morning."

"Hi."

"Made coffee."

"Great." I went to get a cup.

"Can you tell me something?"

"Yeah. What?"

"Where the fuck was all that screaming coming from," he took a sip, "and who the fuck was screaming?"

Pouring a cup, I told him what I knew. "It seems Russ was sleeping with Donna, and it looks like Jody came out early this morning..."

"Holy shit. She *caught* them?"

"Looks that way."

"I don't get it. I thought those two didn't like each other. Of course, lately it seems she doesn't like anybody, but I thought he couldn't stand her."

"That's what I thought."

"What's going on up there now?"

"When I walked by Jody was sitting at the edge of the bed crying. She and Donna had just gone at it, and she had finished screaming at Russ who was sitting up in bed."

"Where's Donna?"

"In her room with Patty."

We sipped our coffee quietly for the next minute or so probably thinking the same thing.

"Ever get caught with your pants down?" he asked gingerly.

"Naw." I made it sound like I've never been that stupid.

"Me neither. Well...Russ has been wanting to dump Jody, so this should do it."

I wasn't so sure but agreed. "Guess so."

"We better get our asses to the beach soon. Things will be pretty uncomfortable around here today until Donna or one of the other two leave."

"It looks like our little summer home is disintegrating before our very eyes," I said.

"There might just be the four of us out here next weekend."

"Maybe."

"By the way, thanks for letting us use the room last night," he said.

Speaking of strange bedfellows. "Yeah, I was going to ask you about Debbie."

"I'm sorry. I should have told you. She's a great lay." He grinned and put out his palm.

I didn't smack it. "I didn't mean that."

He kept his palm out. "Okay, but don't leave me hangin'."

I smiled then smacked it.

"Thanks."

"What I meant was you couldn't stand her either."

He looked down into his coffee cup. "Sometimes I'm a jerk." He looked up smiling. "Don't agree with me."

Smiling again I said, "I won't."

"I figured she was an airhead. You know, the way she dresses and calling herself an actress when she's still waiting for her shrink to give her the fucking green light to go on auditions. Then yesterday when she discussed the jingle with me, I realized she wasn't such an airhead after all. From there we got into some heavy topics. She's actually quite bright and very sweet. Last night when she came out in her usual goofy outfit, it sort of all came together. I thought she looked kinda pretty, sexy." He shrugged his shoulders and lifted his eyebrows. "Go figure."

"Makes sense to me."

"On a very basic level I needed to get laid. Everything else turned out to be a bonus." He picked up the coffee pot and poured some into my cup.

"Thanks."

He poured himself another cup. "I've finally got to stop being so critical of women, or of people in general for that matter. Shit. When I'm honest with myself I'll admit I'm no Cary Grant."

"That's okay. Nobody is. I recently read where Cary Grant said even he isn't Cary Grant."

He looked into his cup again. "Guess I still have a lot of work to do on myself."

"Yeah. We all have to work on ourselves..."

"Anyway, enough of this serious shit. It's not good for my health." He walked over to get a clean cup from the cabinet and poured coffee into it. "I'm going to bring this into Debbie. She's going to love me for this. Breakfast in bed." He giggled. "I'll see you on the beach."

"See you there."

Walking towards the bedroom door, he stopped, turned to me and said, "Thanks again for letting me use the room."

"It wasn't much of a sacrifice since Patty wanted us to stay in her room. But you're welcome."

He started to giggle again. "Tell you one thing, there was a lot of fucking going on in this house last night."

"We certainly did our part." As he turned, walked to the door and quietly opened it, I recognized the new running shorts he was wearing. "Hey," I called in loud whisper, "those are my running shorts."

He looked down at them, turned to look at me and whispered back, "Oh yeah. Thanks. I knew you had good taste but they're a little tight around my balls."

Before I could answer, he hurried in and closed the door.

Chapter Twenty-Eight

I was still in the kitchen drinking coffee when Patty walked in. I greeted her with, "Hi. I was just going to come and knock on your door to see if you wanted to come out to the beach."

She looked upset as she got two cups out of the cupboard and filled them with coffee. "I don't think I want to sit in the sun today. I have some work I want to go over with Donna, and since she won't come out of our room until the coast is clear, I'll work with her in there."

"She's hiding out, huh?"

"I'm pretty much fed up with her antics. I can't believe she went after Russ. She really fooled me with that one."

"Surprised the shit out of me."

"She kept telling me how she couldn't stand him."

"Well, I didn't think he was interested either."

"Do you know how many different guys she's brought home over the past

206

few months?" She didn't give me the time to answer. "Some of them I wouldn't go near with a ten foot pole."

"If any resemble Felix da Cat, I've got a pretty good idea of what they are like."

"I've talked to her over and over about this. She agrees with me, tells me I'm right, then brings home another guy a few nights later. She won't go to a shrink because she doesn't believe she's hurting herself."

She had never told me Donna was bringing home most of the NYC male population. If Donna wanted to hurt herself or worse, that was her business, but she was jeopardizing Patty's safety, as well.

Now I was concerned. "It's not safe for you if she keeps bringing home strangers to fuck."

Patty looked pained. "Don't you think I know that?"

"If she doesn't stop and if I were you, I'd move out."

She took a sip of coffee. "That's my next step."

"Stupid bitch."

"Chris," she said exasperated and sounding even more annoyed with me, "I hate that word."

"Sorry."

We stood in silence for a few moments. I felt like going upstairs and beating the shit out of Donna, even though I knew I'd never hit her, and basically had never hit anyone in my entire life, except for the usual sibling tussles with my brothers when we were growing up. Besides, what good would that do, I reasoned. She was in enough pain, a junkie injecting herself with come. Cock was just her drug of choice. And, I guessed, like any addict she was in her denial stage, not giving a damn about who she hurt.

"I was thinking," Patty said, "that I'd stay out here tonight and have dinner with you. I really don't feel like going back with her."

"Great. Maybe we can go out to Montauk for dinner if you like."

"That sounds good to me, but I can only stay if I can make the 7:03 tomorrow out of Amagansett. Would you mind getting up that early and driving me?"

It was music to my ears. I'd get another night with her and we'd have the house to ourselves. "Of course not."

"Great." She picked up the other cup. "I'm going to bring this cup to her and do some work."

"I guess Russ and Jody are still in their room."

"Yeah. I heard them, or I should say I heard Jody crying as I passed the door. Poor thing." She shook her head back and forth and frowned before giving me a quick peck on the lips. "See you later."

I watched her walk out. Her tee-shirt fell an inch below her ass. In all the excitement this morning, I forgot that I had been working an inch higher than where that shirt ended. A buzz went off in my balls.

I looked at my watch. It was 10:30. I figured I'd go out to the beach, but first I'd go get my swimsuit in my bedroom. Just before I went to knock on the door, I heard the bed squeaking and heavy moaning. There was no point interrupting. I had shorts on, they'd do just fine.

In the living room was someone's towel and lotion. I grabbed them and headed for the beach.

The beach was empty except for an older couple reading a newspaper under an umbrella. There was a haze covering the sky like thin nylon that the sun was trying to burn away, but so far didn't have the necessary heat to do the job. A cool breeze, with a hint of September in it, came in off the ocean that was extremely calm, its surf gently licking the shore. I spread my towel out, put some oil on and lay down. I was surprised to find I was still rather tired. In a few minutes after closing my eyes, I was sound asleep and no doubt snoring.

Two little kids playing nearby woke me. I propped myself up on my elbows. I had no idea how long I was out. The beach was still rather empty. There was a young couple who seemed to be the owners of the kids who woke me, a girl who was by herself and doing some kind of yoga on her blanket, and two guys in lounge chairs working on some beers. In the distance, Atlantic Avenue beach seemed to be filling up. Looking over my shoulder to see if anyone was behind me, I spotted Debbie heading in my direction. As usual there was no way I could have missed her. She was wearing Dr. Denton's pointed sunglasses and was shaded by the pink umbrella she held over head.

"Hi, Chris."

"Debbie," I said smiling, "The bedroom is back at the house."

"Stop making fun of me," she said playfully. "Wearing this is a stroke of genius. You know how I hate the sun. These even cover my feet." She lifted her right foot to show me for emphasis.

"Sit," I playfully demanded.

She plopped down next to me.

"Where's Aaron?" I asked.

"You mean my guy," she said, tilting her head to peer over her glasses.

"Branded him already, did ya?"

"Why not? I haven't branded a guy in quite some time. And to answer your question, sir, he'll be down in a few minutes."

A beach ball that the two little kids were playing with rolled next to her. She picked it up and threw it back to them. They both yelled, "Thank you."

"Aren't they adorable?" she gushed.

I lifted my head to watch them run away with the ball. I wasn't so sure they were adorable, so I just laid my head back to face the sun.

"Isn't it cool how everything turned out?" she said.

"What do ya mean?"

"You and Patty getting together and now Aaron and myself."

"Together" was a loose term. What did it really mean? I wondered how long "together" meant. A few weeks, a month, a weekend or did it mean until Labor Day? I wanted her reaction to the other couple who got "together."

"You're forgetting Russ and Donna getting together," I noted.

My comment made her gasp, "Can you believe it? That Donna is something else."

"She sure is."

"Who ever thought those two would get together?"

Now "together" meant something else again.

"I thought," she said sounding very perplexed, "that they didn't like each other."

"That's what I thought."

"And then to be caught by Jody. The way she was yelling. The betrayal she must have felt. Poor thing."

"That's what Patty said."

"What's that?"

"Poor thing."

"Oh. It's just part of the universal sisterhood. When a sister gets hurt we all feel for her."

"How would the sisterhood respond to Donna's actions?"

She thought for a moment. "Someone who is mixed up, I guess."

"How convenient. I guess the sisterhood knows how to take care of its own."

She picked up a tiny pebble pretending to be mad at my comment and threw it at my legs. She missed. "Don't be a wise guy."

"If you promise not to stone me."

She smiled. "What a surprise to find out that you and Patty have been together."

"Only because she wanted to keep things quiet but not as big a surprise as you and Goldstein."

"It is a surprise for me, too. I mean I was interested in him, but at the beginning of the summer I was more interested in you."

"The better man won." But she didn't seem to hear what I said.

"I found him cute, not in the handsome sort of way but in the way he acted. Besides looks aren't that important and let's face it, I'm no Liz Taylor." She looked at me for my reaction.

I made some quick adjustments on the reply I gave to Goldstein. "I recently read that Liz Taylor said that even she isn't Liz Taylor."

She smiled appreciatively. It worked. "Although," she went on, "he was kind of a wise guy with me. Never took anything I said seriously. Some of the things he said were downright rude, but something inside me told me he didn't mean it."

"I wanted to reassure her. "I'm sure he didn't mean it." I thought I'd throw in a little bullshit too. "He was just playing hard to get."

"I realized the best way to get to him was through his work since he is so obsessed with it. The jingle was the opening. Then we just talked about a lot of things. I guess he thought I was a bit of a ditz but found out otherwise. Last night it just all came together." There was that word again.

Debbie had a childlike innocence about her that was actually appealing. I could see Goldstein really going for it, since he had some of that innocence himself. I was glad they (dare I say it) got together.

She took off her sunglasses, "Aaron really is a wonderful guy you know."

I could see by the look on her face that if I ever doubted it, I should put those doubts to rest. "I know he is." Out of the corner of my eye I saw Goldstein walking towards us. Now I really thought he was a wonderful guy since he wasn't wearing my new running shorts. "Speak of the devil."

"Hi," he said then bent down to give Debbie a kiss under her umbrella.

"I could kiss you all day," she said sounding like she meant it.

"Don't let me stop you, babe, or should I say, baby. You have your Denton's on," he said smiling.

"Do you want me to take them off? I have my bathing suit under it."

"No, leave 'em on. I know how much you hate the sun. Not only that, you look cute in them."

"You're sweet."

Before he could answer, I jumped in. "Are Russ and Jody still in their room?"

"I didn't see Jody, but I saw Russ as I was leaving. He didn't look good. He was dressed and had his overnight bag packed."

"Did he mention anything about what happened?"

"Since he didn't bring it up, I didn't ask. He did ask where you were though.

I told him you were down here." He turned to Debbie. "Want to go for a walk?"

"Okay," she said, sounding excited.

He took her hand to help her up. "See ya later, Chris."

"See ya later." I watched them walk away. They passed the older couple who were still reading the paper. The husband looked at Debbie as she and Goldstein walked by, went back to his paper, then shot another look at Debbie, no doubt. He turned to say something to his wife who looked up from her paper in their direction. They both smiled at each other before going back to their reading.

I guess I was feeling protective of Debbie, or I was used to the way she dressed, but I felt like saying to the older couple, "What's so funny, she just hates the sun. And she's smarter than we are! We'll probably end up with skin cancer."

I watched Debbie and Goldstein walk down the beach until they were spots. Debbie was quite sweet even if she did dress weird, and Goldstein was a good guy and basically harmless. I was glad they got together whatever the hell that word meant.

"Well, I'm still alive."

I jumped and looked up. It was Russ. I was busy thinking about Debbie and Goldstein and hadn't heard him walk over.

"Sorry, didn't mean to scare ya." He had on a short sleeve shirt, shorts and loafers.

"That's okay. Doesn't look like you're dressed for the beach."

"Nah. We're going back to the city." He sat down in the sand and stared out at the ocean. "Can you believe all that bullshit this morning? Sorry about the screaming."

"All you have to do for me, if you wouldn't mind, is answer two questions that should pretty much clear things up."

"Shoot."

"I thought you couldn't stand Donna and what the fuck was Jody doing out here? I thought she wasn't coming out the entire weekend."

"You're right, I can't stand Donna, but that doesn't mean I can't stand her body. I always thought she had a hot little bod."

I had to agree. "I agree with you there."

"When we got in last night I was pretty ripped."

"I know, you kept telling us how you couldn't stand Donna."

"After I crashed on the couch, I think you guys went upstairs, I just conked out. Then around four o'clock, I'm not sure, the door opens and Donna comes in. She was pretty ripped too and pissed about the guy she was with. For some reason she said he turned out to be a dork. Then she wanted to know why I was still on the couch and wasn't it a shame that we both weren't getting laid. I was still kinda drunk, laughed and said there's always me, not thinking she'd take me up on it. When I got up to go upstairs, she just followed. I thought she was heading into her room but she followed me into mine. I told her I was just kidding but the next thing I knew we were sucking face."

"You defenseless baby."

He smiled. "What can I say? That's how it went down. Besides you know I've been needing new pussy."

As a male, I had to ask the mandatory question. It was expected. "So, how was it?"

"Great. I didn't have to do much, she did it all and then some. The woman's an animal. When I was about to come, she made me shoot in her face, then smeared it into her skin. She said there's a lot of protein in semen and good for the skin. Is it true?"

"I've read that somewhere." No wonder her skin has a healthy glow. "So was it worth it?"

"After I came it was."

"Even with Jody finding out? And what is she doing here?"

"Shit," he said disgustedly, sounding like this was the part of the story he wanted to forget. "Her mother started to feel better and since she missed me so much, she thought she'd come out this morning and surprise me."

"Did she ever."

"It's not that she missed me, it's more like she fucking doesn't trust me to be alone for an hour."

"Of course she was wrong," I said with a wise-ass grin.

"C'mon. This was a first."

"Just kidding."

"So we're sleeping then jolted awake by Jody standing in the doorway screaming. At first I thought it was a nightmare until Donna started yelling back and stomped out of the room. There I was under the sheet buck-ass naked. The funny thing was I couldn't say anything, what was the point? I was caught with my pants off. All I kept wishing was that I had a gun so I could shoot her, just so she'd stop yelling. You don't know, but when she yells, nothing can shut her up until she runs out of steam."

"Yeah, she was breaking a few windows."

"Ya know, the funny thing is I almost have her believing we weren't doing any fucking."

"Are you kidding?"

"Nope. I told her we were all drunk or stoned last night, and Donna just ended up in the wrong room. I didn't even know she was in bed with me. Even if I wanted to have sex, I was too drunk to do anything."

"And she's buying that?"

"Yep."

"Tell her I have some swamp land I want to get rid of."

He sort of smiled at my comment.

Then I said, "Ya know you've been waiting to get out of the relationship. You might use this as some kind of opening."

He thought for a second. "No. This wouldn't be the right opening."

I was beginning to think there'd never be a right opening for him. "Yeah. You're probably right. So I guess you guys won't be coming out next week."

"That's what you'd think. But no. She said she didn't want that slut to ruin our last two weekends and since we paid for them, we should come out."

I was surprised. "Should make for an interesting two weeks."

"I gotta get goin'. We're taking the 2:25 back to the city, he said getting up and brushing the sand off his butt. "Anyway, see ya next week." He leaned over to shake hands.

"See ya." I laid back down and closed my eyes when I heard Russ call me. I sat up and turned to look in his direction.

He was walking backwards as he yelled, "It was worth it," then turned and hurried over the dune.

Chapter
Twenty-Nine

Patty and I couldn't decide what we wanted to eat but we knew we wanted to eat it in Montauk. There were very few good restaurants in the area and strangely enough the fish houses were mediocre at best. The fish portions they offered were usually rather small and bland tasting. It made you wonder how badly depleted the surrounding waters actually were. The plight of the once thriving commercial fishing business was well chronicled in the local papers and from time to time, the city papers. Families that had been fishermen for centuries had been calling it quits. Factory pollutants and oil spills hadn't helped matters.

The biggest catch now were tourists who were taken on excursion boats; blues and bass still seemed plentiful. And there always seemed to be enough sharks to go around. On occasion *The Post* would run a picture of some guy grinning next to a few hundred pound shark that was hanging upside down from a chain. Underneath the photo the caption would say how many hours it took the guy to haul him in. I hoped one day there'd be a photo of one of these guys hanging upside down from a chain and a shark standing next to him grinning and holding onto a can of beer. *The Post* would probably run that photo on the front page with the caption, "Shark Lands 250 Pound Man After Four Hour Struggle" But there were still commercial fishing boats and fishermen who worked the water, taking from it whatever they still could.

Twenty-seven stretched like a piece of masking tape from Amagansett, between Napeaque and the ocean, until you could take Old Montauk Highway. It always felt like the flattest area of the island. The restaurant Lunch, sitting on the oceanside, was always packed, and even Sunday nights were no exception. Neither of us felt like waiting for an hour or two before getting a table. Across from it was the Inn at Napeaque. Patty told me she ate there once; the food wasn't very good and it was rather expensive. Two good reasons in my book not to set foot in there. A few clam stands along the way didn't appeal to us either.

A little further on was the Sun Downer that always looked like a motel to me. This time, however, we both noticed a wooden plaque which said "Condos" hanging under its neon sign.

"Could you imagine buying one of those? They're so small! It was definitely a motel in a previous life," Patty said.

"Without a doubt, but now that its come back as condos creates a strong argument for reincarnation."

Patty looked at me and smiled.

When the highway split, I always took Old Montauk Highway because it was, as the sign pointed out at the entrance, the scenic route. Here the road dipped and rolled like the waves it ran parallel to. Ocean views peeked between houses that were built on the bluff. The homes on the left side of the road were built on hills or stilts so they all had great vistas. When we passed Gurney's, a well-known resort that was only partially visible from the road, Patty suggested we might stop there for a drink later to watch the sun set. But we still hadn't decided where to eat.

Entering Montauk, Patty said, "I know where we can eat. Shagwon's. It's a local fish place right up the road."

"Sounds good to me. Let's do it." I was glad she had come up with a place. I was starving.

Montauk is a blue-collar town with nothing hip about it. Here you see families strolling along the streets, hair piled high on young women, bleached by a hair dresser and never the sun; tank tops on their boyfriends—young Sylvester Stallone look-alikes with small gold crosses hanging from chains around everyone's necks. It's Queens and Brooklyn on vacation spending a weekend or a week in the affordable motels that cluster along the ocean.

Shagwon's was an old building in the middle of the street, almost lost among some delis and gift shops. The front door led into the bar; it was dark and filled with locals. An exhibition football game flickered silently from a TV over the bar. The men were fishermen, the women, their wives or girlfriends. They all seemed to be talking fish, weather or sports. The guys were lean in tee-shirts, baseball caps and jeans. Their skin was weathered, workmen's leather. Their accents were different from anything heard in the city or the rest of the Hamptons. Perhaps after a man had fished for years, it's just the sound of the ocean that has dried in his throat.

The restaurant was in a room to the right of the bar. It, too, was dark, rustic, with a white tin ceiling that you find on occasion in very old buildings. On the walls were old photos of how Montauk looked during the early part of the century. Basically stark, windswept, and desolate. There were also photos of Bill Fisher, who I had read about once in Dan's Papers.

Fisher was a millionaire, who in the early twenties decided he wanted to make Montauk a resort as popular as Miami had been at the time. The Miami of the North. There were photos of the Montauk Hotel under construction. It's a big Tudor building on a hill you can see when you drive out to the docks. It's empty now and has been for years, so is a strange building in the center of town near the lake. It resembles the hotel, but it's a narrower six or seven story structure. Over the years it has become a town landmark.

Fisher also wanted to build canals. Although he didn't complete them, he did build the lake before the crash of '29 wiped him out and ended any further building. The only building he constructed that is still thriving is the Montauk Yacht Club. They'll come back as condos. If I stayed out here long enough, I actually could believe in reincarnation.

Our dinner was delicious. The chowder we had was thick, creamy and full of clams. My cod was tasty and, more importantly, there was a lot of it. Patty said her stuffed flounder was great. All through dinner, however, Patty was relatively quiet. I figured she was still upset about Donna.

Over coffee I said, "You've been kinda quiet tonight."

"I guess I have been."

"Don't worry so much about Donna. She'll come around."

"I'm not worried about her. I guess I'm just tired. We didn't get much sleep last night."

"That's true."

"Let's get the bill, then how about driving out to Gosman's and watch the sunset? It's more casual than Guerneys."

"Okay, I'll get the check so we can get going."

Gosman's sits at the mouth of the Montauk Harbor overlooking Long Island Sound. It actually resembles a big garage; the side doors slide up so its large dining room, except for the roof, becomes an open terrace. You can eat and watch a variety of boats come in and out of the harbor. The restaurant is nuzzled next to a square stuffed with a tourist trap of shops. The fish Gosman's serves is, again, mediocre, but thousands of people who come there basically eat up the scenery.

We parked in the lot across the street from the restaurant, then walked out on the large breakwater that runs alongside the mouth of the harbor. I had never seen a sky so beautiful, vibrant with deep orange and red streaks against a blue expanse. I put my arm around Patty's shoulder. I had expected her to put her arm around my waist, but surprisingly she kept her hands in her pockets.

We stayed until the sky grew darker and the day faded, then got back into the car and headed home.

Patty remained quiet until we got close to Amagansett. "I know what," she said excitedly, "let's go skinny-dipping."

The thought of jumping in the ocean naked and at night didn't do much for me. I remembered that the ocean was pretty calm earlier in the day but I still wasn't thrilled with the idea. "It sounds like fun but the ocean was really rough today."

"I don't mean the ocean. I never swim in the ocean."

"Don't you need water to go skinny-dipping?"

"Funny. We'll go to Acabonic Harbor. The water is always calm and warm."

The idea still didn't make my top ten but she was depressed, and calm and warm made things more palatable. "Okay, how do we get there?"

We took the first right before the Amagansett train station. Patty couldn't remember the name of the road, but it's a small beautiful stretch that runs between a golf club and a field before it twists and turns through a wooded area. Where it forked we went right. Within minutes the road became a narrow strip bordered on both sides by water. Houses lined up also on both sides of the road. They stood on stilts for protection against high tides that might wash in beneath them and, no doubt, over the road as well.

The road ended at a small beach that faced a channel connecting the small portion of the harbor to the right with the bay itself on the left. Across the channel, which even I could reach if I threw a rock, was another small beach and a road. It seemed to be a continuation of the road we were on. The channel looked like it cut the road in half. We got out of the car.

Patty was excited. "Isn't it beautiful?"

It certainly was, and I was glad she was no longer down. There were millions of stars and although the moon wasn't entirely full, it looked pretty happy the way it was grinning up there. If I had to go skinny-dipping, this was the night to do it.

Patty started getting undressed. "C'mon. Get your clothes off."

I began to unbutton my shirt. The beach was rather rocky. Patty walked gingerly toward the water. It made her ass shake. I kept my eyes on it until I climbed out of my BVD's.

She waded into the water, dove in, then came up with her head tilted back to keep her hair off her face. "It's incredible," she yelled.

"I'm glad it's incredible," I yelled as I made my way over the rocks, "but is it warm?"

"Like a bath."

I dipped my foot in to test things first. It was warm. No problem. I closed my eyes, dove in and swam to Patty.

She put her arms around my neck and gave me a quick kiss. "Isn't this great," she said still excited.

"Sure is."

She let go and swam out into the bay.

I couldn't get over how warm the water was. I hadn't been able to get in the ocean, except for the time I went after Goldstein, because it stayed so cold. I began doing a leisurely breast stroke towards Patty who was a few yards away, and enjoying the surge of freedom that came over me from swimming naked.

The water was so calm that it reflected the stars. They looked like they were floating on the bay. As I swam I fantasized that I was swimming through the sky, bumping into the stars from time to time. Astronomers seeing me through their telescopes would, of course, think my cock was the Big Dipper. I made myself laugh at the thought, gagging on the water I swallowed in the process. Then they'd think I was some newly discovered star formation and end up naming me the McCauley Constellation.

Patty who was still a few yards away turned towards me. "Wait there." She then dove under.

I stopped swimming, floating for a few seconds on my back then righted myself up and looked to see if she surfaced. She should have come up by now, I thought. At that moment, the opening scene in Jaws flashed through my head. I immediately bent my knees, pulling my legs closer to my chest. Didn't want to attract any shark that might be nearby and it was a good thing my cock wasn't any Big Dipper. I got more nervous, turning myself around looking for her.

"Patty," I yelled. No answer. "Patty!" I yelled even louder this time. My heart was starting to beat rapidly. Where the fuck was she? I dove under knowing I wouldn't be able to see anything. And I didn't. Just a black liquid mass. I surfaced again yelling, this time as loud as I could. "Patty!"

Suddenly she shot up smashing through the surface right in front of me. It scared the shit out of me; great relief followed.

"What the fuck did you do that for?" I said angrily.

She looked confused. "Do what? And don't curse at me."

"You stayed under so long I thought you drowned."

She raised her voice. "I didn't stay under that long. For your information, I can stay under a lot longer."

I calmed down but was still angry. "I'm getting out." I turned and swam through the stars back to the shore.

We dressed not speaking to each other.

Driving back, I wasn't quite sure how to get to the house but I didn't want to ask her for directions. Once we left the Bay, I made a left turn. A minute or two later, I knew it was wrong. I drove another twenty minutes. It should have taken only about fifteen minutes or less to get back to the house.

Patty finally said, "If you would talk to me I could tell you how to get home. If you don't we might be driving around here all night."

Fuck. "You're right. Listen, I'm sorry for yelling and cursing."

"That's okay. You were just worried. I shouldn't have stayed under so long. It was inconsiderate of me. Now make the next left."

We were back at the house in ten minutes.

Chapter Thirty

The alarm went off at 6:00. I reached over, shut it off and told Patty to wake me when she wanted to leave. All I had to do was throw on my tee-shirt and shorts. She yawned, waited a second or two before climbing over me. I had just closed my eyes when Patty shook me.

"Chris, it's 6:45. Sorry, but it's time for that ride."

I yawned, got up, stretched and fumbled into my clothes.

At the station were two businessmen with slicked back hair and suit jackets hanging over their arms and a college kid in a tee-shirt and cutoffs waiting for the 7:03. I turned off the engine and told Patty she might as well sit until the train arrived.

"Would you like to hook up one night in the city, go to a movie?" I asked. "An Officer and a Gentleman is supposed to be pretty good."

"It sounds nice, but I don't think so. I'll probably be working late every night on a new pitch we're making."

I hoped she wasn't still mad at me about last night. Although she was pretty quiet during dinner too. Maybe it was Donna and work. It was just that she was never depressed around me before, or quiet. I didn't know how to read it. "Well,

I'll call you, of course."

"Sure," she said as if she owed me the reply. "Here comes the train." She leaned over and gave me a quick kiss before getting out of the car. "In any event, I'll see you next weekend."

"Okay. Safe trip." I watched the train pull away.

At first I was going to rush back into bed, but I had never been up this early out here. There was a haze that wouldn't burn off for another few hours. It tended to muffle the town the way an unexpected snowfall muffles the city. I decided not to rush home, to enjoy another quiet Monday, grab a cup of coffee somewhere. Nothing in Amagansett would be open yet. Dresners in East Hampton had the best coffee and the best donuts. They made them in the window, placing the round circles of raw dough on a little machine with a conveyer belt that would drop each one into boiling oil. Then they'd take them out and shake them in a bucket of cinnamon or powdered sugar. My mind was made up. I headed for the donuts.

Instead of staying on Montauk Highway, I took Further Lane, which ran parallel to it and into East Hampton, and which was one of the most beautiful roads in all of the Hamptons. It was also considered one of the chicest. On such a beautiful quiet morning, it was the perfect route to take.

At the stop sign coming out of Further Lane was a green Mercedes. The driver looked familiar but I couldn't place him. Getting closer and just before making the turn, it dawned on me who it was: Paul Simon. A flash of excitement passed through me. I watched him turn towards Indian Wells in my rearview mirror.

All through high school I was a huge Simon and Garfunkel fan. Of course, I didn't recognize him right away. I was used to seeing him with a guitar in front of him, not a steering wheel. When he split with Garfunkel, I was a little bummed, but his first solo albums were great, and in college I saw him in concert at Carnegie Hall. But lately he hadn't done much. He wrote and starred in a movie, One Trick Pony, that flopped and so did the sound track from it. I usually don't pay attention to critics since they're just frustrated artists, but they were right this time about both the movie and the album. Paul was washed up, his best work behind him. Yet he was driving a Mercedes, probably lived on Further Lane, was worth millions and keeps getting all those royalties. I stopped feeling sorry for him even though he'd more than likely spend the 80's doing 60's revival rock shows with groups like Tommy James and the Shondells or Jay and the Americans on the bill.

The homes on Further Lane in Amagansett that weren't on the ocean were traditional looking. They weren't very large but were impeccably manicured, with an abundance of colorful flowers and shrubbery. Lawns were expensive lush rugs that looked like no one had ever set foot on. As the Lane stretched into East Hampton, the homes like a crescendo grew in size becoming stately mansions.

On the ocean side, driveways (the length of roads) divided lawns the size of football fields and the homes you couldn't see were even more beautiful. They had to be or they'd be visible from the road.

Where the trees and homes momentarily stopped, the Maidstone Golf Course opened like a large green palm, which held the Maidstone Clubhouse on its fingertips so it wouldn't fall into the ocean. It sat there like a huge wasp Tudor fortress, painted in a proper light tan—nothing toe brown or dark, thank you.

Just beyond, where Further Lane meets Egypt Lane, there is a large pond almost the size of the small lake with an old fence protecting it from the road. Complete with swans sliding across its surface, it could pass as a Constable landscape.

Further Lane ended with Guild Hall and its signs pushing the clothesline painting exhibit for the weekend. I made a right and could almost smell the donuts. The Jitney was picking up passengers at the bus stop across from the Hunting Inn. It was the only active spot in town—the rest of it was still sleeping.

I made a left onto Newtown Lane pulling over right across from Dresners. Unfortunately, it was dark. The signs were obvious, but I wanted those donuts. I got out of my car and crossed the street to be absolutely sure. The little machine with the conveyor belt of raw dough was idle and empty. The note on the door said it would open at 8:30. I wasn't about to wait for almost an hour. I thought about what might be open, because at any rate I needed coffee more than fresh, hot, delicious donuts. Shit. Who was I kidding? I needed the donuts more than the java.

The only place open would be Buckets, the deli down the road near the train station. Buckets, where the sandwiches are overstuffed, like the girls behind the counter, where the donuts are stale and the coffee bitter like the girls again who always seemed pissed off for working there.

Maybe because it was so early, the girl working the cash register seemed even more pissed off than usual. I ordered a coffee and a donut. When she gave me my change, I said, "Thanks." I'm sure she said, "You're welcome," although I'm also giving her the benefit of the doubt. It was more of a grunting sound.

On the sidewalk, I took a sip and a bite. The coffee was extremely bitter and even though the donut was fresh, it was fresh from a Hostess box and not a tiny conveyor belt. I dumped both into a nearby trash can, drove home and went back to sleep.

•

I spent the week writing some poems, typing them up and sending them off to literary magazines with the usual strange names: Fink Stink, Cow Coconuts, and Frog Drool.

On Tuesday morning, a banging on the front door woke me. I got out of bed to say hi to Bessie Tennessee. I never thought of her as just Bessie, it was always with her last name tacked on, as if it were some sort of title. Queen Elizabeth. Catherine the Great. Bessie Tennessee.

She was putting the vacuum together. "Hi, Bessie."

She looked up. A big grin spread across her face. "Mornin' Professa Chris." She gave me a title too. "Sho is hot out today. Ha."

"Already?"

"Yup. Look what I brought ya."

She looked in the direction of my gift. Two sacks of potatoes were leaning against the wall. I was touched. "These for me?"

"Yup. Brought dem straight from da potata house. Packed 'em myself. Picked only da best spuds for ya. I knowed you'd know the difference being Irish and all. You is Irish ain't cha?"

"Yes, I certainly am."

"Dats what I thought. Youse Irish folks knows a lot about spuds and drinkin'. Ha." She smiled.

"Yeah, most of us do, but you didn't have to go through the trouble. Can I pay you for them?"

She looked sternly at me. "I don't want no money. Dey is a gift and it weren't no trouble. Youse a nice man, and dats why I bring dem. Ha."

I was flattered. No wonder her husband kept coming back, she treated him like a king. "Thank you very much." I wasn't sure what I'd do with all those potatoes except give them to my dad. I wanted to try some out on him anyway. "I'm sure my dad will love some of them."

"Is he Irish too?"

"Born there."

"Well, be careful. I know how dem Irish is. You can make some strong drinks outta dis. Make sure your mama cooks 'em up and he doesn't make no potata brew out of 'em. Ha." She started laughing and shaking her head back and forth, "Dem Irish."

I smiled. "I'll make sure Mom cooks 'em."

•

I went to South Hampton on Wednesday to have a look around the town. I had passed through it but never stopped to check out the shops.

Twenty-seven between East and Bridgehampton was dotted with a few homes and vegetable stands. The traffic was a little heavier because of the Hampton Classic, a horse show that runs every summer during the last two weekends in August in Bridgehampton.

The fields I passed were now growing rows of corn. Most fields looked like they had changed clothes, from potatoes in July to corn in August. The stalks were growing quickly. Just a week or two before the sun was just beginning to tug them out of the soil. Now they were already the size of small forwards for the New York Knicks.

Many of the larger fields looked more like they were growing homes instead of crops. There is a field on 27 between Watermill with an abandoned Carvel ice cream stand. The first weekend I drove out it was very dark. I thought the field was a bay and in the distance the tiny lights clustered near each other were a fleet of fishing boats. That Sunday returning to the city, I anticipated going past the bay. To my surprise, it had mysteriously dried up into a potato field and what I thought to be fishing boats were recently built homes.

According to *The East Hampton Star* many farmers had been selling off sections of their fields or entire farms to developers. Of course the new homes and condos are destroying the bucolic beauty of the area but you really can't blame the farmers. They made a lot of money, and very quickly, selling to developers. The kind of money they could never have made working the soil. The flip side is they are destroying the unique beauty of the area. New Yorkers were at it again. We were destroying the surrounding waters, single-handedly destroying fishing and now we were attacking the land. You had to hand it to us, we knew how to maim and destroy. If there was another war, the President should just send in New Yorkers. We'd destroy the enemy country in no time.

I entered Job Lane and found a space right in front of another Book Hampton. They were all over and convincing me that the Hamptons included East, West, South and Book.

The town was a little larger than East Hampton. There was even a Saks blended in well with the little blue blood shops and boutiques. I eventually strolled into the Parish Museum and spent some time gazing at the Long Island watercolors on exhibit. Getting hungry, I crossed the street and went into the Driver's Seat for a burger. I had brought in a *Newsday* with me and saw that An Officer and a Gentleman was playing at the South Hampton Cinema which was just a block away. Patty had her chance. I'd see it by myself.

Except for Richard Gere, and the corny ending, it was a pretty good movie. It took place in the Pacific Northwest where the Gere character goes for six weeks of officer training. The men, on the first day of their arrival, are warned about the local girls who'll try anything to get out of their dull town and dull lives. Even go so far as to trick these guys into marrying them.

That's where Debra Winger comes in.

The best part of the movie: when she lays eyes on Gere, the look on her face says more than pages of dialogue could. That look says she's not like the other girls. She is already gone on Gere and she'll love him forever if he'd just take her to bed. Which he does, of course, at a local motel. There's this scene where they are naked and she's riding his cock. I would have given anything to switch cocks with Gere. But he's the one who ruined the movie for me, simply because he tries too hard to be cool. There's this thing about cool. If you're not born cool, forget it. You can't manufacture it and you certainly can't fake it. The difference between born cool and fake cool is the difference between Steve McQueen and Richard Gere.

Halfway through the movie, I wondered when Gere was going to say, "cunt." He said it, at least once, in all his movies. He must have a clause in his contract that says he has to say "cunt," otherwise he will not take the part. I made a bet with myself that he'd say it within the next ten minutes.

Gere and Winger end up looking for Gere's best friend who dropped out of school to marry a local blonde bimbo. However, she dumps him because she figures now that the guy can't be an officer, there's no way they can live happily ever after. The bimbo ends up telling Gere why she dumped his buddy who ends up killing himself over her. Squinting his eyes, Gere looks at her with all the macho he can muster and says (you guessed it) "cunt."

Driving home I thought about how Winger looked at Gere. The last woman to look at me like that was Laura. I'd been so hurt, angry and the last few months with her were so bad, I forgot about the good stuff. For instance, those Debra Winger looks she'd give me when we first met; how she worried when I wasn't feeling well; how she nursed me through a bout with the flu, and even sending me flowers for no special reason other than she felt fortunate to have me in her life. Yep. Laura wasn't a witch, she was a human being with real blood flowing through her veins. If she were just a witch, why would I miss her so much? Maybe part of the reason our relationship was so terrible those last few months was that I didn't know how to let go and even when I knew how, I wasn't about to.

I had called Patty twice during the week. The first time I left a message. The second time I didn't, figuring she owed me the return call that never came.

Friday, I got up late, went for a slice of pizza, watched the Belushis fight, then sat on the beach for the afternoon. I was a little upset about Patty. Why was she being slightly distant? I went through the possibilities all afternoon on the beach. It could be that she was upset about Donna and feeling unsafe with the "fuck buddies" she brings home. Maybe it was Donna and the new business they were working on. Maybe it was just work related. For a brief moment I even considered that she and Donna were lovers. But I quickly blew that outlandish idea out of my head. Before Becky and the Dutch Motel it never would have crossed my mind. Donna loved cock too much and so did Patty for that matter.

I finally decided it had to do with me. Patty probably wanted the relationship to move in a more serious direction. But there was no way I could do that. I also considered what Becky had said to me in my office, about using Patty as methadone to get over Laura. Maybe Patty was a little more methadone than I cared to admit. That being the case, a more serious direction for us would have to wait. I needed time. Maybe she's trying to hide how she feels. I convinced myself that she threw out bait when she brought up her goals in my apartment but I didn't bite. Maybe she was really in love with me after all. I decided I'd sit her down at the opportune time over the weekend and clear things up.

Kevin Pilkington

Chapter Thirty-One

I was reading a magazine in the living room Friday night. No one had arrived yet. I began wondering if Russ and Jody would actually come out again, when I heard laughing in the driveway. Goldstein and Debbie opened the door and continued laughing as they tried fitting through the doorway with their bags and their arms around each other.

"You guys are going to have to let go of each other if you want to get in."

They laughed even more at my suggestion before letting go. They greeted me, dropped their bags on the floor, then sat on the couch.

Goldstein looked at me smiling, "How goes it, my man?"

"Just fine; and I see things are just fine with you two."

Debbie was bubbling, "Can you believe it? We actually spent every night together this week."

Goldstein looked at her, smiled and put his arm around her then said to me, "I had to drag my ass into work every day exhausted."

Debbie patted him on the leg, "Poor baby," she said then gave him a kiss on the lips.

I smiled. "And they said it wouldn't last."

"Yeah, but what do they know," Goldstein said as he squeezed Debbie.

Debbie looked at Goldstein even though she was addressing me. "What a week. It was wonderful and I feel wonderful. In fact, even my colitis hasn't bothered me."

Goldstein hadn't stopped smiling. "That's because of all those Vitamin D injections Dr. Goldstein administered."

They both giggled and gave each other a quick kiss.

Goldstein looked at me. "I guess Russ and Jody won't be out after last week."

"That's what *you* think," I said.

"What do you mean?"

"Before he left last week, Russ said he almost convinced Jody he didn't screw Donna. You know, some bullshit about being too drunk."

"And she bought that?" he said incredulously.

"Seems so."

"Well, that's good," Debbie added sympathetically.

Goldstein lifted his eyebrows as he mulled it over, then said, "Guess we'll have a full, if somewhat uncomfortable, weekend." He lifted his arm off Debbie's shoulder, rubbed his legs and said to her, "I'll take the bags to my room, this way Chris can use his room tonight."

"Thanks," I said.

He looked at me. "I think while I'm in there I'll just go to bed. For some reason I'm exhausted." He turned to Debbie who smiled at his comment and playfully slapped him on the arm. He got up from the couch, leaned over to where I was and put out his palm. I smacked it gently.

"See ya tomorrow," he said.

"Night."

"Be in in a sec," Debbie said.

"Make it sooner," he said pretending to be tough as he picked up the bags. "I don't like to be kept waiting."

Debbie pretended to be frightened. "Anything you say, master." She watched him leave the room then rested her head against the couch. Her eyes had that Debra Winger glaze in them. "What a wonderful week," she said turning to me. "I know I've said that already, but it has been."

"It sounds like it has been."

"He's such a great guy."

She said it slowly and with such conviction, that even if I had disliked him, her one statement would have been enough to make me think otherwise.

"Well," she said, "I better get to bed." She got up from the couch, walked over to me and kissed me on the forehead. "Good night."

I was surprised and sounded it. "A kiss good night! This is a first."

"Why not? I'm happy and want to share it."

"Thanks," I said warmly. "Good night." She left and I went back to my magazine.

A little later I heard Donna's car pull into the driveway. She was the first to come in. "Hi Chris." She said smiling, just like in the old days, way back in June.

"Hi," I said sounding more surprised that she was pleasant. Patty came in a second or two later. "Hi, Chris."

"Hi."

They both sat on the couch. I was going to ask Patty: How come you didn't call? But she took care of that issue immediately.

"I tried calling you about four times, but I guess I kept missing you."

"Luck of the draw. Guess I was just out of the house."

Donna cut in. "Boy did we have a busy week."

"We worked until about midnight every night on this new business." Patty added.

"At least we got to see An Officer and a Gentleman," Donna said.

I shot a quick look at Patty.

She was just as quick to come to her own defense. "Wednesday was extremely hectic. We were going to have a drink to unwind but Donna saw it was playing a block away and begged me to see it."

Donna picked up on that Patty was probably supposed to go with me. "Oh, were you guys supposed to see it?"

I was glad I saw it. I already got even. "Not really. I saw it on Wednesday too in South Hampton." I said it to Donna but was looking at Patty with a "take that" look on my face.

"Wasn't it great?" said Donna. "Richard Gere was so cool. Don't you think?"

"Yeah. Real cool."

Our movie review was interrupted by the front door opening. Russ and Jody walked in. Jody glanced at Donna right away; with forced peppiness she said, "Hi, Chris, Patty." Donna's name was left out.

Donna did look in their direction. After Patty and I greeted them, Donna said, "Hi, Russ."

Obviously uncomfortable, Jody sounded like she was a bad actress trying to deliver her lines. "Well, I think we will be going to bed now. We are dog tired, aren't we sweetheart?" She looked at Russ. Her smile was uncomfortable as her dialogue.

Russ answered on cue. "Yep, we sure are."

"See you people in the morning," Jody said and hurried up the stairs.

Russ and I said good night. Russ following her looked over at me and raised his eyes to the ceiling. He was just following orders.

Donna looked to see if they were gone. "Now that the coast is clear, think I'll go to bed. I'm beat." Walking out she said, "See you guys in the morning."

"Night," I said.

Patty said, I'm exhausted, too. I'll be up in a few minutes, Donna."

That took care of the is-she-going-to-sleep-with-me-tonight issue. We both sat there quietly.

"Sorry about not seeing the movie with you but I was kinda roped into seeing it."

I was angry she didn't go see it with me and that she made it clear we weren't going to sleep together. I offered a slightly nasty reply: "That's okay. I saw it without you and nobody roped me."

She didn't fire anything back but sounded like she had been scolded. "Oh, I guess that's true."

A few more minutes of silence.

"Chris, I think you and I should talk."

"That's what I was thinking."

"Not now though. It's late. I had a long week and I really am exhausted."

She did look tired. "We'll find time tomorrow or Sunday," I said trying not to sound resentful or angry.

"Well, I guess I'll go to bed then."

She got up and walked slowly enough for me to do or say something. What did she want me to do? Get up, say I was sorry about something I wasn't clear on; tell her I was falling in love and that she should come to bed with me? The only thing I could do or say was nothing. I let her walk by.

I waited to hear her bedroom door shut before I got up and went into my room. I got out of my shorts, took off my tee-shirt, crunched it into a ball and slammed it against the wall. I got into bed doing a slow burn. I was convinced this afternoon that she was falling in love and wanted things to take a more serious turn. But now I wasn't so sure. Maybe she wanted to end things. For some reason the thought of that made me angrier. If that were the case I'd dump her first. Whatever it was I'd find out soon enough.

It also crossed my mind that God could be testing me again since I hadn't been to church in quite some time. Patty had been sitting on the couch in a short jean skirt flashing a lot of leg. As I was getting madder, I was also getting horny. Funny how that works. I kicked around the idea of jerking off, thought better of it, turned on my side, muttered "women" in disgust, and closed my eyes.

I tossed and turned all night. Every few hours I'd wake and look at the clock to check my progress. By eight o'clock I gave up, got out of bed and slipped into a tee-shirt and jeans. I walked into the kitchen thinking I'd make coffee but it was already made. I poured myself a cup and was surprised to find Jody. She was drinking tea and flipping through a magazine at the dining room table.

"Morning," I said.

She looked up from her magazine. "Hi. Good. I see you found the coffee. How is it? I don't drink it myself. Strictly a tea drinker."

It was too strong. "It's great."

She smiled. I had never seen her up this early.

She looked out the glass doors that led onto the porch. "Unfortunately it's not so bright out."

Surprisingly, I hadn't noticed. I looked out at the gray overcast sky. "No, it certainly isn't."

"Russ was snoring louder than the D train. So I thought I'd just get up."

"I can never sleep late out here. Usually the sun wakes me but it certainly didn't wake me this morning."

"Russ tells me you and Patty have been dating," she smiled showing all her perfect teeth and made it sound more like a question that needed a lengthy answer.

I wasn't up to it. "Yep."

"She must still be sleeping." She assumed Patty was in my bedroom.

I didn't want to say that Patty was in her own bedroom, because knowing Jody she'd want to know why. And since I wasn't quite sure myself, and it was a safe bet she was still sleeping, I said, "Yeah, she is."

"There's something I want to apologize for," she said.

I knew what was coming but pretended I didn't. "Apologize about what?"

"For screaming last Sunday morning and waking everyone."

I had to poke a little fun at her. "You mean for blowing the roof off last Sunday? And scaring the shit out of everyone? Forget it."

She smiled sheepishly. "That loud, huh?"

I shrugged my shoulders. "Forget it."

She lost her smile. "Can you blame me though?"

It was best not to answer. I just raised my eyebrows and took a sip from my cup.

"I come out to surprise Russ and I end up getting the surprise of my life." Her face tightened; she whispered. "That little whore taking advantage of him like that."

Taking "advantage" of him. Russ had really worked on her this week.

"What was I to think? They're both nude and in the same bed. I thought they had sex. Wouldn't you have thought that?"

"Yeah. It's what I woulda thought."

"Russ told me you guys were all very stoned last Saturday."

"We were pretty ripped."

"Yeah and that little pig thought she was in her own room. Russ didn't even know she was in bed with him until I started screaming."

"Hummmm," was all I could say.

"Poor guy. I didn't even give him a chance to explain. He didn't even have sex with her. Did he?" She searched my face for a reaction. I wasn't going to sidestep this one. "Jody, are you asking me or telling me?"

"Oh no. I didn't mean it as a question."

The hell she didn't. She was very good at deluding herself but never did it a hundred percent. It was always the ten percent of doubt that tormented her. Russ must have worked overtime on this one.

I wanted to put a lid on things before she really started quizzing me. "The important thing is you two cleared it up."

She smiled. "I just wanted to apologize, that's all."

"Forget it."

I crashed on the couch and looked out the window for the next hour or so.

Russ came down and walked over. "How was your week?"

"Not bad, wrote a little. Mailed some poems. Read. Went to a movie. Very stressful."

"You're the only one who got to spend real time out here and it shows. If you get any darker you'll look like a turd.

I looked back at Jody, who was still reading a magazine, then up at Russ and in a low voice said, "Sounds like you had a busy week convincing Jody nothing happened."

He looked at me like he didn't know what I was saying, looked over at Jody then down at me and in a loud whisper said, "What do you mean, 'convince?' Like I told you before, at the base of any relationship is honesty."

Donna came down around 11:30, passed the table where Russ and Jody were talking quietly. She said, "good morning, Russ and Chris," on her way into the kitchen. Russ and I said, "morning." Jody glared at Russ. Donna came out with a cup of coffee and headed back upstairs.

I was still lying on the couch when Patty came down. It was almost noon. Russ and Jody had gone back to their room and Goldstein and Debbie still hadn't come out of theirs.

"Morning," said Patty.

"Hi."

She looked out the glass doors. "No sun today, I guess."

"Doesn't look that way."

"I have to go into East Hampton to buy some birthday cards for my brother and two friends. Want to take a ride?"

This no doubt meant a ride to East Hampton and to our talk. "Sure," I said.

"Okay, I'll be ready in about ten minutes."

"Just let me take a quick shower first."

"Sure, take your time."

She went back upstairs and I got up and headed for the bathroom.

I made it a quick shower and was back in the living room waiting for Patty in fifteen minutes. When she came down, Goldstein and Debbie came into the room.

"You guys are finally up?" I said.

Goldstein looked at me and extended his palm smiling. "We've been up all morning and most of the night."

I smiled and smacked it.

"Aaron!" Debbie said sounding a little embarrassed and like a little girl.

He put his arm around her waist and she gave him a quick kiss on the cheek.

"Where are you guys going?" asked Debbie.

"To East Hampton. I have to get some cards," said Patty. "You guys want to come?"

Debbie said, "No, we're going to the beach."

"But there's no sun," I added.

"Exactly," Debbie said excitedly. "It's just perfect for me."

"Oh yeah," I said. "It would be perfect for you."

In the car Patty said, as she watched them walk towards the beach, "Boy those two are going hot and heavy."

"Every night this week," I said.

"Really? That's great."

Montauk Highway and East Hampton were more crowded than usual, with everyone who would have been on the beach if the sun were out. Patty and I were small talking as if we hardly knew each other. We were both anticipating our talk; we just had to stumble upon the right time and place. It was somewhere close by.

I parked in the big lot next to the A&P. We went to the stationary store near the men's clothes store, the Latham House. After twenty minutes of looking at cards and still not picking one, I told Patty to take her time but I was going to wait outside. She came out after about twenty minutes.

"Sorry I took so long."

"No problem."

"It's just that the cards always have to be perfect."

"Are they?"

"I think so. Would you like to stroll? There's really no point going back to the house right away, since it's a no beach day."

"Sounds like a good idea," I said.

We walked away from the stores, crossed the street then strolled past the Hunting Inn and further towards Guild Hall. We didn't say much but I could tell we were strolling towards the talk.

We ended up walking as far as the large pond that farmers once used for their livestock three hundred years ago. Next to it is an old cemetery filled with fading names and dates on stones from the seventeen and eighteen hundreds. Both the pond and the cemetery create an historic charm that just goes to prove that if you are dead long enough you can become an intricate part of the scenery. Something to look forward to after you die, if you are willing to wait.

I said to Patty, "Let's go in and read some of the stones."

I spotted the Fisher and Gardner families who must have been the same prominent families who helped settle the area and gave the names to Fisher's Bay and Gardner's Island. The oldest stone I found was dated 1725; Patty found a 1720. We looked around for another fifteen minutes or so until we came upon a grave built like a low stone table. Joshua Babcock had been in there since 1800. Patty sat on the edge where Joshua's feet must have been. When she looked at me I realized we had found the place to talk and this was the time.

"Who should start," she asked cautiously.

"Ladies first."

"Okay. There's a problem here."

"There is?"

"Yes." She looked down at her feet.

"Go ahead, tell me," I said coaxingly.

She looked up and sighed. "I think you're a great guy. You're warm, caring, considerate, and have a great sense of humor."

I liked the adjectives. "Thanks."

"And... I really have enjoyed my time with you, not to mention we have a sexual chemistry, and you also happen to be a wonderful lover."

Wonderful lover. I really liked the sound of that. I never thought of myself as a "wonderful lover." Chris McCauley, Stud. It had a nice ring. And the way she was starting off, I was becoming more convinced that she might be falling in love with me. I was beginning to relax. Maybe I would have to dump her, but I was going to have to be honest and let her decide.

"But there's a problem."

Here it comes, I thought.

"There's this ghost," Patty said sounding both frustrated and annoyed.

That threw me. I didn't get it. "What ghost? What are you talking about?"

"Your old girlfriend."

I was still confused. "Who? Laura?"

"Yes. Laura."

My voice went up an octave. "Laura! I don't see Laura. In fact I haven't seen or spoken to her since last spring."

"I know but you aren't over her yet."

I felt myself get angrier because she was right. "What are you talking about?"

"Do you realize how many times you have mentioned her when you are with me?"

I tried to recall if I had and how often.

She saw me race. "See, you don't even realize you do it. If someone is intelligent, you tell me how smart Laura is. When you were drinking at Bay Street, you kept telling me how beautiful she is. Last Saturday I did something with you I never dreamed of doing with anyone and you almost called me by her name. Do you know what that felt like? And I know darn well that you stayed in the Laundry to see if that blonde in the back was her."

I had no idea I was being that bad or that obvious. I felt like an alcoholic who thinks he is hiding the fact that he has been drinking, is trying to act sober and thinks he is getting away with it but everyone else knows he's sloshed.

I couldn't say anything.

She went on. "You told me you broke it off with her but you act like she ended the relationship. If you did end it maybe you're just regretting you did. Maybe you felt you made a mistake."

All I could get out was, "I didn't make a mistake."

"The fact is, as nice as things have been with us, it's always been the three of us. You, me and her."

I didn't want to own up to it but I didn't want to deny anything either. "Really?"

"Yes, really."

We both remained silent for a bit.

She began again. "I think, Chris, that you need more time to get over her before you become involved in another relationship."

"You mean this one, don't you?"

"Yes. This one. You're not being fair to yourself and you're certainly not fair to me. I would like to continue seeing you on our terms when she is no longer around. Until then, until you break your, your *obsession*, I don't think we should continue seeing each other."

I didn't fight for Patty. I sensed it's what she wanted. Not that I didn't want to, a lot of me did. It's just that I was tired. Even though I broke it off with Laura in April it felt like yesterday. And since I spent months fighting for her, I had nothing left over to fight with for Patty.

Patty's eyes were filled with tears. "So what do you think?"

"I think you should do what you think is best."

"Okay then."

We were silent again until Patty said, "Wasn't there something you wanted to talk to me about?"

"No. It doesn't make any difference now. Let's go back."

Chapter
Thirty-Two

We said nothing to each other as we walked to the car. Driving back to the house, it felt like we said even less.

Donna was flipping through a magazine when we walked in. Jody was at a safe distance on the back deck talking to Russ. Donna put her magazine down. She looked up at Patty and said, "Did you get the cards you wanted?"

"Yeah, I did. Let me show you," Patty said going over to sit next to her taking the cards out of the small brown paper bag.

I never realized buying cards was such a big deal or even that interesting. Maybe it was another one of those woman things a man would never fully understand. Just one more item to add to a very extensive list. I headed for my room; I needed to get my file and to do some work on my nails to make myself feel better. But before I could there was a knock on the door. I said to the girls, "I'll get it," but they were so busy talking about the cards, I don't think they heard it.

I opened the door to face a policeman in his early twenties, with red hair, a very bad case of acne and a somber look on his face. He was holding a clipboard with some paper on it. I thought he was going to ask for a donation for the police department like the fire department did the week before.

"What can I do for you, officer?"

He sounded like the military. "I am sorry, Sir, but I have the unpleasant duty to report an accident."

I felt the muscles in my stomach tighten. Donna and Patty stopped talking in back of me to listen. "What kind of accident?"

"A drowning, sir."

"Who? Where?" I said raising my voice.

He lifted up his clipboard and started flipping through a form. As he was searching, he said, "A quarter mile up the beach in the direction of Montauk. Oh, here it is, sir." He squinted. "A Mr. Goldstein."

I felt everything inside of me drain into my feet. I think I heard Donna or Patty gasp and one of them shriek, "Oh, God!" I pushed past the cop who was still flipping through his form. I began to jog towards the beach. At first I felt disoriented and wasn't quite sure where I was going until I heard the cop yell, "Wait, sir!" The sound of his voice cleared my head like a splash of water, reminding me where I was headed. I broke out into a sweat and into a full run.

With the sky still overcast there wasn't anyone on the beach except for the small crowd in the near distance grouped around a jeep ambulance and police car. I was running at full speed but the sand was making footing difficult. I was in a dream again, the faster I pumped my legs the slower it seemed to be taking.

The closer I got I started chanting to myself, "Please, Aaron, don't be dead. Don't be dead you bastard."

I finally got there running around the front of the ambulance and squad car that were facing the water. There must have been about twenty people mulling around them. In the middle of the car and ambulance was a body covered with a white sheet. I had to see him for myself. I began slowly walking over to the body.

"Wait a minute, sir," another police man with another clipboard in his mid-fifties said to me.

I looked him in the eye. I was sweating and out of breath. "It's a friend of mine." It was obvious by the way I looked and the tone of my voice that I meant it. He looked at me then nodded his head that it was alright for me to look.

I tried to kneel down but felt so exhausted I actually fell on my knees. I waited briefly to get my wind back and to find some strength, then slowly pulled the sheet back and looked into the closed eyes of Debbie.

The shock of seeing her knocked what little wind I had left out of me. I put both my hands into the sand to brace myself in case I passed out. Goldstein became Debbie. This was a nightmare I wanted out of in a hurry. I hoped I'd wake soon and it would be over. I had closed my eyes then opened them. I wasn't sleeping, Debbie was still there. I stared at her. I had never seen anyone dead before and it seemed like I still hadn't. She looked like she was sleeping, the way she always looked in the bed next to mine.

I then heard someone say, "God!"

I looked up at Russ. He too was out of breath.

"Debbie, not Goldstein," I said as if he couldn't see for himself.

"I know," he said. "The cop gave you the wrong name. He called you but you didn't hear him. Goldstein is in the ambulance. They gave him a sedative. Shit, Chris, I can't believe this." His voice started to tremble. "She looks like she's just sleeping."

The girls came up beside him. Jody looked quickly at Debbie before turning and burying her face in Russ's chest. She began sobbing. Russ put his arms around her but kept looking down at Debbie.

Patty and Donna both started crying, then wrapped their arms around each other. Donna said angrily, "What in God's name happened? Where's Aaron?"

The older cop came over. "Are you all friends of hers?"

Russ answered him. "Yeah. We all share a house." Jody kept her face buried in his chest.

I looked up. "Can you tell us what happened?"

"According to Mr. Goldstein, they were walking when the deceased..."

"Debbie," Patty interrupted angrily, "her name's Debbie."

He looked at her then continued where he left off. "Decided she wanted to go for a swim, which she proceeded to do. Unfortunately it's a drowning accident. A wave or a cramp probably caused her to panic. Mr. Goldstein can't swim and ran to the nearest house for help, but when they got back it was already too late. He's in the ambulance by the way. He was given something to calm him down. I have to fill out a few more forms, then she'll be taken to South Hampton Hospital where her family will be contacted." He looked at all of us. "Sorry," he added before walking away.

The sky had begun to clear and the sun started peering through the clouds. I leaned over and placed the sheet over Debbie's face.

Jody lifted her face from Russ's chest, looked down and said, "Hurry, Chris, cover her hand too. You know how she hates the sun."

Chapter
Thirty-Three

The paramedics wanted to take Goldstein to the hospital to keep him overnight but he insisted on staying with us. Russ and I held onto him as we all walked back to the house; he was heavily sedated but would sporadically say something about trying to save her, then break into sobs.

Russ and I brought him to his room. When we got him into bed, he looked over in the corner, noticing Debbie's overnight bag and some of her clothes. He began sobbing again. We told him to get some rest and closed the door.

The girls were sitting down in the living room. Patty with a tissue in her hand kept wiping her nose at one end of the couch. At the other end, Donna stared blankly at the rug, her face red and eyes swollen from crying. The only sound was coming from Jody, whimpering in the chair across from them. Donna looked up at her and through clenched teeth said, "Can't you shut the hell up?"

Jody looked at her and stopped long enough to get out, "*You* shut the hell up!"

Patty jumped in. "Why don't you *both* shut up!"

I went to sit between Donna and Patty; Russ sat on the arm of Jody's chair.

Donna looked at me. "I guess we should spend the night here," she said.

Jody looked up at Russ, "Can we leave this evening?" she asked.

He snapped, "Wait a minute," at her then looked at me to see what I had to say...

"I'm sure we all don't want to stay here tonight but Aaron won't be in any shape to leave until tomorrow."

Russ said, "That's for sure."

"If you guys want to leave, go ahead but I'll stay and drive him home in the morning," I added.

"In that case, we all stay," Russ said.

"None of us are in any shape to drive anywhere," Patty added.

Jody looked up at Russ again. "But you and I take the train. We can leave tonight."

Although Jody was being self-centered as usual, I didn't blame her for wanting to leave. I wasn't looking forward to spending the night in my bedroom with Debbie's bed next to me.

Donna looked at us, "I guess we should call her mother?"

"I'll call her tomorrow from home," Patty said. "The police are contacting her now. I don't think I should call tonight."

"What about her father?" I asked.

"He died a year ago in a car accident," said Donna.

"Christ," Russ said, "and now this. Poor woman."

•

I couldn't sleep that night and really didn't expect to. I kept seeing Debbie lying under that sheet on the beach. I tried avoiding looking at her bed, it was still left the way she made it the previous week.

I couldn't lie on my back because I saw it in the corner of my eye so I turned on my side and faced the wall. None of it made sense. She was so happy with Goldstein this week. Then I thought of him and how important it was for him to remember how happy he had made her during the punishment he was sure to inflict upon himself for not being able to swim. I hoped for his sake he'd understand he was the cause of her happiness, not the cause of her death.

I had all but forgotten about my talk with Patty until it seeped back into my thoughts. I just let it go. In the scheme of the day's events, it wasn't worth going over.

I had dozed a while. When I woke, I felt wide awake and turned to look at the clock. It was 5:30. I decided to get out of bed and out of the room. Getting into my shorts and tee-shirt, I quickly walked past Debbie's bed. As I turned to avoid any eye contact with it, I heard Goldstein talking to someone in the living room.

Patty was sitting on the couch in her big tee-shirt listening to him discuss the accident. In the living room I could hear the showers going upstairs and Russ and Jody's voices behind the closed door of their bedroom.

"Morning," I said.

Patty turned and smiled. Goldstein who was dressed in jeans, a shirt with one of those little green alligators and wearing sunglasses, kept talking. He didn't notice Patty turn to face me or hear me. He kept talking about not being able to swim. As I went to sit in the chair across from them, he noticed me and stopped talking.

"Morning, Chris," he said.

"How are you doing?" I asked.

He stared at me for a few seconds before saying, "I'm still alive."

I didn't answer.

"Everybody is up and wants to get going," Patty said.

I wanted to get out of there, too. "I can certainly understand that."

"I thought," Patty said, "since the first train isn't until 8:00 you could give Jody and Russ a ride home. This way they won't have to wait around for two-and-a-half hours. We'll take Aaron back because Donna and Jody will never sit in the same car together."

"That's fine with me." I looked at Goldstein. "I'm sure Mr. Goldstein would rather ride with two sexy women rather than me anyway," I said in a futile attempt to make him smile, just a little. Instead his shoulders started shaking as he began sobbing. Patty leaned over and rubbed his leg for a few minutes to comfort him.

He reached up, worked his fingers in under his sunglasses, and began rubbing his eyes. "I'm sorry. Sorry," he said.

I didn't know what to say except, "It's okay. It's okay."

He adjusted his glasses and put his head back against the couch and looked up at the ceiling. "I keep seeing her laughing and then the wave crashing over her. Then not seeing her at all. Looking all over. Running out into the water as far as I could go. Waves knocking me over. Panicking. I couldn't see her and was afraid she drowned. If only I could fucking swim, I could have gone out and saved her."

He lifted his head up and looked at both of us. "The only thing I could do was run to the nearest house."

"You did the only thing you could do, Aaron," Patty said compassionately.

"It was," I added. "Even if you knew how to swim, you probably wouldn't have found her in time."

He looked at Patty and me as if he might be starting to agree with us before putting his head back against the couch again.

Russ and Jody came down the stairs with their bags.

I looked at them and said, "I'm going to give you guys a lift home. The next train isn't for another two hours."

"Great," Russ said, "thanks."

"Thanks," Jody added quickly. "I would like to get going as soon as possible."

Patty looked over at them, "I'm going to take Aaron."

Jody looked at her. "Thanks," she said, which meant she was grateful that she didn't have to ride with Donna.

"How are you doin'?" Russ said to Goldstein who didn't answer.

I looked at Russ and just raised my eyebrows, then said, "Give me a few minutes to get ready so we can get going."

"I'm going to get ready too," Patty said getting up. She lowered her voice and said to us, "After I speak to Debbie's mom and find out about what she's going to do about the funeral, I'll call everyone."

I didn't bother to take a shower. It would have taken too much time. That's how quickly I wanted to get going. I threw a few things in my overnight bag. I decided I'd come out one day next weekend to get the rest of my stuff and also get the rest of Debbie's stuff and bring it to her family. It took me all of ten minutes to get ready.

Patty and Donna were coming down the stairs as I was heading into the living room. Patty had been as fast as I had been. Russ and Jody were sitting quietly with Goldstein who still had his head against the couch. Russ looked up at me and said, "Ready?"

"Yep." I looked around at everyone and they were ready too. The first and probably last mass exodus from the house.

"Let's rock," Donna said.

I was the last to walk out, made sure the door was locked, and slammed it shut with a little more force than intended.

Just before we got into the car Patty said, "I'll get in touch with you guys about everything."

"Everything" meant the funeral arrangements. She carefully avoided "funeral" for Goldstein's sake as well as for everyone else. It was a word none of us ever expected to use in connection with our summer house. It just didn't fit in with the beach, sea, or sun.

I pulled out first. Patty, who was driving, followed me out. The streets and towns all the way out to the Expressway were virtually empty. It was much too early for the Hamptons to be awake. There was a dampness in the air and the lawns and trees were thick with dew. Where the clouds were starting to break, the sun was peeking. It was going to be a beautiful warm day, a perfect beach day.

I kept checking for no reason to see if Patty was behind me. She remained a few cars back until we reached the L.I.E. and then I lost her. Russ, Jody and I didn't say anything to each other the entire ride. The three of us were simply drowning in our thoughts. I got us back to the city in an hour and twenty minutes. The fastest time ever.

•

The city was very warm which meant my apartment would be very hot. Walking in, I immediately headed for the A.C., flipped it on high and fell onto the couch. Exhausted, I stared out the window at the building across the street until it began to blur from the tears in my eyes. I began crying uncontrollably. I kept at it for some time before falling asleep.

I ended up sleeping most of the day away—got up once at noon to take a piss and knock down a beer. Then went back to sleep and woke up starving around 5:00. I left the couch to get some Chinese food for supper. I was gone for no more than half an hour. Coming back and placing the food on the kitchen table, I saw there was a message on my answering machine.

Pushing playback, I heard, "Chris, it's Patty." She sounded tired. "I spoke to Debbie's uncle. Understandably her mother couldn't come to the phone. They are going to bury Debbie tomorrow but it's just for the immediate family. They did invite Aaron. On Wednesday afternoon at one, they're going to have a memorial service for friends at the Woods Chapel in Manhasset. It's easy to get to. Take the L.I.E. to Exit 50. When you come off it make a left and stay on that road for a mile. The chapel is on the right. So that's it." There was a slight pause, then she said, "Oh, yeah. I called Jody and Russ. So I guess I'll see you Wednesday. Bye, bye."

At first I felt disappointed. Patty did not want to talk to me or if she did, she did a good job of hiding it. I thought about calling her back anyway, with some crap about my machine not working properly and not being able to make out the entire message but then thought better of it. I then proceeded to get mad at Laura. This time there was no hurt involved and my anger had a different angle. If it weren't for Laura coming between us, my relationship with Patty would still be going. It was a first.

I guess I never really considered Patty my girlfriend. A fundamental problem. All summer Laura was my girlfriend and Patty was the girl I dated. Now that Patty wanted to dump me and no longer wanted to even be considered my girlfriend, that's exactly what I wanted her to be. Shit. I reached into the bag, took out the first container I got my hand on along with a plastic fork, and headed over to the couch.

I thought about her message and how there had always been a safe distance between me and words like bury, funeral, and memorial service. Luckily I had been sheltered—no one I knew had ever died. An aunt and my grandparents had died but I was too young to fully comprehend what it all meant. Just recently a friend of my dad's had died of a heart attack. Of course it was terrible to hear, but it always seemed more natural for my parents' friends to die. It was part of being in that age group.

It was just something else they did. But no one should die in their twenties, funerals aren't supposed to take place now. Who has time to even consider dying when you are still trying to find out where life starts?

I thought about Mrs. Gelfand and wondered how she would ever get over the loss of her daughter. For a parent there couldn't be any greater tragedy.

I opened the container. It was brown rice, but at that moment there was no way I could eat anything the color of sand.

Chapter
Thirty-Four

I spent most of the next two days lying on my couch looking out the window. I felt too emotionally drained and depressed to do much else. I noticed how in the afternoon, the sun would reflect off a window about thirty stories up in an apartment building on 79th Street. From my vantage point a clear day meant the sun was simply peering down at the city from the picture window in the condo it owned.

I called Goldstein on Tuesday to see how he was doing and if he wanted a ride out to the memorial service. He said he was doing okay but the funeral on Monday was painful. Debbie's mom was a strong woman and told him how glad she was that he made Debbie so happy during her last week on earth. He went on to say he took the week off from work, added on some extra hours with his shrink and thanked me, but didn't need a ride since a car service from his agency was driving him out.

Wednesday was a little bit cooler than the previous three days, and the humidity that draped over the city like a damp rag had lifted. Although it wouldn't take me over an hour to get to Manhasset, I left a little early in case traffic was heavy. It turned out that they were doing road work in Queens, of course, and cars were moving at a snail's pace.

I reached the chapel at exactly 1:00. It was a large yellow square with one stained-glass window in the front. There were quite a few cars in the parking lot in the back: I grabbed the first space I could find and hurried inside.

There was a small black plaque in the hall with Debbie's name in white letters on it and a small arrow pointing to room one. I walked in and quickly surveyed the area. There were about fifty or sixty people of various ages sitting in folding chairs waiting for the service to begin. I took one of the three remaining empty chairs in the last row nearest the door.

I looked around for Patty and the others. I spotted her sitting down the aisle, in the first seat of the middle row. Next to her was Donna. They were both dressed in stylish black dresses. Goldstein was across the aisle too in the second row and Jody and Russ were two rows behind him.

In front of the room was a closed gray curtain. There were numerous flower arrangements in front of it in a variety of colors. Debbie would have approved. The walls were wallpapered in dark green patterns which brought out the colors in the flowers even more. The room possessed a moldy smell that hurled me back twenty years. It was the same smell my grandmother's dark living room possessed because no light ever filtered through its closed curtains. She never entertained in it and when I did sneak in there it was just to spook myself, to experience the thrill of getting scared. Within a few seconds of entering, I'd turn and run out with that moldy smell stuck in my nostrils for hours.

The rabbi walked out from a door to the left. He was on the short side, in his mid-fifties, and dressed in a well-tailored black suit. He looked at us for a few minutes with such a compassionate expression that his face almost seemed to glow, between his thick salt and peppered hair and beard. He said he wanted to begin the service with prayers. He began reciting them in Hebrew for the next ten minutes or so. I had little idea what he was saying, but he chanted them, and the constant flow and rhythm of his voice soothed me more than prayers I had known in English. I closed my eyes, bowed my head.

After finishing the last prayer, he kept his hands together as if he were still praying and began to speak to us. "How wonderful to see so many faces on this solemn occasion. It's a testament to the love Debbie Gelfand brought to the world in the brief period of time God granted her to walk among us."

As he continued, I looked for the faces I knew. Goldstein, in black suit and sunglasses, listened intently to what the rabbi was saying. Every few seconds he would reach up with a hanky and dab his nose. Russ was also listening intently, but Jody was looking down into her lap. At first I thought she, too, was listening to the rabbi until I saw her bring up her right hand and examine her fingernails a bit more closely. Then she brought up her left for a closer inspection of her bright red nails.

"...we all knew and loved Debbie for her strength and compassion as well as for her weaknesses. After all she was a human being. She was one of us..."

I looked at Patty. She seemed to be hanging on every word the rabbi was saying. I noticed, for the first time, how her nose curved up at the end. It was a cute nose, not the perfect nose I always thought Laura had. Of course I thought Laura's was perfect because I looked at it with imperfect eyes. I never loved her for her weaknesses. When you create an ideal there are none. When you love a statue you have created, you will eventually have to accept the fact that marble is cold. I had finally accepted it. Mulling things over on the couch during the past two days, I finally figured out that if you let yourself accept someone's weaknesses, you can love what's real. Patty is real. Marble just doesn't become her.

"It is always difficult for us to accept the death of a loved one. When death lurks outside the home of the aged or the terminally ill and finally gains entry, we can accept the inevitable with a bit more understanding. But when death sneaks into the back door and steals one so young there is always shock, disbelief, and the deeply felt pain of sudden loss."

Death had been lurking at the front door of my relationship with Laura for months. It's just that I had tried not to let it in. But when it did get in, I acted as if it had snuck in the back door. The shock and disbelief shouldn't have been quite so deep because it was a gradual losing—not a sudden loss. In this instance, death was much more noble than I gave it credit for. It kept knocking on the door like a patient, dark gentleman.

"I had known Debbie since she was a little girl. I'm sure that she is looking down and grateful that you are all here. And knowing her the way I did, I'm sure she wants us to go on, to remember her and her spirit as a means to enhance our lives. So continue to mourn her passing, and then rejoice in her spirit as a way to heal. When you think of her, you will smile because she more than anyone enjoyed her short life and understood the old saying, 'Life is for the living.'"

I remember Goldstein saying that Mrs. Gelfand was happy Debbie spent the last week with him. He had made it a happy one for her. If I had died at any time since breaking up with Laura, I would have gone to my grave depressed and despondent over her. No way to spend my last week on earth. I'm alive and my relationship with Laura is dead.

That's right: it's over.

Life is for the living, just like the rabbi said. Patty has been full of life. What an ass I'd been to ignore it. Now all I had to do was get Patty to believe that from now on it would just be the two and not the three of us. I wanted to run over across the aisle and tell her why she should give us another chance. This was a memorial for Debbie. May she rest in peace. And it was a memorial for Laura. May she rest in peace and live on to a ripe old age.

The rabbi finished his eulogy with another prayer in Hebrew. When he concluded, a woman who because of her strong resemblance to Debbie I knew immediately was Mrs. Gelfand was escorted out of the room. The rabbi said she would receive us as we left the chapel. With that said everyone got up and made their way towards the door to form a line and offer their condolences. I looked over at Patty to try to make eye contact, but she had turned to talk to Donna.

Since I was so close to the door, I got in line. There were only about eight people ahead of me. Mrs. Gelfand was receiving us in the lobby. Standing next to her was a tall man with thick white hair the color of clouds who looked to be in his early sixties. As I got closer, Mrs. Gelfand's resemblance to Debbie was startling. She was the same height, had the same nose and similar curly hair. From a distance, if I didn't know better, I would have sworn it was Debbie. Getting closer, the extra lines on her face and hidden flecks of gray hair clarified their age difference. Still, she could have passed for Debbie's older sister.

At first I thought I'd say that I was one of Debbie's friends from the share house when I expressed my condolences. But when there was only one more person ahead of me, I changed my mind. I extended my hand to Mrs. Gelfand, she took it in both of hers and smiled. The smile came from her heart along with the pain that was etched in the lines of her pale face.

"Mrs. Gelfand, I'm Chris McCauley, a friend of Debbie's. I just wanted to express how sorry I am. She was such a lovely girl."

"Thank you. Thank you," she said, her voice quivering ever so slightly. "It's just such a shock. She was such a wonderful daughter. I couldn't have asked for a better one. I'm going to miss her a great deal."

Before I could say anything, she said, turning to the older man next to her, "This is my brother, Jim Gelfand. Debbie's uncle."

We shook hands. "My condolences, Mr. Gelfand."

He smiled. "Thank you for coming, Chris."

I wanted to say something else to Mrs. Gelfand, but she was already talking to the couple behind me. I smiled again at Mr. Gelfand and walked towards the door. I was glad I didn't say that I was in the share house with Debbie. In a strange sort of way it would have made me feel guilty. Not that it was my fault exactly, but it was the house's fault. If Debbie hadn't taken a share maybe it would never have happened. Of course, it was foolish thinking, but I would have felt like an accomplice. An accomplice to the house.

I waited in the parking lot. I wanted to see the others. Patty and Donna were the first to appear. They walked over.

"It was a beautiful eulogy," said Patty.

I nodded my head in agreement. "It was."

"Mrs. Gelfand. She looked terrible," said Donna.

"She's been through a lot over the past two years," said Patty.

We then stood there quietly until Donna said, "We'd better get back to the office."

I wanted to talk to Patty, but this wasn't the place and I wasn't going to take the time either.

"Yeah, we should get going," she said.

I tried to stay with them for no other reason than wanting Patty standing next to me for the few extra minutes.

"Did you see Goldstein?" I asked.

"Yeah," she said. "He seems to be okay. I saw Russ and Jody but we didn't get a chance to talk."

More silence.

"We really better go," said Donna. As she turned to walk to the car she said, "See ya, Chris."

"Take care."

Patty and I looked at each other as if we both wanted to say something.

"Well," she said, "take care."

"Yeah, you too." I said, surprised to discover a lump in my throat. I watched her walk to the car. She looked great in black.

Jody and Russ walked up behind me.

"Chris," I heard Russ say.

I turned.

"Hi, Chris." Jody said smiling, showing a lot of teeth.

Russ looked glum and Jody looked like she could have been leaving a party.

"Hi," I said reaching out to shake Russ's hand.

"It was nicely done," Russ said so quietly I almost couldn't hear him.

"Weren't the flowers great? All those colors," Jody said excitedly as if she had just seen a Broadway play.

Russ and I looked at her but didn't say anything.

Russ turned to me. "We spoke to Goldstein before the service. He seems okay."

Jody motioned with her hand like she was shooing a fly away. "He'll be just fine." Making it sound like he was just getting over a bad cold. Then she looked at Russ. "We better get going, Sweetie. You promised me lunch."

Russ didn't answer her and didn't look at me. I sensed he was embarrassed. Embarrassed by Jody's cheery attitude and probably because he was still with her. All summer, all he had talked about was getting out of the relationship. Although the Donna episode might have been the wrong way to get going on the road to freedom, it certainly had been a way. And he was embarrassed because I knew he was full of shit. Whatever the reasons were he needed to be with her, no matter how miserable she made him. Which, in the grand scheme of things, is just fine. Every man picks his poison. Just don't bitch about giving it up as you keep reaching for it.

"Do me a favor Sweetie," Jody said to Russ. "Will you put on the air conditioner and cool off the car before I get in? You know how I hate getting into a hot car."

Russ didn't answer her but was about to obey. He put out his hand. "Well, Chris. It sure was a strange summer."

I shook his hand. "Yep. It certainly was."

"I'll give you a call. Let's get together soon."

I knew neither one of us for different reasons had any intentions of picking up a phone. "Yeah. We'll get in touch."

"Take care." He walked over to his car.

I said to Jody, "Since when do you guys have a car?"

"It's a rental," she replied, watching Russ walk away and as if to make sure he was out of hearing range before talking to me. "You know, Chris, ever since that incident with Donna, our relationship has gotten better. It's amazing."

Here we go, I thought. Let's keep the illusion alive. At first I started to get angry, then I just felt sorry for her. I wanted to say: You two have one of the most fucked up relationships I've ever come across and what's "amazing" about it is that you two manage to stay together. Instead, I said, "That's good."

"Yeah. We talked things out the way we always do and have a clearer understanding of each other's needs. I know now that they didn't do anything that night. I have to learn not to be so quick to accuse. And as Russ says, honesty is everything. Even our sex life has gotten better, which I thought was an impossibility since it was so great to begin with."

251

I nodded my head but said nothing.

Russ honked the horn. Jody looked in the direction of the car. "My Sweetie's calling. I better get going." She leaned over and gave me a quick kiss on the cheek. "Take care, Chris, we'll be in touch."

"Take care."

She hurried off to the car. I was glad to see her go.

I waited for Goldstein. I watched as the steady stream of mourners leaving the chapel became a trickle. He finally appeared looking even taller in his black suit and sunglasses. I was surprised that when I put out my hand to shake his, he wrapped his arms around me instead. I was touched by his unexpected show of affection, returned his embrace, and patted my hand on his back.

"Well, that's that," he said.

"It was a nice service."

"Yeah. I think Debbie would have really liked it," he said making it sound like a question.

"I'm sure she would have." I was going to tell him that if he wanted to talk over the next few weeks, I'd be there to listen. He could call at any time of the day. It didn't make any difference. If I could help alleviate some of the pain and guilt, I'd do anything I could. But before I got a chance to say it, he spoke first.

"Chris, I wanted to ask you a question."

"Sure, Aaron, what is it?"

"It's important."

I put my hand on his shoulder. "Go ahead, ask. What is it?"

"There's a new jingle we've been working on."

It wasn't what I expected to hear. I took my hand off his shoulder and I must have had a surprised expression on my face because he continued with a touch of urgency in his voice.

"Oh. It's not like the other jingle. This one I think is much better. It really comes across with the goods. I'd like your opinion."

"Yeah, sure."

"Great." He looked over my shoulder. "There's my ride. I'll call you in a few days." He leaned over and gave me a quick embrace and patted me hard on the back. I kept my hands at my side. "See ya," he said smiling, taking off his sunglasses and sticking them in his breast pocket. Then he hurried off and got in the back seat of a Buick, greeted the driver and waved to me as they pulled away.

I felt a little foolish. There I was feeling sorry for him, wanting to help in any way I could and all he was concerned about was another jingle.

I walked back to my car and shook my head, thinking about Goldstein. I

252

should have known better than to have worried about him. It was obvious he was going to be just fine.

Chapter Thirty-Five

I drove out to the house on Saturday morning to gather up the few things I had left there. Also, I wanted to pack up any of Debbie's belongings to give to Mrs. Gelfand.

There wasn't much traffic. I hadn't thought there would be. Even though it was Labor Day weekend, anyone who was thinking of going to the Hamptons was already there. So that meant the L.I.E. would be almost spotless, and it was. There was only a minor traffic slow up near Westbury, but there wasn't another hitch the rest of the way.

Although a beautiful holiday weekend was predicted, it had been rather overcast since late Friday afternoon. It made me feel better since this wasn't how I planned to spend Labor Day weekend. I had imagined us all lounging on the beach soaking up rays. That's what I envisioned at the beginning of the summer. I thought the same thing just two weeks ago, of course, with slight variations on the theme.

However, Walter wouldn't be lounging with us, and Donna and Jody wouldn't be speaking to each other, along with some other minor tensions. But I never figured anything like this: one of us would be dead or the rest of us not wanting anything to do with the house or the Hamptons. I was beginning to catch on. In life the only certainty besides death was uncertainty.

I was surprised to see Donna's car parked in the driveway when I pulled up to the house. She or Patty or both came out probably to gather up their things too and tie up any loose ends. I had planned to call Patty and talk about us, but I decided to rehearse things over with myself before I picked up the phone. I needed a few rehearsal days and I wanted some distance from Debbie's memorial service. In short, I thought it best to let things settle. Talking about us still seemed insignificant in the shadow of death.

Walking into the house, I didn't hear anything at first, then heard something coming from the direction of my bedroom. I walked into the kitchen and looked down the hallway. The bedroom door was open, Patty was bent over Debbie's bed, with her butt facing me. She was wearing a pair of cut offs, football jersey and sneakers. On the bed were some of Debbie's clothes that she was putting into a bag.

"Hi," I said.

She straightened up quickly and spun around to face me and almost fell back onto the bed in the process. When she looked at me the shock on her face settled into relief. She closed her eyes, exhaled and said, "Oh, it's you."

"I'm sorry," I said walking into the room. "I didn't mean to startle you."

"I know. It's just that the house is so quiet and I didn't hear you. And you know, getting Debbie's stuff together and all."

"You beat me to it. I was going to get her stuff along with mine. I wish I'd known you were coming. I could have saved you a trip."

"That's okay. I had to get some things Donna and I left here last week."

"Is Donna here too?"

"No. She didn't want to come out. She said she's had it with this place."

I was glad Donna hadn't come out. This was the perfect opportunity to talk to Patty. "I can understand that." I looked down at Debbie's bed and the few items of clothes. "I guess she didn't leave much here."

Patty turned and looked down at the clothes. "No. This is all I could find."

"Are you going to bring it to her mom?"

She nodded. "Yeah. I thought I'd drop it off on my way back."

I wasn't crazy about the tone of her voice. It was polite, as if she were just an acquaintance. It was the sound of distance.

"I should get this stuff packed and get going. I promised Donna I'd have the car back by 3:00. She has to go to her nephew's birthday party."

"Let me help you get this stuff in her bag."

"Thanks."

I went over and opened one of Debbie's overnight bags. We both began filling it. "Did you get your stuff together?" I asked as we packed.

"Yeah. It's already out in the car. I'm all set."

I kept trying to decide when to bring "us" up. I felt like a runner at the starting line, knowing the race as going to begin at any moment but feeling fidgety and nervous during those final seconds before it commenced.

"That's it," I said as I placed the last piece of clothing in the bag.

We looked at each other.

Patty smiled, "Thanks." She then looked around to see if there was anything else to take, even though she knew there wasn't. "Well, I guess I should get going," she said.

"Let me grab my things. We can leave together."

"Okay. I'll check my room one last time."

"Leave Debbie's bag. I'll carry it."

When she left, I rushed through the dresser drawers, grabbed whatever I had in them and threw it into my bag. I felt like I was running out of time and I was. I began rehearsing what I was going to say but none of it sounded right, so I stopped planning. I'd just say whatever came into my head from my heart and hope I'd make points with her.

I grabbed my bag and Debbie's and hurried into the living room, and waited until Patty came down with her suitcase.

She smiled, "That's it."

"Okay. We're out of here." I opened the door for her. She thanked me and walked to her car. I slammed the door, making it sound like a starting gun at the beginning of a race. I put my bag down next to my car and brought Debbie's over to place in Patty's trunk. As she looked for her keys, I said, "I've been wanting to talk to you."

She found her keys and looked at me saying rather meekly, "About what?"

Maybe it was the tone of her voice or the way she had looked for keys, but in that very brief moment I changed my plans and I'm still not sure why. Perhaps it was the events of the past week. Or maybe along with getting older, I was one of the few lucky guys who was about to begin the maturing process as well.

"About my still being stuck on Laura."

She didn't say anything; she just waited for me to go on.

And I did. In the new direction I hadn't been planning. I didn't feel like I was in a race and standing at the starting line, wanting to get off to a good start as soon as the gun sounded. My stomach calmed and I lost all sense of urgency. Instead I felt more like a quarterback who goes into a football game with a designed play, steps up to his offensive line to take the ball, but as he looks over the opposing team, he realizes the play will never work. So instead he calls an audible: a new play to at least pick up a few yards. Suddenly, all I wanted to do with Patty was pick up a few yards.

"I thought about what you said to me in East Hampton the other day, about how I wasn't over her. And I wasn't. But at least I'm over all that obsessive bullshit now."

She searched my face to see if I were telling the truth. "If you mean it, I'm glad for you. It means you can get on with your life."

"Yeah. It does. But I wanted to make sure that you knew that even if I was messed up, I never took you for granted. I always knew you were a special person with a warm heart and values I admired."

The expression on her face softened. "Thanks," she said, rather softly and almost seemed to have a difficult time getting it out of her mouth.

I went on. "All that physical stuff was icing on the cake."

She stared at her keys again. "It sure was."

Smiling I added, "And you got great legs. Did I ever tell you that?"

A faint smile appeared on her lips. "No you didn't," she said quietly, "but you should have."

I found the next few words difficult to get out of my mouth, as if they were too thick for my throat. "I just wish we could have met a little later, after I had gotten all my emotions straightened out on my own time and not on yours."

Her eyes began to fill but no tears ran down her face. "Me too. I guess we had chemistry, but our timing was a little off," she said then looked down at her keys again.

We both said nothing for the next few minutes until Patty said, "I better get going."

I just nodded my head in agreement as she turned and went to put her bags in the trunk. "Let me help," I said, "put this stuff in the trunk."

After we slammed the trunk shut, she got in, started the engine, then rolled down the window.

I leaned over and said, "I really enjoyed the time we spent together this summer and getting to know you."

She smiled. "We sure had our moments."

"Yeah, we sure did," I added somberly before a few more seconds of quiet began.

"Well, I really should get going," she said hurriedly, in a vain attempt to avoid the emotion that surfaced in her voice.

"Okay then, have a safe trip."

"You too, Chris."

I thought about giving her a quick kiss goodbye but thought better of it, just stepped back as she pulled out of the driveway. I watched her drive down the road until she turned onto Bluff and both she and the summer were out of sight.

I stood there staring at nothing for a second or two longer feeling slightly drained. I was feeling surprised at myself for not trying to hold on, and also pleased with myself for recognizing it was time—time to let go. I turned around, threw my bag in the back seat, started the engine and headed for Montauk Highway and home.

I took Bluff and slowed up in front of Atlantic Avenue beach to take one last look. It was still overcast, but since it wasn't raining, I guess everyone was out to get their last official bit of beach on the last official weekend of summer. I was glad I wasn't on it with them. I pulled away and made a right onto Hand Lane so I could pass through the town of Amagansett to get a final look.

The town looked empty. It must have been on the beach too. As I passed Stephen's Talkhouse, I noticed a tall blonde walking past it, but I didn't bother to get a better look. Not while I was right next to her, that is. I waited until I was further down the road, then shot a quick glance in my rear view mirror. I still couldn't quite help myself, but at least I knew I was at a safe distance. Her face was a blur.

CPSIA information can be obtained at www.ICGtesting.com
Printed in the USA
LVOW090234070712

289134LV00001B/26/P